A LITTLE LOVE SONG

A LITTLE LOVE SONG

MICHELLE MAGORIAN

EGMONT

EGMONT
We bring stories to life

For Alix Pirani and Sheila Robins, with thanks.

The author and publisher would like to thank the following for
permission to use copyright material:
'Little Love Song' (Horatio Nicholls/Leo Cochran) © 1930 Reproduced
by permission of EMI Music Publishing Ltd, London W1F 9LD
'You're as pretty as a picture' (McHugh/Adamson) © 1938, Robbins
Music Corp, USA. Reproduced by permission of EMI United
Partnership Ltd, London W1F 9LD
'I'll be seeing you' words and music Sammy Fain/Irving Kahl
© Redwood Music Ltd.

First published in Great Britain 1991
by Methuen Children's Books Ltd
This edition published 2015
by Egmont UK Limited
1 Nicholas Road, London W11 4AN

Text copyright © 1991 Michelle Magorian
Cover illustration copyright © Lucy Davey

ISBN 978 1 4052 7696 2

www.egmont.co.uk
www.michellemagorian.com

5896/17

A CIP catalogue record for this title is available from the British Library.

Typeset by Avon DataSet Ltd, Bidford on Avon, Warwickshire

Printed and bound in Great Britain by the CPI Group.

MIX
Paper
FSC FSC® C018306

One

Rose gripped the handlebars and pressed hard against the pedals. Bumping and juddering along the uneven country road her black braids slapped her back. Above her, the sun appeared intermittently between leaden clouds. Once she reached the top of the hill she stood still, gasping for breath, her legs shaking uncontrollably. Below her, an expanse of pale green sea brushed against a tiny village and the surrounding coves and cliffs.

Two tiny lanes broke off from the main street of the village and led down to a jetty. The coastline to the left of it curved into a small V-shaped bay where a handful of boats were moored, except for one with a red sail which swayed and leaned through the water. On a narrow peninsula stood a manor house.

Three whole months here, she thought, three blissful months of no school. Three months when she could write for as long as she wanted. She just hoped she could finish one really decent story, one that she didn't have to keep writing in fits and starts and shelving for months at a time. She felt so hemmed in, by her age, by her school, by her family. The war had been going on for nearly four years and what had she done? Nothing, aside from collecting bits of salvage, and helping raise miserly amounts of money. If she didn't have to go back to her wretched school she could have registered for call-up in five months on her eighteenth birthday.

She glanced back over her shoulder. There was no sign of her sister. She pushed off again. She knew she was being mean but she had so little opportunity to be by herself that she wanted to make the most of it.

Careering down to the village she took in the cluster of whitewashed cottages with their grey tiled roofs. There was a strong whiff of fish. She stopped at the foot of the hill, left her bicycle by the wall of the end cottage nearest the beach and swung open the gate. A short plump woman in her fifties answered the door. She was holding a long empty pea-pod.

'Excuse me, is this Salmouth?' asked Rose. 'I'm not a foreign spy,' she added, pulling out a crumpled identity card from her pocket.

'That's right, dear.'

'I'm supposed to be meeting someone at the church. Can you tell me where it is?'

''Tis jest up and round a bit.' She waved the pod in the direction of the street. 'You jest carry on up this here road, past the two lanes and the corner pub, then takes the first turning on yer right. You can't miss it.'

A strange scuffling noise from the floor caused Rose to glance down. An ancient dog had flopped into a wrinkled heap at the woman's feet.

'This is Rumple,' announced the woman, and she gazed fondly at him.

Rose squatted down and ruffled his fur.

'On holiday, are you?' the woman asked.

'Sort of.'

'That's nice. We don't see many people down here now, what with most of the beaches havin' barbed wire round 'em and petrol being rationed. It's bicycle or shanks's pony if you want to get around here.' She paused. 'And Harold's carthorse. But he looks as old as Rumple.'

Rose grinned. 'Who? The horse or Harold?'

The woman laughed. 'Why both!' she said.

Rose stroked the dog's chest. 'I think Rumple is very nice.'

'Oh, everyone's fond of him. He misses the boys though, don't you, old thing?'

Rose was about to ask but stopped herself.

'That's my four,' explained the woman. 'All in the forces. John's in the navy. He's in India. Robert's in the R.A.F. He's stationed in Norfolk, and my other two are in the army. Keith's in the Far East and the youngest, Barry, is in a P.O.W. camp in Germany.'

Rose stood up. 'Oh, I am sorry,' she said quietly.

'At least I know he won't be doing any fightin' for a while. And I can send Red Cross parcels to him. Will you be stayin' long?'

'Three months,' answered Rose guiltily. 'My mother's an actress. She's going abroad with E.N.S.A. They take shows out to the troops. She's sort of evacuated me and my sister out here till she comes back. There's a woman who'll be looking after us. It's all arranged.'

'Oh well, I expect I'll be seeing a lot of you then.'

Suddenly Rose found herself holding out her hand. The woman looked surprised for a moment and then gave it a vigorous shake. Her palm felt warm and firm, Rose noted.

'My name's Mrs Clarence.'

Rose smiled. 'I'm Rose, but most people call me Roe.'

'Where are you stayin'?'

'Lapwing Cottage.'

The woman frowned. 'Sure it's *Lapwing*?'

'Yes. Why?'

Mrs Clarence stared at her for a moment.

'I didn't think the major would be rentin' it out again. Still, no harm, eh?'

There was an awkward silence.

'Must dash,' said Rose and she backed down the garden path to retrieve her bicycle.

She cycled up the main street past two lanes and a pub on the corner and turned into a lane on her right. A hundred metres up a slope stood a small grey-stoned church with a bell tower. She hopped off the bike and leaned it against a tree just inside the church gate. As there was still no sign of her sister, she decided to run down to the harbour and take a quick look.

She headed towards an empty fishmonger's shop at the corner and peered in. Two inert crabs decorated the window shelf. They peered back at her. She was about to walk past the bookshop next door when she caught sight of her reflection in the dusty glass and scowled. Why did she have to be the awful-looking one in the family? Trust her to be the thin ugly one with a Cinderella for a sister. The ugly duckling who would never, never turn into a swan.

She thought of Diana, green-eyed, tall and built like a perfectly proportioned Greek statue. Rose's eyes were dishwater-grey and she had such small breasts she was sure no one would notice if she wore a brassiere or not.

A small bell jangled as she pushed the door of the bookshop open. Hundreds of second-hand books were scattered in neglected piles across the floor. She stepped gingerly over them and tried to manoeuvre her way round the central bookcase. In front of a book-lined alcove stood a cluttered table and chair. Beside it, wide wooden stairs sloped up to the next floor.

'Hello,' said a voice from above. 'Can I help you?'

Rose jumped.

A faded pair of baggy corduroy trousers was making its way

down the stairs. The owner of the trousers was the scruffiest-looking man Rose had ever seen. His brown hair stuck out wildly and continued round his chin and mouth into a shaggy ginger-streaked beard. His skin was so pale that his large brown eyes appeared almost black. She guessed he must be in his late twenties or early thirties, but it was difficult to tell.

'No, thank you,' she replied politely. 'I was just looking.'

'Holidaying, are you?'

'Sort of. We're here for three months.'

'Three months!'

'Yes. We're staying at Lapwing Cottage. Do you know it?'

He flinched. 'Yes,' he said quietly. 'I know it.'

Suddenly she was conscious of how out of place she must look in her navy gymslip and school blouse and she reddened. She pulled her watch hastily from her pocket and moved towards the door.

'Must dash. Er . . . what times are you open?'

'Nine till six. And watch out for that pile of books. You're about to go flying.'

She left the door banging behind her. As she tore up the lane she muttered angrily to herself. Why on earth had she blushed like that? But she knew. It was the man's eyes. They had met hers with such frankness and amusement that it alarmed her. It was almost as if he already knew her.

She skidded round the corner and sprinted in the direction of the church.

Diana was leaning wearily against the church wall, her bicycle propped up against her, her cardigan knotted round her waist. She looked worried. As soon as she spotted Rose, she threw back her thick chestnut plaits and straightened up.

Really, their mother was ridiculous making them braid

their hair, thought Rose. Diana was almost twenty-one! Rose would gladly have had hers cut if she hadn't been afraid of looking like a boy.

'Have you been waiting long?' asked Rose.

'No,' said Diana, 'but that's not the point. You shouldn't have gone on ahead. You could have got lost. Then what would I have done? I don't even know if this is Salmouth. The signposts have been taken down.'

'Oh, but it is. I've asked.'

'Country people often give strangers the wrong directions in case they're the enemy.'

'We hardly look like German parachutists,' said Rose, and she started to giggle. 'Has Mr Thingummy come yet?'

'No. It's a good job he hasn't,' said Diana. 'It'd have been embarrassing if I'd had to tell him I'd lost you. And his name is Mr Partridge.'

'Oh yes. So it is.' She stuck out her stomach. 'Afternoon,' she drawled. 'I'm Mr Pa-a-artridge.'

'Please,' begged Diana in a whisper. 'Here he comes.'

A tall stocky man with a red face and a large belly was walking in their direction. A battered cap which appeared to have shrunk was perched precariously on his balding head.

'Afternoon,' he said leaning back. 'I'm Mr Pa-a-artridge.'

Diana avoided looking at Rose.

'You're the Miss Highly-Robinsons, I take it?'

'Yes. How do you do?' said Diana politely.

'So, you're havin' a go at Lapwing Cottage?' he said, ignoring her outstretched hand.

'Yes. We've been looking forward to our stay there,' said Diana, smiling and glancing up the lane. 'Which one of these cottages is it?'

'Oh, it ent in the centre of Salmouth. It's along they cliffs.'
And he waved his hand towards the sea.

'But I was told it was in Salmouth,' she said.

'It's that all right, but Salmouth stretches outward quite a bit.'

'I see. Is it far?'

''Bout a mile or two.'

'Oh,' said Diana, disappointed.

The man smirked, turned on his heel and headed for the main street.

It took all their strength to push their heavily loaded bicycles up the slope from the beach to the coastal path above the cliffs.

'He could at least offer to help,' panted Diana.

But Mr Partridge strode on ahead, pausing only now and then to make sure he was being followed. Rose hauled her bicycle over a small rock, and wheeled it past Diana. She was determined to keep up with Mr Partridge. She was beginning to feel tired but she was blowed if she was going to show it.

Mr Partridge was now well ahead. Rose gave her bicycle a determined push. Once she had caught up with him, she kept up a steady pace alongside.

Gazing out at the sea she felt a flutter of excitement. 'Yes,' she said firmly. 'I'll learn to swim this summer.'

'You won't do no swimming round here,' said Mr Partridge. 'That little beach in town's the only one for miles that ent got barbed wire round it. It's a funny old beach too. Dangerous. The sea's up to yer knees one minute and over yer head the next. No. You won't get no chance to swim round here. Not unless you go to one of the coves, and then you can only get to

7

those by boat. And no one'd let you borrow one. No. Ent no hope of you swimmin' round here.'

Oh yes there is, Mr Doom and Gloom Pa-a-artridge, thought Rose.

After what seemed like five days, Rose spotted a small white unkempt cottage, with weeds and brambles growing wild round it.

Mr Partridge stopped. 'There she be,' he said.

Rose gaped at it. 'Rightyho,' she said, matter of factly. She stared at all the unploughed wilderness. It puzzled her to see so much land being wasted. In London, people were even growing carrots in window boxes. 'I'll wait for my sister, Mr Partridge, if you'd like to go on.'

He nodded and carried on walking.

'On no!' cried Diana, when she saw the cottage. 'That's not it, is it?'

'I'm afraid so,' said Rose.

'We can't possibly stay here.'

'It's not so bad,' said Rose.

'Oh well, as long as I can have a hot bath,' Diana began weakly, but she was too tired to finish her sentence.

'Here goes then,' Rose whispered.

They pushed their bicycles forward and headed for their holiday home.

Mr Partridge was waiting for them by a small wooden gate. The paint had been stripped off by wind and salt spray. He pushed it open, and they struggled up the overgrown pathway, towards a door. It was unlocked.

Mr Partridge lowered his head and entered the kitchen. At the end of one of the whitewashed walls stood a black range.

In the centre of the room was a scrubbed wooden table and three chairs.

Rose noticed a large oil lamp on the table. No electricity, she thought, or gas. She opened the window over the sink and stuck her head out. Standing in the middle of wild flowers, unpicked vegetables, high grass and apple trees was a solid black object.

'A pump!' she yelled. 'We've our own pump!'

'Mr Partridge,' began Diana, eyeing the sink, 'where are the taps?'

'Taps? There ent no taps here, ma'am. That's what the pump's for.'

Inside a cupboard to the left of the sink were three cups, three plates, three sets of cutlery, one saucepan, two glasses, some jam jars, a wooden tub, a broom, a bucket, a mop and various cleaning materials. On one of the shelves were a jug of milk, a bowl of eggs, bread, and a pat of butter, a teapot and enough tea to make a few pots.

'Mrs Partridge has laid the range for you.'

He pointed to where piles of wood were stacked neatly in order of size beside it. 'The major likes to give you a head start, see.'

Diana clasped her hands anxiously. She stared at Mr Partridge and opened her mouth but no sound came out.

'I'll show you where the latrine is,' he said.

Rose and Diana followed him out of the kitchen into a narrow corridor. As he opened the door into the garden, Rose spotted a zinc tub hanging on a hook behind it. 'That's the bath, I suppose.'

He nodded.

In the garden stood what appeared to be a miniature shed.

Mr Partridge had no sooner lifted the latch when one of the hinges broke and the door crashed into an awkward diagonal. They peered in. A square wooden seat with a hole in it stood over a deep trench.

'What happens when it gets full?' asked Rose, mesmerised by the depth of the pit.

'You won't stick it long enough to find out. You're our third lot to stay. The others didn't last a week. Too scared.'

'Why? Is it haunted?'

'Roe, don't ask such silly questions!' exclaimed Diana.

'So they say. Miss Hilda, that's the lady who used to live here, were a bit mad, see.'

'Really! What, screaming mad?'

'Roe!'

'Oh no, she weren't dangerous, like. Well, not that I know of.' He lowered his voice. 'She was just a bit *queer*, you know. See that door in the corridor, that's where her things are. They're all locked up. Been in there since last autumn when she died.' He straightened up. 'Since her death I've been collecting the rent for her brother Major Withers, which,' he emphasised again, 'ent never been for long. Still, you're all paid up till the end of September so that's one job I won't have to do, isn't it?' And he gave a smug smile.

'No,' murmured Diana.

'You won't need me to show you the bedrooms. My wife left clean sheets and pillow cases up there for you. If you need to use a telephone,' he added significantly, 'the nearest one is at the farm over the hill. That's the Acres' place. 'Course I wouldn't stay if I was you. If you got ill or died of fright it'd be months before your bodies were found.'

They stood by the steps and watched him leave.

'Thank goodness he's gone,' said Rose. She gazed back at the garden. 'Don't you love it?'

Diana looked doubtful.

'Take no notice of him. He's just trying to scare us off. Let's start unpacking, before Miss Hutchinson arrives.'

Diana paled. 'Oh no. I knew there was something I had to ask! I don't know what time she's supposed to be arriving.'

'Oh, come on!' said Rose. 'Let's get started.'

She dragged her two pairs of bicycle bags up the stairs, her sister trailing on behind.

They found themselves standing in a sparsely furnished bedroom, facing the main garden. A pile of freshly laundered sheets was stacked on a single bed.

'This is Miss Hutchinson's room, I suppose,' said Diana.

Rose slipped quickly out of the room and opened the next door off the landing. It was a tiny hallway room. She guessed it must have once been part of the landing. In front of the garden window was a table and chair. The table would be ideal for her writing. Let's hope Miss Hutchinson doesn't bag that, she thought.

She carried her bicycle bags into the bedroom but when she saw the view from the far window she dropped them and ran towards it. Flinging it open she leaned towards the sea. Clusters of lilac-pink flowers grew out of the wall and shook as a salt breeze wafted in. Rose breathed in deeply.

It was certainly a strange cottage. The main garden was at the side and the front door faced the lane. To her it seemed lopsided. She felt that the front of the cottage ought to face the sea.

She drew herself back into the room. Two mahogany beds stood on either side of the garden window. She grabbed the end of one and pulled it on its castors towards the coastal window.

She hung her gymslip and dress in the wardrobe and dumped the rest of her clothing in the chest of drawers.

She had just changed into a pair of shorts when she heard shouting coming from downstairs. She ran out of the room.

Diana was in the kitchen holding a letter.

'It was on the table,' she said. 'It's from Miss Hutchinson. She's been called up!'

Two

'He knew all the time,' muttered Rose. 'He must have hung around until we'd gone upstairs and then sneaked in with the letter.'

Diana sank into one of the chairs. 'I'd better ring Mother up and tell her we're coming home,' she said.

'We can't do that,' said Rose. 'She'd drop out of the E.N.S.A. revue.'

'That's hardly our fault, is it? Miss Hutchinson should have let her know sooner.'

'But she didn't,' said Rose slowly, 'and Mother doesn't even know now.'

'She'll be awfully shocked when she does,' said Diana, 'especially when she knows we'll have to spend the night alone.'

'Not if she doesn't.'

'What do you mean?'

'We don't have to tell her.'

'Let her think Miss Hutchinson is with us tonight?' said

Diana. 'And then break the news tomorrow so she won't worry?'

'No.' Rose paused. 'I mean, not tell her at all.'

'I don't understand,' said Diana.

Rose dragged a chair out and sat down. 'The rent's all paid up. Why not just stay anyway? Let Mother think Miss Hutchinson's here and that everything is fine.'

'*Lie* to her?' said Diana, aghast.

'It's only half a lie. After all, everything *is* fine, isn't it?'

'It certainly isn't.'

'Diana, you can't tell her. She'll back out of doing this show and let someone else take her part. You know she will.'

'We could wait until she's gone and stay with Aunt Em.'

'She starts rehearsals at Birmingham Rep. next week,' Rose reminded her.

'We can't stay here on our own.'

'Why not?'

'Who's going to cook our meals and wash our clothes?'

'We don't have to have meals. We can eat sandwiches and dip our clothes in a bucket of water every now and then.'

'And who's going to chaperone us?' asked Diana.

'We can chaperone each other.'

'But what would people think? Two girls on their own?'

'We're not girls.'

'You are.'

'But you're not. A lot of people are married by your age.'

'Look at you,' said Diana, waving her finger at Rose's shorts. 'As soon as you're out of Mother's sight, you go and put those things on. I bet she doesn't even know you've packed them.'

'Aunt Em thinks they're all right.'

'That's because she made them.'

'Diana, this is Salmouth, not London. They're far more respectable than skirts. At least the wind can't blow them up and show your knickers.'

'Please,' said Diana, shocked. 'Don't use that word.'

There was a moment's silence.

'Well,' said Rose. 'What do you think?'

Diana shook her head.

'We can't,' she said. 'We don't even know how to cook an egg let alone get a range going. And what about ironing and shopping? We wouldn't know where to start. It's no good, Roe, we'll have to go home.' She gave a dismal sigh. 'At least Timothy will be pleased.'

Rose took a deep breath. She was sick of the sound of that boy's name. A besotted lapdog, he was forever turning up on the doorstep with envelopes containing the drippiest poems imaginable. Diana couldn't cope with it but she was too kind-hearted to send him packing.

'I think you're being mean. Mother's heartbroken since Father's death. This is the first time in ages that she's started to look happy again. You know how long it took for Aunt Em to persuade her to go to an audition. And now that she's got the job and has gone to all the trouble of evacuating us out here, so that we'll be nice and safe, while she risks her life and goes off to the Far East, you want to stop the whole thing because you're too selfish and too scared to spend three months looking after yourself.'

'Just look at us,' said Diana. 'We've only been here an hour and we're quarrelling. And that's what we'd be doing all the time. You know we would.'

'Mother's good on stage,' said Rose ignoring her. 'You know she is. She'll boost the troops' morale and . . .'

She stopped. She could see it was useless.

'I suppose I'd better go up to that farm and telephone,' said Diana at last. She looked hesitantly at her. 'Would you like to come with me?'

'No, I wouldn't,' yelled Rose, making for the door.

'Where are you going?'

'For a *long* walk. After all, I might as well make the most of my short stay here.'

'Roe,' began Diana. 'Please . . .'

Rose slammed the door. As she tore down the path, a long sucker caught her blouse and scratched her arm. She pulled it off angrily and flung back the gate.

She sat on a grassy tussock near the coastal path seething, her knuckles pressed hard into her forehead. 'I'll refuse to eat a thing,' she muttered. That'd get her, she thought; that'd make her feel guilty. If there was one weapon she could hold over people it was her ability to go without food for days. That's what she did at school if her pocket money was stopped as a punishment for losing her temper. By the third day of starving herself the teachers' manner towards her changed dramatically.

'Now come on, Rose,' they'd plead. 'You must eat.'

'I'm sorry,' she'd reply, 'but I just don't feel hungry.'

Sometimes it was true. She didn't feel hungry.

She raised her head and stared out at the sea. If she was honest, she was being just as selfish as Diana. She had longed for this holiday. It was the one thing which had kept her sane throughout the summer term. Now they would have to return to London and her mother would be hovering over them all the time. If Rose so much as sat anywhere for a think or a scribble, she would be either made to *do* something, or her mother would want to read what she had written. Rose couldn't bear to show her writing to anyone. Not that she ever did. Except Aunt Em, sometimes. She wondered what Timothy would say if he knew that her sister showed her his poems.

'Oh, Diana!' she said crossly. With her looks she had nothing to worry about, yet she worried about everything and that included drippy Timmy's feelings. 'But what if . . .?' she began, mimicking her sister's favourite expression. How anyone so striking could lack so much confidence beat Rose. Diana had always had it easy, she thought bitterly. She had never been expected to pass exams by her father. She was just loved for herself, whereas Rose was constantly having to win his praise. Now, because she was too frightened to stay, they would have to go home and put up with Timothy. For a moment she felt a flicker of sympathy for her sister. Timothy was the only male in her life who had the courage to come near her. Diana was so beautiful she scared all the others away.

And then she had an awful thought. Suppose Diana was right about him. Suppose Timothy wasn't ghastly and that it was being in love which caused him to behave the way he did.

'If that's what love does to you, I'd rather not have anyone fall in love with me,' she muttered.

She tugged at a large clump of grass and tore it out of the earth.

Not that anyone would. She looked too much like a boy.

'Oh hell!' she yelled, and she hurled the grass into the air.

A gust of wind caught some of the blades and carried them to a ledge. Rose lay on her stomach and looked down. Below her was a cove. It was obviously one of the coves Mr Pa-a-artridge had gone on about; the ones you could only reach by boat.

'Really?' she said to herself. 'We'll see about that, Mr Pa-a-artridge.'

She gripped the rocks and placed her feet carefully on a jutting edge. Peering down she realised that if she swayed from side to side, and stretched her legs out far enough, there was actually what appeared to be a set of uneven steps. She lowered herself down to the next ridge. Halfway down she stumbled and slid down some loose stones, grazing her knee against a piece of rock. She stood still for a moment to catch her breath.

She bent her knees, grabbed a thick branch near her waist and lowered herself carefully on to the next ledge. Now what, she thought. She looked in vain for something else to grip. There was another piece of rock at the end of the ledge. She slid herself along towards it and tested it out to make sure it wouldn't crumble under her weight. It was solid and there was a larger rock underneath. She just needed to lower herself a little bit further and she would virtually be able to jump.

She made it to the large rock and stretched a leg to a ledge which stood diagonally above another one. Don't rush, she told herself. Once she reached the next ledge other ones were easier to find. She leapt on to the ground, threw off her sandals and ran across the beach. The water swirled in from the sea, throwing itself flatly across the sand and up into a fine spray on the rocks.

Rose sank down and pushed her toes into the sand. She felt so private and safe. Surrounded by a semicircle of pink and grey cliffs, her only companions were the seagulls perched high on the ledges above her.

Her anger had somehow left her. Instead, she felt sad.

A gull flew from one of the rocks. She watched it soar and glide and settle on another one.

I ought to go back, she thought dismally. She picked up her sandals, dragged her feet towards the cliff and took a last look at the cove, trying not to cry.

Approaching the cottage she noticed that Miss Hilda's locked room had blackout curtains across the window. They stood out starkly, a dark square patch in the centre of the peeling white walls. Now she'd never have a chance of seeing what was behind them.

Diana was waiting for her at the gate. 'Worried as usual,' muttered Rose.

'What did Mother say then?' she snapped. 'When do we have to go back?'

'I haven't phoned yet. I've decided to stay.'

'Oh,' cried Rose astonished. 'You *are* a brick!'

Diana gave a shy laugh.

'Not really. If I'm home for my twenty-first, Mother will organise a big formal do and invite every relative still living. I'd hate it.' She paused. 'Will you come with me then? I'm not very good at lying.'

'Oh, I feel as if I can breathe again,' said Rose. 'Yes, of course I'll come!'

'Roe,' said Diana quietly.

'Yes.'

'I'm terrified.'

'What of?'

'Of failing at everything. I'm so stupid.'

'I'm the one who fails, remember? You're the one who passed all their exams.'

'That was a fluke,' said Diana. 'And anyway they were secretarial exams. They're hardly as important as . . .' She stopped.

'As what?'

'Oh, nothing.'

'If it helps,' said Rose, 'I'm a bit scared too.'

'Oh dear.'

'But not that scared. Come on,' she said, linking arms with her sister. 'Let's get it over with.'

The next morning, after failing to get into the locked room, Rose examined the garden. Flowers and leaves of varying sizes had long since grown over the borders which surrounded the tiny lawn of waist-high grass. There was a strong whiff of honeysuckle. Rose stood back and stared up at the wall. Pale pink and yellow flowers trailed and sprawled up to Diana's bedroom window.

Wild flowers had invaded the foot of the garden, their yellow, blue, pink and lilac heads bobbing among untended vegetable patches. Rose pushed her way through a clump of green leaves so tall they almost obliterated the rough stone wall which was strangled in undergrowth. 'Rhubarb,' she whispered.

The stalks were green but for a pink glow at the roots. She released them and moved with difficulty through to the wall. Clumps of blackberry bushes appeared to be keeping company with some pale pink fruit. At first she thought they were raspberries, but they were longer in shape.

She turned and gazed at the apple trees by the latrine, under her window, and the two at the end of the garden. Unripe green apples hung from their branches. Thanks to Miss Hilda, they'd be all right for fruit.

She squatted down, disappearing into a miniature jungle. 'What I need to find out is what a weed looks like. It would be awful if I killed a prize marrow by mistake.'

She rose from her hiding place and headed for the kitchen. Diana was sitting at the table, staring with fixed concentration at a shopping list. She looked desperate.

'Don't worry,' said Rose. 'We'll be all right. I've discovered rhubarb, blackberries and something pink in the garden.'

She caught sight of some numbers scrawled down on the paper. 'What on earth are you *doing?*'

Diana looked anxious. 'I'm trying to calculate how many points I've used up. Roe, I don't even know which shops we ought to register at. Miss Hutchinson was going to do all that. Do you seriously think we can do it?'

'Of course we can.' She sat down beside her sister. 'If we can last until next week, we'll be fine. We've enough money for this weekend . . .'

'But Mother's arranged for Miss Hutchinson to collect the money every week from the local post office. I don't think they'd allow *me* to draw the money out instead.'

'I've been thinking about that.' She touched Diana gently on the arm. 'Do you think you can tell another tiny lie? Remember Mother won't be able to see you blushing.'

Diana sighed. 'Go on.'

'Explain that the post office is two miles away, that it doesn't seem fair that it should always be Miss Hutchinson who has to go to collect the weekly money, so could she authorise it to be collected by you *or* Miss Hutchinson? After all, if Miss H. was here and she came down with bubonic plague, we'd be stumped, wouldn't we?'

'What if Miss Hutchinson tells her she's been called up? Mother'll never be able to trust me again.'

'But Miss H. left the letter to be delivered by hand. If you're worried, you could always write to her, thanking her for the letter, and tell her that you've let Mother know.'

'It's awfully risky.'

'You're not backing out, are you? Look, Mother'll be leaving next week. If we can just keep our heads till then, we'll be sailing!'

Diana picked up the list and stared at it.

'I'm sure Mrs Clarence will help us with the shopping,' said Rose. 'She's the woman who directed me to the church. The one I told you had an old dog. The one who didn't think I was a German parachutist.'

Diana smiled.

Rose stood on the tip of the slope. Below her lay the beach. She waited for Diana to catch her up before descending into the village. 'Not long now,' she said reassuringly.

Diana responded with a nod. Speaking was too much effort. She trailed after her. The pinkish dust from the pathway flew up soiling her white shoes.

Rose waited for her again at the foot of the cliffs before heading across the beach. She swung open the gate to Mrs Clarence's cottage.

'Are you sure we should?' asked Diana.

But before Rose had knocked on the door Mrs Clarence opened it, a tea towel in her hands. She beamed. 'Come in,' she said. 'You must be the sister.'

'Are we disturbing you?' said Diana.

'Not at all. I was just drying up the lunch things. You look worn out. I'll make you some tea.'

'Oh, but . . .' started Diana.

'Go on with you. Sit down!'

Diana sank gratefully into a chair.

Rumple, who was slumped by the unlit hearth, raised his head for a brief moment, gave a sniff and let his chin flop back to its original place.

A clock ticked loudly on the mantelpiece. Two photographs of young men in uniform stood on either side of it, a third on the wireless which stood on a table and a fourth on top of a small china cabinet.

'Her sons,' explained Rose.

Mrs Clarence came out of the kitchen carrying two bowls of vegetable soup and several slices of buttered home-made bread.

'We don't want to deprive you of your butter ration,' said Diana.

'There's plenty more where that comes from. We're not so fussy on points here. I've a friend who's got cows. She gives me butter in exchange for a few veggies and a bit of knittin'. Now,' she said firmly, 'you eat that up. I don't expect you got over hearing Miss Hutchinson's been called up yet.'

They stared at her, astonished.

'You'll get used to it. People knowing what's goin' on. I know old Harold, see. He works up at the Partridges' and at my friend's farm doin' odd jobs. So what are you going to do then? Go back home?'

'No,' said Rose. 'We've decided to stay. Without Miss Hutchinson.'

'That's nice. There's someone else who can look after you then?'

'I'm going to look after us,' said Diana suddenly.

Mrs Clarence looked shocked. 'You can't stay up there on your own. Who's going to cook and wash for you?'

'Us,' said Rose.

'I'm nearly twenty-one,' said Diana. 'It's about time I learnt.'

'But you're not brought up to it,' protested Mrs Clarence. 'Would you like me to ask around and see if I can get you a maid?'

'That's very kind of you, Mrs Clarence, but no thank you. Anyway, I don't think you'd find one. Most of them have been called up.'

At this Diana blushed violently.

Rose knew the reason for her sister's embarrassment. It was because Diana still wasn't in uniform. Thanks to their mother's persuasive tactics and much string-pulling, she had managed to keep Diana at home.

'What does your mother say about you bein' on your own?'

Diana opened her mouth and reddened again.

'She trusts us,' said Rose, rescuing her. 'Doesn't she, Diana?'

Diana nodded.

'"There are not many mothers who trust their daughters in your situation,"' Rose blundered on. '"But I trust you." That's what she said.'

Mrs Clarence gave a sigh.

'Oh well, I s'pose it's all right then. You both seem so young though. Still, you all got to grow up quicker now,' and she gazed at them sadly for a moment.

'We were going to ask you about the shops here,' said Rose quickly.

'I'll take you round.'

'Oh, would you?' blurted out Diana.

Mrs Clarence laughed. 'Of course.'

'You don't need me to come, do you?' asked Rose.

Diana looked anxious. 'Why? Where are you going?'

'Only to a bookshop. I can post your letter to Timothy for you on the way.'

'No thank you.'

'Yes. I suppose you'd better do it. I might *accidentally* lose it.'

Mrs Clarence gave a sudden cry.

'You haven't planned to do anythin' this evening, have you?' she asked. 'Only the Women's Institute are havin' a special Kitchen Front talk tonight. It's all about what you can make with yer rations. Would you be interested in comin' with me? You might find it useful.'

'Yes, please,' answered Diana.

Rose stared horrified at them. She couldn't imagine anything more boring. To her relief she realised that she hadn't been included in the invitation.

'And when we come back from the shops,' continued Mrs Clarence, 'I can show you both how to cook a few simple dishes.'

'Oh, Mrs Clarence, that is kind of you,' said Diana.

'I'll be off then,' said Rose abruptly. 'Thanks for the soup, Mrs Clarence,' and she hurriedly made for the door.

Rose had just reached the bookshop when a tall spectacled youth in shorts and sandals came flying out of the doorway. She stepped back quickly. Within seconds he had disappeared round the corner towards the beach.

'Excuse me!' she said loudly after him.

The shop was empty; the door still open. She slipped in carefully. She didn't want the little bell to ring and bring the man down.

Moving swiftly round the shelves she looked for something on human biology. She knew the basics from girls in her dormitory, but their stories contradicted one another and they left too many questions unanswered. She had scanned the biology books at school for any information about how babies came about, but the nearest she got to it was a chapter on the reproductive life of the stickleback.

'Can I help?'

Rose jumped. The book-man was standing on the stairway.

'What?' she said, feeling herself blush.

'Are you looking for anything in particular?'

'No. I was just browsing.'

He slid his hands into his pockets and gazed down at her, making Rose uncomfortable. She was usually the one who played observer. She glanced at his shorts and plimsolls.

'Yes. Derry tells me off for wearing them too.'

'Derry?'

'My young cousin. He's staying here. You must have caught sight of him leaving.'

'I did. He bumped right into me.'

'Ah.' He paused. 'And how are you finding Lapwing Cottage?'

'I love it.'

He smiled, his eyes distant. And then he moved briskly down the rest of the steps.

'You're my first customer of the day. Do you want to be left alone to browse or would you like me to recommend something? You don't have to buy. You can borrow if you like, seeing as you're here for so long.'

She suddenly noticed that her hands were covered in dust. She brushed them against her shorts.

'Am I really your first customer?'

'Yes. They don't go in for reading much here in the summer.

Only when it's raining. I keep a mixture of light and heavy for them down here.'

'Light and heavy?'

'Romances, thrillers, the odd Dickens and a few art books.'

'What happens in the winter?'

'Much busier. At Christmas it's packed.'

Rose noticed that the edges of the man's eyes were pink and that the shadows underneath them had grown darker. She let her hands drift across a set of Agatha Christies.

'How old are you?' he asked suddenly.

'Seventeen and three quarters.'

'Read any D.H. Lawrence?'

'He's banned, isn't he?'

'Some of his books are.'

He walked up the stairs.

'Come on up. I'll find some of his poems for you.'

Rose followed him, groaning inwardly. Memories of standing up in turn at school reciting endless verses of 'How they brought the Good news from Ghent to Aix' for the weekly literature mark came flooding back. She was about to tell him not to bother, but as soon as she stepped off the tiny landing into the next room, she changed her mind.

She had never seen such a bookish living room. Bookcases and shelves stretched upwards to the ceiling and unplaced volumes lay scattered about the floor. Only one wall remained empty. Leaning up against it were paintings and prints. The window above them looked out on to the bay.

In the centre of the room were two large armchairs and a low table. There were books on the mantelpiece, by the grate, and on a stool by one of the armchairs.

'May I open the window?' she said.

He picked up his pipe from the mantelpiece and stuffed it with tobacco. 'Go ahead.'

She flung it open and leaned out. The thunder of distant guns jerked her back inside.

'There's an army camp about fifteen miles inland,' he explained. 'It's probably one of their practices.'

'Oh,' she said and she leaned back out again.

'Now, young lady, let's choose some books for you.'

Oh Lord, he was going to get her some of those awful poems. She followed him into the adjoining room. It was a kitchen that he seemed to be using as a study. In between the range, the sink and the larder were piles of paper. Like the living room it, too, was overflowing with books. A table was pushed up by a window overlooking the sea. It looked like a general dumping ground. He brushed papers and envelopes aside revealing a heavy black typewriter underneath.

'Now where is that damned book?' He pushed his hand through his hair and gave a grunt.

'Actually, poetry isn't one of my favourite subjects.'

'Ah, but this is different,' he said squatting down on the floor. 'Ah ha. 'Ere she be,' he cried, breaking into the local dialect.

He thrust it into her hands. 'I'd be interested to hear what you make of them,' he said over his shoulder.

Rose followed him down to the shop feeling both annoyed at being saddled with a book not of her choice, and flattered that he had lent it to her.

'Thank you, Mr . . .'

'Trelawn,' he said. 'But call me Alec. Everyone round here does.'

Embarrassed, Rose walked hurriedly out of the bookshop.

She could never ever imagine calling someone of his age by their Christian name.

Three

The next morning Rose woke early. She pulled on her black swimsuit, threw her notebook, a towel and shorts into a bicycle bag and crept quickly down the stairs. Out in the garden, she cupped her hands under the pump and gulped down some water. She left a note for Diana explaining she would be back in a couple of hours, and set off.

Once she had reached the grassy tussock above the cove she lowered herself over the edge placing her feet carefully on the ragged set of uneven steps the elements had beaten into the cliff. The bag which was strapped to her wrist swayed awkwardly across her chest. She slid down some loose stones, paused for a moment and then stretched out her leg towards a more solid ledge. By the time she had landed at the bottom, she vowed she would buy a satchel or knapsack.

She threw off her sandals and sat cross-legged on the beach, emptying the contents of her bag and spreading them out around her. Then, taking a good hard look at the sea, she stood up and stepped out boldly. At the water's edge an icy wave swirled round her ankles. She leapt backwards. Step by step she forced herself forward, until the sea was at hip level.

'Ready, steady, go!' she yelled, and she bent her knees quickly.

The water rushed up to her neck. She gasped at its coldness and flung her arms about, walking in Groucho Marx style through the water. She held her chin up stiffly, watching the incoming waves out of the corner of her eye and leaping into the air as soon as they swept near.

She tried the breast stroke but floundered spluttering. A wave hit her with such force that she was blinded for a moment. She staggered to her feet coughing. She attempted the stroke again but was too frightened to take her feet off the ground. Disappointed, she rose out of the water, walked towards her towel, and flopped down on to it. As soon as she had dried out she made her way back. This time she sat at the edge and allowed the waves to swirl over her before venturing deeper. Once in, she dipped her chin into the water and blew a few ineffectual bubbles.

'Well done,' she whispered to herself, and did it again.

She leaned back languidly and gazed up at the cliffs.

Suddenly she had an idea. She leapt out of the sea, grabbed her towel and exercise book and sat down.

'Ballad of a First Night *sans chaperon*,' she wrote.

This would cheer Diana up. She was still depressed after the latest 'I am in torment without you' letter from Timothy. It had been waiting for her when they had returned from shopping in the village.

'Diana sweet, throws wide the door,' she scribbled.
'To step into the dew-kissed grass,
Pulls wide the latrine portal old,
Screams loud as rabbits scurry past.'

She paused for a moment, and then continued writing, crossing out and arrowing words in. She wished she could write what she was really feeling, instead of this rubbish.

'Idiot,' she muttered.

She returned to the poem again. She liked making fun of all the twee stuff they were made to learn at school. She read the next verse out loud.

> 'But cheer up, for the week is new,
> Adventure waits in our abode.
> Let's face those crawlies in the dark,
> And welcome spiders to our home.'

'You can't have "abode" and "home",' she muttered.

She gave a sigh and picked up the D.H. Lawrence poetry, flicking through the index. It looked as though all the poems were about flowers and animals. She wasn't in the mood. She preferred to read about people. She turned to the first poem.

'Discord in Childhood' she read.

It had two verses. Probably some sickly sentimental thing about . . . she stopped. Her eye caught the first line. She read on. By the time she had reached the second verse she was sitting upright. This wasn't poetry. Well, not her idea of poetry.

'And at night when the wind arose, the lash of the tree shrieked and slashed the wind.'

She remembered lying awake in the dorm, listening to the wind, and hearing the branch of a tree scratch at the glass of a window.

She read slowly through the second verse.

'A slender lash whistling delirious rage. Delirious rage,' she repeated.

By the time she had finished reading it, she was near to tears. She closed the book hurriedly and grabbed her exercise book. This time she didn't bother with rhyming. She wrote down the

30

first words that came into her head; a great disorganised flood of them. It didn't matter that they made no sense.

When she finished, she felt deliciously satisfied, even light-hearted.

'You're as pretty as a picture.
Has anyone ever told you before,' she sang.

It was a song her father used to sing to her. It was a silly song. Why her father used to sing it to her was a mystery.

She heard a swishing sound and looked up. A boat with a red sail was passing the entrance to the cove. It swayed briefly, changing tack and slowly sailed in her direction.

'Damn,' she muttered. 'Damn, damn, damn!'

She recognised him immediately. It was the bookman's young cousin. She willed him to go away, but he tacked the boat nearer, loosened the mainsail and hopped out into the shallows.

Suddenly she was aware of her state of undress; of her swimsuit clinging damply to her skin. She pulled her plaits down over her shoulders to hide her chest and drew up her knees. She was angry with him for invading her private place and angry with herself for being so embarrassed.

He hauled the boat up on to the sand. His open-necked sports shirt and white floppy shorts made his lightly tanned arms and legs appear even browner. He stood for a moment, thrust his fingers through his mop of untidy brown hair, and gazed in her direction. One of his spectacle lenses caught the sun so that for a moment it appeared like a small gold disc. He pulled the spectacles off and cleaned them with his shirt. Rose took in the pink ridges at the bridge of his nose. Only one spot on his chin, she observed. Better skin than Timothy's. Thicker, springier hair too. She watched him rearrange the glasses back on to his face.

'Hello,' he said politely. 'Are you on holiday here?'

She nodded.

'How did you find this place?' he said.

'I looked down.'

'But how did you get here?'

'I climbed.'

They stared awkwardly at one another.

'It's very pleasant, isn't it?' he said. 'It's one of the few places that doesn't have barbed wire. Is this your first visit down here?'

'No.'

He looked puzzled. Then his face lit up. 'You must come in the mornings. I always come in the afternoons.' He paused. 'People don't usually bother coming all this way out. How long does it take you to walk?'

'Not long. I'm staying near here. In Lapwing Cottage.'

'You don't mean where Mad Hilda used to live?'

'That's right. Did you know her?'

'Not really. But she used to visit the bookshop quite a bit.'

He took a towel from the boat and sat down on the sand a short distance from her. 'I come here for a month every summer,' he explained. 'This year I'm staying till I'm called up. I'm in the Home Guard at the moment but I'm going to be a pilot in the R.A.F.'

'Aren't you a bit young?'

'I'm eighteen!'

'Sorry. I thought you were younger.'

He frowned.

'What about . . .' She hesitated. 'What about your eyesight?'

'If I can handle a boat single-handed wearing glasses I can fly a plane. And anyway, once I've got the results of my Highers they'll take me all right.'

'What if you don't pass?'

'I've got to,' he said.

He stared out at the sea, shading his eyes from the sun. Rose looked at the boat. It was a clinker dinghy. She knew because, when she was twelve, she had spent a year longing to sail in one. But no one in her family was interested, so all attempts at persuading her father to buy a second-hand one had failed.

'She's lovely.'

'Yes, she's not bad.'

'Do you ever take anyone with you?'

'Crew, you mean?'

'Yes.'

'It's best on your own,' he said matter of factly. 'Why? Do you sail?'

'No, but I'd love to learn.'

'You can swim, I suppose.'

'Not exactly,' she said.

'Oh well, that's that.'

'I've been trying to teach myself but . . .' She shrugged.

'There's nothing to it,' he said.

'Tell that to my lungs.'

He gazed at her thoughtfully. 'How long are you staying here?'

'Three months.'

'That's masses of time to learn. I'll teach you if you like. I'm here most afternoons.'

'Teach me to swim?!'

'If you want. You know,' he said, 'I'm sure I've met you somewhere before.'

'You nearly crashed into me this morning, outside the bookshop.'

He was grinning. She smiled back.

He spread out his towel, and peeled off to a dark green woollen swimsuit.

'Want to start learning now?' he asked.

She nodded.

He ran and dived into the water. Rose hovered at the water's edge. He turned and swam on his back. 'Cold, isn't it?'

The waves swirled round Rose's ankles. She wrapped her arms round herself suddenly overwhelmed with shyness. She had never stood alone in front of a boy wearing a swimsuit.

'Come on in,' he yelled.

'I'm not going out of my depth,' she said.

'Don't you trust me?'

'I won't know till I've had a lesson with you, will I?'

'All right. Keep your plaits on. I'll come inland a bit.'

He swam towards her. Rose moved slowly in up to her waist.

'Face me,' he said. He rubbed his chin with his fingers. A small bead of sweat glistened by one of the thin wisps of hair that grew on his upper lip.

'Breast stroke is probably the best. I'll teach you how to float first though. Turn around and let yourself fall slowly backwards. Let your ears go under.'

Rose gritted her teeth and leaned back. The thought of him looking down at her made her tense up. Suddenly she was aware of her breasts and the hair under her armpits. She collapsed in the middle and sank into a sitting position on to the sea-bed.

'You're supposed to take your feet off the bottom,' he laughed.

'But I'll sink!'

'I'll stand beside you and put my hand underneath you.'

It was even worse when he touched her. It took five tries before Rose relaxed enough to let her feet leave the ground. Time after time she slipped, swallowing great gulps of ocean on her travels down. It wasn't till they had moved on to the breast stroke and Rose could concentrate on the arm movements that she began to feel less self-conscious.

'You're doing splendidly,' he said.

'It's no use,' she moaned, 'I'll never do it. I must have been born with a brick inside me.'

'Rot,' he exclaimed. 'It's only your first lesson.'

They flung themselves on to the sand for a rest. Rose watched him put his spectacles back on. The glass was splattered with wet sand and sea-water.

'You just need practice, that's all.'

'I suppose so. It's very kind of you to help me.'

'It gives me something to do.' He spotted the book. 'What's that?'

'D.H. Lawrence. Your cousin lent it to me.'

He turned away frowning.

'Have you read it?' she asked.

'I'm a mathematician myself.'

'Oh.'

'And I don't read poetry.'

'Why not?'

'It's trivial.'

'How do you know if you don't read it?' asked Rose irritated. And then she remembered, she hadn't thought much of poetry either until she had read this book.

'What's Mad Hilda's place like?' he asked politely, changing the subject.

'You can come and see it if you like.'

'Won't your parents mind me coming?'

'My parents aren't there. It's my older sister Diana who's in charge. And she wouldn't mind.'

'Your parents, are they . . .?' He hesitated.

'My father. Last year. But Mother's still alive. She's with E.N.S.A. She's leaving England tomorrow, off to some desert. We don't know where, of course. That'd give away where the troops are.'

'That's plucky of her. Who's looking after you then?'

'No one. We're looking after ourselves.'

'Just the two of you?'

'Yes.'

'On your own?'

'Yes.'

'With no one to protect you?'

'We'll be all right. My sister's twenty-one. Almost. So will you come?'

'I don't know,' he said reddening. 'I've never . . .' He stopped.

'Been alone with girls?'

'Of course I have,' he said nonchalantly. 'Heaps of times.'

He jumped to his feet and made for the water. 'Come on, skinny,' he said, over his shoulder, 'let's have one more go.'

Rose stood, her hands on her hips. 'My name is not "skinny". It's Roe.'

He stopped and looked at her. 'That's an odd name.'

'It's short for Rose.'

'Oh, I see. Mine's Derry,' he said. 'Short for Derek.'

And still red in the face he turned and dived into the water.

Rose stared after him. What on earth had she said to make him so hot and bothered?

Diana was waiting for her at the gate. 'Where have you *been*?' she called as soon as she spotted Rose.

Rose sauntered up to her. 'To the beach. I left you a note.'

'But you didn't say where you were going or when you'd be back. I've been worried sick.'

'I did. I said a couple of hours.'

'From when! I've been up five hours. It's one o'clock.'

'What!'

'And I bet you've had no breakfast either.'

'I'm sorry. I left my watch behind. I had no idea.'

'What have you been doing?'

Rose opened her mouth to answer.

'You know it's dangerous to spend too long out in the sun,' interrupted her sister.

'I don't burn badly like you.'

'You know I'm responsible for you now,' she said weakly. 'Anyway. I've made us some lunch.'

'I'm not hungry.'

Diana looked alarmed. 'Roe, you haven't eaten all day!'

'Honestly. I'm not hungry. I couldn't eat a thing.'

It was true. Somewhere between the path and the cottage she had lost her appetite.

Within minutes, her rinsed swimsuit was dripping over a hedge, and she had climbed up into one of the apple trees with the book of poems. She browsed through the pages, picking out the odd sentence. Even though she didn't understand some of the words, there was a strange power in them. At times she felt as though she was peering through a keyhole eavesdropping on something very private.

She leaned back against the trunk, her legs dangling at either side of the branch she was sitting on.

'I durstna kiss thee tha trembles so, Tha 'art frit o'summat,' she read.

'Frit,' she repeated. Could it be frightened? Why would the woman be frightened? Rose knew, for often late at night she imagined a man slipping into her bed and holding her in his arms. It frightened her, yet she still found herself imagining it.

She shuddered. She was too restless to read any more. She was bursting to write, but she wanted it to be something she could get her teeth into, like a short story. She had at least twenty ideas for stories but none of them were good enough. She had to come up with a good idea soon, or she'd go mad like Mad Hilda.

The next morning, before anyone was up, Rose made yet another attempt to get into the locked room. She pushed some wire into the keyhole and jiggled it around. It hit a piece of material. She pulled it to one side and peered in. She couldn't see a thing.

A loud knock at the front door made her jump.

'Just coming,' she yelled.

She removed the wire, picked up a fork, penknife and pencil from off the floor, and quietly opened the back door, dropping her burglar implements amongst a clump of weeds.

Then she ran into the kitchen to find Mr Partridge already standing there, a large package in his hands.

'Jest wanted to deliver this,' he drawled and he placed it on the table. 'It's a wireless,' he said, 'from yer mother.'

'How do you know?' said Rose indignantly.

'I s'pose she thinks you need it to keep you out of mischief, not having a chaperone, like,' he said, ignoring her question. 'Waste of postage, ent it? You'll only be sending it back. And I got these from Mrs Potts.' He fished into his pockets and brought out three letters.

'What was Mrs Potts doing with them?'

''Tis her job. She be the postwoman. I had to deliver this, see, so I thought I'd save her the journey.' He stared at her for a moment. 'You been washing your hair?'

'Yes.'

She had no intention of telling him that she'd been for an early morning dip.

'You still managing all right here then?'

'We're managing wonderfully, thank you, Mr Partridge.'

'You don't find the two-mile walk to the village for shopping too tiring then?' he asked.

'It'll make us fit.'

'It didn't make the other townees fit. It finished 'em off. That and the strange noises at night.'

'What a shame,' said Rose and she smiled defiantly at him.

'Well, I'll be leaving you. Don't suppose I'll be seeing you again.'

Rose watched him from the doorway.

'I sincerely hope not,' she muttered.

An urgent whisper came from the corridor. Rose opened the door to find Diana crouching in her nightdress.

'You can come in. He's gone.

Diana caught sight of the package.

'It's a wireless,' said Rose. 'Mr Pa-a-artridge had a good look before delivering it.'

'How marvellous.'

'What, prying into our mail?'

'No, silly. The wireless.'

She began looking round the wall.

'What are you doing?' said Rose.

'I'm looking for a socket.'

'Diana,' said Rose ominously. 'There's no electricity here.'

'You're right,' she said, and she sank into a chair. 'What a disappointment.'

Rose pushed aside the string and packing paper. 'Give us a hand.'

'What's the point?'

'We can use it like an ornament. It'll make the place look more homely.'

Diana smiled. 'You *are* daft.'

They slid their hands into the box and lifted it out. It was a small wooden affair with a criss-cross fretwork design on one side and a large circular dial on the other.

'Whoopee,' yelled Rose.

'Well, it looks nice,' commented Diana.

'Don't you see? It's run on a battery. Aunt Em has one of these. She takes it with her when she has to go away and work in repertory theatres. We'll need to get it recharged, now and then.'

She turned a knob. The deep mellifluous voice which was giving the news was soft at first and then gradually grew louder.

Rose patted it with satisfaction. 'I'll pop into Mrs Clarence's to look at her newspaper, see what's on tonight.'

'I won't be in,' said Diana hesitantly.

'Oh? Are you going to another of those Women's Institute meetings?'

'No. First aid.'

'First aid!'

Diana looked awkward for a moment.

'Yes. I'm going with this girl I met at the W.I. last night. She's pregnant, actually. She's staying at that small seaside hotel in Salmouth. It's being used as a nursing home for expectant mothers.' She swallowed. 'Look, I might as well tell you, her parents threw her out. You see, she's not married.'

'Diana!' Rose was stunned. 'You can't mix with someone like that.'

'Why not?'

'Because people will think you're like her. And when they know we're here on our own . . .' Her voice trailed away. 'We can't afford to get ourselves a bad reputation.'

'I admire her.'

'Admire her? For goodness' sake don't let anyone hear you say that.'

'I'm sorry but I do. I don't think I could cope if it happened to me.'

'But, Diana, it wouldn't.'

'She's great fun.'

'Loose types usually are.'

'Roe, she's not like that.'

'Why isn't she married then?'

'Her fiancé is in the Far East somewhere. She hasn't heard from him in ages. She doesn't know if he's dead or alive.'

'Oh. I see.'

'I'm sure you'd like her. She's the same age as you. In fact,' said Diana casually, 'I was thinking of inviting her here for tea.'

'Diana, you wouldn't!'

'You could meet her then.'

'I don't want to.'

'Why?' She frowned. 'You still don't approve then?'

'It's not that. It's just . . .' Rose hesitated. 'I'd be embarrassed, that's all. I wouldn't know what to say.' She paused. 'Is she, you know, big?'

'Yes.'

'See what I mean. I wouldn't know where to look either. Don't invite her here, *please*.' To Rose's alarm Diana didn't answer. 'I don't understand you, Diana. You know what they say at school about girls who get . . .' She stopped. She couldn't bring herself to say the word.

'Dot doesn't fit that picture.'

'Wasn't there anyone else at the Women's Institute you could have made friends with?'

'Yes. But Dot was on her own. And she looked a bit shy.'

'But how did she get in? Being unmarried and . . .'

'She wears a curtain ring on her finger.'

'But doesn't it look like one?'

'Yes. But everyone was too polite to say anything.' Diana smiled. 'Her look of relief when I sat next to her was so comical she made me laugh.'

There was an awkward silence.

'I'm still going with her to the first-aid classes,' said Diana quietly. 'I like her company. She makes me feel relaxed.'

What about my company? Rose was about to ask. But Rose wasn't interested in the W.I. and Red Cross classes. And even if she did go with her she knew they wouldn't hit it off. Diana's goodness irritated Rose so much it brought out the worst in her and they always ended up squabbling.

'You're too kind-hearted for your own good,' Rose grumbled.

'She's the one who's kind-hearted.'

Rose shrugged. 'If you say so.'

Diana picked up the letters.

'Come on,' she said. 'Let's open these.'

The first letter was from their mother telling them about the hectic rehearsal schedule and the uniform she had to buy, complete with kit for the desert. She had arranged to ring Mrs Acres on the afternoon of 9 July for a farewell call, and she hoped Miss Hutchinson would have got over her shyness of telephones by then to spare a few words.

'That's tomorrow!' whispered Diana.

The second letter was addressed to Diana. It was in Timothy's handwriting.

'Don't open it yet,' begged Rose. 'You know it'll depress you. Open the other one.'

Diana slit the envelope neatly. Inside was an official letter giving Diana permission to collect the weekly allowance from the post office. 'We've done it!' exclaimed Diana. 'We've actually done it!'

Rose snatched the letter and gazed at it. She smiled.

'We'll be all right now.'

Four

After Rose checked the programme listings at Mrs Clarence's, she bought a canvas bag at a tiny fishing-tackle shop.

It was navy blue and so faded from having been bleached by the sun in the front window, that she managed to knock the price down. The only snag was that it was too long and she had no means of shortening it.

She walked into the bookshop with it dangling by her knees. The shop was empty. She had just reached the table in the alcove when a precariously balanced pile of books toppled over. She picked them up and tried to put them back on the already overcrowded table.

The door opened from upstairs. It was Alec.

'I'm awfully sorry,' she said, sending another lot of books careering off the edge.

He stopped halfway down. He looked tired. 'Don't worry about that. It all needs sorting out, I'm afraid.'

He noticed the book in her hand.

Rose could feel herself reddening.

'I see you've brought the poems back,' he said. 'Did you read them?'

'Not all of them.'

'You didn't like them?'

'I think they're wonderful,' she blurted out. 'I just skipped the ones that didn't interest me and read the ones that did.'

He smiled. 'Come on upstairs. The kettle's just boiled.'

They sat either side of the fireplace in two armchairs while Alec poured out the tea.

'How do you ever find anything here?' she asked, taking in the overloaded mantelpiece.

'I don't look very often these days.'

She spotted a book with a blue cover. 'That one,' she said pointing hesitantly at it. 'May I borrow it? It's one of the books banned at my school.'

'Which one?'

'*Jane Eyre*.'

'Good grief! *Jane Eyre* banned?'

She nodded.

He pulled it out and gave it to her. 'Have a look round, and see if there are any other banned books here.'

'Thanks!'

Suddenly she found herself blushing again. She looked hastily down at the floor. She picked up her cup and swallowed some tea. Out of the corner of her eye she saw Alec pick up his pipe from the hearth. She began to feel a tingly sensation all over her body.

'Diana will have a fit when she sees it,' she began quickly. 'She's my sister. She went to the same school as me. She left ages ago. Lucky thing. I've been made to stay to retake School Cert. Still, at least my holidays started early.' She paused. 'A bomb fell on our hockey pitch, you see, and at the end of one of the wings. One of them exploded and one didn't so we all had to evacuate. Then the headmistress's mother died, and the vice-headmistress got jaundice. So we broke up early. Thank goodness!'

Alec smiled. 'Is it really that bad?'

'Bad? It's terrible! At least other schools do voluntary work or knit socks for the troops, that sort of thing. I'm hopeless at knitting but I'd far rather be struggling over plain and purl than be bored to death doing silly mediaeval embroidery and learning the social graces.'

'How long have you been there?'

'An eternity. Since I was eleven actually. What a mistake!'

'Why a mistake?'

'You can't possibly be interested in hearing about life in a girls' boarding school.'

'On the contrary. I'd love to. It's completely out of my range of experience.'

She laughed. 'Well,' she said, taking a deep breath. 'My

sister Diana was one of those model pupils – quiet, gentle, good, hardworking and beautiful. The teachers adored her. Everyone raved about her. Then I came along.'

'And you were compared with her?'

'From dawn to dusk. "Why aren't you like Diana?" "Because I'm not Diana," I'd say. Then I'd get hundreds of lines for answering back.'

'But surely they've stopped comparing you with her now.'

'Oh no. Her legend still lives on. Anyway, that's not the only reason it's so awful.' She lifted her feet for a moment and then put them back on the floor. 'Do you mind if I take my sandals off?'

'Go ahead.'

She slipped them off and tucked her feet underneath her.

'The real reason it's so awful is . . .' She hesitated. 'It sounds silly really. I feel I can't breathe there. There's no room for me to be myself. I have to be on guard all the time.' She paused. 'Even our leisure time is organised. Sometimes I lie awake in bed until old Frosty, she's our housemistress, gives us our last check. She comes round to look at us when we're asleep. I close my eyes and pretend, and then I lie awake in the dark and listen to the sounds outside my window. That's the only time they can't organise me. But, if I do that too often, I fall asleep in class and I'm given double prep as a punishment.'

'Have you told your parents you're unhappy at school?'

'Unhappy?' repeated Rose, startled. 'I didn't say that, did I?'

'No.' He poked the tobacco down further into his pipe and relit it. 'But you are, aren't you?'

Rose was stunned for a moment. She stared intently at an ink mark on the wall. 'Yes, I am,' she said. 'And I have to go back whether I pass my exams or not.'

She hardly finished speaking when she burst into tears.

Alec sat quietly for a while and then handed her a handkerchief.

'Sorry,' she choked out. 'I'm not in the habit of blubbing.'

'Looks like you needed to.'

'You see,' she said, 'I'm always losing my temper. Well-bred young ladies are not supposed to lose their temper, you know, but honestly, if someone is rude to me or says something I don't agree with, it seems stupid to smile sweetly and say, "Yes, ma'am; no, ma'am." Do you know, I've even been sent off to have private talks with the school chaplain? He says that if I don't swallow my anger, I'll spend the rest of my life a spinster. And not just a spinster. I'll be an ugly old spinster because losing my temper so many times will distort my face. Can you believe it?'

'Oh yes,' said Alec wryly. 'I can believe it.'

'Of course I pointed out that the teachers were all spinsters. And soon after, Matron was instructed to withhold my weekend pocket money again. When I asked why, I was told, "You know perfectly well why." "No, I don't," I said. "Don't raise your voice to me, young lady!" she says, raising *her* voice.

'I mean, it's so unfair! And of course there's a whole goody-goody crowd in my House who are out to win the school shield, so every time I get into trouble, they're absolutely foul to me.'

'Haven't you any friends there?'

'As soon as I start getting on well with someone, we're separated. They say it's because we have to learn to mix with the whole community, but really it's because they're scared stiff we'll get *too* friendly, if you know what I mean.'

Alec frowned and shook his head. 'For goodness' sake,' he said. 'Why do your parents make you stay there?'

'Because my sister *loved* it.' She paused. 'And I only have one parent. My father was killed in action last year.' Her eyes filled up. 'Oh lor. Here I go again. Anyway, he's left enough money for me to take Highers and go on to university.' She wiped the tears hurriedly away from her face. 'He died just before I took School Cert. My mother said I flunked it because I was so upset. But it wasn't that at all. I tried extra hard, because I knew how much he wanted me to get it.' She looked down at the handkerchief in her hands. 'I'm awfully sorry, I'm afraid I've drenched this.'

'That's what it's for.' He smiled. 'Let's see if we can squeeze some more watery tea out of that pot.'

The watery tea tasted wonderful. Alec began talking about the D.H. Lawrence poems and together they looked through the book and told each other which poems and which lines they liked best. 'Listen to this,' he'd cry, and he would read out a couple of lines and look at her, waiting to see her response.

As Alec talked, she had the strangest sensation of coming home. Names of authors she had never heard of came drifting across the room. 'Oh, I'd like to read that,' she found herself saying. 'I'd like to read something by her.'

When she finally left the bookshop, she ran without stopping along the beach, weaving in and out of the half a dozen holiday makers. She broke into a trotting motion and started singing, 'Run rabbit, run rabbit, run, run, run,' gliding over each hill, sliding eagerly down dips. She felt as if, had she leapt, invisible wings would have carried her sailing to the top of the cliffs and on to the coastal path.

It was five a.m. when Rose finished reading *Jane Eyre*. Rolling over on to her stomach, she gave the blackout curtain nearest her a good tug. Outside, the sky was a wash of pale green and lilacs.

She turned down the oil lamp, slipped out of bed and drew the other curtains. The window by her bed was open. She leaned out, trembling. She was too exhilarated to sleep now. The image of Jane returning to the blinded and disfigured Rochester, their passion for each other unshaken, was so beautiful and so powerful. It was stupid of the teachers to deny her that experience. More than stupid. Wicked.

She stayed at the window and watched the sky's colours dissolve into pale blue. She felt as though she was on the brink of a great journey. The flowers in the wall looked so vibrant in the dawn light that she decided to pick one. She edged over the sill and stretched out an arm down to them. She managed to pick one of the smaller flowers, the larger ones were too rooted in the wall. She was about to draw herself back into the room when she noticed something dark and soft sticking out of the brickwork underneath the sill. At first she thought it was a leaf but when she touched it, she realised it was oilskin. She wiggled it gently at first before realising that half the brick was loose. She pulled it out. Wedged underneath it was a small bundle.

'What on earth . . .?' she whispered.

She replaced the brick hurriedly and withdrew into her room.

Inside the bundle was a thin canvas bag. She emptied its contents out on to the table. A large key and a roll of muslin dropped out. Rolled in the muslin was a piece of paper wrapped round two small keys.

Rose opened it carefully. It was a letter, written in a large vibrant hand.

Dear Lover of this View,

I thought you might appreciate my hidey-hole being here. The large key will open the door to the middle room downstairs. I had another one made when I overheard Mr P. telling Mrs P. that my brother had given him instructions to lock as many of my possessions as was possible in there, in the event of my problematic heart giving out.

Enjoy what's there.

The contents of the bureau will explain everything. For your sake, keep it a secret, however difficult you may find that. If my brother ever found out he would make it impossible for you to remain here in Salmouth. He would prove black was white if it meant avoiding a family scandal.

Love

'Mad' Hilda

Rose stared at the letter, astonished that her curiosity should be so easily satisfied. She twisted the large key over and through her fingers and then returned it to the bag. No, she decided, she had no right to pry. She was about to wrap the muslin round the small keys when she stopped. Mad Hilda must have written the letter for a reason. Perhaps it was important to her that someone looked through her things.

It was still early. If she moved quickly she could have a good look before her sister was awake.

The room was packed. Leather books, trunks, cane chairs, cases and velvet and chintz curtains were squeezed all the way round a writing bureau. Faded oriental rugs were rolled up and squashed into a corner. A wooden crate was stuck between a large box-shaped gramophone and a case full of records.

She edged herself in, climbed on to the crate and leaned towards the window, hooking back the black piece of material to the side to let the light in. She hauled herself over the box and stretched out an arm towards a pile of books crammed in between a brass table and a trunk. They were old children's books, their heavy covers embossed with gold lettering.

Nearby were poetry books, and novels by Dickens, George Eliot, Tolstoy and, much to her surprise, D.H. Lawrence. She couldn't imagine someone old reading him. It was difficult to see the other books. They were too well buried. She manoeuvred herself backwards and looked in the wooden crate. Wrapped in cushion covers and tablecloths were ornaments and pieces of pottery. Rose's favourite was a young dancer. The girl was balanced on one foot, her other leg flying behind her, her arms outstretched. The sight of a solid object which had movement delighted her. She wrapped it up carefully and eased it back into the crate.

She decided against attempting to pull the gramophone records out in case they broke. She longed to be able to open the trunks. She suspected Miss Hilda's clothes would be packed in there. But it was impossible. She would have to empty the room out first.

She tried to push open the roll-top lid of the writing bureau but it was locked. The smallest key was rather ornate. She suspected it belonged to the desk. She stood with one foot on the crate, and the other balanced on a bamboo table, praying that her pyjama trousers wouldn't split. As she eased the key in, it gave an encouraging click. She slid the lid back. Inside were several books tied together in pairs. She picked up the nearest pair and undid the ribbon. As soon as she opened them, she knew they were diaries. She closed them hurriedly and was about to put them back when she remembered the key. If Miss Hilda hadn't wanted anyone to read them she wouldn't have included it in the bundle.

She picked one up. It was fairly dull really. Accounts of day-to-day life at the beginning of the century, reminder notes to visit Mrs So-and-so, mending to do. Disappointed she opened the other one. It puzzled her. It was a diary too, but more autobiographical. The first one had been written as the day's events were happening; the second in retrospect, almost as if Miss Hilda were introducing herself.

She read the first page:

I was born in 1885 and christened Hilda Mary Charlotte Edith, daughter of Brigadier and Mrs Withers. We were a small family. I was the youngest of four; the only daughter.

She opened another page at random.

I rarely saw my parents. Occasionally Nanny allowed them to visit us in the nursery.

It was a bleak room on the top floor. My youngest brother Richard and I pleaded to pin drawings on the walls or put flowers on the sills, but we were always prevented from doing so. My two older brothers couldn't see what all the fuss was about. Being older they thought themselves rather superior.

In books, nannies always taught their charges lovely songs and told them fairy stories. Not ours. Day after day we had to sit still in that dreary little attic surrounded by ugly bits of discarded furniture. We had one tiny piece of brown cloth on the bare floor and we ate our unappetising meals at a scrubbed deal table.

Only the night nursery had pictures. They were battle paintings extolling the glories of certain regiments. There were stuffed animal heads on the walls too. When the candles were blown out their marble eyes glinted in the dark. They terrified me.

Rose skipped the next few pages and read on.

Richard was always my favourite brother. Although he was two years older than me, being delicate we seemed much of an age. I loved to fuss over him when he was ill and he loved to be fussed. My older brothers had no time for me. Being a girl, what I had to say was of no interest to them.

Rose removed her foot from the bamboo table and looked for somewhere to sit. She squeezed herself into the corner of a laden cane chair, and continued reading.

Unlike my other brothers, Richard wasn't strong enough for the rigours of boarding school. He stayed at home with me. Even so we had different teachers. I had a governess, he a male tutor. We were allowed to share some lessons, provided we didn't speak to one another.

Rose closed the book, still disappointed. She had expected some exciting, incoherent ravings, not a description of Miss Hilda's childhood. There appeared to be no signs of her madness at all. She remembered Mrs Clarence saying that it was during the last war that she went mad. She did a quick addition. That would make her twenty-nine at the start of it. A later diary might tell her.

She picked one up, only to discover once she had settled herself back into the chair again, that it was a box of photographs. Two of them were printed on glass. She was about to lower the lid when she noticed a girl's face. She pulled it out. The girl looked about Rose's age. She was dressed in a white blouse and tie, and long dark skirt. Her hands were resting on the handle bars of a large bicycle. On top of the girl's long wavy hair was a straw boater. Rose stared at the girl's face. The girl stared solemnly back at her.

Above her, the stairs creaked. She was about to thrust the photograph in the box when she noticed some writing on the back. Scrawled in ink were the words: *At last I'm allowed a bicycle. July 1902.*

The latch on the sitting-room door clicked open. Rose flung the box into the bureau and locked the lid. She checked that the door was closed, and stretched across the room, to unhook the curtain.

Footsteps passed by her.

As soon as she heard the kitchen door close, she slipped out, dived into the sitting room, pushed the latch up noisily, opened and slammed the door, retraced her steps back to the kitchen and threw open the door.

Diana was standing at the sink. She gave Rose a tired smile. The kettle was perched on a small primus stove on the table.

'I couldn't sleep,' she said.

Rose stared at the primus. 'Where did you get that?'

'Mrs Clarence gave it to me. It's so we don't have to have the range lit all the time. I thought I could use the range to bake lots of things in one go, and then we could eat them cold with salads.'

'You're becoming so organized!'

'I'm not a natural at it. You should have seen me last night. I sat with Mrs Clarence at a table, with a piece of paper, and between us I managed to sort out the chaos in my head. I'm all right as long as I don't panic.'

Rose leaned against the sink. 'So why couldn't you sleep?'

'Because I *am* panicking. I felt so useless at Mrs Clarence's. Do you know I had to ask her how to boil an egg! I don't think I can cope.'

'You're not backing down, are you?'

'No. This is my one chance of learning to cook before I get married. If I get married.'

'Of course you will,' said Rose reassuringly. 'I'm the one who'll be the spinster aunt.'

'Then why has no one wanted to take me out?' She paused. 'Then I keep thinking about Timothy. Am I being selfish staying here?'

'No,' said Rose firmly.

'He's suffering so much, Roe, and I don't know what to do. I try to be kind but it's not enough. Do you think I could learn to love him?'

'No!'

'Neither do I. Oh, Roe, I dread his letters. I don't know what to say to him when I write back and I feel guilty all the time for causing him so much pain.' She sighed. 'Then I thought of Mother going away. I kept imagining one disaster after another. Honestly, Roe, I don't think we'll be able to get away with it. She's going to smell a rat when she doesn't speak to Miss Hutchinson today.'

'Just say she's twisted her ankle. She'll believe you. She believes anything you say.'

'I know. That's why I feel so ashamed. I do hope we're doing the right thing.'

'I'm sure we are. I just have this feeling that if she goes now it'll put her back on her feet.'

'Roe, that's not the real reason you want her to do it, is it?'

Rose fought back a smile, but found it impossible. 'Not altogether, but it's so nice not being supervised, don't you think?'

'I'm not so sure.'

The kettle came to the boil. Diana whisked it off and poured the water into the teapot on top of some leftover tea leaves.

'How was the first-aid class?'

Diana opened the larder door and grabbed some cups and saucers. 'Marvellous!' She settled down at the table and pushed the cups in Rose's direction. 'You pour.'

'Did you do broken limbs, or how to drag people through blazing buildings?'

'No. We learnt how to take a pulse and were shown pressure points so that if someone's bleeding we'll know how to stop it. Next week we're doing shock and . . .' She stopped.

'Yes? And what? Diana, you're blushing.'

'Am I? Oh.'

'Come on, you might as well tell me.'

'We're going to learn about having babies. I mean, giving birth to them.'

'You're not!'

'Dot asked if we could.'

'That was a bit brazen, wasn't it?'

'I don't think so. There were other expectant mothers there, too. They were just too shy to ask. So Miss Johnson, she's the lady in charge, is going to arrange for a midwife or a doctor to speak to us next week and I'm going to take notes.'

'You're not serious, are you?'

Diana nodded.

'But why?'

'Because yesterday, when Dot and I were out walking I suddenly thought, what if she starts having her baby right here? What on earth do I do?'

'You'd really stand by her if she started giving birth somewhere?'

Diana looked startled for a moment. 'Yes,' she said, surprised, 'I hope I don't have to but yes, I would.'

'You suddenly seem so brave,' Rose murmured.

'Me? Brave?' Diana shook her head.

'Yes. I couldn't bear to go to anything like Red Cross. I'd only have to hear blood mentioned and I'd be on the floor.'

'Once you know what to do you don't feel so queasy.'

'Perhaps,' said Rose. She twirled her empty cup round the table. 'Mother would have a fit if she knew you were learning about babies.' And were walking around with someone like Dot, she thought silently. Suddenly she had a sneaking admiration for her sister for not caring what people thought. Rose knew she would still be too embarrassed to be seen with them and she was ashamed at being so buttoned up.

'I know,' said Diana.

'Did she tell you anything about, you know?'

'A little. She said she'd give me a booklet about the rest of it, the night before I get married.' She leaned back in her chair. 'I'm dreading this phone call. I hope I don't start to blub. I'm not used to her going away.'

'Yes,' said Rose quietly. 'It's usually us, isn't it?'

Rose swallowed back her tears. What she had really wanted to say to her mother was, 'Take care. Don't die.' Instead, she blurted out, 'Have a wizard tour!' like something out of a school story.

To Rose's surprise, Diana seemed more relaxed since the phone call. She was listening to a very unfunny comedy show on the wireless and actually smiling. Usually it took her at least two days to shake off the glooms after receiving a Timothy-letter. Tonight, less than twenty-four hours later, she looked positively serene.

'I'm going to have an early night,' Rose said suddenly.

Diana looked up. 'See you in the morning then,' she said

and she returned to listening to the wireless.

Rose climbed up the stairs. She had just reached the landing when she found herself thinking of the photograph of Mad Hilda as a girl, and the note at the back of it. It was the word *allowed* which was tugging at her. 'At last I'm *allowed* a bicycle,' she murmured. Could the girl have been forbidden to ride one as a punishment? Perhaps girls in those days weren't encouraged to ride them.

She stopped at the top of the stairs. 'That's it!' she cried. 'I knew there was an idea for a story here.'

She ran into her room, grabbed her notebook from the table, and propped up the pillow behind her.

'Is she tall? Medium build? Excitable? The patient sort?' She began scribbling. 'Ambitious? What kind of school does she go to?' She stopped. 'If she did go to school. Oh hell, I don't know anything about Victorian or Edwardian life.'

She glanced doubtfully at her scrawled questions. No, she *had* to write the story. She knew vaguely what it was about already. It was how the girl had managed to persuade whoever it was to allow her to have a bicycle.

She sank back, relieved. At long last she had something to get her teeth into. She always felt as though she was existing on half her blood supply when she wasn't working on a story.

'Let me see,' she said. 'Helen? Deirdre? Gwyneth?' There was no hurry for her to think of a name yet. When she'd found the right one, she'd know instinctively. She drew one of the pillows towards her and hugged it tightly.

'Oh *good!*' she said.

By the following afternoon, her euphoria had dwindled.

Derry was waiting for her in the cove.

Rose lowered herself down on the first ledge and reached out for a familiar piece of rock.

'Do you need a hand?' he yelled.

'No, thank you,' she grunted and immediately lost her foothold and slithered past the next ledge. She flung her arms out, and hit her elbow. When she finally regained her balance, she paused for a moment and pressed her forehead into the rock before climbing down.

'You should have let me help,' he said.

'I'm all right,' she insisted. 'Just a bit off form, that's all.'

She dumped her bag on to the sand and flung herself down beside it.

'Cheer up, old girl,' he said.

'My mother's leaving today.'

He sat next to her. 'So. You should be proud of her. You should feel pleased.'

'Well, I don't feel what I *should* feel. I feel what I feel. All right.'

'There's no need to be so bad-tempered about it.' He turned away.

'I'm sorry,' she said. 'It's just that the phone call was awful. I suddenly realised that she was leaving the country. And I didn't even know where she was going. I wanted to say so many things to her, but we just sort of talked politely about this and that. It's difficult when you can't see someone's face. I hate telephones. I'd much rather write letters.'

'Would you? I hate writing letters.' He stood up. 'Come on, let's have our swimming lesson.'

She hauled herself to her feet and stumbled slowly towards the sea. It wasn't till she had reached the water that she noticed an old black rubber tyre covered with light brown rectangles.

'Where did that come from?'

Derry scowled. 'Alec. I mentioned I was teaching you to swim.'

'I like the patriotic patches. Did you put them on?'

'No. He did.'

'That was kind of him.'

'I suppose so.'

'Have you quarrelled with him or something?' asked Rose.

'Sort of.'

'What about?'

Derry shrugged impatiently. 'Look, do you want to learn to swim or not?'

'Of course I do.'

'Well then, come on.'

She wet her arms and legs and moved in up to her waist.

They repeated the arm and leg movements of the breast stroke alternately. Derry held her arms while she did the leg movements with the tyre around her middle. After a while she attempted to do it on her own, but she was so afraid of putting her head in the water that she floundered helplessly.

This time he only gave her the one lesson. Afterwards they flopped down on to the sand for a rest.

Rose's gaze drifted in the direction of the dinghy. 'Why is the name of the boat painted out?'

He looked startled. 'I don't know,' he snapped. 'Does it matter?'

'No. But why are you getting so fussed about it?'

'I'm not getting fussed!'

'Yes, you are. You nearly bit my head off.'

'I'm sorry. I don't like being asked lots of questions.' He jumped to his feet. 'Let's *do* something,' he said. 'Got any ideas?'

Rose thought for a moment and then smiled. 'Yes. When we were little my father used to dig a car for us in the sand. You could even sit in it. Let's make one.'

'No. Let's make an aeroplane!'

'All right.'

She knew they were acting like children but she was enjoying herself so much she didn't care.

They scooped away at the sand with their fingers. It was a laborious process. Eventually they dug a long rectangular ditch, carved a seat out for the pilot and another small hole and seat for the rear-gunner.

They clambered into it, and then proceeded to do countless bombing raids. Rose was the rear-gunner. She crouched into a tight ball.

They constantly had near misses. She became wounded but carried on bravely, still firing at Jerry. Then Derry was hit in the arm, a wing caught fire, but with masterly skill, he managed to land the plane just before the petrol supply was about to give out. He cut his way through the damaged plane and dragged out the wounded rear-gunner.

'Just a scratch, sir,' remarked Rose matter of factly. 'What about you?'

'Oh, arm's a little shredded, that's all. The plane's had a bit of a prang but she'll take to the sky again. Mission was a ripping success.'

After the heroic pilot and rear-gunner had been patched up they decided to destroy the sand plane.

'I'm a Mosquito pilot,' yelled Derry running over to the cliffs. 'And I'm dropping a bomb on target. Eeeoow!'

Rose ran to the other side of the cove and gathered herself for a flying leap.

'I'm a Hurricane,' she yelled. 'Nee ya ow!'

Together they jumped on to the plane making exploding noises and laughing. Neither of them would leave the mound, but continued to jump up and down till they had exhausted themselves and there was nothing left.

It had begun to grow cool and Derry decided to return to the village.

Rose helped him push the boat out.

'See that peninsula?' he said, stopping to point to where the manor house stood. 'One day I intend to go to the other side of that. I need to read a bit more about sailing though, and look at some maps. But as soon as I've studied them I'll take you round there.'

'Really!'

'Of course. As soon as you can swim.'

She stood in the water and watched him leave. Once he was out of sight, she ran out, put her sandals on quickly, and with her belongings stuffed higgledy-piggledy into her bag, she clambered up the cliff face, so that she could follow the sail as the boat headed for the village.

How extraordinary, she thought, that as well as teaching her to swim he wanted to take her sailing too.

'An ugly old thing like me,' she whispered. His kindness astonished her. But then Rochester had loved plain Jane, hadn't he? Not that there was anything romantic between her and Derry. She smiled thoughtfully. 'I wonder what Diana will make of him.'

Five

'Come on, Derry,' she said. 'We're almost there.'

Rose opened the gate. Derry hung awkwardly in the lane.

'My sister's not an ogre.'

He gave a tight smile and followed her up the path.

It was the following afternoon.

Diana was sitting at the kitchen table peeling potatoes and cutting them into pieces. She looked up. 'This is Derry,' Rose announced. 'Derry, my sister Diana. Derry's on holiday here, too.'

Derry's jaw dropped. Speechless, he gaped at Diana, his face growing more scarlet by the second.

'I met him at the bookshop,' said Rose breaking the silence, 'and then bumped into him down at the beach.'

'The beach?' he began dazed. 'Don't you mean the . . .'

Rose trod on his foot.

'Won't you sit down, Derry?' said Diana. 'You look a bit hot.'

'Well, actually, he came to give a bit of advice on the garden,' said Rose, rescuing him.

'All right. But you will stay for tea, won't you?'

Derry nodded.

'Thank you,' he gulped.

'Come and see the garden,' said Rose, dragging him out of the kitchen.

Rose flung open the back door. They manoeuvred themselves past the bicycles that were propped up by the wall, and sat on the doorstep.

'Well,' she said. 'What do you think?'

'Rather crowded, isn't it?'

'I love it. It really feels alive.'

'It won't be for much longer if the weeds take over.'

'Oh. Perhaps we'd better start weeding right away then.'

'Are you sure it's worth it? You'll be leaving soon.'

'I told you, we're here till the end of September. My mother arranged it all.'

Derry stared at the riot of snapdragons by his feet. 'Your sister is very beautiful,' he murmured.

'I know. She tends to scare people off because of it but she's terribly shy. I'm glad you said you'd stay to tea. Come on,' she said, 'I'll take you on a guided tour.'

It wasn't long before they were tugging at the long strands of convolvulus that were obliterating several large shrubs and a hydrangea bush. They crawled into the undergrowth searching for roots.

'What you need to do,' said Derry, 'is to throw the weeds into a pile and make a compost heap out of them. You'd better wait till it's rained though. It's hard work pulling weeds up from dry ground.'

They threw an armful of convolvulus over the end wall.

'Look, why don't we water the garden and then weed it?' suggested Rose.

'No. It wouldn't sink in enough.'

'Oh.'

'Anyway, at least we've a plan of campaign.'

'We?'

'I thought perhaps I'd help,' he blurted out. 'Do you mind? It'd give me something to do.'

'Mind?' laughed Rose. 'Of course not. The sooner the weeding's done, the sooner I can plant vegetables. There must be something I can plant that will pop up while we're here. Even if I only manage to produce one measly carrot it would help our food supply.'

Diana called out to them, to come in for tea. Derry hung back, reddening.

'Don't worry,' said Rose. 'It won't be so terrible. Just remember what I told you.'

'I'm afraid we're a bit short of china,' said Diana in the kitchen.

'I'll drink tea out of a jam jar,' said Rose.

'No. I'll do that,' said Derry politely.

In the centre of the table were scones, a loaf of bread, some small cakes and a pot of jam.

'Where did you get the jam?' asked Rose.

'From Mrs Clarence.'

Derry stood awkwardly in the doorway unable to take his eyes off Diana who was already seated. Rose persuaded him to sit down.

No one spoke.

'Roe,' said Diana quickly, 'have you one of your poems handy?'

'You don't write poems, do you?' said Derry, surprised. 'You don't look the type.'

'Only nonsense sort of poetry.'

'Have you?' said Diana.

'Sort of. But I was going to save it till we needed cheering up. But if you want it now . . .'

'Oh yes,' she begged.

Rose dragged out a folded piece of paper from her shorts pocket and shook the sand out of it.

'I hope I can read it. I've crossed bits out so often.'

She peered down at her scrawled handwriting, and stood up.

'"On Trying to Have a Bath",' she announced. 'It's a sonnet. You know. Fourteen lines of iambic pentameter and all that.

'The steaming warmth of bathroom joys has fled.
No more the leisured soak at turn of tap.
A grey zinc tub we have now in its stead
Where, emptying our saucepans in a flap,
We try to fill this portable 'tureen'
With water piping hot and not lukewarm,
So we can stew ourselves to pearly clean
For cleanliness we know is *très* good form.
Alas a tepid plunge is all we get,
And weary from the stoking of the range
We fill, refill, and constantly regret
Those sweeter days that left us less deranged.
To compensate, we strip wash at the sink.
That way, we feel more happ'ly "in the pink".'

Derry and Diana clapped vigorously. Rose bowed and sat down.

'That end bit was a bit rude,' said Diana laughing. 'We have a gentleman present.'

But the poem had broken the ice. Derry, at long last, appeared relaxed.

'Got any more?' he asked.

'Tons. But they're all at home.'

She took a piece of bread and spooned some jam on to it.

'I must say,' said Derry with enthusiasm, 'these potato scones are splendid.'

Diana, who was pouring the tea, smiled. 'Thank you, I'm quite pleased with them too. It's my first attempt at them.

I don't know if Roe explained but I'm the cook here.'

'And I'm the washer-upper.'

'Don't you ever cook?' asked Derry.

'Not if I can help it,' said Rose, 'I loathe it.'

'And I've found I love it,' said Diana. 'So it's working out quite well.'

'But aren't you getting any help at all?'

They shook their heads.

'It doesn't seem right,' he said gazing at Diana.

There was an awkward silence.

He's never looked at me like that, thought Rose wryly.

'Derry was telling me about Miss Hilda,' she said suddenly. 'He actually saw her.'

'Did you?' said Diana.

'Yes. She just looked a bit odd, that's all. I don't know why people believed such extraordinary tales about her.'

'What tales?'

'About her being a witch.'

Diana looked alarmed.

'Hang on,' said Rose. 'Supposing she had been a witch, she might have been a good one. What made them think she was one anyway?'

'They say she used to grow herbs and use them as medicine.'

'I thought you said people were too scared to come here.'

'Did I? Oh, I don't know. Honestly. I didn't take much interest in her.'

'I wish I'd been here when she was alive.'

There was another awkward silence.

'Would you like some more tea?' said Diana.

'No, thank you,' said Derry politely.

'It's nice for Roe to have met someone of her own age. I

67

think it's a bit dull for her in the school hols. When do you go back?'

'I'm eighteen!' he said, mortified.

'Oh. I'm so sorry. I thought since you were home that you . . .'

'I'm waiting for my exam results before I sign up for the R.A.F.' he explained hurriedly.

'He wants to be a pilot,' added Rose.

'That's marvellous,' said Diana. She looked guilty for a moment. 'I think I might go into the W.A.A.F. when I join up. If they'll have me.'

'Diana!' exclaimed Rose.

'I've got to join up soon,' she murmured, 'and I'm afraid I'm too cowardly to face the munitions factory.'

'But why the W.A.A.F.?'

'Every time I see a plane, it makes me shudder. I think to be a pilot or a rear-gunner or anybody in an air crew must take so much courage. They seem so helpless up there. I just feel that if I was in the W.A.A.F. maybe I could do something down below to help them. I'm afraid I have no idea what. I don't care really. Even if it was just cooking eggs and bacon for them or making tea I'd feel I was contributing something.'

'I should feel very proud to know that you were rooting for us chaps while we were in battle,' said Derry.

'This is beginning to sound like a very slushy film,' commented Rose.

'Goodness, look at the time,' interrupted Diana. 'I'd better get a move on. I'm going to first aid tonight,' she explained, 'and it'll take me a bit of time to get there. Will we be seeing you again Derry?'

'I hope so,' he said hoarsely.

'It's my twenty-first in a couple of weeks. We're having a little celebration here. Do come. It'll be nice for Roe to have company.'

Rose groaned inwardly. How could her sister be so innocent? Couldn't she see from his rapturous gaze that, as far as he was concerned, Rose had ceased to exist? Derry began mumbling incoherently but Rose knew he had accepted the invitation.

Rose cupped her chin in her hands and stared out into the garden. She was sitting in the tiny room next to her bedroom. In spite of wearing her swimsuit and having the table drawn close to the open window, she still felt hot. She studied the scribbled notes she had made over the last fortnight.

Alec had lent her several books on the Edwardian period. When she had tentatively asked if she could borrow some she had expected him to pry and ask her exactly what she was going to write or laugh at her. Instead he had seemed genuinely interested in her request and had ploughed through rooms of books to find what she was looking for. She had scoured the books knowing she would only use a tiny portion of the information she had collected, yet it felt as though she had hardly skimmed the surface. But it was Hilda's diary that had been most useful. It was when Miss Hilda was seventeen that her favourite brother had died. He was only twenty. Miss Hilda's elder brothers were already serving in her father's old regiment, so that she suddenly found herself quite alone.

We scrubbed the kitchen table, everyone pitched in to help, Miss Hilda had written. *Father and Mr Mackie carried Richard down into the kitchen. The doctor arrived and we waited in the living room while he carried out an appendicectomy. We prayed that Richard might be strong enough to recover, but he never regained consciousness.*

When he died it was as though my heart had been ripped apart.

Rose opened her notebook.

'Come on, concentrate,' she muttered. 'Think of the story, not Miss Hilda. You've got to start writing sometime.'

For the last few days, she had been besieged with scenes about her fifteen-year-old heroine Edith. Only that morning while she was cleaning her teeth at the pump, Edith and her governess were having a quarrel inside her head.

Her hand was shaking as she picked up her pencil. She took a deep breath.

'Hello,' came Derry's voice. It sounded as though he was in the kitchen.

Her heart fell. It was obvious he liked Diana better than he liked her. She recognised the signs, having been through it many times. It was a good job she hadn't depended on him for her swimming lessons. Instead she continued practising on her own in the mornings.

Now whenever he arrived at the cove, he would suggest they return to the cottage to do a spot of gardening. Once there, he would sit and stare at Diana ignoring Rose while she weeded the garden unaided.

Rose couldn't bear the thought of another Timothy dropping in on them. Still at least he wouldn't be writing poetry. Suddenly she found herself longing for Derry to notice that she was female too. And not just good old tomboyish Roe. She was a fool to have introduced him to Diana. She didn't have a chance of his attention with her sister around.

There was another voice in the kitchen now. It was Mrs Clarence's. Rose picked up her watch from the table. No wonder Derry had come to the cottage. It was well past two. He must have wondered where she'd got to.

She flung back the chair.

Downstairs Mrs Clarence was seated at the kitchen table. A scythe, a pair of garden shears and a can of oil were leaning up by the door. She was laughing.

Derry was standing with his back against the sink.

'Oh,' Mrs Clarence panted. 'I should have come on the inland route. I know it's longer but at least it don't have as many dips and bumps as that cliff walk. I'm getting too old for it.'

'It's nothing to do with age,' said Diana pressing a tiny round piece of pastry into a baking tray. 'I've only just got it into my stride.'

Mrs Clarence leaned across to look.

'Those look marvellous.'

'I'm rather pleased with them too. You know, I'm getting quite a kick out of seeing what I can make with only a few ingredients.'

'There must be something wrong with me,' said Rose. 'I haven't the slightest interest in cooking whatsoever. The thought of it bores me stiff.'

'The thought of *food* bores you stiff,' remarked Diana.

'I suppose I'd better tackle the lawn,' said Mrs Clarence, 'before I get too settled.'

'You don't have to,' began Diana.

'Nonsense. It'll be nice to be able to sit out on it tomorrow. You're only twenty-one once.'

Rose could have hugged Mrs Clarence. If it hadn't been for her she would have given up the garden in despair, long ago. Derry talked about helping, but after ten minutes of digging, or building the compost heap, he lost interest, and avoided anything resembling weeding. It was too finicky, he said. Girls

71

had smaller fingers than boys so she'd better do it.

Mrs Clarence had spent a whole day with her, helping her to weed. She pointed out where vegetables had 'shot' themselves, turning into yellow flowers through being left unpicked. She showed Rose which tiny leaves were weeds and which were not, and then between them they picked up the trails of deep pink roses from the ground and draped them along the walls. Then they had discussed whether or not they ought to dig up the lawn and plant vegetables. It seemed such an extravagance to leave it.

'I think Miss Hilda would like us to keep it though, don't you?' Rose had said without thinking, and Mrs Clarence had given her an odd look.

'Yes,' she said. 'I think she would. And after all it's such a tiny lawn.'

Lawn was hardly what it could be called now. Standing waist-high in seeded grass, it resembled a cornfield.

Mrs Clarence took off her cardigan and hung it on a branch on one of the apple trees.

'This takes me back a bit,' she murmured, and she swung the scythe neatly through the grass.

When they had finished trimming a neat edge round the mowed lawn Mrs Clarence lowered her voice. 'About tomorrow,' she whispered, 'I've managed to persuade an old friend of mine, called Ben, to bring his accordion with him. Lots of people from the village are coming too. Alec says he'll lend us his gramophone, and we'll all bring some records with us. We can have a bit of a dance on the lawn.'

'Does Diana know?'

'Oh no. It's tip-top secret.'

'I won't breathe a word.' She frowned. 'I'm surprised

people here are so friendly. I thought it took years to accept "foreigners".'

'It does. But we've all had to learn to mix a bit more with all the newcomers coming in and out. People here admire you, you know.'

'Admire us? Why?'

'Mr Partridge ent too popular here, see. And he's always managed to put the fear of the divvil into anyone who's stayed here. They're ever so pleased he hasn't succeeded with you two. And, a twenty-first is something special too. Let's face it. There's not much to celebrate at the moment. They've taken to Diana. They want to give her a day to remember.'

'I hope it will be,' said Rose quietly.

'Anything up?'

Rose nodded. 'A letter's arrived from Timothy. Diana hasn't seen it yet.'

'Is that the boy who pines for her?'

'Yes.'

'You're going to have to give it to her sometime.'

'I know. Do you think it'd be wrong of me to keep it from her till after the party?'

'Won't she think it strange he's forgotten her birthday?'

'I suspect she'll secretly feel rather relieved.'

Mrs Clarence gave a conspiratorial smile. 'I should accidentally mislay it then.'

'Good,' said Rose, relieved. 'Honestly, he's beginning to make *me* feel guilty too.'

There was something else Rose wanted to ask but she wasn't sure how to approach the subject.

'So it's just people from the village coming, is it?' she began lamely.

'Oh no. Diana's invited some of the young married women from the hotel. The ones who go to the first-aid classes. And Dot.'

This was just what Rose had feared. She stared at Mrs Clarence for signs of disapproval.

'I'm glad,' said Mrs Clarence. 'Dot's a kind soul. The other unmarried women daren't leave that hotel, they're that ashamed. Dot can't be doing with that hangdog approach. She says she doesn't want her child seeing his mother apologise for her existence. Did you know that her parents threw her out?'

'Yes, Diana told me.'

'And that they want to have the baby adopted and for her to go back to London as though nothing has happened?'

'No, I didn't. But how on earth is she going to manage on her own?'

'She'll have to get a job of some sort.'

'But no one will want to have anything to do with her once they know she's . . .' Rose hesitated.

'An unmarried mother?' finished Mrs Clarence for her. 'Yes, I know. Her parents said that if she comes back on her own, there'll be a job waiting for her.'

Rose struggled for something to say which would sound vaguely sympathetic but all she could manage was, 'Oh, poor thing.'

'She doesn't feel sorry for herself.'

'I'd throw myself off a cliff if it was me.'

'Oh, go on with you. Anyway that won't ever happen to you. You've got a loving family.'

Rose glanced in the direction of the kitchen where Derry was hovering awkwardly by the window trying to talk to Diana.

No. It definitely wouldn't happen to her. She'd be lucky even to get kissed, she thought.

'Cheer up, love,' said Mrs Clarence. 'You look as if you've got all the world on your shoulders.'

Rose plucked away at a small blade of grass. 'Mrs Clarence,' she said slowly, 'there's something else I've been meaning to ask you.'

'Yes?'

'It's about Alec.'

'What about him?'

'Why isn't he in the services? I mean, I know he's not in the Home Guard so I can't quite understand . . .'

'He *is* in the services, my love. The army. He's a very brave man. You know he was awarded the Military Medal for his contribution at Dunkirk.'

Rose was stunned. 'No,' she murmured. 'No. I didn't. I had no idea.'

'Oh yes. He was a private then. All the officers in his company were dead. The men were panicking and he just took over. He could have left with them but he stayed on the beach to help. He saved a lot of lives.'

'He never said a word.'

'Didn't think he would.'

'Is he on leave then?'

'In a manner of speaking.'

'Is he ill? He always looks so pale.'

'Why don't you ask him yourself? He'll be able to explain it to you better than I can.'

'I've tried to, but it never seems the right moment. And I've hardly seen him lately.' She paused. 'I've asked Derry, but I only have to mention Alec's name and he practically bites my head off. Don't they get on or something?'

'Not since Alec's illness.'

'But that doesn't make sense. If he's ill it's not *his* fault, is it?'

'I don't think Derry sees it that way.'

'Mrs Clarence, do you really think Alec would mind me asking?'

'I don't know. He might, what with Derry's reaction and then that girl Louise breaking off their engagement.'

Rose swung around. 'Engagement!' she repeated.

'Didn't you know?' asked Mrs Clarence.

'No.' Shaken by this sudden revelation, Rose was left speechless for a moment. She had never imagined Alec being that close to anyone. 'I thought he was one of those old bachelor types,' she said.

Mrs Clarence suppressed a smile.

'And you say she left him because of this *illness*?'

'Yes.'

'But why?' said Rose astounded.

'If you really want to know, my love, ask him.'

Diana stepped out into the garden, her hair still loose. She was wearing a pale green cotton dress with dark green and red flowers printed on it. It had broad shoulders and short sleeves and was buttoned to the waist with four dark green buttons. She slipped her hands into the V-shaped pockets and glanced down at her bare legs and brown lace-up shoes.

'Do I look all right?' she asked nervously. 'I was going to put on my stockings but it's so hot.'

'You look beautiful,' said Rose.

Diana smiled shyly.

'I'll put your hair up for you,' said Mrs Clarence.

'You're not fussed about me wearing shorts, are you?' Rose asked. 'All I have is that awful prissy dress which makes me look twelve, or my school gymslip.'

Diana shook her head. She gazed out at the garden. 'You've made it so lovely,' she said. 'I never expected anything like this.'

She looked quite moved. Bunting hung from the apple tree, hedges and walls. At the end of the tiny lawn stood the kitchen table, now covered in a white tablecloth. Plates of cakes and sandwiches were arranged around a large ornate cardboard cake. A key made out of silver paper had been placed in the centre. Hidden in the cardboard was a small fruit cake made with well-wishers' fruit and egg rations.

Derry was the first to appear. He arrived wearing white flannels with fake turn-ups, a white shirt and cravat and white shoes. His hair was greased to one side and his spectacles gleamed.

'Goodness!' cried Rose. 'You do look smart.'

'Do I?' he said grinning. 'Do I really?'

He glanced round swiftly. Mrs Clarence and Diana were carrying plates to the table.

He blushed and stuck his hands awkwardly into his pockets.

Suddenly Diana gave a cry. They whirled round.

Coming at a snail's pace was the oldest nag Rose had ever seen. Seated in the cart it was pulling were a dozen or so young and middle-aged women from the Women's Institute and Red Cross class. As soon as they saw Diana they stood up in their patched and darned summer frocks, and cheered. A short stocky man in his fifties was squashed in amongst them, beaming. He was carrying an accordion.

Diana looked near to tears.

'Surprise! Surprise!' chuckled Mrs Clarence.

Rose didn't know it but Dot was sitting in the front with a young man who was holding the reins.

'That's my son Robert. He arrived home unexpectedly last night. He's on leave. I hope you don't mind him coming.'

'Mind?' laughed Diana. 'Of course not.'

A tall cheery-faced man with cropped sandy hair and a handlebar moustache, he was dressed casually in flannels and an open-necked shirt and cravat. Although Rose knew from Mrs Clarence that he was barely twenty-three, the lines in his face gave him the stamp of an older man.

Rose watched him as he unhitched the back of the cart, and gave the women a hand-down. They ran up the path clutching their own cups and plates, their arms filled with flowers and vegetables.

'Happy birthday, love!' said Dot and she flung her arms round Diana's neck. Diana buried her face into her shoulder and put her arms round Dot's large waist.

'Oh,' she cried. 'This is wonderful.'

The women spread their gifts out on to the table. Rose strolled across the grass to take a look. They really were exquisite; dark red and white sweet williams, long tapering blue delphiniums, red roses and deep pink rambling ones like the ones which now trailed their walls. Next to the vegetables were jars of pickled cauliflower and gherkin jammed compactly together in pale green and cream rows, home-made biscuits and cakes, jams and bottles of wine.

From behind came a loud shriek. Diana had unwrapped Dot's present.

'An onion!' she yelled. 'Oh, Dot, how on earth did you find it?'

Rose swung round and stared at the seventeen-year-old girl she had been dreading to meet.

'Don't ask me,' said Dot waving her hand. 'I nearly had me baby with all the effort.'

'But I can boil this up in stews and soups. This'll make everything taste so much better. I shall put it in the middle of the table,' she said.

Against her will Rose found herself drawn to Dot. She was a plain-looking girl. Her mousy hair was short and wavy with a side parting, and her nose, which was small and round, was placed firmly above a wide mouth. It was her sense of humour which made her attractive. Her eyes were a deep blue and seemed to mist over every time she threw back her head and peeled into laughter. She had a light laugh which was so infectious that it made Rose want to giggle. Apart from her bulge, Rose thought her dreadfully thin. She noticed the brass curtain ring her sister had mentioned on her wedding finger.

Rose gazed at her sister. She looked radiant.

Robert Clarence walked past her carrying a gramophone. A short plump woman with fair hair was following him with a wooden record case. Rose suddenly realised that Alec wasn't there. She made her way through the chattering women to Mrs Clarence who was offering sandwiches to a dumpy woman with freckles. Mrs Clarence held out the plate to Rose.

'Is that Alec's gramophone?' Rose asked.

'That's right.'

'Oh. I thought he'd bring it himself.'

'Did you invite him?'

'No. I just took it for granted he'd come.'

'Diana doesn't know him. You should have asked him.'

'Yes,' she murmured. 'I suppose I should.'

She felt disappointed. It would have been nice to have had someone there she felt at ease with and yet to her surprise she also realised she was glad. She wanted to keep her friendship with him private, wanted to keep it apart from the scrutiny of Diana.

'Excuse me a minute,' said Mrs Clarence. 'I want to introduce your sister to Robert.'

Rose turned away.

The accordion-player was sitting on a chair by the table mopping his forehead with a handkerchief. She dashed across to him.

'You must be Ben.'

He nodded. 'When do you think theys'll want the dancin' to start?' he drawled.

'After the food, I expect.'

She handed him a drink, picked up a plate of cakes and began offering them round. Dot was heading towards her.

There was no escape.

'You're Roe, ain't you?'

Rose nodded.

'Di told me about the poems you write on her birthday. She's dying to hear this year's one. When are you reading it out?'

'I haven't written anything.'

'Go on with you, stop pulling my leg.'

'Honestly, I haven't.'

How stupid, she thought. What with being so involved with researching and writing down ideas for her story, she had completely forgotten.

'She's ever so looking forward to it,' said Dot. She looked alarmed for a moment. 'You are joking, ain't you? You have written something, haven't you?'

Suddenly the most wonderful idea occurred to Rose. If she could pull it off, it might kill two birds with one stone.

'Yes. But it's not exactly a birthday poem. I'll be playing a character. Would you ask people to get cushions from inside to sit on?'

''Course I will.'

'I'll need time to get changed though so don't let anyone back in afterwards. I want it to be a surprise.'

As soon as the cushions had been carried out to the lawn Rose moved swiftly into the cottage. She grabbed a piece of boiled beetroot from the kitchen larder, nipped out into the corridor and slipped the key into the door to the locked room.

When everyone was seated Robert Clarence lifted the arm from the record and put it back on its holder. He saw where Diana was sitting, and strode purposefully towards her. 'May I sit next to the birthday girl?'

Diana smiled. 'Yes, of course,' she said.

He slipped in happily beside her. 'What is she going to do?' he asked.

'I'm not sure,' said Diana, lowering her voice. 'She always writes me a silly poem on my birthday, but Dot's been acting rather mysteriously so I think she must be doing something a little different.'

The back door opened slowly and the chatter subsided.

'Blimey!' whispered Dot.

Rose drifted out of the doorway, her left arm raised to her forehead, her right arm trailing behind, a piece of paper clasped between her fingers. Around her unplaited hair which fell outwards in countless waves, she wore a thin gold band. A burgundy velvet curtain was draped and arranged in a robe with gold braid criss-crossed around her chest so that she appeared to be a mixture of a Pre-Raphaelite painting and Ellen Terry. She had smeared beetroot on her lips and underlined her eyes with burnt cork.

She gave a cough and clutched the paper so hard that it became crumpled. Someone laughed and was immediately shushed. Rose gave a watery smile. Diana stifled a giggle. Rose lifted her head and gazed out over the audience and into the distance.

'You see before you, one who is tortured with the pains and passions of love,' she began expressionlessly, 'but I know, indeed I can sense, that all of you here will be sympathetically receptive to these deep and searing longings which I am here forthwith about to share with you, for lo, we have all known what it is to love.'

By this time, several of the women had begun laughing, for they realised that Rose was making fun of all the endless recitations they had had to endure politely at various village concerts.

'And now I shall begin my burning lament.' She lifted up the scrap of paper.

> 'Poem of unearthly passion,' she moaned.
> 'When I recline upon the barren heath at night,
> I gaze forlornly at the weeping frozen moon
> It wafts so limply in the fragrant midnight sky
> Away from all that's dear, yes, you have guessed,
>   it's you.'

As Rose continued to read in her dreary way, the laughter reached such a pitch that she was forced to stop. Even when she carried on, she found it necessary to pause between sentences until the laughter had subsided.

Derry, who was apoplectic, removed his spectacles and wiped them on his shirt.

Rose raised one arm weakly.

'Up in the sky where lovers' darts do toss and turn
I see our love writ clearly in the distant blue.
It says, my dearest precious own sweet one,
There lies the story of dear me and fondest you.'

She let her arm drop limply to her side, and was halfway into a mixture of a bow and a curtsy when everyone erupted into cheers and loud applause.

She backed clumsily towards the door and closed it behind her.

'She's a marvel, ent she?' cried Mrs Clarence. 'Her face! Talk about deadpan.'

'And that monotonous voice!' laughed Diana.

Derry leaned towards them. 'I didn't know she could write anything so marvellously awful. '*The weeping frozen moon!*' he choked.

Dot appeared in the doorway with the lighted cake, Rose following. Ben played an introductory note. Diana, who was standing listening to Robert Clarence, swung round. 'Oh,' she cried.

As Dot walked across the lawn with as much grace as she could muster, there was a chorus of 'Happy Birthday' and:

'Twenty-one today, twenty-one today.
She's got the key of the door,
Never been twenty-one before.'

It was then that Rose noticed Robert Clarence. She was used to seeing people staring with adoration at Diana but never with such a steady gaze. Diana turned to look at him and his face softened. It shook Rose. They both looked so vulnerable.

Suddenly the realisation that no one would ever look at her like that caused such sadness that she could feel her eyes growing wet. She blinked quickly, resumed her jolly manner and dashed round handing out pieces of cake and loganberries and cream.

Four of the women paired up and began foxtrotting and quickstepping round the lawn to Ben's accordion. Soon other couples joined them. Robert Clarence moved continuously amongst the faded floral dresses, taking it in turns to dance with the women, trying to make up for all the absent men.

Derry sat awkwardly on a chair by the table and watched. After a while Robert stopped changing partners and stayed with Diana.

Dot and Rose, who had been doing a strange kind of dance of their own, sat on the grass at the edge of the lawn.

'Don't they look romantic,' sighed Dot, as Robert and Diana glided past them.

'I suppose so,' murmured Rose feeling both jealous of Diana and pleased for her.

Later, when Ben took a short break, someone put some swing records on. Rose watched in amazement as four of the girls whirled about the grass at breakneck speed.

'What kind of dancing is that?'

Dot was astounded. 'Jitterbugging! Blimey, you have been cut off in your little boarding school.'

'Don't remind me. I know.'

'It's even better with blokes,' said Dot. 'They can throw you around on their hips.'

Diana and Rose stood at the gate. The horse and cart now faced the hill. The women had gathered up their cups and plates and had climbed into the cart, their faces flushed, their arms sunburnt from the glare of the afternoon sun. Mrs Clarence and Dot sat on either side of Robert on the seat.

'I'll see you tomorrow,' he said.

Diana nodded.

As the horse began its slow plod up the lane Rose and Diana waved. They leaned over the gate and watched it crawl up towards the hill. It wasn't till it was out of sight that they returned to the garden.

The table and chairs were now indoors. The only remnants of the party were the coloured flags hanging from the trees and hedgerows. The girls wandered slowly back to the kitchen.

'Oh, Roe,' said Diana smiling. 'It's been a wonderful day. Twenty-one!' she said. 'I can't believe it. I can vote. I can marry.' She reddened. 'Not that I'm thinking of it. And now I've met Robert. Oh, Roe, he wants to take me out tomorrow. And I've accepted but I don't know if I should have done. I feel so guilty.'

'Whatever for?'

'Timothy.'

I'm the one who should feel guilty, Rose thought.

Diana gave a puzzled frown. 'It's funny he didn't remember my birthday. Perhaps his card has got delayed in the post.'

'Diana,' interrupted Rose quietly. 'I have a confession to make.'

'Oh?'

'You know that poem I read?'

'Oh yes. It was marvellous. I haven't laughed so much in ages.'

'Diana, I didn't write it.'

'What do you mean?' She looked puzzled. 'Did you find it in a book?'

'No.' She swallowed. 'I found it in this.'

She drew the envelope from her pocket and slid it across the table.

'It's addressed to me.'

'It arrived yesterday. It's from Timothy.'

'So he did remember. Roe, it's open.'

'Yes. That's what I'm trying to tell you.'

Diana frowned for a moment and then she realised. 'The poem, it wasn't . . .?'

'It was.'

'Oh, Roe, that was cruel. Those were his feelings you read out in front of everyone.'

'I know.'

'How could you do such a thing? Is there a letter with it?'

'Yes. I didn't read that.'

'How considerate of you.'

She snatched the envelope and stormed out of the kitchen.

Rose watched her stalk angrily to the foot of the garden to read it. It was as if she wanted to make as much space between her and Rose as was possible.

Rose gave a sigh and picked away at the grain on the table. She was about to make a hasty retreat to her room when she heard a loud shriek. She leapt up and looked out of the window.

Diana's back was shaking violently and she was making

short staccato gasps which sounded like a mixture of weeping and a fit.

'Hysteria,' whispered Rose alarmed. 'Oh my goodness. You're supposed to slap someone's face when they're like that. I've never hit anyone before.'

She raced out into the garden but stopped once she reached her. 'Diana,' she began hesitantly, 'are you all right?'

Diana nodded. But Rose noticed her wiping her face with her hands so she knew she was crying.

Rose was devastated. 'I'm awfully sorry, Diana, I never meant . . .'

And then Diana turned round, her mouth open, the strange gasping sound still erupting from her throat. And Rose smiled. She had been right. Diana was hysterical. But not in the way she had envisaged. Diana was hysterical with laughter.

'Oh, Roe, if only you knew,' she gasped. 'This is the best present I could have had. He *is* a pompous ass, isn't he?'

Rose nodded beaming.

'Thank you! Thank you! Thank you!' and she flung her arms round Rose's neck.

They hugged each other tightly. It was the closest Rose had felt to her sister in years.

'Oh, Roe,' Diana laughed. 'I'm free! I'm free of him!'

Six

Derry scowled.

'Why do you want to see Alec?' he asked.

Rose leaned her bicycle up against the shop window.

They had used the inland route to the village, the one Mrs Clarence had mentioned.

She threw her plaits back over her shoulders. 'I just want to ask him about something, that's all.'

He gave a shrug and leant his bicycle up next to hers.

The bookshop was empty of customers and as messy as usual. They stepped over numerous dusty piles and edged their way up the middle of the steps where books had now been stacked on either side. They found Alec kneeling on the sitting-room floor, surrounded by more books. He was dusting them. He looked up and smiled.

'Hello, stranger,' he said.

'You haven't bought *more* books,' said Derry, disgusted.

Rose sat on the floor and picked one up. She observed Alec's grubby crumpled clothes and the dark shadows under his eyes. She wondered if he ever slept.

'I'm awfully sorry about yesterday,' she said. 'I never thought of inviting you. I just took it for granted you'd come.'

'How did it go?'

'It was marvellous. Didn't Derry tell you?'

'No!' snapped Derry and he walked out and slammed the door.

They listened to him stamping upstairs. Embarrassed, Rose stared into the book she was holding.

'Has Derry talked to you about me?' asked Alec.

She shook her head. 'Mrs Clarence told me a little.'

'What did she say?'

'That you're in the army. That you were given the Military Medal for what you did in Dunkirk.'

'Oh,' he said surprised. 'Did she?'

'She thinks you're a very brave man.'

He gave a short laugh. 'She must be the only person who does.'

'Why do you say that?'

'Didn't she tell you?'

'No. She said you had some kind of illness and that your fiancée and Derry hadn't reacted too well to it. Is that true?'

He nodded.

'Is it . . .?' she faltered. 'Is it that you're a conscientious objector? Is that it?'

'It's a bit late for that,' he said wryly. 'No. I cracked up. What they call a nervous breakdown. I tried to keep going. I thought that work was the best cure but I started having blackouts. I was supposed to have been sent to an army psychiatrist for treatment but they're rather overworked now. I was lucky. I had this crazy Irish doctor instead. He kicked me out of hospital and sent me home. He said, "The trouble with you English, is that you still treat death like a great taboo. You pretend it isn't there. Go away with you," he said, "and grieve."'

He shrugged. 'I suppose that's what I've been doing.'

Rose put the book back on the floor. 'Was it really terrible, what you went through?'

'Yes. But no more terrible than many other people's experiences. Some survive and bounce out of far worse ones.'

'And that's why Derry thinks you're . . .' She stopped.

'A coward? Yes.'

'Do you?'

He pulled at the bridge of his nose with his fingers. 'In a way. I think even Louise thought that. She could understand me being in a state of shock, but she couldn't take the crying. Men aren't supposed to do that sort of thing, but once the dam broke, I couldn't stop.' He gave an awkward smile. 'Some days

I would bawl my way through my entire handkerchief supply. I think I must have been carrying a well around inside me.'

'Do you still cry?'

'Occasionally. When something jogs my memory. But I feel more anger than anything. Anger at the loss of life. My friends. That sort of thing.' He paused. 'In November I shall have a check-up to see whether I'm A1.'

'And if you are?'

'I don't know. It'll either be back in the fray or a desk job.'

'You don't mind me asking, do you?'

'No.'

'Now I understand why you weren't embarrassed when I blubbed.'

He laughed. 'Yes. I'm afraid I've had lots of practice at it.'

A lock of his hair had fallen into one of his eyes. Without thinking, she pushed it to one side.

'So what have you been doing all this time?' he said suddenly. 'Have you started that story yet?'

'Yes. This morning. But it's not going too well. Alec,' she said slowly. 'There is one other thing.'

'Yes?'

'Do you know Dot?'

'She's one of the mothers from *Hôtel Maternité*, isn't she? The young woman Mrs Clarence has taken under her wing.'

'Yes. Is it really called *Hôtel Maternité*?'

'No. It's just my name for it. So what about her?'

'I'd like to get her a book.'

'On bringing up babies?'

'On having them.'

'Ah.' He scratched his head. 'I know I have a couple of books on that, but where they are . . .'

'Well, if you come across them.' She stood up. 'I'd better go now.'

He looked sad. 'You're not shocked by what I told you?'

'No. Just a bit puzzled. I'm afraid I don't know anything about breakdowns.'

'Won't you stay to tea?'

'I'd love to, but I've already been invited to Mrs Clarence's.' She turned to leave.

'Roe?'

'Yes.'

'Don't give up that story.'

She smiled. 'I won't.'

She had followed the diaries up until the outbreak of the last war and a little beyond. In her early twenties, Miss Hilda had turned down several proposals of marriage, and it was assumed, especially since her mother had become ill that she would remain unmarried and stay at home to look after her parents. Her brothers agreed that she was unmarriageable. Already, they thought her a little odd.

Of her suitors, Miss Hilda wrote, *I found the men such bores and I couldn't help but compare them to my darling brother Richard. Sadly they never came up to his standards. Perhaps I was being unfair, but I couldn't bear the thought of being intimate with a man I couldn't respect or love.*

Rose settled herself back on the cane chair, with another pair of books from the bureau and untied them. One was leather bound and shabby. It was an album. Inside were handwritten poems, some jingoistic, some funny and lyrical. A few thank-you poems dedicated to 'Nurse Hilda'. In amongst them were sketches, drawings and signed photographs of young men in uniform.

Rose opened the other book. It was an account of Miss Hilda's experience as a voluntary nurse. She began reading. Her shock was immediate. As she turned the pages rapidly, clutching the book, it was as though someone had taken hold of her roughly and had shaken her. She read about the overcrowded wards where nurses tried desperately to save twenty or more lives at a time; of men who cried out deliriously, of those who finally woke up only to find a limb missing or who shrieked, 'I can't see! Where are my eyes?'

Then there were the men whose raw skin blistered and seeped from the mustard gas, men who fought for breath with burnt lungs, men who would never father children, men who would never walk again, men who shook and rattled and wept.

Looking back, Miss Hilda had written, *remembering what I had witnessed, men dying day after day, perhaps it seems surprising, considering my sheltered upbringing that I was not overwhelmed by it all, but I appreciated the fact that I was alive and healthy, and like all of us, I did the best I could.*

I noticed that the men who were recovering, grew restless, so I brought in an album, and asked each of them to fill one of the pages. It was a way of keeping them occupied. Originally I had two albums, but my family found one and burnt it.

Rose was staggered. Why on earth would they want to burn it? She opened the album and gazed at the photographs.

'I wonder how many of them survived,' she murmured.

She returned to the diary.

His name was Matthew. He was six years my junior; twenty-five. How he had managed to survive two years of the war I'll never know. When he was brought to the hospital it was the fourth time he had been wounded.

It was his eyes which first drew me. As dark and as brown as his hair, they radiated such warmth, humour and intelligence.

It wasn't long before I was hauled in to see the charge sister and was discouraged from fraternising with Matthew. It was all I could do not to smile. I had always considered myself an unattractive plain sort of woman, hardly one likely to 'flirt' with patients as some of the younger nurses were accused of doing if they were pleasant to the young men.

One day Matthew asked if he could write in my album. When he returned it to me I found an envelope inside with 'H' written on it. I had to wait until the women in my bedroom were asleep before I had the time and privacy to read it. When I did, it took all my self-control not to laugh at his description of life as a patient, under the watchful eye of nanny-like sisters.

From that day, we communicated via the album.

Rose turned each page rapidly as she followed the account of Miss Hilda and Matthew's courtship; their coded sayings; the private jokes; the blossoming of love.

By the summer, Matthew had grown strong enough to be allowed in the gardens with some of the other soldiers.

Occasionally, Miss Hilda was able to go outside with him too, but the nurses were always under the eagle eye of a sister who made quite sure there were no improprieties.

One day they sat at either end of a bench. Matthew pretended to be engrossed in a book. By some lucky chance they remained together, undisturbed, for half an hour, and in that time he proposed and she accepted.

We planned to be married, as soon as he was discharged from the hospital.

Matthew wrote to my father and asked for my hand in marriage. He explained that he was not a rich man but that he could provide a comfortable home. Before the war he had worked as an editor for a publishing company.

Then followed a series of letters.

Hilda's older brother arrived at the hospital. He was on leave, and his father had ordered him to bring Miss Hilda back, and put an end to her nonsense.

As Rose read on she felt as though she was being dragged through a nightmare of misunderstandings. Miss Hilda's family ridiculed her behaviour, laughed at Matthew's age, implied that perhaps all the hard work as a voluntary nurse, which they had disapproved of in the first place, had unhinged her mind. Within three weeks of Matthew's proposal, Miss Hilda was called in to see the matron. The matron's manner was icy. She informed Miss Hilda, that her mother was ill, that they were grateful for all her help, but duty to one's family came first and that she was to go home immediately. On her return to the ward she discovered that Matthew had been discharged.

Rose lowered the book.

'No,' she breathed.

Miss Hilda had gazed at his empty bed, stunned. She couldn't believe that her one chance of happiness had been deliberately taken away from her.

A soldier handed her one of the albums.

'Nurse,' he whispered, 'Matthew asked me to give this back to you. He said you weren't to let it out of your hands until you'd looked inside.'

Miss Hilda had turned hastily away. Tucked in between two of the pages, she found a folded piece of paper with an 'H' on it.

She just managed to slip the note under her cuff when

the charge sister moved briskly towards her and snatched the album from her hands.

'I believe you should be packing,' she snapped.

Miss Hilda had stumbled out into the corridor and across to her room in the nursing quarters. Even there, she was not alone. She had to wait until she was out of the hospital grounds before she could read the note.

'My dearest Hilda,' he had written. 'It seems your father has influence in high places. He has contacted the commanding officer of my regiment and I am to be sent post-haste to France.

I have one week of leave before I go.

My dearest one, I quite understand if you refuse my next request, but I would like so much to spend that week with you.'

He had then given an address where he could be contacted.

Rose whipped through the pages.

'Please,' she begged. 'Please go with him.'

I informed my parents, by letter, that I would be home as requested, but that there would be a delay of a week as a ward of forty soldiers had arrived unexpectedly and that they were all seriously injured.

I met Matthew at Waterloo Station. He had bought me a wedding ring. It felt so natural and so right when he slipped it on my finger. As far as I was concerned I was already joined to him and he felt that too.

We boarded the train like a newly married couple on honeymoon.

Passengers sensed it too, for they smiled at us, and we bathed in all their small kindnesses on the journey.

As Rose closed the book she discovered that her hands

were shaking. She leaned back and gazed at all the carpets and boxes, the wicker chair and the old gramophone and reached out and touched them. She felt so close to Miss Hilda.

She sat up sharply. She could hear laughter and voices in the lane. She leapt out of the chair and unhooked the curtain. By the time she had reached the kitchen and had put a saucepan of water on the primus for tea, her sister walked in. She was not alone. Towering in the doorway, carrying the shopping was Robert Clarence. Rose found herself avoiding their eyes in case they had seen the curtain swinging back across the window. But she needn't have worried. They seemed oblivious of her.

'Tea!' gasped Diana, dropping into the chair. 'Just what I need.'

Robert dumped the shopping on the table. Rose stared at them. They were both beaming like a couple of Cheshire cats.

'If I'd known you were going shopping,' she said, 'I would have come with you.'

'I didn't plan to, but once I was there I didn't like to waste the journey.'

'Did you post your mail?' Rose asked significantly not knowing whether or not to mention Timothy in front of Robert.

Diana nodded and laughed. 'Yes. It's over.' She turned aside. 'Robert knows all about it.'

'Oh,' said Rose.

'Would you like me to unpack these bags?' he asked.

'No,' said Diana, 'let's have tea first.' And she drew a cake and a pot of honey from one of the bicycle bags. 'Look what Robert's mother has given us.'

Rose had never seen such a transformation in a person.

Her sister was so relaxed. Could being twenty-one make such a difference? Perhaps it was because she had shaken off Timothy. And then she noticed Robert with his elbows on the table gazing at her sister. And to Rose's amazement Diana didn't seem in the least perplexed. And then the penny dropped. That's why Diana was so relieved when she could break off the relationship with Timothy without guilt. She was in love with Robert! But how could she fall in love with someone so soon? She hardly knew him.

'Roe?'

'What?'

'Penny for them.'

'Sorry. I'm in a bit of a dream.'

'You've been working on your story then.'

'Yes.'

'Are you all right?'

'Me? Yes. Why?'

Now it was Diana who was staring at her. Rose rubbed her face with her fingers self-consciously. 'Have I a smudge?'

'No.'

'What is it then?'

'Oh, nothing,' said Diana. 'You suddenly look older, that's all.'

Seven

'But she's not old enough,' objected Diana.

'Don't be daft,' said Dot. 'She's seventeen and a half.'

'Three quarters actually,' put in Rose.

They were in Mrs Clarence's kitchen discussing the forth-coming dance. It was Dot who had announced that the American G.I.s were organising one at a village five miles away.

Diana was leaning up against the sink with Robert. She frowned. 'I don't know. I do think seventeen is a bit young to start meeting men.'

'But I've told you,' Rose interrupted, 'I just want to *dance!*'

'There's going to be a proper band there,' said Dot. 'If I wasn't carrying this ole thing around,' she said patting her stomach, 'I'd be there in a flash.'

Rose was swallowing down a desire to say, 'Look I'm going anyway. I don't need your permission.' But Diana had been so happy since Robert's appearance that she didn't want to spoil their last days together before his leave was up.

'But who's going to escort her?' said Diana. 'You won't be there, Dot, and neither will I.'

'Oh?'

She blushed.

'Diana will be having dinner here,' said Robert. 'It's my last night.'

'Do you really want to go?' asked Diana.

'Yes. What about that Harold you mentioned, Mrs Clarence?'

'Harold?' said Diana looking interested. 'Who's he?'

'The man who owns the horse and cart,' said Mrs Clarence. 'He's ninety-two.'

'There's Derry,' Diana said. 'He might go with you. I'll ask him.'

'If he agrees,' said Rose, 'you won't worry about me then?'

'No.' She sighed. 'Though he's a bit young too.'

Rose gave Dot a quick smile. Since reading about Hilda and Matthew she had warmed to Dot and they had struck up an easy friendship. Now, thanks to Dot joining forces with her, Rose suddenly realised she would be able to go to her first dance!

Dot grabbed her by the arm.

'Come on,' she yelled, 'you're going to have a proper jitterbug lesson,' and she dragged her into the sitting room. Within minutes, she and Rose had folded up the table, pushed it to one side, and placed the chairs up against the walls.

'Now,' said Dot, jiggling a knob at the front of the wireless, 'with any luck we'll be able to get the American Forces Network.'

Mrs Clarence stood in the doorway. As soon as she heard the first strains of a clarinet she threw up her hands. 'Oh no, not that jazz!' And she retreated hastily into the kitchen.

'This is going to be a bit difficult to demonstrate with me extra luggage but here goes.'

Rose who was already caught up in the rhythm was swaying from side to side.

'Now you'll 'ave to imagine that I'm a man,' said Dot.

'It's all right, I'm used to leading. I'm always the man at dance classes.'

'Well, you ain't going to have woppin' great G.I.s pretending they're young ladies just so's you can lead them.'

Rose began to copy Dot but was imitating her so exactly that she was even taking into account the slightly heavy swing of her body with her well-advanced pregnancy. Dot leaned on the sideboard and giggled.

Suddenly the music stopped and an announcer introduced a Geraldo number.

'Jealousy!' they yelled.

They walked slowly into a clinch and proceeded to do an

exaggerated tango round the room. Dot turned her face and began mouthing the words.

Rose shrieked with laughter. So much so that Robert and Diana came to see what was happening.

They both whirled round the floor, Dot continuing to mime singing while Rose gave arch and smouldering looks. Dot stood stiffly like a Spanish dancer and Rose grabbed one of Mrs Clarence's roses from a vase and stuck it into her mouth.

'Ouch!' she said, and spat it out rapidly.

She swanned back into Dot's arms. Dot lunged forward, threw her back over her knee, lifted her up and twirled her into a low curtsy.

'You're both mad,' exclaimed Robert.

Diana looked anxious.

'It's all right,' said Dot. 'I feel fine. I haven't felt so good in ages.'

She twiddled the wireless knob again. There was a strange swooping sound. She moved the knob back carefully and turned the volume up. The room was filled with a male American voice.

'It's like watching a film without the picture,' said Rose.

'Boogie-woogie,' yelled Dot. 'Let's swing.'

Robert burst out laughing. 'Come on,' he said grabbing Diana's hand. 'Let's get out of here before we're trampled to death.' And they fled through the front door.

Rose and Dot stumbled and spun across the room. Rose kept laughing, not because she found it funny but because the music was so exhilarating. The next number was slow. She could imagine it being played in a sleazy nightclub, the empty glasses on the piano, and couples leaning exhausted in each other's arms.

'Oh, come on,' said Dot to the wireless. 'How can I teach her the jitterbug, if you keep giving me these lovey-dovey tunes.'

The next number was 'Take The "A" Train'. Rose led Dot in a speedy quickstep.

'They got to have a good number soon,' Dot panted.

'This is marvellous,' said Rose. 'I've never heard such wonderful music. I feel I could dance forever.' She paused. 'What's this tune?'

Dot gaped at her. 'You must know this one!'

'No. I don't.'

'It's "In the Mood". Good old Glen Miller.'

She began to swing Rose round again. 'That's it,' she yelled. 'Back and round and back and round and away!'

'Oh, Dot,' gasped Rose, stopping for a moment to stare at her.

'Keep going, gel. Don't stand there gawpin'. That's right. Swing!'

It was an exhausting process learning the jitterbug, and they soon became grateful for the occasional slow blues number when they could sink back into their chairs for a breather.

'You wait, Rose my girl,' gasped out Dot. 'You'll be in tip-top form by Saturday. I'm absolutely determined.'

'I wish you could come too.'

'Get on with you. Once you get the swing of it you'll be all right. Hah! Hear what I said! The *swing* of it!'

Rose groaned.

'Oh,' said Dot, 'I thought that were quite clever.'

She took Rose's hand. 'Come on!'

By mid-afternoon they decided to leave Mrs Clarence in peace and walk back to the cottage to continue practising there.

They strolled past the beach and up the slope to the coastal path. They didn't speak much at first, not out of awkwardness, but out of a desire to drink in the day. Every now and then Rose glanced at Dot out of the corner of her eye. She envied Dot's easy manner. She wished she could be as relaxed.

'Dot,' she began hesitantly. 'Do you like being female?'

''Course I do. Don't you?'

'I'm not sure.'

'I'd hate to be a man.'

'Why?'

'Because they get sent to the front for one. And anyway, they can't have babies, can they?'

They stopped. Rose slipped off her sandals, and sat down, dangling her legs over the edge of the cliffs.

Dot lowered herself beside her.

'Dot. I don't know if it's worth me going to that dance. I can't see Derry dancing with me.'

'Why ever not?'

'He doesn't see me in that way.'

'So. There'll be others there falling over their feet to get to you.'

'Not with him there. I wish you could come.'

'Good job I can't. He wouldn't be seen dead with me around.'

Rose felt herself reddening.

'It's all right,' said Dot. 'I'd better get used to it. Looks like I'm going to have to cope with that sort of thing for a long time.'

'I used to feel embarrassed,' Rose confessed.

'About what?'

'Meeting you. But once I did, those feelings disappeared.'

Dot smiled. 'Good.'

They stared out at the sea. It was smooth, like a mirror that had been tinted pale green.

'Did you love him?' said Rose quickly.

'Oh yeah. Still do.'

'You think he's still alive?'

'Yeah. I'm sure I'd feel it if he weren't.'

'Do you mind me asking?'

She beamed. 'No. I've been dying to talk about him for ages. I can't at the hotel. I mean, there, we're all supposed to be victims of the Immaculate Conception. Even the marrieds are treated like convent schoolgirls. Not that we see much of them. The nurses do their best to keep us separated. We shouldn't even be in the same building, but somebody who was organising it all slipped up.'

'Why do they keep you apart?'

'In case we corrupt them.'

'You're not serious.'

'Yeah. What makes it really stupid is that I bet half those women only knew their husbands for a couple of weeks while they was on leave before marrying them. Me and Jack have been walking out together since he was fourteen. The only reason we didn't get married was because of me dad. He wouldn't give us permission. He wanted to keep me at home to look after the kids, and work on his stall.'

'How could he be so cruel!' said Rose angrily.

Dot was surprised at this unexpected outburst.

'Yeah,' she said softly. 'You're right. It was cruel.'

'Is that why . . .' She hesitated. 'You did what you did?'

'Out of spite? No. It just sort of happened. We didn't plan it or anything. We didn't think about the consequences. We was too happy, I suppose. That's why I was caught.'

She gave Rose a steady look. 'You understand, don't you?' she exclaimed. 'You really do understand.'

'Yes. I don't think I would have done if I hadn't . . .' She checked herself. 'If I hadn't come here. But yes, I do.'

Dot gazed into the distance.

'I was so mixed up, when he joined the army. I was that proud of him but I was narked too. I didn't want him getting himself killed. We talked such a lot about the future, you see. And I wanted us to have one.' She turned. 'I know this sounds daft but we knew when we was *twelve*, we'd get married.' She looked away. 'Bit late now.'

'What will you do after you've had the baby?'

'I dunno. I keep thinking of all sorts of things, like getting some kind of job with short hours. I could work in munitions, of course. They have nurseries attached to them. I'd like to get trained in something, but honestly I don't think I've a hope in hell.'

'Why not?'

'Because of being an unmarried mum. If I could pretend to be widowed, it'd be all right, see. I mean, honest, Roe, any fool can see this is an old brass curtain ring,' she said, twisting it round her finger. 'If I could save up enough to buy a proper wedding ring then I'm sure I could get some kind of work. But I can't even afford baby clothes at the moment.' She paused. 'I did try getting work on that farm near here.'

'Mrs Acres' farm?'

'Yeah. But she went all tight-lipped, and kept staring at this effin' thing on my finger. I knew she knew. And she knew I knew she knew.'

'What was he like?' asked Rose.

'Jack?'

She nodded.

'Small and skinny with an enormous conk. I used to say, "Neither of us are oil paintings, are we, Jack?" "You'll do," he'd say. "You can't have a kiss and a cuddle with an oil painting."' She looked serious for a moment. 'Sometimes he'd be given leave out of the blue and he'd turn up in the market and stand in front of me dad's stall. And I'd just go barmy. I'd yell, and dance around and hug him. I didn't care. Me dad used to get that mad.' She turned away shyly. 'We did it in Epping Forest. We borrowed bikes and went there for a picnic. Our parents thought it was safe enough for us to go on our own. I think they thought it was too cold for us to get up to any hanky-panky. I mean, it was November!' She paused. 'It was one of those lovely warm autumn days. I remember the earth smelt sort of damp. We wheeled our bikes into the trees and just kept going. We felt like we was the only people in the world.

'We lay this big blanket down on the leaves and started our picnic. I don't think we stopped talking or taking the mickey out of each other for hours.

'Then it got sort of dusky and, I don't know, it just happened. We just loved being together so much. And doing it made us feel even closer. I dunno how long we stayed there. I know it got dark and it took us ages to find our way out.'

'Was it just the once?'

'No. We did it again a couple of times. I think we would have done it more but it kept raining. Epping Forest was the only place we could be private.' She reddened. 'Are you shocked?'

'No.'

'You know something,' she said, and her eyes started to fill, 'I'm that grateful to have Jack's baby inside me. Honest, Roe. I'm so bleedin' proud.'

Rose took her hand and squeezed it.

Dot dragged her arm across her eyes. 'Thanks, mate,' she said shakily.

They stood up and carried on walking.

Rose's dress was a faded pink-patterned affair with puffed sleeves and a frilly collar. With the help of Dot and Mrs Clarence, she dyed it a rich burgundy, padded the shoulders, replaced the collar, cuffs, and buttons down the front, with black ones and made a belt from the material which had been used for tying a bow.

Rose's only pair of party shoes were black patent ones with button-down straps. They were at the bottom of a cupboard in London, much to her relief, for she felt like Shirley Temple in them and they pinched her toes. Instead, she bleached her socks and polished her walking shoes.

On the evening of the dance, she laid her dress over the bed in Mrs Clarence's room and took her underwear into the bathroom. She had decided to wear the new blackout bloomers that Aunt Em had made for her. They were a bit cumbersome but at least they weren't patched or darned.

Alec had given her a bar of scented soap. She was so thrilled with it, that she had even used it to wash her hair.

For the last few days, she had practised the jitterbug until her entire body ached.

She sank back and attempted to luxuriate in the shallow amount of bath water they were allowed, with her hair bundled up into a turban to keep it from getting wet.

She rubbed the sweet-smelling lather into every nook and cranny of her body, even between each toe. She dried herself leisurely, slipped into her brassiere, vest and knickers, and, with a bucket, scooped out as much bath water as she could into a large barrel by the bath. Mrs Clarence liked to use any spare water for the garden.

Her towel wrapped round her, she made a quick sprint into Mrs Clarence's bedroom and dressed. She hadn't a clue what to do with her hair. She couldn't wear it in plaits. Diana might have second thoughts if she looked too young.

Dot popped her head round the door. 'You look crackin',' she said.

'What am I going to do with all this wretched hair?'

Dot sat on the end of the bed and took a good look at it. 'You could either have it in a single plait, or loose.'

'It'll end up looking like a bush if it's loose. I think the single plait is about the best idea.'

Dot brushed it out vigorously and weaved it into one long plait. She left Rose to hold it while she went downstairs to search for a ribbon.

She returned, waving a long strip of dark red curtain braiding. 'This is the best I can do,' she said. 'Mrs Clarence was going to cut it but I've thought of a better idea. I'm going to replait this with the braid.' She moved her fingers swiftly through Rose's hair separating each piece. 'Then I'll tie it round and round into a bow with what's left.'

When she had finished, she walked over to the dressing table, where a blanket was hanging over the mirror.

'Don't touch that,' said Rose. 'I put it there, so I wouldn't get depressed.'

'But you look lovely.'

'Please,' she begged, 'I feel much happier when I've forgotten what I look like.'

Dot shook her head. 'I dunno. Sometimes I can't make you out at all.'

Rose took a deep breath. 'I suppose I'd better make my entrance.'

Mrs Clarence, Diana and Robert were waiting for her at the foot of the stairs. Rose noticed that Robert had his arm round Diana's waist, and that she was looking a little flushed.

'Oh! You seem so much older,' Diana said, surprised.

'Thank goodness for that!' exclaimed Rose.

'You look lovely.'

'M'm,' said Rose in disbelief.

'That's what I just told her,' said Dot.

'You do,' added Diana. 'Honestly.'

'Thanks.'

Dot was hopping excitedly from one foot to the other, doing a strange kind of jig.

'Don't you think you should sit down,' said Diana.

'Oh Di, di diddli di,' said Dot, collapsing into a chair.

Diana laughed.

'Oh dear,' said Rose. 'I suppose I'll just have to twiddle my thumbs until Derry arrives.' She sat down, and shifted restlessly. 'I feel so nervous, as if I'm about to take School Cert. all over again.'

There was a knock at the door.

It was Derry in his Home Guard uniform. 'The horse and cart are here,' he announced. 'Harold's tied her to your fence, Mrs Clarence. He's put some tarpaulins in the back, because it looks like rain.'

He stared at Diana, and then at Robert. 'I thought you'd

be wearing your uniform,' he said. 'That's why I wore mine.'

Robert gave a puzzled smile. 'I don't understand,' he began.

'Oh,' cried Diana. 'Did you think we were coming?'

'Yes,' he said reddening. 'When you asked me I thought . . .' His voice trailed away.

'Oh, I am sorry. No, it'll just be you and Roe.'

Derry looked devastated.

So much for my first dance, thought Rose.

'You'll have a much better time without us,' said Robert.

Derry, who appeared rooted to the spot, gave a quick nod.

'I'd better take you outside then,' he said to Rose in a monotone.

Rose followed him to the lane where the horse and cart were tied. Without a backward glance he climbed up into the seat. Rose clambered up behind.

Mrs Clarence and the others stood by the gate.

Dot walked over to Rose and rested her hands on the seat. 'Don't worry, love,' she said. 'You'll have a smashin' time.'

Derry shook the reins. Dot stepped back.

'Stop!' yelled a voice. 'Stop!'

Alec was sprinting down the street. He was holding a tiny corsage of pink and white roses. He ran up to them and stopped on Rose's side.

'Let me pin this to your dress,' he said. 'You must wear one for your first dance.'

'Oh, Alec,' she cried. 'They're beautiful!'

He lifted her down and attached the sprig of flowers beside her collar.

'You look the belle of the ball,' he whispered.

Rose couldn't answer. She was smiling too much. Suddenly she wished he was coming too. She had broached the subject with him in the bookshop, but when he hadn't shown any interest, she hadn't liked to pursue it. She assumed he couldn't dance and, anyway, it would have been awkward to have him and Derry in the same company.

He helped her back up to the seat.

Derry shook the reins, and they began to jog forward. Rose turned round and waved. As they drew away, she noticed Alec handing Dot a small package.

'It's a book,' she breathed. 'Oh good.'

They headed towards the road which would take them out of Salmouth, and on to the one for Tindlecombe. Rose leaned forward excitedly. She glanced at Derry out of the corner of her eye. A slow trickle of sweat was working its way down the side of his spectacles. He wiped his forehead with the back of his hand and stared silently into the distance. It was obvious he would rather be anywhere than with her. If only Diana had made it clear she wasn't coming, it wouldn't have been such a terrible shock for him. But then, she thought ruefully, if he had known, he wouldn't have agreed to partner her.

He gave the reins a sudden flick. 'I suppose you cooked this up between you,' he muttered.

They stood in a queue at the hall's entrance. Sounds of noisy chatter and piano music came from inside.

'It all sounds rather vulgar,' said Derry.

It all sounds rather marvellous, thought Rose.

A stout American G.I. was sitting at a table collecting money for tickets. Rose looked round hurriedly for some seats.

'Quick!' she said urgently, seeing three by a table.

She made a quick dash for them. Derry strolled sulkily after her.

The hall had been decorated with lines of coloured flags. In one corner, by a raised wooden platform, there was a table where drinks were being sold, and on the other side, a doorway, which led to the lavatory.

She slung her cardigan over the back of a chair and sat down. 'What do we do now?' she asked.

'Wait,' said Derry.

'When does the dancing begin?'

'How should I know? Don't ask so many questions.'

He stood up. 'I'll get you some powdered lemon,' he said and headed towards the refreshment table.

As soon as Derry left her, she was joined by two G.I.s.

'May we join you, ma'am?' said one touching his hat. He glanced at the two empty chairs.

'I'm very sorry but there's only one going free.'

The men shrugged, turned on their heels and walked to the other side of the hall.

Derry returned with their drinks.

'What's that you're drinking?' asked Rose.

'Cider.'

'Oh, let me taste.'

'I don't think you should. It's not really for young ladies.'

'Oh, go on.'

'Roe, Diana said I was to look after you.'

'I know. But you don't have to be so serious about it.'

'Well, I am.'

Rose looked around the hall. She had never seen so many American uniforms. The few young men who were farm labourers, and therefore not eligible for call-up, stood despondently near the main doorway.

In the midst of the general buzz of chatter, a middle-aged

man was playing a medley of old favourites on a stand-up piano on the platform. 'Ladies and gentlemen,' he announced, 'we'd like to start the evening with a tune entitled "Little Brown Jug".'

As more uniformed musicians squeezed on to the stage, the G.I.s swarmed around the tables and within seconds the floor was filled with dancing couples.

Suddenly the thought of making physical contact with a man seemed extraordinarily intimate to Rose. She had been used to dancing with girls or teachers. She noticed several young men glancing in their direction, looking first at Derry and then at her.

'Would you like to dance?' asked Rose tentatively.

'Not yet,' he snapped. 'I'm not in the mood. And anyway it's up to me to ask you, not you to ask me.'

A young man came over and asked him if he could dance with her.

'No,' said Derry coolly, before Rose had a chance to speak.

'But why?' she said, when he had left them.

'He's not an officer.'

'But I want to dance.'

'I'm sorry, Roe, but he asked for my permission and I promised . . .'

At that moment Rose felt a hand at her elbow. She looked up to find a man in his early twenties looking down at her. His blond, almost white, hair was shaped into a crew cut. Rose had never seen such blue eyes.

'May I have the pleasure, ma'am,' he said.

'Yes, *please!*' she blurted out. 'I mean. Oh.'

He laughed and held out his arm for her to take. Ignoring Derry, Rose slipped her hand round the crook of his elbow.

'Who's the boy scout?' he whispered, as they squeezed in between the partners on the floor.

'My brother,' she lied.

'Oh, sorry.'

'It's all right. He's a bit down in the dumps tonight. He'd rather be with someone else.'

In spite of Dot's lessons, Rose stood awkwardly in front of him, not knowing quite where to put her hands. He seemed to sense her hesitation and placed his hand firmly behind her waist. His fingers sent a warm glow through the base of her spine. She swallowed. This was nothing like dancing with the schoolmistress.

'You put your left hand on my right shoulder,' he said gently.

'Oh yes, of course,' she stammered.

He took her other hand and they moved round the floor in a mish-mash of a foxtrot. After she had trodden on his toe for the third time she stepped back.

'It's no good,' she said in despair. 'I can't do it. I'm so used to leading.'

'You are?' he said.

'At dance classes I always play the part of the man.'

The soldier shook his head. 'You English have some strange customs.'

She laughed. 'I go to an all-girls school.'

'Am I the first man you've ever danced with?' She nodded.

'Holy Moses!'

'And you'll probably be the last,' she added dismally.

'No. I'm honoured. Look,' he said, 'I gotta swell idea. See these boots I got on.'

She glanced down. 'Beetle-crushers, we call them.'

'Well, they're pretty darn strong. How's about if you stand on them and I just move us around. Nobody'll notice.'

'But I've already crushed your feet enough as it is.'

'Yeah, but that was unexpected. This way I'm prepared. Come on, try it.'

Gingerly she placed her feet on his. He gripped her firmly and manoeuvred her into the centre where it was most crowded.

'Do you think I'm doomed to dance like this for the rest of my life?'

'It's not so terrible, is it?'

'I suppose not.'

'Anyway, once you get the feeling of going in the opposite direction, you'll pick it up. If you can learn it one way, you'll be able to do it the other way.'

She smiled. 'I reckon so,' she said imitating his accent.

'Oh, taking the mickey, eh!' and he swung her round.

After they had danced for a while he escorted her back to her chair.

'May I sit with you?' he said. 'I see you have an empty chair.'

'Of course.'

'Are you thirsty?'

'Very.'

'I'll get you a cider.'

As she watched him dart through the crowd to the refreshments table she was aware of two angry eyes burning into her back. She turned to face them.

'Did you have to dance quite so close to him?' Derry snapped.

'I'm afraid I did. You see, I was standing on his feet.'

'Very funny.'

'I was.'

She felt the soldier's presence by her side. He was carrying a tray with two glasses of cider and an orange on it.

'An orange! Where on earth did you get it?'

'We ordered a whole lot especially for the dance.' He pushed it in her direction. 'It's for you.'

'Thank you.'

She picked up the glass of cider and began drinking it. Derry's face was thunderous.

'Oh, it's nice,' said Rose. 'It tastes a bit like lemonade.'

'It's scrumpy. You can't drink too much of it though, it's lethal.'

After they had rested, they returned to the floor.

'My name's Tony, by the way,' he said as he swung her gently past the other dancers.

'Mine's Rose.'

'A rose by any other name. Something, something, something. That's about the only Shakespeare I know. Sounds a real old English name, Rose.'

'Yes, I suppose it is.'

'I hope you don't mind,' he said, when they were taking a break, 'but I'm going to ask some other ladies to dance too.'

'Of course I don't.'

'But I want to dance with you again for sure.'

She watched him as he slipped through the crowd to a plump young woman on the other side.

Rose danced with two other men, but she still hadn't found the knack of not leading, and after several painful mishaps she was back in her chair, watching again. Derry was stumbling around with a Land Army girl. Since he had expressed his belief, on the journey, that he had been manipulated into being a dance partner for Rose, Rose suspected she would be the last person on earth he would ask for a dance. She looked around for some way of amusing herself.

It was then that she became aware of the orange peel. Marmalade, she thought. If I can collect enough peel, Diana could make marmalade.

She picked up the tray casually and wandered round with it, picking up the skins from the tables. She hardly dared look up in case she met any of the girls' eyes and they were having the same idea as her. As soon as the tray was full she walked slowly past the band towards the doorway which lead to the lavatories. A queue of girls was waiting outside. She slipped past them into a little caretaker's kitchen at the back. Quickly, she knelt down behind a covered table, placed the tray on the floor and lifted her dress up. Grabbing the peel in large handfuls she threw it into her knickers, pulled the leg part up to her thighs and spread the peel around evenly. She let her dress fall and gave a relieved sigh. There wasn't a bump to be seen.

By the time she had returned to her chair, Derry was escorting the Land Army girl back to her group of friends.

'What have you been doing?' he asked suspiciously when he rejoined her.

'Powdering my nose. Derry, why don't you want to dance with me?'

'That's obvious, isn't it?'

'I didn't get you here under false pretences. Honestly.'

'I brought you another cider,' said a voice.

It was Tony. He placed the glass on the table and sat beside her. 'Ain't they a swell band?' he said, gazing at the platform.

'Oh yes,' she breathed.

'They're professionals, you know. They get called up same as everybody.'

He placed his hand firmly under her elbow. 'Like to try dancing again?'

'Are you sure you want to?'

'You bet.'

They found a spot in the crowd again and Rose placed her feet on his.

'You know,' he said, 'we could start a new craze with this kinda dancing. I reckon it'd be real popular.'

He held her close and they began moving round the floor again. Rose was acutely aware of the orange peel. She hoped it didn't make her feel too lumpy.

'Anything worrying you?' he asked.

'Oh, no. I was just remembering something that I hope I did all right.'

The music stopped abruptly and the pianist yelled out, 'O.K, you cats, get swingin'!'

About two thirds of the couples left the floor.

'Best get outa the way,' said Tony leading her to her chair. 'Could get dangerous.'

'What's happening?'

'People are going to be jitterbuggin'!'

'Jitterbugging! Oh, can't we join in?'

He looked at her, amazed. 'You mean you can do it?'

'A bit. Can you?'

'Sure I can. I love it. Come on.'

The ran back on to the floor. Tony grabbed her hand and she started twirling and spinning.

'Hey, you're good,' he exclaimed. 'You're real nimble.'

Not only did Rose's confidence soar but the more exhilarated she felt, the more relaxed and carefree she became. Derry stared at her open-mouthed. Gradually the surrounding couples began to whisper to each other and stopped to watch. Tony and Rose, who had become aware of the sudden attention, swung and whirled around each other. What they hadn't noticed was that the band were all mesmerised by their performance and didn't know whether to stop playing or to keep going, for Rose had quite forgotten that one of the reasons why the jitterbug was so frowned upon, was that it revealed young women's underwear. Unbeknown to her, the entire hall was not only transfixed by her heavy black bloomers but also by the strange shapes that seemed to be moving around inside them. What Rose also didn't know was that Aunt Em had used strong elastic for the waist and old elastic for the leg. Countless eyes now watched as the leg parts of her knickers slowly worked their way down to her knees.

Derry sat with his hands over his face. 'Why?' he whispered to himself desperately. 'Why?'

Suddenly the leg elastic, unable to withstand the strain of its contents and the jitterbug any longer, finally disintegrated. Peel flew in all directions. Derry sank his face into his hands. The band stopped and Tony and Rose froze and stared at the floor.

Rose lifted her head slowly, aware of every fibre of her body burning. Her face hot, she backed towards the exit, pushed the large blackout curtain aside and stepped outside into the night. She broke into a sprint and ran and ran till she reached a stile by a field. She leaned against it, her heart pounding.

What was she going to do? Her cardigan was hanging at the back of her chair and her purse was still on the table. How would she get them back and how could she face Derry? He was bound to tell Diana.

She was sitting there trying to fathom out an answer when

she heard footsteps. She began walking again. Someone called out to her. She turned. It was Tony.

'Why'd you run off?' he said. 'I been looking for you everywhere.'

'How could I stay?'

'People thought it was real funny.'

'I bet they did.'

'Hey, where's your sense of humour? They were just a bit surprised, that's all. But you've really broken a lot of ice. People are laughin' and talkin' like crazy. I reckon you've jest about created a legend in these parts.'

'Now tell me something that'll cheer me up.'

'Look, honey, they really admire your dancing and they think it was real neat to hide that orange peel. I guess we've a lot to learn about your struggles with rationing and that. It would have bin great if your elastic hadn't have given out.'

He suppressed a smile. 'Oh boy, you shoulda seen the speed that peel went. It flew everywhere. A piece of it went flying straight into one of the trumpets. I never seen such a bull's-eye.'

'It didn't, did it?'

'Cross my heart and hope to die. We had to call the nurses from the American Red Cross to help patch up the injured. It was a hell of a good job it wasn't banana skins.'

She burst out laughing. He took hold of her hands.

'Please come back. We're going to follow your English tradition and end the evening with "The Anniversary Waltz" and I want that dance with you.' He squeezed her fingers. 'I haven't had such a swell evening in a long time.'

She blushed. 'All right.'

'Zowee!' he yelled, whirling her around the lane. He stopped and crooked his arm for her to take. 'O.K. ma'am. Let's go.'

Rose hoped they would be able to slip back into the hall unseen, but as soon as she was spotted there was pandemonium. Before she knew what was happening she was presented with a large bag of orange peel, and everyone applauded.

'You'd best stick to the slow numbers for a while!' yelled out a Land Army girl. 'You don't want to chance the rest of the elastic.'

Tony took the bag from her and carried it over to the table. To Rose's relief, Derry was smiling.

'I give up,' he remarked.

'So you're that gal's brother?' Rose heard two G.I.s say to Derry, as she moved back to the floor.

When 'The Anniversary Waltz' was announced Rose found herself surrounded.

'I'm sorry,' she said. 'But I've already promised this one.'

This time she didn't stand on Tony's feet. She let herself sink into his arms. When the dance finally came to an end he kissed her on the forehead.

'You know, I didn't mention it before, but this is my last evening in England.'

She was about to ask where he was going but she remembered that he wouldn't be able to answer her even if he knew.

'It's bin a swell evening, Rose.'

'For me too.'

She opened her mouth to speak but stopped herself.

'What is it?' he said.

'Your hair. Can I touch it? I just wanted to know how it feels.'

He lowered his head. She pressed her hand down on the top of his crew cut. 'Oh, it's soft. I thought it'd be prickly, like a hedgehog.'

He escorted her to the table and walked with her and Derry to the stable, the bag of orange peel in his arms.

A light rain had started to fall. It felt refreshing after the stifling atmosphere of the blacked-out hall.

Rose was just about to climb on the cart when he took hold of her arm.

'Rose,' he said, 'if I didn't have someone waiting for me back home, I'd be real proud to have you be my gal.'

She was astounded. 'Me?' she whispered.

He handed her the orange peel. 'So long,' he murmured, and he kissed her on the cheek.

Rose hardly spoke a word on the journey home. She sat in a daze, a tarpaulin wrapped round her shoulders, while the fine rain trickled down her face. She thought back to the beginning of the evening when Derry had been so nasty to her. It didn't seem to touch her now. Tony had made her feel human again. Perhaps there was hope for her after all. Perhaps she was only ordinarily ugly as opposed to disgustingly ugly. She rested her fingers against her cheek. Her first dance, she thought, and instead of being the wallflower of the year she had ended up actually being kissed.

When she turned she found that Derry had been staring at her. He smiled and asked her if she was comfortable enough. She smiled back, amazed that he had asked.

Two days later a jeep drew up outside Lapwing Cottage and an Italian-looking G.I. leapt out. Derry and Rose were sitting out in the garden.

'I'm looking for a dame called Rose,' said the G.I.

Rose stood up. 'That's me.'

'Parcel for you, ma'am, from Tony and the gang,' and he

handed her a large bulky package over the hedge.

Diana opened the kitchen window. 'What is it?'

Rose was still staring at the retreating jeep.

'What?' she said startled. 'I don't know. I suppose I'd better open it.'

She unwrapped it on the kitchen table and found several smaller parcels. There were tins of fruit, corned beef, ham, bars of chocolate, scented soap, razor blades and oranges. The soft parcel she kept till last.

'Oh!' she cried, and she spread her fingers along the silky contents. 'They're beautiful.'

Inside, neatly folded, lay a light adjustable suspender belt, nylon stockings, and several pairs of lacy, shell pink French knickers.

Eight

Rose crossed her legs, the diary crooked in her arms, her knees jutting up and over the armrests.

We didn't waste a moment, she read. *We talked little of the past, and nothing of the future. Instead we talked about ourselves. I had never met a man who could talk so freely, not since my darling Richard had died.*

We stayed in a little inn in a coastal village, rather like Salmouth. We lunched out, preferring to take a picnic. We both loved the sea, and walked along the sands talking endlessly.

One day we picnicked on a grassy slope overlooking the bay and saw no one all day. We could have been the only two people in the world.

Rose sank back against the curtains, hugging herself. That's what Dot had said about her and Jack. Is that what it felt like to be in love? She felt feverish and slightly breathless. It was frightening and exciting all at the same time. It was as though she was in love too, only there was no one for her to love.

We hardly slept at all that first night. Overjoyed at lying in bed together, we held hands. It was such an exquisite sensation that we could barely move. We kissed and murmured and whispered to one another till the dawn.

It wasn't till the third night that we were joined as man and wife. I was so content lying in the dark with Matthew's arms around me.

Rose swallowed. She was trembling.

Our loving was so tender. I remember how we smiled over breakfast. We were always smiling. I couldn't help it. I only had to look at Matthew's mouth smiling back at me, and I laughed.

Rose read swiftly, whisking the pages back. She slowed down at the end of their week together.

When we said goodbye on the station, I had to use all my self-control not to cry. Matthew leaned out of the carriage window and clasped my hands so tightly that they hurt.

'My darling Hilda,' he said. 'I do love you so. You will wait for me, won't you?'

I nodded. It was an absurd question for him to ask.

As the train pulled out of the platform I remember thinking how a few hours earlier we had been lying in bed together. For the first time we had fallen asleep early. When we woke, we discovered our sleep had been so deep that we had hardly moved; our arms and legs were still draped over one another.

It was the last page in the book.

Rose stretched out her legs and balanced herself by placing one foot on a box and the other on a trunk near the bureau.

Once she had found the diary which followed, she collapsed back into the chair. The diary lay unopened on her knees. She stared at it for a moment. She had such a feeling of foreboding that she wasn't sure she could face reading on.

'I must,' she whispered. 'That's what Miss Hilda wants.'

She flung back the cover.

I moved back into the dull strictures of life with my parents, taking care of my invalid mother.

My elder brother was killed at Ypres and we all went into mourning. His death only made me more conscious of Matthew's absence.

I rose early so that I could meet the postman before the mail was delivered. For nearly two months Matthew and I were able to correspond, and then the letters stopped. I tried to find out what had happened to him, but I seemed blocked at every attempt, not being next of kin, but also, I suspect, by my father's regimental friends.

Four months after Matthew and I had parted I was summoned to the drawing room. I was quite unprepared for the young man who sat there. I could tell from his uniform that he was from Matthew's regiment. I seem to remember my parents sitting stiffly on chairs. I saw only the soldier.

As soon as I entered the room he sprang to his feet. We stared silently at one another. My father was speaking but I couldn't hear him. I remember I felt sick, that there was a rush of warmth to my face though my hands were icy.

I heard my father say, 'What you have to say can be said in front of us. My daughter has no secrets from us.'

You daughter has nothing but secrets, I thought.

Eventually I moved towards him. I knew why he had come.

'It's about Matthew, isn't it?' I said.

He nodded.

'He felt no pain,' he started awkwardly.

But then they always said that. I have no clear recollection of what else he said. It seemed as though he was in some dream in my head.

I remember offering to see him out. We walked through the grounds and stopped at the heavy ornate gates, which seemed more like prison gates than ever. The soldier gave me a letter. I thanked him and stood quite still, the letter clasped in my hand.

Without looking back I headed swiftly for the coastal path. I didn't dare to return to the house. I was frightened that Matthew's letter would be snatched from me. I quickened my pace, and began to run, half-stumbling, and it was then that I began to cry.

Rose stopped. Her jaw was clamped and the back of her nose stung. Suddenly she remembered being summoned to the headmistress's study. And how she knew, without the headmistress having to say a word.

Rose couldn't believe it; couldn't believe that someone as warm as her father could be dead; couldn't believe that she would never hear his voice again, or see his eyes light on her proudly; that he was gone; that he was never coming back.

And her whole body ached as it had done then.

She dragged out Alec's handkerchief from her shorts' pocket and hastily blew her nose.

Before I knew what was happening I found myself standing, howling out at the sea. On and on I screamed. I felt calmer after my strange wailing. I could breathe again. It was then that I realised I had been in a state of mourning for four months. From the moment Matthew's train had drawn out of the station, I had known we would never see each other again.

On my father's estate, there was a deserted cottage. It stood on a small lane which broke away from the coastal path. I had been using it as a refuge, hiding all sorts of treasures under the floorboards. For some reason I felt safe there. I made for it immediately.

As soon as I had reached it, I shut the kitchen door behind me and tore open his letter.

It was tucked between two pages. Rose hesitated for a moment before unfolding it.

It was written in a swirling italic hand.

'My dearest Hilda,

From the moment we met, we accepted I was living on borrowed time. If you should ever receive this letter it will be because that time has finally come to an end.

I would like to believe that I have died for some great cause. If the carnage of this war will prevent all future wars, then perhaps my life won't have been entirely wasted.

My dearest one, you are still always in my waking and my sleeping thoughts. I wrap our week together round me. It warms and comforts me.

I know I can't expect you not to grieve. If I had survived and you had died, I would have walked to the four corners of the earth and howled.

Don't cling on to grief, that's all I ask. I have seen it consume some women. Have done with it and enjoy living, for my sake. If I have given you anything of worth, then my life will have had some value. My own dearest Hilda, if I could only hold you in my arms again. Promise me, my darling one, promise me that you won't live half a life. Promise me that you won't allow your family to suck the life from you.

I love you. I always will love you.

Matthew.'

Rose folded the letter carefully and slipped it back into the diary.

I remember how I slumped to the floor weeping. I sat there, my back against the door, my hands resting on the tiny swelling under my dress. The baby would keep his memory alive. No one could take that away from me. I was so confident that at last I had beaten my family.

How very naïve I was then.

Rose was about to turn the page, when she heard someone in the kitchen. She sprang forward and closed the door. Footsteps passed her hiding place. She held her breath.

To her relief, whoever it was had stepped into the garden and had shut the door behind them. Rose slipped out into the corridor.

Derry was standing on the lawn. As soon as Rose strode out to join him she was aware of attempting to act jolly, even though the diaries had upset her badly.

Without thinking she said, 'Diana's not here.'

He blushed. 'I didn't come to see Diana,' he stammered. 'I came to see you.'

He was holding a paper bag. He thrust it forward. 'They're seeds. For your garden.'

She took them.

'I thought you might want a hand with weeding,' he went on.

Rose stared back at him. She felt dazed. Her head was still swimming with Miss Hilda's words.

'I haven't called at an inconvenient time, have I?'

'No,' she lied. 'No. I needed a break.'

'What have you been doing?'

She tried to think. 'Working on my story.'

'What story?'

'The one I've been borrowing books for, from Alec.'

'Oh.'

It was funny that she had never told him about it.

'Let's start weeding then, shall we?' he said.

'Yes,' she said brightly. 'Let's.'

They started at the foot of the garden.

She felt so buffeted and raw after reading Miss Hilda's diary that she found it difficult to speak. She wished he would go away.

They tugged up some convolvulus which had wrapped itself round the stems of a clump of honesty.

'I thought we'd got rid of this,' said Rose attempting to make conversation.

'It always comes back,' said Derry.

'That's what Mrs Clarence said.'

'Is that where Diana is? At Mrs Clarence's?'

'Yes. Sorry.'

'Oh no,' said Derry quickly. 'It's not that. I really did come to see you. I've been meaning to apologise to you for days but it never seemed the right moment.'

Rose shrugged. 'That's all right. It means I can surprise you.'

'How do you mean?'

'I can swim now. Well, a little. I've been practising every day.'

'That's wizard! Why didn't you tell me?'

'You've had your mind on other things.'

He reddened again. 'Yes. I suppose I have. Actually it's not your neglected swimming lessons I want to apologise for, though I am sorry about that too. It's for the way I treated you at the dance. I was foul.'

'It was all a misunderstanding,' Rose began.

'You were so popular!' he interrupted. 'So many men wanted

to dance with you. I was a fool not to have been nicer to you.'

'It's all right, Derry, you don't have to . . .'

'And I've seen the light,' he rushed on. 'About your sister, I mean.'

'Oh?'

'It was just an infatuation for an older woman. I'm more mature now.'

Rose stared at him, but he looked just the same.

'It's just as well,' she said. 'I'm afraid her heart is elsewhere.'

'Robert?'

'Yes.'

'I'm rather surprised they should get on so well, coming from such different backgrounds.'

'You mean N.Q.O.C.D.'

Derry stared at her blankly. 'What's that?'

'Not quite our class, dear.'

'Oh, I see. Well, yes,' he added awkwardly.

'Derry, he's the first man who's actually talked or listened to Diana. It's a terrible handicap being shy and beautiful. It's a nightmare being gawked at silently all the time.'

Though I wouldn't mind a taste of it, Rose thought.

'But Robert hardly ever took his eyes off her,' said Derry.

'But it was different. He didn't look as if he was in pain.'

'I think you ought to know that his father was a farm labourer,' he said. 'And he didn't go to a very good school. Robert, I mean.'

'He got a scholarship.'

'To a *grammar* school,' pointed out Derry.

'Yes, I know. Still, I prefer him to that awful Timothy. At least Robert has a sense of humour.' She paused. 'I hope Diana knows what she's doing. She doesn't really know a lot about men and I think he's serious about her.'

'You don't think he'd take advantage of her, do you?' said Derry startled.

'Oh no. Diana would be too shocked.'

'People behave differently in wartime, you know.'

Like Miss Hilda and Matthew, she thought. She shook her head. It wasn't the same.

'No,' she said simply. 'Diana wouldn't. It's not in her nature. She's too conventional. She'd rather die a virgin than not be one when she marries.'

'I didn't mean her,' Derry blurted out. 'I wouldn't dream of implying that Diana would willingly ever . . . you know.'

He turned away and took a hefty tug at the convolvulus again.

They fell silent for a moment.

'By the way,' he added nonchalantly, 'I wanted to talk to Robert about his bombing missions before he left. I thought it might be useful for when I become a pilot. But he kept changing the subject.'

'Perhaps he didn't want to talk about them.'

'Why ever not? I'd be proud to.'

'Maybe he wanted to forget about them for a bit before going back.'

'I suppose so.' He took a sideways look at her. 'And I suppose he and Diana needed to make the most of every moment they had.'

'Yes.'

She remembered an incident one afternoon at the cottage. She had just returned from a swim, and as she came up to the gate, she had heard sounds of sobbing coming from the kitchen. She ran up the path. The door was open. Diana and

Robert were standing in the kitchen. She was weeping on to his chest while he held her, stroking her hair and comforting her.

'What's the matter?' Rose had cried, thinking perhaps there had been a telegram with bad news about their mother.

'Look at it!' Diana had wailed. 'Just look at it! It's completely sunk!'

On the table was a freshly baked cake with a hollow middle. 'It's the last straw,' she snuffled into Robert's chest.

For a moment Rose could only stare stupefied at Diana's dishevelled hair, and at the flour on her blouse and skirt, and then she started to laugh.

Eventually Diana saw the funny side, but now, on reflection, Rose remembered the way Robert had held her so tenderly in his arms.

'Penny for them,' said Derry.

'I'm sorry. I was thinking about Diana and Robert. You're right. They did have to make the most of the time they had.'

'I think everyone must nowadays, don't you?' he said with meaning.

'Oh yes,' Rose agreed. She was reminded of Miss Hilda's account of her grief over Matthew's death. She couldn't bear the thought of Diana going through that. She was too vulnerable to survive it. 'I hope nothing happens to him,' she added quietly.

Derry stared out at the sky. 'I don't know,' he said. 'I think I'd much rather go out with a bang while I'm still young. And die for my country. I'd hate to be middle-aged.'

'Don't say that.'

'No one would miss me anyway,' he said airily.

'Of course they would. What about your parents?'

'They'd be glad to see the back of me. I don't think they

wanted me in the first place. They'd have much rather it had been just the two of them. I'm always in the way.' He gave a short laugh. 'When I'm there.'

'Derry, I'm sure that's not true.'

'Would *you* miss me?' he said suddenly.

'Me?' She blushed. 'Of course I would.'

He smiled.

For a moment neither of them spoke.

'I wonder if Dot's husband has been killed,' said Derry pointedly.

'Yes,' she whispered. 'I don't know which is worse, not knowing so you can keep hoping, or being told there is no hope.'

Derry hesitated. 'Roe, there's something I think you ought to know.'

'Yes?'

'It's about Dot.'

'Oh.'

'You know that ring she wears?'

'It's a curtain ring.'

He gasped. 'You know then?'

'Yes.'

'And you're still friendly with her?'

Rose touched his arm. 'Derry, they loved each other. They'd known each other since they were children.'

'You mean,' he gulped, 'you don't mind?'

'No.'

Derry gaped at her. She removed her hand hurriedly and looked away so that she didn't see the horrified expression on Derry's face before he recovered himself.

'Actually, I'm *glad* you feel that way, Roe. That's how I feel.'

She swung round. 'Do you really?' she said. 'I thought you disapproved of her.'

'What made you think that?' he said innocently.

'Something she said.'

'Oh no. I was just a bit surprised she was allowed out, being unmarried, that is . . .'

'She's the only one who is,' interrupted Rose. 'The other unmarrieds spend their time knitting and examining the floorboards. They have the vicar round to read to them. Dot says she doesn't know who's more embarrassed.'

'But why do they let her out and not the others?'

'She just walks out.'

'And they don't stop her?'

'They tried to once. They locked her in a room but she climbed out of a window. They got such a fright seeing her dangling above the drainpipes, they never did it again. Mrs Clarence helps too. She tells the matron she needs someone to clean for her, but as soon as Dot gets through the door she whisks her off to the back garden and points her towards a deck chair. Mrs Clarence says she likes her company.'

'Is that why you mix with her? Because she goes there?'

'No. I admit I didn't approve of Diana's friendship with her at first but something changed my mind.'

'What was that?'

'Just a book I read.'

'So you do believe in that sort of thing before marriage then?'

Rose took a deep breath. 'In some circumstances. Yes. Are you shocked?'

'No, no,' said Derry eagerly. 'I agree with you. Things are different now. I mean, in peacetime killing people is wrong, but now it's quite the opposite. I think it's the same sort of thing with . . .' He faltered. 'When you're you know.'

'In love?'

'Exactly.'

Rose was astonished. She felt relieved; less alone. She was tempted to tell him about Miss Hilda's affair and the fact that she had become pregnant too, but then she remembered Miss Hilda's letter asking its reader to keep the contents of the room a secret.

'Though if it was me,' he continued, 'I'd make sure nothing happened, if you know what I mean.'

Rose didn't but she wasn't going to let on for fear of looking naïve.

'That's nice,' she said, hoping it was the right thing to say.

There was another awkward silence.

Derry cleared his throat. 'I've asked Harold if I can borrow his horse and cart tomorrow.'

'Has he agreed?'

'Yes, and I was wondering,' he paused, 'if you'd let me make it up to you. The dance, I mean. And come to Gynmouth with me. To the pictures.'

Rose stood by the gate watching out for him, her hand shading her eyes.

As soon as she spotted the horse and cart on the brow of the hill she flung the gate open and sprinted up the lane. Derry waved.

His hair was sleeked down neatly from a side parting, and he wore his white flannels, white shirt and cravat outfit. He had actually dressed up for her!

'I'm awfully sorry,' she panted out to him, 'but my sister wants to come too.'

His smile disappeared. He looked devastated. 'To the *pictures?*'

'Oh no. She just wants to do some shopping.'

He grinned. 'That's not too bad then. Do you want to ride with me?'

Rose nodded and hauled herself up beside him.

Diana was still in the cottage when they arrived. Rose and Derry waited for her in the garden.

When she finally appeared, Rose couldn't have been more surprised, for she was decked out in a hat and gloves.

'Do you mind sitting in the back, Roe?' asked Diana. 'Seeing as you're not in your best dress. I'll sit in the cart when we return, I just want to keep my dress from getting crumpled. It doesn't matter on the way back.'

'All right,' said Rose.

As Derry clipped the back section of the cart into place, he winked at Rose. Rose, not knowing quite what was expected of her, winked back. Derry smothered a laugh.

Derry helped her sister up to the seat and turned the cart. Rose plumped up the cushions and settled back. She suddenly felt happy. Her short story was going well, and, thanks to Robert's appearance, she and Dot had spent more time alone together and had grown quite close. And now there was Derry's sudden interest in her. It had never occurred to her that any boy would ever ask her out, let alone be disappointed when he thought her sister might be coming with them! It astounded her that Derry actually wanted her company all to himself. And he seemed genuinely sorry for having been mean to her.

She saw him in a different light now. He was quite handsome really, underneath his spectacles.

The cushions made her feel hot. She leaned forward for a

moment. 'Phew!' she gasped. 'I'm baking back here.' She pulled herself up to her feet and clung on to the back of the seat. She bumped against Derry's back. 'Sorry,' she blurted out.

'That's all right,' he said, turning to grin at her.

Rose sat back in the cart and drifted off into a daydream about her story. She could see Edith in her long skirt cycling down a bumpy lane. She woke with a start, as the cart clattered over a large stone. They passed a row of terraced houses and turned into the main street of Gynmouth. Rose sat up sharply.

For one and a half months Rose had forgotten the devastation of war.

They jogged slowly past piles of rubble and torn buildings with broken and boarded-up windows. The intact windows had the usual strips of brown tape criss-crossed across the glass. Compared to London, the damage was minuscule; compared to Salmouth, it was a blitz.

'Oh, this is ridiculous,' said Diana suddenly and she pulled her hat and gloves off and threw them in the cart.

'What are you doing?' asked Rose.

'Making myself more comfortable.'

Derry dropped Diana off, and he and Rose walked past queues of women standing outside grocery and butcher's shops and crossed over the square towards the cinema.

The film was *Mrs Miniver*. Rose hid her disappointment. She would have preferred something lighter, like a Will Hay comedy.

'Have you seen it before?' asked Derry.

'No.'

She stood awkwardly next to him as they queued at the box office. There were only three other people in front of them; another couple a little older than them, and an elderly woman.

Derry stared enviously at the young man. He was in R.A.F. uniform.

The box office was a tiny cubicle. A thin elderly woman, who was jogging a grubby toddler in her arms, took the money and gave Derry two square pieces of newspaper with numbers on them.

They made their way to the swing doors and stood outside them with the others.

'Why don't we go in?' said Rose puzzled.

'Got to wait till Mrs Piegarth done all the tickets,' drawled the old woman. 'Then we'se got to hand 'em back to her.'

Mrs Piegarth poked her head out of the window to see if there were any more customers. She slipped back inside, opened the side door still holding the child, and hooked back the swing doors. The light from the street flooded the tiny auditorium.

Rose was halfway down the aisle when she realised she was alone. Derry was standing by the stalls. Bewildered, she turned back to join him. 'I thought you'd want to be near the front,' she whispered, 'because of your eyesight.'

He looked hurt.

'Sorry.'

'That's all right.'

Mrs Piegarth took a last look round and closed the doors.

Rose shifted in her seat. It was strange to be sitting next to Derry in the dark. Gradually her eyes adjusted. Once she could see the outline of the chairs, she relaxed. From behind came a whirring sound. A shaft of light was streaming from a tiny square in the wall. From the faint gurgling sounds from behind it, she suspected that Mrs Piegarth and infant were also in charge of the projector.

The programme began with the Pathé News with its endless newsreels concerning the progress of the war, and insistent propaganda about Digging For Victory. And then it was *Mrs Miniver*.

As the film began, Rose suddenly became aware that something was moving with painstaking slowness along the back of her seat. Derry was staring with fixed concentration at the screen but one of his arms was lying at the back of her chair. Gradually his fingers closed over her left shoulder. She froze, not knowing whether to smile at him, lean back, or what. He gave Rose's shoulder a squeeze.

It wasn't a cheering film. It ended with a sermon, stressing that the fight against Hitler was not only in the skies and on the beaches, but also in England on the home front. After it was over, there was a plea for people to buy war bonds. Derry removed his arm and stood up politely. Rose walked past, her face hot.

They staggered blinking into the sunlight, and then stared at one another, embarrassed. After what seemed an eternity Derry said, 'Let's look at the shops.' They wandered through the streets, but the shop windows were filled with ugly utility furniture and dark clothing, their faded coupon numbers propped beside them.

A green and yellow bus passed by. They stopped to stare at it. It looked so bright against the drabness of the town. And then Rose spotted a second-hand bookshop and her spirits lifted.

'I don't want to look in there,' said Derry. 'I've had enough of books to last me a lifetime.'

Rose was disappointed, but for some reason didn't protest.

They sat on a bench in the centre of the town square. The

mottled statue of an unnamed soldier loomed behind them.

'I wonder where Diana is,' she said.

'Look,' said Derry pointing. Diana was stepping out of the town hall. 'What on earth has she been doing *there*?' he asked.

Rose shrugged. 'Perhaps it's something to do with Dot. Once she has her baby, she'll have to give up her green ration book and have a blue one. She's probably making inquiries for her.'

They waved to her.

'I'll get the cart,' said Derry. 'You wait here.'

Diana sat in the back, leaving Rose and Derry room on the seat. She seemed much more relaxed, and kept humming snatches of songs to herself.

It wasn't until they were a couple of miles from Salmouth that she dropped her bombshell. 'I might as well tell you,' she announced. 'I've signed up with the W.A.A.F.'

Derry pulled the cart to a sudden halt.

Rose whirled round. 'What!' she yelled. 'Diana! You haven't!'

'I'm afraid I have,' she said.

'But why?' Rose asked. 'Why on earth didn't you wait till we'd left Salmouth?'

'Because Mother would have been back by then. And you know how upset she gets every time she thinks I'm leaving. Also, I didn't know if my courage would last till then.'

'I thought they weren't taking on new recruits,' said Rose. 'I thought they were keen on girls going into munitions.'

'They are. I mentioned I'd be quite willing to do that but . . .'

'I don't believe you!' cried Rose.

'I hardly believed I was saying it myself.'

'So what happened?'

'They asked me about myself. I told them about my secretarial training and then I mentioned the first-aid classes. I asked if there was any chance of joining the nursing section but they said they only took trained nurses, but would I be interested in the administrative side of hospital work? I was so thrilled they just laughed. They said they couldn't promise anything but that they'd put in a good word for me!'

Rose saw her holiday coming to an abrupt end and her one chance of romance being dashed away. And there was her short story. She'd never be able to finish it at home.

'So when are you going?' she asked dismally.

'I don't know. I explained that Mother was abroad and that I was looking after you until September. When they heard you were only seventeen they asked if there was anyone else you could be left in charge of in case I'm called up before then. I mentioned Mrs Clarence. I thought you'd rather stay in Salmouth with her than have to stay in Birmingham with Aunt Em. Do you think now is the time to tell her about Miss Hutchinson not being here?'

'Not unless you're called up before September. There's no point, is there?'

'I suppose not.'

'Who's Aunt Em?' asked Derry.

'My mother's best friend,' explained Rose. 'She's *in loco parentis* should anything happen to my mother. I don't know why. She's the complete opposite of my mother. Unconventional, mad.'

'Why can't she come here and look after you?' interrupted Derry.

'She's working at Birmingham Rep.'

'Oh,' he said, disapproval in his voice.

'It's all right,' said Rose. 'She doesn't kick her legs in the air. She does plays.'

'Derry, I'm sorry you should have to hear all this family business,' said Diana. 'How embarrassing for you.'

'Not at all,' he said gallantly. 'I don't mind.'

'Oh, Roe, I hope I don't spoil your holiday,' she added.

'There's one and a half months to go. You might not be called up in that time.'

'But if I am.'

'Don't worry. We'll sort something out.'

Diana was looking anxious again.

'It'll work out fine,' Rose reassured her.

Diana sighed. 'I hope so.'

Derry shook the reins and they jogged on towards Salmouth. He glanced aside at Rose and raised his eyebrows. Then, to Rose's utter amazement, he put the reins in one hand and gently linked his little finger in hers. Rose could feel every inch of her skin stinging.

It was then she remembered having once seen Robert and Diana doing the same thing. Perhaps Derry had seen them too, and this was his way of showing his feelings.

And then it dawned on her. Was it possible that Derry was trying to tell her that he had fallen in love with her?

Nine

Rose thumped her pillow again and sank back into it.

The window was open. A breeze caused the curtains to billow so that one brushed her face. It was no use, she thought, sleep was out of the question. She couldn't stop thinking about Derry. She wondered if he would want to see her again. She went through every remark he had made, every loving look. She dwelled on the feeling of his arm across the back of her chair, his fingers touching her shoulder, the squeeze. He must like her. But he hadn't *said* anything. He hadn't said, 'I'll see you tomorrow.' Might she have said or done something to put him off?

She pushed the bedclothes down to the foot of the bed, and rested her head in her hands. Dot was about to become a mother; Derry a pilot and Diana had signed up for the W.A.A.F. And she? She was indulging in summer 'hols' before returning to her schoolgirl state. She felt such a baby.

She sat up. It was a waste of time lying in the dark and stewing. She grabbed a jersey and pulled it on over her pyjamas.

In the tiny room adjoining her bedroom, shadows from the nearby apple tree flickered over the papers that were strewn across her table. She drew across the blackout curtains and lit the lamp. Gathering up her notes and books, she piled them in a heap on the floor. All that remained on the table was the exercise book with the story about Edith. She sat down and began whispering it out loud, crossing out words and sentences, tightening here and there, and substituting any word she had already used. When she reached the final sentence, she pushed the chair back, walked up and down excitedly and then returned to whisper it through all over again. Finally, when she felt she couldn't do any more work on it she clasped her hands above her head.

'I've done it!' she cried inside her head. 'I've actually done it. A whole story!'

Too exhilarated for sleep, she picked up the lamp and made for the stairs.

She stood the oil lamp on Miss Hilda's bureau, unlocked the roll-topped lid, and slid it back. With a diary in her hands, she settled back into the cane chair and reread the final paragraph.

I was so confident that, at last, I had beaten my family.

How very naïve I was then.

Rose turned the page.

For two more months I managed to keep my confinement a secret. I let out my dresses and took to wearing capes. At every opportunity, I walked out along the coastal path to the cottage. Out of sight, I could relax.

At the cottage I kept pieces of wool, cotton, lace and muslin, and made preparations for the birth. I hid the baby's clothing and my wedding ring in a canvas bag and laid it under a floorboard. Over this, I threw a piece of matting.

I was able to take occasional trips into Gynmouth. Wearing my wedding ring, I opened a savings account under the name of Mrs Tomlinson, though I had little idea as to how I was to earn enough money to save.

I had planned to tell my parents that I would be staying with a friend who was expecting a child, have the baby under my married name, somewhere far from home, and then return with it, saying it was the child of my widowed friend who had died in childbirth and entrusted it into my care.

One morning one of the housemaids blundered into my bedroom while I was still dressing. I'll never forget the shocked flush on her thin young face. She gaped at my shape, and then bowed and backed from the room, apologising profusely.

Still in my state of undress, I could not run after her. I was stunned for a moment, and then hastily returned to binding myself in. The binding had prevented my parents from noticing I was with child. Once dressed, I walked briskly along the landings and down the endless polished stairs towards the kitchens, but I knew before I reached them that there would be too many servants busying themselves there. I prayed that, until I could speak to the girl in private, she would keep her discovery to herself. Alas, I was unable even to catch sight of her.

That afternoon I took what was to be my last walk. On my return I was informed that my father had been called away on urgent business and that my mother had retired to her bed and was on no account to be disturbed. I ate supper alone and was served by two of the servants who stood silently in the shadows, never leaving me alone for a moment.

The following morning, so as to avoid a repetition of the previous day's episode, I went to lock my door. There was no key. Thinking I must have left it on the outside I turned the door knob, only to discover that I had been locked in. I sank down on to the bed, my heart beating.

Rose turned the page and leaned forward so that the pool of light from the oil lamp fell more centrally on to Miss Hilda's whirling hand.

The windows of my room were too high for me to try to climb down, and I also had the baby to consider. Eventually I heard footsteps treading lightly on the landing, and whisperings. I stood by the door, but nothing happened. The whispering continued.

'Now come on,' I said, knocking firmly on the door. 'Let's stop this nonsense.'

There was no answer. By then I had begun to shake. All day I remained, without food, locked in my room. Fortunately I still had my chamber pot. As dusk began to close in, I heard two vehicles draw up outside. I leaned out of the window to look. One was a van *which reminded me of the ambulances which brought patients to the hospital. The other was my father's carriage.*

Two men emerged from the van. I heard my father's voice and the tramping of feet over the loose stones. Some ten minutes later, the key turned in my door. I stood with my back to the windows. The door opened, and the two men I had seen were standing in the doorway. They were rough types in greatcoats. I was conscious of attempting to hold my ground.

'And what is all this about?' I think I said rather stiffly.

Before I could say more, they strode swiftly across the room, seized me by the elbows and dragged me bodily towards the landing.

The more I resisted, the tighter was their grip.

Downstairs I heard weeping. The poor little housemaid probably.

'Let me go, sir,' I raged.

'Come along quietly, miss,' said one of the men as if to a child, 'or we shall have to restrain you and that would make us all very unhappy, wouldn't it?'

My feet barely touched the ground, so strong were they.

I remember my father standing silent and expressionless in the hall.

Rose was enraged. She gripped the book tightly and raced through the pages. What followed was an account of the asylum; of Miss Hilda's imprisonment there; of how her baby son was snatched from her minutes after it was born: how they brought him to her at set times so that she could feed him; and how she was informed that after six weeks of breastfeeding, he would be taken away for adoption.

Miss Hilda had no way of leaving the asylum; her father had her certified as insane. Rose shivered. She pulled the velvet curtains towards her and wrapped them around herself.

They thought it would be humiliating for a woman of my class not to have a wet nurse for my baby. They were shocked when I wasn't.

They called me mad because I fought to keep him. But I had felt him grow within me, had seen him briefly at his birth, had held him in my arms and nourished him from my own body.

When they tore him from my arms for the last time, they strapped me down, and until I had learnt to stifle my screams, they would not set me free. They could not see my darling Matthew in my son's eyes. They insisted I forget I had ever given birth; that I must obliterate my past. They called this sanity.

Rose was unable to read any further. She felt sick. 'She wasn't mad at all,' she muttered. She flung the diary back into the bureau. She had to get out of the room. Outside in the garden, padding through the wet grass, she was surprised to find it was already growing light. She stood in the middle of the lawn trembling violently and gasping for breath.

It was then that she thought of Dot. Could someone put Dot into an asylum? Could her father? After all, she was only seventeen. If he could stop her marrying . . . She must find out. She had to help her if she was in danger. She grew breathless again. She raised her head. Against the pink of the sky the leaves were a lush dark green, stark and rich. She breathed in deeply letting the garden soak into her and soothe her. She turned slowly, savouring the smells of the damp earth and the ripening apples.

Above her a window opened. Diana leaned out yawning. 'Hello,' she said surprised.

Rose glanced up at her. The last thing she wanted to do was to have a chat. She was desperate to stay on her own for a little while longer.

'I'm going into the village. I was just about to call you and tell you,' she lied.

'Have you had breakfast?'

'Yes.'

'Really?'

'No.'

'Roe!'

'I'm not hungry. Look, I'll see you later.'

Alec opened the door.

'What brings you here so early?' he said. He placed his hands on her shoulders. 'Are you all right? You look a bit pale and wan.'

'I'm just tired. I couldn't sleep last night.'

He smiled sympathetically.

'And,' she continued, 'I'm a bit nervous.'

'Of what?'

'You reading my story.'

He grinned. 'Is it finished?'

'Yes.'

'Do you have it with you?' he said.

'In my bag.'

'Come on up. We won't be disturbed. Derry won't surface for another four hours.'

So that's what Derry did in the mornings, she thought. How odd.

Up in the sitting room she tried to hand Alec the exercise book, but he insisted she read it aloud.

She emptied an armchair of several piles of local newspapers. 'Are these for salvage?' she asked.

'No. Some of them have pieces I've written in them. I keep meaning to cut them out and catalogue them but I've never got round to it.'

'Were you a journalist before you ran this shop?'

'I wrote articles about local goings-on. A sort of gossip column.'

'Did you get paid?'

'A little.'

'Gosh. Are you writing anything now?'

'No. And stop procrastinating.'

They sat opposite one another in the armchairs. She watched as Alec hunted round for some tobacco, the pipe in his mouth. She could see he hadn't slept either. The rims of his eyes were so pink, they looked raw.

He leaned back excitedly. 'Fire away.'

Rose stared down at the opening page and swallowed. 'It's called "Free-wheeling". I know it's not the most marvellous title but I thought it would do temporarily.'

'Stop apologising and get on with it.'

Her hands were shaking. She wondered if he noticed. She was afraid; afraid of being so upset if he didn't like it that she would never be able to write again.

She began. As she read, her mouth grew steadily drier. She kept her eyes down, gripping the book, while sweat trickled down inside her blouse. She had reached the crisis: Edith's flight through the night on her bicycle, her mad dash through the woods to get a doctor for her sick brother. On and on she read, to where Edith's parents discover she had been taught to ride the bicycle, in secret, by the gardener's boy.

The room seemed so quiet, it was unbearable. Rose couldn't even hear Alec breathing. When she had finished, Rose closed the book and looked up to find him staring at her. His pipe was still unlit.

'It wasn't *that* awful, was it?' she blurted out, unable to stand his silence any longer.

'What do *you* think?'

She reddened. 'I don't know. I mean, I have all these pictures in my head but my vocabulary is so limited. Often I can't find the word I want, so it's always less than I'd like it to be.'

'But?'

'The characters are real to me,' she said earnestly. 'I really care about them.'

'So do I,' he murmured. 'For what it's worth, I think it's publishable.'

'Publishable!'

He stood up swiftly and went to one of the bookcases. Before Rose had time to think, he had thrown a dozen or more paperbacks and magazines on to her lap. 'They're short-story magazines,' he explained. '*Penguin New Writing* publishes articles as well, and reviews. A lot of the magazines are crying out for new short stories now.'

'They are?'

'Have a browse. I'll make us some breakfast.'

She wedged herself back in the corner of the armchair and drew up her knees. The only magazines she recognised were *Horizon* and *Lilliput*. She picked up the Number One edition of the *Penguin New Writing*. It was slim, and dark orange in colour. At the bottom a small penguin appeared to be dancing.

She looked at the list of authors printed on the cover. She had vaguely heard of George Orwell but none of the others. She scanned the titles and rested on one called 'Sense of Humour'.

Inside, opposite the title page, was a photograph of the editor, a man called John Lehmann. She began to read his biographical notes.

'". . . is in touch with young authors from India to

America,'" she murmured. 'Gosh. It seems awfully highbrow. "Has worked as a literary critic for many periodicals, and is at present engaged on the amplification of his study of modern English literary trends . . ."'

She turned to the biographical notes at the back and looked up the writer of 'Sense of Humour', a man called V.S. Pritchett.

'Oh my goodness,' she cried.

Alec appeared at the kitchen doorway. 'What is it?'

'It's about one of the writers in here. It says he left school at sixteen during the war. I suppose that must be the last war. He didn't go to university. He left school at sixteen!' she repeated. 'And now he's a well-known story writer. I mean it's possible, isn't it?'

'Of course it's possible.'

'I don't expect that to happen to me but . . .' She stopped. What on earth was she saying? 'Oh, Alec,' she breathed. 'What an idiot I am. I know what I want to be. It's been staring me in the face.'

He leaned casually against the door frame, his hands in his pockets.

'You know too, don't you?' she said.

'Yes.'

'Then why can't I say it?'

'Because it means so much to you?'

'Yes. It's me, you see.'

He smiled. 'I know.'

'Oh, you're laughing at me!' she protested.

'Sorry, ma'am,' he said, with mock sheepishness, and he bowed and retreated to the kitchen.

She turned to the V.S. Pritchett story and was immediately

drawn into it by the dialogue. It flowed so smoothly that her eyes drifted effortlessly down the page.

Alec handed her a piece of toast and jam and a cup of tea. She mumbled her thanks and carried on reading. She quite forgot he was in the room, until she came to a part in the story where the young man was comforting his weeping girlfriend and one thing began to lead to another. Rose found herself blushing. She looked up briefly. Alec was reading too. Her story! When she had finished she discovered her tea was cold. She gulped it down quickly.

'Take them with you,' said Alec. 'I'm afraid I only have five of the *Penguin New Writing*. I've been ordering them, but often they're destroyed en route in a bombing raid and I've given a lot of them away to servicemen.' He leaned forward. 'Now, about your story. I've been thinking.'

'That you've made a mistake. That it's not as good as you thought.'

'You don't have much confidence in yourself, do you?'

'Nil.'

'Belt up for a moment and listen.'

She held her lips together with her fingers.

'Can you type?'

She shook her head.

'I can. And what I suggest is that I type it out for you. I'll make two copies in case a bomb disposes of it.'

Rose removed her fingers. 'You really are serious about it, aren't you?'

'Now,' he said, ignoring her. 'Do you intend to change your name?'

'I haven't thought about it. It's a pretty awful one.'

'Rose? I rather like it. Much better than Roe.'

'I mean my surname. Highly-Robinson. We're always being teased about it.'

'Tell you what, I'll start getting on with it. When you've decided on a surname I'll type it in afterwards.'

'I'm not really taking this in,' she said lamely.

'I can see. You look as though someone's hit you over the head with a blunderbuss.'

'It's the first step, isn't it? Do you know, as soon as I receive my first rejection slip, I'll have it framed and put on the wall. Then I'll know I've really started. Mm. This jam is scrummy.'

He laughed.

'What's so funny?' she said.

'The way you talk sometimes.'

'What's wrong with it?'

'It's just a little quaint. Terribly girls' boarding school.'

'Oh,' she said crossly. 'I don't write like that, do I?' she added, alarmed.

'No.' He smiled. 'Nothing like.'

'That's a relief. The sooner I can shake off that place, the better.'

'You still don't want to go back, do you?'

'Of course not. It's not a passing phase, you know.'

'Who said it was?'

'My parents.' She spread some jam on to another piece of toast. 'They've been telling me I'm going through a phase about leaving, for six years now. How long is a phase, I ask you?'

'I would guess it's until you stop disagreeing with them.'

'My poor father wanted me to go on to university and take a science degree.'

'That's unusual.'

'Times are changing, my gel,' said Rose hanging on to

invisible lapels. 'Gels have got to be educated just the same as boys. You go into science.'

'And your sister?'

'He didn't bother with her. *I'm* the one that has to go to university.'

'Why not her?'

'Because she's beautiful. Even in the school plays, I always get cast as a man. But I can understand that, I suppose.'

'I can't.'

'I'm hardly female-looking, am I? Without all my hair I'd look like a boy.'

'Is that what you want to be?'

She shrugged. 'I used to, desperately. I was my father's last hope for a son. I did try doing all the things he wanted me to do, because I don't want to end up just getting married and being stuck at home. I want to be able to earn my own living, so I really tried at all the "boy" subjects, like mathematics, but I just wasn't good enough and I didn't really enjoy them. I ended up liking the wrong things, like acting and English and history.'

'I'm a little confused,' said Alec. 'You're saying that in order to be independent, you not only have to have a degree but it also has to be a science degree because that is supposed to be a male subject.'

'Yes.'

'What does that make the men and women who don't have degrees in science?'

'Oh, I don't know. I'm so mixed up. The problem is, I don't want to be male and I don't want to be female.'

'I see,' said Alec slowly. 'Well, the first problem's solved. So, why don't you want to be female?'

'I told you, I don't want to be trapped in a house. If I *had* to get married I'd like to be the one that goes out and earns the money and I'd like the man to stay at home and do the cooking.'

Alec rose and extricated his pipe from between two books on the mantelpiece. 'Sounds like you don't want to be your *idea* of what a woman should be.'

'Exactly.'

'So be the way you want to be.'

Rose stared at him.

'Or better still, be the way you are,' he said.

'Don't try to change,' she stammered. 'Is that what you're saying?'

'Yes.' He laughed. 'Funnily enough, you'll probably change more when you stop trying. Are you all right? You look shocked.'

'I am. I'm not used to hearing someone tell me to be the way I already am. I usually only feel that when I'm on my own or when I'm writing.'

She leaped over Mrs Clarence's gate and sprinted across the beach looking for Derry. To her dismay, she saw that his boat had left its moorings.

She hadn't meant to stay at Mrs Clarence's for long, but had fallen asleep in a deckchair in her garden after chatting with her and Dot. She had been so worried about what might happen to Dot's baby that, before she could stop herself, she had blurted out, 'Could Dot's father sign her over into a lunatic asylum?' Then she had to explain hurriedly that she had read it in a book somewhere.

Dot had looked upset but Mrs Clarence had declared firmly that Dot would move in with her and be her official evacuee and that they would face the 'authorities' together. And Dot had calmed down.

Rose shinned swiftly up the rocky section which led to the coastal path and ran. Clambering up the hilly parts, skidding back on her heels on the downward slopes, she pushed herself forward, stumbling and gasping, stopping only briefly to rest her hands on her knees to catch her breath.

The sky gave a loud rumble. That'll keep the harvesters busy, she thought. The air was oppressive. She gazed seaward. There was still no sign of the boat. There didn't seem enough wind for Derry to have sailed as far as the cove unless he had left hours ago. He could be sitting there now wondering why she wasn't there, and thinking she wasn't interested in seeing him again.

She retrieved her bag and broke into a steady trot. By the time she spotted the cottage, she was beginning to feel sick. She drove herself on, past the lane, on towards the cove. There was no one there. She sank into the grass at the opening and stared stupefied at the deserted cove. The boat had been dragged up on to the sand. It sat there empty, tilting to one side. Footprints trailed away from it.

Of course, she thought, he must have gone to the cottage! She hauled herself to her feet and staggered back along the path. The gate was open. She tucked her blouse into her shorts and threw her plaits back over her shoulders. Then with all the nonchalance she could muster, she strolled to the garden at the side.

Derry was sitting on the step, cleaning his spectacles on his shorts.

'Hello,' she said.

He put his glasses on and looked at her. She walked lightly

towards him, dropped her bag down by the step and glanced around. 'Where's Diana?'

'You just missed her.'

'Where's she gone?'

'I don't know. We didn't talk. I saw her from the coastal path cycling over the hill.'

'Oh.'

So they were alone. She hovered, too shy to sit near him.

'I suppose . . .' she began.

'I heard . . .' he interrupted.

They laughed awkwardly.

'You begin,' she said.

'I heard you'd been round to the bookshop.'

'Yes. Alec lent me some books. Well, they're mostly short-story magazines.'

'I see.' He frowned and looked away.

Rose felt so tight inside she thought she would burst. 'I know about his nervous breakdown,' she blurted out.

He whirled round. 'It doesn't run in the family, you know,' he said. 'I'm not like that. I won't back out when things get too much.'

'Of course you won't.' She hesitated. 'I don't think he was deliberately backing out. He told me the doctor ordered him here to recuperate.'

Derry stared gloomily at the ground. 'You don't know what it's like,' he muttered. He clasped his hands tightly. 'Do you know he *cries*? One night I was walking past his room and I heard him weeping like a baby. A grown man!'

'But isn't that to do with his illness?'

'I don't know. I just know if any of my friends find out, I'll never live it down.'

There was an embarrassed silence. 'It's awfully close, isn't it?' he said at last.

'Yes. I think there might be a storm.'

'That'd be good for the garden.'

'But not for the harvesting.'

There was another silence. Every time Rose thought of something to say, she immediately censored herself, so she said nothing.

'Roe,' said Derry quietly. 'Come and sit down.'

She blushed. 'All right.'

As she squeezed in beside him, he slipped his arm round her waist.

I'm going to die, she thought, I'm going to die.

He took her hand. 'About Alec,' he murmured.

'Yes?'

'It hasn't made you want to have nothing to do with me, has it?'

Rose was astounded. He was afraid *she* wouldn't like *him*! It was unbelievable. 'Why on earth should it?'

'It's not the sort of thing people talk about.'

'Isn't it?'

'No.'

'Derry, there's something that's been puzzling me. I hope you don't mind me asking, but Alec seems a bit old to be your cousin. He looks as though he's in his thirties. How old is he?'

'I don't know. Twenty-five. Twenty-six.'

She gasped. 'Are you sure?'

'He can't be much more than that. He was eight when I was born. My aunt and uncle had him when they were middle-aged. They couldn't have children, you see.'

'You mean, they thought they couldn't.'

'Yes,' he said hurriedly. 'Yes, that's right.'

He looked uncomfortable. 'Those apples will be ready soon,' he said suddenly. 'I'll help you pick them.'

Rose gazed at the neatly planted vegetable patch, and the tiny wild daisies and small pink flowers which were sticking out of the stone wall. Three butterflies hovered above the lilac flowers of a small buddleia shrub, closing their wings as they settled on the cone-shaped clusters of petals, opening them up again to give a flash of their deeply coloured black and orange wings.

Derry watched her out of the corner of his eye. He pulled her close to him. They sat there for some time staring out at the garden, neither of them speaking or moving. Eventually Derry shifted position.

'Let's go to the cove, shall we?' he said.

'All right. I'm afraid I can't stay too long though.'

They stood up and walked to the gate; a shy distance between them. They stepped into the lane, their hands in their shorts pockets. Derry glanced aside at her. 'I shall be starting training soon,' he said.

'Are you sure you want to be a pilot?' she asked.

'Positive. Why?'

'It's so dangerous. Once you're in a plane, you're a sitting target.'

'You must think of Jerry being the target.'

'I suppose so,' she sighed.

'Once the results of my Highers come through I'll be called up in no time. They're desperate for pilots, you know. I'll probably start training in a fortnight. Maybe sooner. That's why I want to make the most of this time. Just in case it's my last summer.'

Rose stared ahead. She remembered Robert Clarence

saying that the R.A.F. were having to teach the young men so quickly nowadays, that many of them actually died in training accidents. She suddenly found herself panicking. Supposing, like Miss Hilda, Derry was her one and only chance of love. She had visions of her sister going off and getting married, while she stayed at home to look after her mother; the spinster aunt to her sister's children. She shuddered.

'Are you cold?' asked Derry.

'No. It was just being reminded of the war.'

They climbed down the cliff to the cove and sat in the sand.

'Honestly, Roe, I don't mind dying young.'

He let his hand drift down one of her plaits. 'I don't suppose you'd unplait your hair for me, would you?'

'Yes. If you like.'

'I'll do one and you do the other.'

They began untwisting them.

'It's very frizzy,' she said. 'Quite the wrong sort of hair to have long. I'd much rather have it short.'

'You mustn't have it cut. You'd look like a boy.'

She was alarmed. 'I don't *now*, do I?'

'Of course not.'

When her hair was undone he placed his hands underneath it and spread it out across her shoulders. It made her tingle.

He hesitated. 'Roe, I'd love to see what it looks like against the sand.'

She blushed.

'Just so I could compare the colours,' he added.

She lowered herself on to her back. Derry moved closer.

'It's so dark,' he murmured.

He pulled it upwards and outwards, so that it encircled her head like a large black halo.

Rose sank into the sand's warmth and closed her eyes.

It was heavenly to be touched. So many times she had hugged herself in bed at night, stroking her skin with her fingers, imagining that someone else was doing it. And now it was really happening to her.

'Such beautiful long hair,' said Derry. 'It really is your best feature. That and your eyes.'

She opened them. 'But they're such a nothing sort of colour. All bluey, greeny, grey.'

'It's the shape. They're very large.'

She remembered some line in a Chekhov play. One of the characters had said something like, 'I know I'm plain, because people tell me what nice hair and eyes I have.'

Derry put his hands in her hair again, and then, bit by bit, he edged in closer and lay down beside her.

'I know,' he said suddenly. 'Let's play roly-poly.'

'What's that?'

'Didn't you play it when you were small?'

'I don't know. What is it?'

'You go up to the top of a hill, lie down and roll all the way to the bottom.'

'Oh yes. I was always getting into trouble for that. I used to come home with grass stains all over my dress. But it's too dangerous here.'

'Not down the cliffs, silly. Along here. On the beach.'

'All right.'

'We have to hold on to one another,' he said.

'What?'

'It's more fun.'

'Oh. All right then.'

They wrapped themselves round each other and began a rocking motion.

'Ready!' yelled Derry. 'Steady. Go!'

Rose gave a shriek as they pushed off, and forced themselves round, like a rolling human sausage. They lay apart on the other side of the cove, shaking with laughter.

'Oh, that was wonderful,' panted Rose. 'Let's do it again.'

Derry was trembling from head to foot. He grinned. They clung on to one another and began rocking again.

'Here we go!'

Giggling hysterically, they tumbled and rolled across the sand.

'Again!' said Rose when they had collapsed on the other side.

Derry gazed at her. Fine white sand was scattered over her dark skin and hair. 'You're covered,' he murmured.

'You too.'

She stretched her fingers out tentatively and brushed away the sand from his face. Her hand stopped at his mouth. She removed it hurriedly.

They stared at one another. Eventually the hand that Rose was leaning on grew numb. She shook it vigorously. 'It's gone numb,' she explained.

'I'll squeeze it back to life for you.' And he kneaded it firmly with his fingers.

She gasped. 'I've got pins and needles now. They're awful, aren't they?'

When her hand felt normal again, Derry pushed her gently back on to the sand. He leaned forward to kiss her.

Rose sat up startled. 'You won't lose respect for me, will you?' she asked suddenly. 'I'd hate you to think . . .' She trailed off.

'Of course I won't.'

They gazed at one another in silence, not moving.

'It's been a splendid afternoon,' said Derry at last.

'Yes,' agreed Rose. 'It has.'

He cleared his throat. 'May I see you again?'

She reddened. 'Yes. If you'd like to.'

Suddenly he leapt to his feet. 'I'll be Tommy and you be Jerry,' he said eagerly.

She stared at him, stupefied. 'I don't want . . .' she began, but he was already running to the rocks, hiding and dodging behind them, making bomb sounds.

She couldn't take in this dramatic change in his behaviour. One minute he had been about to kiss her and now he wanted to go back to playing childish games. Suddenly she remembered the diaries, Matthew's death in the trenches, Miss Hilda's descriptions of the wounded. And Dot lying in the deck chair, her hand resting on her belly feeling her baby kicking, not knowing whether her Jack was dead or alive. And it came to her more forcibly that war was not a game; that being burnt in an exploding plane was agony; that bullets hurt, that women like Dot weren't interested in living with the memory of a dead hero. They'd much rather have an ordinary sort of fellow, who was alive.

Derry ran across the sand in front of her ratatattatting a volley of machine-gun fire.

Rose gazed numbly back at him.

'What's up?' he said. 'I've just thrown three grenades at you and you're still alive.'

'What? Oh. Sorry,' and she collapsed on to the ground.

'Hopeless. What kind of death is that?'

All right, all right, thought Rose angrily. 'I'll give you a real one, if that's what you want. She stood up, and as he machine-gunned her, she gave a horrifying scream and sank howling on to the beach. After shrieking and writhing, she finally death-rattled into stillness.

'You don't have to overdo it,' he said sullenly. 'Now you've spoiled it.'

'*I* spoiled it?' she exclaimed. She stood up and brushed the sand from her legs and arms.

They stared at one another for a moment before looking hurriedly away. Then, still not speaking, they made their way back towards the cliff.

Ten

Rose stared miserably out of the bedroom window. She had had another sleepless night. Every time she had closed her eyes she kept hearing Derry's disgruntled voice saying, 'Now you've spoiled it.' She was furious with herself. Her one chance of a boy paying attention to her and she had mucked it up.

'Stupid idiot,' she muttered. 'Why didn't I just play the game?'

'Hello.'

Rose jumped. Diana was standing at the door. 'Sorry. I didn't mean to startle you. I thought you'd be asleep. There's no need to leave this now,' she said, waving a note. 'I'm going to Mrs Clarence's. Robert's phoning so I need to be there early.'

'I didn't hear you come in last night,' said Rose.

'That's because you were so fast asleep.'

Rose was about to protest that she was sure she hadn't slept a wink but stopped herself. She didn't want Diana to know she was worried about anything.

'How was the first-aid class?' she asked.

'Marvellous.' Diana sat at the end of Rose's bed.

Rose climbed back under the covers and hugged her knees. 'What did you learn?'

'Exercises.'

'Exercises! What have they got to do with first aid?'

'They were the sort you do to prepare yourself for childbirth.'

'And *you* did them?'

Diana smiled. 'Yes. Dot and I volunteered first. Then Mrs Clarence.'

'She didn't!'

'One of the old ladies yelled out, "Bit late for you, ent it, Mrs Clarence?" In the end everyone was doing them.'

'But who told you what to do?'

'This Land Army girl. She'd had some training in physical education. She was incredibly persuasive.'

'So you still didn't get your talk from Dr Clarke?'

'Yes, but not for a while. The exercises were to fill in time. The woman in charge of the first-aid class had received another message to say he'd be late. Poor Dot. She really thought he wasn't going to turn up again.' She began to giggle. 'You should have seen what this Land Army girl had us doing.'

'Sounds fun,' said Rose enviously.

'You haven't heard the best yet,' continued Diana. 'When the doctor did turn up we all had our backs to the door except Gillian, the Land Army girl. She had just got us doing hip exercises. We had to imagine we were belly dancers. The trouble was, the only music the first-aid teacher could provide on her gramophone was a Strauss waltz.'

Rose began to smile. 'Go on.'

'So there we were,' said Diana. 'A group of women aged seventeen to seventy with our arms raised, moving our hips around and concentrating like mad to this crackly music when suddenly we hear this male voice behind us saying, "A Viennese harem! Well, I've seen everything now!"'

Rose shrieked with laughter. 'What did you do?' she cried.

'Nothing at first. We were too stunned. And then everyone collapsed and we couldn't stop laughing. Respected members of the community were leaning against the chairs and walls, weeping hysterically. To cap it all, Gillian announced we would end off with some relaxation exercises and asked the doctor to join in.'

'And did he?'

'Yes! He lay down on this threadbare carpet beside us, giving little snorts of laughter and then, after some breathing exercises, it went quiet. The next thing I heard was Gillian gently pulling us back awake and loud snoring coming from somewhere. Dr Clarke had fallen into a deep sleep.'

'Oh no.'

'Dot was devastated. She was convinced she would never have her questions answered before her baby was born.'

'So what did you do?'

'Drank our cups of tea round him till he woke up. I think he was glad of the nap. He's had to come out of retirement, even though he's well into his seventies, and he's forever dashing from village to village. Anyway, he gave an excellent talk.'

'About what to do if . . .?' Rose began.

'We found ourselves on our own with someone in labour?

Yes. The most important thing to remember, he told us, is to keep calm. That helps the woman stay relaxed so that nature can take its course.'

'Is that all?' asked Rose.

'Oh no. He gave us lots of information. I've written it all down in my notebook. You can borrow it if you're interested.'

'Thanks.' Rose laughed. 'You know, you've really cheered me up.'

Diana smiled. 'Good. Were you feeling a bit gloomy?'

'Yes. But I'm all right now,' said Rose quickly, resisting the temptation to talk about Derry.

Suddenly Diana shot off the bed. 'Oh lor, the telephone call! I must fly or I'll miss it.'

Rose waved her off at the kitchen door, regretting she hadn't confided in her. Perhaps it was for the best though.

Diana still saw her as a child. If she suspected there was anything going on between her and Derry she would never allow them to be alone together. She sighed. She wouldn't know until the afternoon if he wanted to see her again. Until then she had hours to kill.

She decided to return to Miss Hilda's diary. The room was airless. She hitched back the blackout curtain, left the door ajar and began reading.

Miss Hilda described the condition of the asylum; its sparsely furnished, crowded wards; its smells of disinfectant mixed with human excrement; the bars on the windows; the cells.

I was forced to support a paradox, she wrote. *I had to convince the nursing staff and doctors that I had not only forgotten what had happened, but also I regretted it; that my affair with Matthew had been some kind of illness.*

At first I refused. After all I had been brought up to believe in being honest, but I quickly realised that honesty was my jailor, so I began to lie.

In my thoughts I kept Matthew's memory alive. I lived through our courtship day by day, hour by hour. I tried to remember every conversation we ever had, everything he had written in his letters. I had tasted happiness. I knew it was within me to recreate it and experience it again. I had to cling on to that knowledge.

The nurses taunted and abused me, calling me a high-class whore, saying they hoped my little bastard had been drowned somewhere. If I didn't howl with mental or physical pain, I was considered depressed. If I shouted back in anger at their cruelty, I was locked in a steam bath, trussed up in a straitjacket or given drugs.

Throughout all this I had this strong belief that it was important to retain my physical fitness. I walked the wards as much as possible, and developed a series of exercises which I could carry out in secret. As long as I was able to keep my body and mind alert I felt I had a grip on my sanity, for I believed that if I broke down in that institution, I would become as mad as the inmates and most of the nursing staff.

I did my best to keep clean, brushing my hair in the morning with my fingers and plaiting it (I had no brush or comb) and washing my face and hands.

In the spring of 1919, I received an unexpected visit. It was my brother Edward. He had returned from Africa. I was surprised he had come. I wondered if my father knew of his visit. The visiting room was bare, but for two chairs which faced one another. Two female attendants stood either side of me. They gave us ten minutes. I longed to ask after my son. Was he alive and well? Had he been sent to an orphanage? Had he been adopted? But I knew that any acknowledgement of his existence was considered part of my illness and would reveal to the authorities that I had still not been cured. I knew, too, that if I asked after my parents, my father in particular, I would be in grave danger of losing my self-control.

Rose read through Miss Hilda's account of their stilted conversation.

'And the war is over now, you say?'

'Yes. Last November.'

'Will you stay in the army?'

'For the moment. But I must start thinking of the estate, now that Father is living on his own. You did know about Mother?'

'No.'

'She died a year ago.'

I attempted to say, 'I'm sorry,' but I couldn't seem to form the words.

'Is there anything I can send you?' he asked.

'Books,' I said smiling. 'Writing materials, a brush and comb, hairpins, soap.'

He didn't return my smile.

'I don't know when I shall be able to come again,' he stammered. 'I'll send you what I can.'

I watched him hurry for the door, his struggle with the door knob, his look of panic when he realised that it was locked.

'Don't worry, Edward,' I said. 'I'm sure Father hasn't signed you over, too. I expect they'll let you out after they've taken me away. After all, you haven't had a baby out of wedlock.'

The attendants seized my elbows and dragged me to the door.

'Or didn't you know about your nephew?' I yelled.

For a month they punished me, only they called it 'treatment'. They shaved my head so that my 'poor' brother would have no need to send me a brush and comb. My hands were tied to the end of the bed so that I was unable even to wash myself and I was informed I would have no use for the writing materials my brother had sent.

Later I asked if I could help on the ward, but the nurses scoffed at my V.A.D. experience. V.A.D.s were 'potty-emptiers'. If I was really interested I could do that type of work.

So I made it my job to ask the women who were incapacitated when they needed bedpans, and managed to obtain permission from one of the visiting doctors to clean the patients up when they were incontinent.

I grew fond of the women I nursed, but rather like a mother to children who would never grow up. I had my moments of despair when one died, or committed suicide, but my despair was most acute in May, for I would remember the warm baby I had held so fleetingly in my arms.

In 1924, seven years after I had been brought to the asylum, my brother visited me again. This time we were in the presence of a doctor, and my attendant nurses stood further away. My brother had put on weight. He was stout, had lost some hair, and had a high flush to his cheeks. The conversation was as stilted as our last one had been. Then to my surprise, the doctor spoke.

'I hear you have been helping the nurses,' he said.

'Yes,' I answered. 'But only in small ways. I couldn't hope to be as skilled and professional as they are.'

I felt like a veritable Uriah Heep, but my survival was what was paramount in my mind and I knew that the two nurses would report everything I had said to the others.

'And you feel in good health?' he went on.

'Yes, thank you. I am well looked after.'

I remember there being an awkward pause as he observed the state of my shift and hair. He pressed his hands on his knees.

'Good,' he remarked. 'I'm glad to see you are progressing.'

My heart leapt! Progressing! I glanced at my brother.

'And how is army life?' I asked politely.

He shifted uneasily in his chair. 'I'm no longer in the army. I l̶ɇ̶ft̶
two years ago.'

'You're looking very well,' I lied. 'Civilian life obviously suits you.'

'I'm married, too,' he added.

'Oh, I am pleased for you, Edward.'

I did not dare ask if he had any children.

'Is there anything you need?' he asked.

One glance, and he could have answered the question himself.

'An Old Testament would be welcome,' I said. 'And perhaps some
other uplifting book. Pilgrim's Progress?'

They smiled. Joy of joys, they smiled!

'I'm sure that can be arranged,' said the doctor.

'And perhaps a little news of the outside world? A newspaper!'

They frowned. I had gone too far.

'Only, of course, if you think it would be beneficial,' I added
hastily.

As I was escorted to the door, my brother began to speak quietly
to the doctor. I had hardly reached the doorway when I heard the
doctor say softly, 'Please accept my condolences, Major Withers. The
brigadier was a fine man.'

I froze for an instant, but only an instant. Years of practice at not
betraying my feelings took over, and I continued walking. If my father
was dead, it meant that Edward was now my legal guardian, that is
if the law had not changed in my absence.

A week later I received a parcel and letter. Inside the parcel was
a Bible and Pilgrim's Progress, a brush, comb and hairpins, a large
square of soap, a pen, a bottle of ink, paper, envelopes, handkerchiefs
and a tape measure.

'Dear Miss Withers, the letter read,
    I hope these gifts will bring you comfort and inspiration.

I have enclosed a tape measure and would be obliged if you
would send me your measurements.

Yours sincerely,

Mrs Edward Withers'

I wept quietly. I suspected that 'comfort and inspiration' was to be
provided by the Bible and Pilgrim's Progress, but to me, the comfort
was in the soap and hairbrush, and the inspiration lay in those white
sheets of paper and the pen and ink. Oh the glory of having clean
brushed hair! My head felt lighter, as though the grease and dirt had
been weighing heavily on it. I had no mirror so that when I pinned it
up, I had to use the reflection of myself in the windows, which was
difficult, as the bars obscured most of my face.

I was sent some clothing.

On one of the doctor's rare visits I asked if I might have access
to more laundry facilities, so that I could do my own washing and
ironing.

He was pleased. 'Good progress,' he called it.

Three months later, I was taken to the visitors' parlour to meet
my sister-in-law. I had not known such a place existed in the asylum!
A fire was blazing in the hearth, and nearby, a vase of flowers had
been placed on a table. I longed to touch and smell them. I wanted to
warm myself in front of the fire, to spread my arms along the woven
rugs. Meekly, I sat opposite Mrs Withers.

She was in her fifties; a plump woman of medium height. I was
shocked to see traces of powder and lipstick, having been brought up
to believe that only women of easy virtue painted their faces. Luckily
I had had some warning of the change in hemlines from the clothes
she had sent, otherwise I would have found it impossible to have
concealed my shock.

A maid brought in a tea-tray and placed it on a small table

beside us. There was silence as she poured three cups of tea.

'I enjoyed the psalms, Mrs Withers. I found them uplifting,' I began.

She smiled approvingly. 'Oh, did you? Yes, I find them so, too,' she crooned.

There was another silence.

'And you are well?' I ventured.

'Yes, thank you.'

Another silence.

'And my brother?'

'Oh yes, Major Withers is quite well.' She paused. 'I expect he told you about the brigadier.'

'Not exactly,' I said.

'Oh, I see,' and she blushed.

'I expect he didn't want to upset me,' I added hastily.

'Ah, yes.'

More sipping of tea.

Desperate for something to say I blurted out, 'I hope you don't mind me saying so, Mrs Withers, but that is such a charming hat you are wearing.'

In fact I thought it hideous. It looked like half a bucket made out of felt with a mangy orange flower attached to it.

'Why, thank you,' she gushed. 'Perhaps I can send one to you so that you can wear it when you go for walks.'

'You've been too kind as it is.'

'Nonsense!' and she gave a slight wave. 'It would give me nothing but pleasure.'

She looked puzzled for a moment. 'And you are quite recovered from your illness?'

I hesitated. 'That is for the doctor to say.'

'It must have been so difficult nursing all those wounded men,' she went on. 'I'm sure the strain would have made me ill, too.'

She looked at me with blank innocence. If that was the story my brother had invented, then I wasn't going to contradict her.

'Oh, we're very pleased with her progress,' put in the doctor, 'very pleased indeed.'

True to her word, Mrs Withers sent me a black hat, a cloche hat she called it, together with a black coat and black gloves. From then on she came once a week to visit me and I was allowed out for walks in the walled courtyard.

One afternoon, she blurted out, 'Miss Withers, do you think you could cope without a maid or gardener?'

I was dumbstruck.

'Don't alarm yourself,' she continued hastily. 'If you think you couldn't manage, we'll wait until we can find ones for you. Oh dear,' she said glancing at the doctor. 'I fear I might have said too much. But servants are so fussy nowadays. I mean, so difficult to come by. And the cottage is miles from anywhere and terribly exposed. And I think they're a bit scared of being out there all alone by the sea.'

With me, I added internally. I was thinking rapidly. And then I realised which cottage she meant.

It was the doctor's turn to look alarmed.

'Are you feeling unwell?' he enquired. 'You seem a little pale.'

'I'm feeling quite well. It was just a bit of a shock. I wasn't expecting it. I'm sure I could manage without servants, Mrs Withers,' I added swiftly.

A few months later I was summoned to the parlour to see my brother. I had been given no warning of his visit.

'The doctor and I have been discussing your welfare,' he began. 'I have agreed that you should be allowed to be released from his care, and live in the outside world again.'

I held my breath and kept as still as still. I was the acquiescent rock.

'There will of course be certain conditions. If you agree to these

173

conditions, then you may live at the cottage. I shall arrange to have eggs and milk delivered there and will give you a small monthly allowance for food and other sundry items.'

'And the conditions?' I asked softly.

'That you never mention the misdemeanour which happened seven years ago and that, if you do, I will inform the person or persons concerned that your words are the ravings of a mad woman, and I will have you taken back here immediately.'

Noticing that my hands had clenched into fists I clasped them meekly.

'And I may go to the shops in Salmouth?'

'If you wish. But not to the manor,' he added firmly. 'If an emergency should arise, you can inform Partridge.'

Partridge, I thought, the gardener's boy. He must be a grown man by now.

'I shall make sure you are given the basic requirements, such as furniture. Partridge's wife will deal with linen, cooking utensils, that sort of thing.' He paused. 'Have you anything to say?'

'I think your offer is most kind.'

He cleared his throat. 'So you agree with the conditions?'

'I agree.'

'And you have fully repented your past?'

'Of course,' I lied demurely.

It wasn't until February 1925, after eight years of imprisonment, that I walked out of that institution.

I was forty years old.

Eleven

Rose walked briskly along the coastal path. She felt purged, as though she had lived through Miss Hilda's long dark tunnel and had emerged with her into the sunlight, a survivor. She swung her bag carelessly over her shoulder and drank in the raggedy fields, the squawking of hungry gulls, the scent of sea air. Everything about her seemed sweeter and more vibrant.

There was no sign of Derry at the cove. She was surprised to find she was relieved, and that disturbed her. She swam the width of the cove twice and then lay on her stomach on a towel, jotting down ideas for another story. None of them excited her. She returned to thinking about her change of name and decided to choose her mother's maiden name, Jolliffe; Rose Jolliffe.

Suddenly, she caught sight of the red sail. She sprang to her feet, and waved. He grinned and waved back, tacking the boat into the cove. Together they hauled it up on to the beach. He took hold of her hand. As they walked towards the cliff face, she felt her legs growing weak. Her skin was stinging and a strange ache seemed to swell up into her throat. As soon as they had sat down, Derry put his arm round her.

'I'm glad you turned up,' he said quietly.

'Oh,' she murmured. 'Are you?'

'I thought you'd still be cross with me.'

'Snap,' said Rose and she drew her fingers along the sand. Derry stroked her arm.

'Roe?' he said, drawing nearer.

'Yes.'

'May I kiss you?'

Startled, she gave a nod. As he came towards her she wasn't sure whether she ought to close her eyes or not. She closed them hurriedly, conscious that her right hand was filled with sand, and wondering if she ought to let go of it.

'Unplait your hair again,' he said.

While she did so, he sat back and watched her. He kissed her again letting his hand move down the side of her swimsuit and on to her thigh.

She stiffened. 'Derry, you mustn't do that.'

'Why not?'

'Because I don't think you should.'

'Don't you like it?'

'Yes.'

'Then that's all right.'

He continued to stroke her leg. As his hand moved upward, she grabbed it, and sat up sharply.

'Derry, you mustn't.'

'I'm sorry. I got carried away. You're not angry with me, are you?'

Rose shook her head. She loved it when he touched her; loved putting her arms round him; and yes, she loved it when he stroked her. She was grateful he wanted to spend his time with her at all. Yet there was something wrong.

'It's just, I don't want you losing respect for me,' she stammered.

'I won't,' he said. 'I promise.'

He put his arm around her again.

Gradually she relaxed, and allowed her head to rest on his shoulder.

'When I'm on a bombing mission,' Derry whispered, 'I shall have these memories to take away with me and treasure.'

The following morning Rose crept out of the cottage early, leaving a note for Diana on the kitchen table. She had heard Diana coming home late from Mrs Clarence's so she assumed that Robert was all right.

She headed straight for the bookshop and told Alec of her change of surname. He had finished typing her Edith story. There, in cold print, she read it through as though someone else had written it. Repetitions leapt out at her. She drew line after line through unnecessary sentences and altered words.

'I'm awfully sorry,' she said, when she handed it back.

'It's all right. I only made one copy. I guessed you might like to have another session with it.'

Rose sank back into one of his large armchairs. She loved being in Alec's living room. She felt at home. She had intended to broach the subject of love, pretending that she and Derry were two characters in a story she had read, saying she didn't understand the feelings of the female character, and could he? But once she was with him she was swept back into Edith's world again and she and Alec got involved in talking about writing and books. Then to Rose's amazement, he mentioned Miss Hilda.

'You knew her?' she exclaimed.

'Oh yes. We were old friends. That's why it's so odd you should be staying there and doing the same sort of things as she did.'

'What do you mean?'

'She'd borrow books as if she was researching. Sometimes she'd get books in Gynmouth too. She loved reading.'

'I know,' said Rose, remembering the books in the locked room. 'I mean, I know because I've seen some of her books in the cottage.'

His face grew taut. 'I suppose I ought to offer to buy them,' he said quietly. 'I'd hate to think of her favourites just lying there.'

'No, don't.'

He stared quizzically at her. 'You want them all to yourself, eh? Don't worry, I'll wait till you leave.'

'No, you mustn't!'

'Rose, what's going on?'

She reddened. 'I'm not supposed to know about them. They're locked up in a room between the kitchen and the living room.'

'Ah, yes. I know the room.'

'You do?'

'I used to go there frequently.'

'You did?'

He laughed. 'Yes. Why the astonishment?'

'I didn't realise. You didn't say. What was she like?'

'Full of verve, quick-witted, amusing, affectionate. I think you would have liked her.'

'Did she talk much about her past?'

'Sometimes.'

'She wasn't mad, you know,' she blurted out.

Alec looked at her oddly. 'Who told you about her being mad?'

'Oh. Mr Partridge, Derry, Mrs Clarence.'

'I know she was put into an asylum. She told me one evening, when she was in her cups.' He paused. 'You said her books are in a locked room?'

'Yes. I've found a way of getting in. Mr Partridge has put as much of her stuff in there as he possibly can. I sometimes sneak in and sit amongst it. I like it there.'

'What makes you so sure she wasn't mad?' he asked slowly.

She hesitated. 'Just a feeling.'

'Yes. I felt the same. She was one of those women who was before her time. Didn't conform, you know. I think those dull old blighters of her relations had her locked up because she was too full of life for them to handle. Anyway, at least her brother got her out, even if he did refuse to have anything to do with her.'

They fell to discussing what to do with Rose's story. Rose suggested, since the main character was fifteen, that perhaps a magazine for girls might like it. Alec disagreed.

'Let's go for the top,' he said. 'Let's try *Penguin New Writing* or *Horizon*.'

It was during her walk back to the cottage that Rose got the seed of an idea for another short story. She remembered Miss Hilda's comment about Partridge being the gardener's boy and that had set her daydreaming. She liked the idea of writing about a gardener's boy, perhaps the same gardener's boy who had helped Edith; a story from his point of view.

As soon as she reached the cottage, she sprinted up to her study and began to browse through the photographs in her books, jotting down notes. She knew she would scrap most of them, but in the past she had discovered that if she wrote them all down, they would lead her to the one idea which would finally excite her.

The door swung open. It was Derry. He stood and stared at her, taking in her dishevelled plaits and flushed brown face, her shorts and bare feet, the papers and books scattered untidily across the small table and floor.

'Why didn't you answer me?' He looked hurt.

'I didn't hear you.'

'But I called out.'

'Honestly, I go deaf when I'm writing.'

He frowned. 'What are you writing?'

'Just some ideas for a short story.'

'A humorous story? Like your poems?'

'Not exactly.'

'Oh.'

As he walked in, Rose felt invaded.

'What are the old books for?'

'Research.'

'I came to the cove but you weren't there.'

'I'm sorry. I didn't notice the time. And you didn't say when you'd be coming.'

'You walked two miles to see Alec though,' and he scowled.

She took a deep breath. She might as well tell him now. 'He's typing out a story for me. He thinks it's publishable standard.'

'Well, he can't know much, can he?'

'What do you mean? He's had lots of articles published in newspapers and magazines.'

'How can someone who hasn't even got School Cert. write a publishable story? I think he's being cruel, raising your hopes like that.'

'Charles Dickens didn't have School Cert. Charlotte Brontë didn't have School Cert. Neither did Shakespeare.'

'Don't you think this has all gone to your head a bit? You write one short story which Alec keeps going on and on about.'

'Does he? I didn't know that.'

'And now you think you're as good as Shakespeare and Dickens.'

'I don't. But trying to get something published is an important start. I've learnt an awful lot just by imagining a stranger reading it.'

'I just hate to think of you building up your hopes for the story and then being disappointed when no one wants it.'

'How can you be so sure no one will want it?'

'I mean *if* no one wants it.'

'I don't suppose anyone will. But it doesn't matter. I'm taking the risk, that's what's important, like being a pilot. That's risky.'

'That's different,' he said grandly, 'that's for your country. I mean, there is a war on, you know.'

Rose felt acutely depressed. Derry put his arm around her shoulders, and gave her a squeeze.

'It's just that when you weren't in the cove waiting for me, and then I found you were thinking about a story, I was a bit rattled, that's all,' he said. 'You can write all the stories you like after I've gone. You're making my last days before I start training, the happiest ones I shall have in my whole life.'

'Please, Derry, you know I don't like you talking like that.'

'I have to be realistic. Very few pilots survive. I'd much rather accept the fact and get as much out of life as I can.'

He sounded so grown-up, thought Rose, while she was behaving like a schoolgirl. She tried to smile, and slipped her arm shyly round his waist.

That afternoon, as they lay in the sand, Derry returned to stroking her legs and finally she allowed him to touch her breasts through the swimsuit. What puzzled her was that, in pleasing him, she was displeasing herself. If she was in love with him, she ought to feel pleased. Instead she longed to leap up and do something else.

The air was oppressive and clammy. By late afternoon, the sky suddenly became overcast.

'Here comes the storm,' said Derry. 'I don't think I'll risk sailing back. I'll leave the boat here.'

They dragged it further inland, tied the painter round a jutting rock and clambered up the cliff face. Rose was relieved to be moving again. She gripped the rocks and hauled herself up while Derry struggled on behind.

Once on the coastal path the dark clouds which had gathered began to move swiftly across the sky. Rose and Derry sprinted along the path and up the lane then leapt over the gate and flung the kitchen door open.

At first Rose thought the note on the kitchen table was the one she had written that morning, until she recognised her sister's handwriting.

'Oh no,' she whispered.

'What is it?' asked Derry.

'Robert didn't phone. Diana's gone back to Mrs Clarence's to wait again. I hope nothing's happened to him.'

Derry closed the kitchen door. The cottage suddenly seemed deathly quiet.

'You'd better borrow my bike and go back by road,' said Rose hurriedly. 'There's going to be a downpour.'

'I wouldn't leave you here by yourself.'

'Oh, I'll be all right. I'm often on my own. I'm used to it.'

'Don't you want me to stay?' He sounded hurt again.

'Of course,' she stammered. 'I just don't want you to get caught in the rain.'

A loud rumble set the window rattling and the kitchen grew

dark. Rose heard herself making polite conversation about the weather. She couldn't bear Derry sitting there, staring at her.

'Have you any food?' he asked.

'I'll have a look.'

As she opened the cupboard her loose hair fell across her face. She twisted it and stuffed it down her blouse.

'How about bread and Marmite?'

'What about something cooked?'

'We don't do much cooking. It means lighting the range. We could have a salad and cold carrot pie. And I could boil up some potatoes on the primus if you like.'

'Yes. That'd be nice.'

She poured water into the sink from the bucket.

Suddenly he stood up. 'Would you change into your dress?' he said.

Rose swung round. 'What?'

'Your dress. You know, the one you wore to the dance. Would you put it on?'

'Whatever for?'

'For me.'

'But it's for special occasions. The only other dress I have here is my gymslip.'

'But this is a special occasion. We're having a meal together, aren't we? Go on, Roe,' he pleaded. 'Put it on. You look much nicer in it.'

He pulled her hair out from her blouse. 'That's better,' he said. 'You must never have it cut.'

She gave a resigned nod and made her way silently to her bedroom. She removed her dress from the hanger, slipped her shorts and swimsuit off, took a pair of knickers from the chest of drawers and put her dress on.

Downstairs Derry glanced at her bare feet.

'You haven't put your nylons on,' he said disappointed.

'I'm saving them. They might get laddered. Anyway I feel more comfortable without them.'

'It doesn't look as good though. Put them on, Roe. Go on,' he begged. 'Just to please me.'

Rose returned to her bedroom and sank on the bed. 'Oh Lord,' she whispered. 'What on earth's happening to me?'

She pulled the nylons on carefully, twisting them round to make sure that the lines were straight.

Returning to the potatoes downstairs, Rose had the sensation that she was in a portrait Derry had created, and that if she stepped out of it, she would make him unhappy.

There was a tightness in her chest. She tried to breathe but nothing happened. For a moment she panicked.

'Are you all right?' he asked.

'I feel a bit breathless, that's all.'

'It's this storm. Once it breaks it won't feel so airless.'

'Yes. I expect that's what it is.'

She raised her head. Outside it was growing darker. She took an oil lamp out from the cupboard and drew the blackout curtains, plunging them into darkness. As she struck a match, she noticed her hands were shaking. She inserted the glass funnel over the lighted wick and lowered the glass bowl round it. The amber globe sent long shadows sprinting along the walls.

She placed the saucepan of potatoes on the primus. 'I'll put the blackout up, upstairs,' she said.

She had hardly reached her sister's bedroom, when a crack of lightning shot across the sky. There was a loud crash of thunder and monsoon-like rain hurtled down.

She flung open a window on the garden side, and leaned out. A fork of lightning sent her darting back inside. Even with the window shut, the noise was deafening. As she stood there, she realised that if her sister hadn't already been caught in the downpour, she would probably remain wherever she was until it had calmed down. Until then she and Derry would be trapped together.

'It's a heck of a storm, isn't it?' Derry shouted up the stairs. 'I'll just have to stay here till it stops.'

By the time the potatoes had boiled and she had laid the table, she had lost her appetite. She poured the water into Diana's 'making soup' bowl, and placed the saucepan on the table.

'Help yourself,' she said. 'I'm not hungry.'

She watched him eat. Hating the silence between them, she made stilted conversation about how nice it was to eat by the light of an oil lamp. After Derry had finished eating he took the lamp through into the living room and sat down on the large sofa.

Rose stood in the doorway.

'Sit down,' he said.

She perched on the edge.

'No, further back,' he urged. 'You're miles away.'

Rose wanted to run away, or yell at him to go home, but it was still raining heavily outside, so she did as she was told.

Derry drew her close. Once they were nestled together she felt better.

'I'll never forget these moments, Roe,' he murmured. 'I think you're an awfully good sort.'

They listened to the rain beating against the windows, neither of them speaking. It was Derry who broke the silence.

'I think I'll have to stay the night,' he said.

Rose did not move.

'Good job I'm here, eh? Otherwise you'd be sleeping here on your own. Do you have a spare bed?'

'Yes, but it's in my room.'

'That's good. We could chat to each other in the night. Then if you got scared of the lightning, you'll have me nearby to protect you.'

'I don't get scared. I like a good storm. I always think it's the sky's way of getting all its bottled-up feelings out of its system. You know. Losing its temper and having a good howl. I always feel calmer after a storm.'

Derry gazed imploringly at her. 'Please, Roe,' he urged. 'This will be the only chance we'll ever have of spending a night together. Please.'

'All right,' she murmured. 'I'll make up the bed in there.'

Upstairs, she made up his bed and changed into her pyjamas, moving laboriously, as if her body was willing her to slow down.

'Call out, when you're decent,' he said excitedly.

She slipped into bed and drew the sheets up to her neck. She glanced at the oil lamp, not knowing whether to turn the wick down or not. Instead, she called out to him.

He peered awkwardly round the door.

'Do you want me to turn out the lamp?' she asked.

'No, no,' he said. 'I'll do that after I've undressed. Just keep your eyes closed.'

Rose sank back into her pillow, her eyes shut. 'After you've done the lamp,' she said, 'could you draw the curtains? It's nice to see the dawn coming up.'

'The dawn! I shall be asleep when that happens.'

'I like to see the night too. I feel as though I'm sleeping in a coffin if the curtains aren't open.'

'All right,' he said.

She heard him approach the bed; heard his gasp as he touched a hot part of the lamp. But there was no sound of the curtains being drawn.

'I'll draw them myself,' she muttered, irritated.

'No, don't!' he said urgently. 'Keep your eyes closed.'

'All right,' she said, puzzled.

She heard the curtains swish as he shook them along the brass curtain rail and waited for him to move away so that she could open her eyes. Something heavy landed beside her, and the spring of her bed squeaked.

'Derry? What are you doing?'

She felt him move closer.

'Roe,' he began uncertainly. 'Let me come in beside you. I won't do anything, I promise. We could just cuddle, like on the beach.'

'No,' said Rose, shocked. 'We can't!'

'Why?'

'Because it's wrong.'

'Not if we just cuddle.'

He placed his hand very gently on the sheet where she gripped it. 'Please,' he whispered. 'There's nothing wrong in us just sleeping together.'

'We might do it in our sleep. I'll get pregnant.'

'It doesn't happen like that. You have to be awake to do it.'

'Always?'

'Yes.'

'But if that's true why shouldn't people sleep together if they're not married?'

'I don't know.'

'You're absolutely sure it can't happen in your sleep?'

'Positive.'

She released the sheet. He drew it aside and slipped in beside her. She opened her eyes. He was smiling. He slipped his arms around her and drew her close. This feels wonderful, she thought. If he could just be content to hold her like this. His hand moved across her breasts. She stiffened.

'Sorry,' he said, but he kept his hand there.

The window pane gave a sudden rattle.

'Oh look,' she whispered.

Trickling down the glass were lines of wet silver. A branch from one of the apple trees bobbed up and down, its leaves and fruit dripping.

Derry was staring at the buttons on her pyjama jacket. Clumsily he started to undo them. It suddenly occurred to her that she had never seen her breasts face on; had never looked at them in a mirror. Derry was seeing more of her than she had.

He placed his hand over one breast.

'Are they all right?' she asked anxiously.

He nodded, smiling.

'Please,' he whispered, moving his hand down. 'Please, Roe.'

'No!' And she gripped his hand even tighter. 'That's enough! What sort of girl do you think I am?'

He took his hand away.

'It's wrong, Derry.'

'Oh no, it's quite normal. Honestly. I've read all about it.'

'I can't, Derry. I wouldn't be able to face you ever again. I wouldn't be able to face anyone.'

'I won't lose respect for you if that's what you're thinking.

It's because I care so much for you. Please, Roe,' he added plaintively. 'Don't break my heart.'

She sighed. 'No, Derry.'

He let go and turned his back on her.

Rose was bewildered by his sudden withdrawal. As she stared silently at the outline of his back, a faint smell of socks came wafting up from under the bedclothes.

Outside the rain continued to fall.

She had been awake for some time. She lay quite still, not daring to move; afraid of waking Derry, yet even more afraid that Diana would return to find them in bed together.

She eased herself out horizontally. Derry gave a small grunt and rolled over to the space she had vacated. She paused for a moment, gathered up her clothes and tiptoed swiftly out of the room.

Once she was washed and dressed, her hair brushed and plaited, she felt more relaxed. She picked some small blue and yellow flowers from the other side of the garden wall and placed them in a jam jar on the wooden table. She put out bread and margarine, and rinsed the teapot out. A kettle of water was on the stove. All she needed to do was to light it.

She opened the kitchen door and let the morning air suck the dust of night out. It was cooler than usual. She leaned in the doorway in her shorts and blouse, rubbing her arms for warmth and listening to the bird song.

She returned to the sitting room, threw open the windows and garden door and switched on the wireless. They were playing oboe and flute music on the Home Service. As she sat outside on the steps everything about her and within her all seemed to be moving together; the music and the fresh scents of the garden, the thrill which filled every curve of her body, all made one living breathing picture. For a moment she wanted to share it with Derry, but the music swept through her with such intensity that she found it impossible to move.

'Please, Derry,' she urged. 'Do hurry and get dressed.'

As soon as the kettle had boiled, she made a pot of tea and called up to him. There was no answer. She ran up the stairs only to discover that he had gone back to sleep. She rocked him desperately from side to side.

'Wake up!' she cried. 'Wake up!'

He groaned and threw his arm over his face. She shook him again. He opened his eyes.

'You went back to sleep,' she explained. 'There's a cup of tea downstairs.'

'Can't I have it in bed?'

'Derry, Diana will be back soon. You must get up.'

He manoeuvred himself to a sitting position. 'I don't have to. When she comes, I can just come down dressed and pretend I was fetching something from your room.'

He took hold of one of her plaits and started to undo it. 'Come back to bed,' he cajoled.

She shook the plait away from him. 'I don't want to. Come on, Derry, do get a move on.'

He scowled and threw himself back into the pillow. 'I'll get up when I feel like it.'

Rose stared at him flabbergasted. 'I think you're mean and inconsiderate!' she yelled. 'You don't care about my feelings at all. All that talk about love, I don't believe a single word of it. If Diana comes home and finds you up here, I never want to see you again.'

She turned her head swiftly so that he wouldn't see her tears and fled from the room, slamming the door.

Moments later, he appeared in the kitchen looking sheepish. 'Sorry,' he mumbled. He lowered himself into a chair. 'I don't like getting up early, that's all. It makes the day too long.'

She pushed a cup of tea towards him. He took it without a thank-you. He didn't even seem to notice the flowers and how nice she had made the table look.

As soon as he had finished eating she whipped the plates from under his nose. 'I want to get everything washed and cleared away before Diana comes back,' she explained.

'Yes, of course,' he sighed. 'But how about going to the cove after that?'

Rose dreaded another session of arguments and counter-arguments. All she wanted to do was to collapse in the grass and close her eyes.

'Don't you want to sail round the peninsula?' he asked.

'Of course I do but . . .'

'Well, come and show me how your swimming is progressing and I'll see if it's good enough for me to take you.'

Swimming, she thought. Now *that* she didn't mind.

The boat lay on its side in the sand. It was filled with water. It hadn't been very sensible to have tied it to a rock, thought Rose. It could so easily have been dashed to pieces.

'I'll go back for a saucepan,' she suggested.

'It's not worth it. We've tipped most of it out. The sun will probably dry out the rest. If it doesn't, then we'll try and bail her out. Come on.'

He was sitting on the sand at the back of the cove, patting a spot beside him.

'I thought you wanted to see me swim.'

'Yes, of course,' he said hurriedly. 'I forgot.'

She dropped her bag and sandals and climbed out of her shorts and blouse. Suddenly she felt self-conscious standing there in her swimsuit for she remembered what Derry had been doing to her the previous night. She avoided his gaze and made her way towards the sea.

She stopped by the boat and let her hands drift along the boom and mainsail longingly. She turned. 'If I can swim well enough today, will you really take me sailing in it?'

'Of course.'

She gave it a friendly pat and eased herself into the icy water, her shoulders hunched against the coldness. 'Are you watching?'

He nodded.

'I'll walk over to those rocks and swim from edge to edge.'

As soon as she reached them, she sunk into the water and began to swim steadily towards the rocks at the other side of the cove. She was doing the breast stroke, raising her head and taking in great gulps of air, swimming in a slow leisurely rhythm so that she wouldn't tire herself out. She pushed herself away from a rock with her foot and turned to make for the other side. She was conscious now only of the surface of the water as she rose and dunked her head into it. Through the fine spray, she saw the dark rocks on the other side.

She turned again. She was beginning to enjoy it now. She counted in her head, although there was no pressure to reach any particular number of cove lengths. On and on she swam, till her limbs seemed to dance in the water. She felt graceful; strong.

'It's all right,' called Derry. 'You needn't swim any more.'

She ignored his cries and carried on, pushing and dipping, pushing and dipping.

Eventually she stopped, not because she was tired, but because she felt satiated. She rose slowly from the water and loped out. Her spine felt extraordinary, as though someone had massaged it. She felt at ease; exhilarated.

'Well?' she said, smiling and sinking into the sand beside him.

'You proved your point long ago,' he said grumpily.

'I thought you'd be pleased.'

'Didn't you hear me call?'

'Yes, but I wanted to go on.'

'Why? There was no need.'

'I was enjoying it.'

She drew up her knees and gazed out past the rocks and the peninsula, out, far out to the horizon where the sky sank clear into the sea. Her lips were wet and salty and the water from her plaits was streaming in rivulets down her back.

'I'm bored,' he said.

'Are you?' she exclaimed. 'Why not come in for a swim?'

'It's too cold.'

'We can go sailing now,' and she touched his arm excitedly.

'The boat needs more time to dry out.'

'It'll only get wet again in the sea.'

'Don't keep going on about it!'

'Sorry.' She paused. 'You seemed so keen on the idea earlier on.'

There was an uncomfortable silence.

'I've some books in my bag, if you want to read one.'

'I've grown out of stories, thanks.'

Derry seemed so strange. One minute he treated her as if she was the most attractive girl in the world, and the next moment he'd say something which made her feel small.

She took a jotter out of her bag and flicked it open.

Derry sat up abruptly. 'I thought you weren't going to do that until after I'd gone.'

'I'm only jotting down a few ideas, in case I forget them.'

He watched her as she wrote rapidly across the page, totally absorbed.

'Roe?' he said.

'M'm.'

'You're being very mean.'

'What?' she murmured absently.

'Ignoring me like this.'

'Sorry. Won't be a minute.'

In her head, a boy in woollen knickerbockers was running up a hill, a fierce wind throwing the sea from the cliffs below into a crashing spray which rose up as high as the path. A light from the window of a stone cottage shimmered in the darkness. She closed the book.

Derry was scowling. 'Very few people get anything published, you know.'

'That's no reason to stop writing.'

'Of course it is. It's a waste of time otherwise.'

'No, it isn't. When I finish a story I feel I've achieved something. And I get more from reading other people's stories. It makes me more alert. I start eavesdropping on people's conversations, and observing them more closely and . . .'

'I haven't noticed you doing that today. I might as well not have been here.'

'But, Derry, I swam so that we could go out in the boat together.'

'Are you sure you don't like me just because I've got the boat?'

'Of course not!'

'I bet if I said we wouldn't go anywhere in the boat you'd soon lose interest in me.'

'That's a terrible thing to say!'

'You're always going on about it.'

'But you were the one who suggested it in the first place.'

He shrugged his shoulders, and stared gloomily at the sand. Rose gazed at him feeling helpless. Everything she said and did seemed to make his misery more acute.

'I thought you'd be more understanding,' he mumbled. 'I've probably only got a few days left.'

She watched his hand picking away at the sand. She hadn't meant to upset him.

'I'm sorry.'

He looked up swiftly. The old desperate look that she had come to dread was back.

'Perhaps it'd be better if I went home,' she said.

He shook his head frantically. 'No, Roe. I want you to stay. You know I do.'

And so the whole wretched to-ing and fro-ing began all over again, with Rose wanting to run away, and then berating herself for being such a coward. As they lay on the towels in a secluded corner at the back of the cove, Rose hung on to Derry, her chin pressing into his shoulder.

'Oh, Roe,' he said excitedly. 'You really care about me. I can feel it. You really do.'

'Do I?' Then why did she feel so awkward with him?

'Roe!' he began. 'Would you consider . . .?' He paused. 'I mean it would be a great honour if, before I leave here, that is . . .' He swallowed. 'If you'd let me go inside you. You know?'

Rose drew herself away from him. 'No! Derry, how could you suggest such a thing!'

He knelt up beside her. 'It's because I love you.'

She shook her head vehemently. 'I'll wait till I'm married.'

'But there's no time for us to do that,' he said urgently.

'Derry, it's out of the question.'

She stood up angrily, and marched off to where her clothes lay. Derry ran after her.

Suddenly she began to cry. 'I'm so fed up with it all.'

He took her hand and stroked her knuckle repeatedly with his finger. 'I'll tell you what,' he said. 'We won't talk about it any more. All right?'

She gave a shrug. She felt worn down. 'Oh dear,' she sniffed. 'I must look a mess.'

'You do rather. I'll look away while you sort yourself out.'

She picked up her shorts, dragged a handkerchief from her pocket and blew her nose. And then she noticed whose handkerchief it was.

'Derry!' she exclaimed. 'What will you tell Alec? He'll be wondering where you've been.'

'I'll just tell him I slept on the couch at the cottage.'

'But I'm going to tell Diana I was alone.'

'He doesn't know her, does he?'

'Not really. No.'

She stuffed the handkerchief back into her pocket. 'Does it look as if I've been crying?'

'No.'

He went to put his arms round her but she stepped away from him.

When they had pushed the boat back into the water, Rose didn't bother to climb up to the path to watch him sail back towards the village. Instead she remained in the cove and slowly replaited her hair.

Twelve

'Please stay here tonight,' begged Diana.

'I'll be fine on my own,' Rose insisted. 'I managed all right last night without being murdered.'

They were standing outside Mrs Clarence's gate, Rose's bicycle resting against it.

'But there was a storm then,' pointed out Diana. 'No one dangerous could have reached you. I would have come back if it hadn't been so bad.'

'I know you would,' Rose reassured her.

'But I have to stay here tonight,' Diana stammered. 'I must be here in case . . .' She frowned anxiously at Rose.

'Of course you must,' said Rose. 'I understand. Honestly.'

'So why don't you stay here?'

'Because I've an idea for another story set in the same period and all my reference books and notes are in the cottage.'

'Couldn't you bring them back here?'

'There'd be no point. Mrs Clarence or you would want to talk to me. Or Dot would be popping in for a chat.'

'I thought you liked Dot.'

'I do. That's why it'd be impossible to think about the story, let alone write anything. There'd be too many distractions. I must get as much as possible done in case you're suddenly called up.'

'Oh, don't,' said Diana.

'You're not getting cold feet, are you?'

'No. It's just that I feel responsible for you and I don't think I'm doing a very good job.'

'Don't worry about me,' she said cheerfully and she clambered back on to her bicycle. 'I'll be fine.'

As soon as she opened the kitchen door Rose spotted the envelope on the table. She sat down slowly and tore it open.

One glance at the slip of paper inside and she knew. The previous year she had passed all the subjects except French. This year she had passed French and failed Geography. No School Certificate.

She stared numbly at the words. Although she had told everyone that she probably wouldn't get it, she realised that she must have had a glimmer of hope. She slumped her head into her arms and sobbed like a baby.

Hours later, she dragged herself out into the garden, splashed her face at the pump and sat in the middle of the lawn, exhausted and dejected. She heard the gate being opened. She sprang to her feet, hoping it was Diana.

It was Derry.

He stopped by the kitchen window and stared at her. 'Have I called at an inconvenient time?' he asked.

Rose felt dazed. 'Inconvenient?' she repeated.

'I'm sorry I'm late,' he blurted out.

'Late?'

'I meant to come earlier, to the cove, but . . .' his voice trailed away.

'Oh, that,' she said lamely. 'I didn't go there today. I didn't feel like it. I got my School Certificate results this morning. I failed again.'

'Oh,' he said relieved. 'That's what's upset you.'

She turned away.

'So you've been here all day then?'

'Yes,' said Rose blankly. 'No one else knows. Not even Diana. She's staying at Mrs Clarence's. Robert still hasn't phoned and she's getting rather worried.'

'I see.'

Rose started to thump the ground with her fist. 'I hate school. I hate it! It's stupid.' And with that she burst into tears.

Derry backed into the wall. 'Is there anything . . .?' He wavered. 'Would you like a cup of tea?'

'Tea!' she yelled. She wiped her face roughly with her hand. 'No. We'll have some of Diana's wine. She won't mind.'

'Not for me, thank you.'

They sat on the steps, Rose hardly conscious of him, a cup in her hands. The wine made her tears flow even more rapidly. Derry sat holding his knees.

'Is Diana staying at Mrs Clarence's tonight?' he asked.

'Yes.'

'Don't worry,' he said matter of factly. 'I'll stay here with you.'

Rose was alarmed. 'I'll hardly be good company,' she muttered.

She stared down at her handkerchief and twisted it violently in her hands.

'It's not the end of the world, old girl.'

'It is. As long as I have to stay at school, I'm just living in a childish ivory tower. It's as if everybody and everything is trying to stop me from growing up. I feel so hemmed in.'

'Roe, there's something I have to tell you.'

'You haven't been called up, have you?'

199

'Not yet. But I went into Gynmouth this afternoon and registered. I had my exam results, too. I passed my Highers.'

'Derry! Oh congratulations! Here I've been blubbing away feeling sorry for myself and all the time you've had to swallow down your good news.'

She took hold of his hands and squeezed them. 'Well done.'

'So that's why I registered immediately.'

'Yes, of course.' She sighed. 'I do envy you. I'm not exactly looking forward to being called up, but I feel so left out.' She released his hands. She felt like an unborn gosling, trapped inside a shell which was so small it had become painfully uncomfortable; so small that she could hardly breathe.

Derry touched her shoulder and moved closer. 'Everything's different now, I mean, well, we have even less time . . . Roe. Look at me.'

But she couldn't. She stared with fixed concentration at the stone wall, aching all over. She lowered her head. 'Derry,' she began.

She wanted to say, 'I don't think I love you,' but perhaps she was running away from love. Confused, she forced herself to look at him. And then wished she hadn't. His face had that earnest desperate expression imprinted on it.

'I'd think it a tremendous honour,' he blurted passionately. He put his arm round her.

She wished he would put his other arm round her too and crush all the aches away. No, she didn't. What was she thinking? She had to say no.

'It'd give me courage,' he went on quickly. 'When I'm flying. Something I can treasure. Perhaps,' he added hesitantly, 'it would give you more courage, too, for when you go back to school. Something to think about when you're feeling a bit under the weather.' He paused. 'Something to help you feel more grown-up.'

She wanted to yell, 'Help!' She wanted Diana to appear. She wanted her mother to arrive and say, 'I'm back.' Someone, anyone, to come and rescue her. She felt so sad and tired, and the wine was making her feel muzzy.

'Say yes, Roe. Please say yes. It'll be wonderful. I promise.'

She imagined him lying in bed with her and holding her tight and she remembered how Matthew had wrapped the time he and Miss Hilda had spent together round him 'like a warm cloak'. And then there was Dot. She had done it. She seemed to think it was wonderful, too. So why was she holding back?

And then she remembered a Pearl Binder story in one of the *Penguin New Writing* magazines. It was about a young pilot who had not returned to his digs. The landlady had gone upstairs to help the adjutant sort out the dead pilot's belongings.

'So little . . . the smart dressing-gown, slippers pressed to the shape of his young feet, the girl's photograph, the brown-papered novel, his flying charts and neat log book . . . Less than eight hours ago he had emerged, whistling cheerfully from the bathroom, and laughed over his shoulder as he passed her on the stairs. Now he was not.

She cried a little that night, thinking over the day, cried that he had gone out ignorant of fulfilment . . . ignorant even of passion.'

The passage had made a deep impression on her at the time. Now suddenly the reality of Derry being dead came home to her.

'Now he was not,' she murmured.

'Will you, Roe?' Derry pleaded. 'For me.'

She would have to do it. Not to agree would be so selfish.

'Are you sure I won't get pregnant?' she whispered.

He gripped her shoulders. 'Positive. I know how to prevent it. Just leave it to me.'

She opened her mouth to speak but there was no sound.

'You will then?' he said beaming. 'You will?'

'You don't mean *now*, do you?'

'Oh, no, we'll wait till it's dark. I'll go upstairs and get everything ready.'

And he fled upstairs.

It sounded like an operation, she thought.

She rested her head against the doorway, fatigue sweeping through every muscle. She longed to dissolve into the greenness of the garden and disappear. Her mind began to drift. If he'd just hold me, she thought, just for a moment. That's all I want.

'Goodbye. Goodbye. Goodbye,' she whispered.

A strange silence passed over the cottage. She watched the twilight creep with deadening slowness around her and the shadows from the garden lengthening across the tiny lawn.

It was as though she didn't own herself any more, as if somehow she had handed her body over to Derry but her mind had remained distant.

He tugged the sheet away from her hands and slipped in beside her.

'It's so dark,' she said. 'I can't see you at all.'

'It's better that way.'

He sat stiffly beside her. Rose accidentally brushed against his chest. He was naked. She withdrew her hand swiftly.

'It's all right,' he reassured her. 'I'm still wearing my underpants.'

'You smell of peppermint.'

'It's your toothpaste. I borrowed some. I hope you don't mind.'

'No, of course not.'

'You're supposed to lie down,' he said.

Like a lamb to the slaughter, she thought. What on earth made that sentence pop into her head? Startled, she brushed it aside and slid slowly down into the bed.

'Derry,' she whispered. 'We don't have to do it tonight, you know.'

He moved swiftly down beside her, his fingers at the buttons of her pyjama jacket. 'We *do*,' he said earnestly. 'We'll never have a chance like this again. We *have* to do it now.'

'But, Derry . . .'

'You're nervous, that's all. It's normal. All girls are.'

'But there's no hurry, is there? Couldn't we just hug a little first?'

'Look, Roe,' he said firmly. 'I know what I'm doing. Don't go giving me instructions.'

'I didn't mean . . .'

She longed to say, 'Derry, just hold me. Today I failed my father again, and the thought of his disappointment in me is too much to bear. And I miss him. I don't want him to be dead. I want him back.' She swallowed down a huge lump in her throat.

She tried to push against Derry with her hands. He was weighing so heavily on her, she could hardly breathe.

'It's all right,' he said. 'I know what to do.'

'Derry, you're crushing me!'

'It's all right. You'll be all right.' Her pyjama jacket lay in a heap at one side, one arm still inside a sleeve. She attempted to stop his hand at her trouser leg, but he was too strong and it slid out of her grasp. Now it dangled from one ankle.

'Derry, I'm not ready.'

'Yes, you are,' he said, puzzled. 'Oh, I see, your jacket isn't properly off,' and he pushed it away from her shoulder.

'No, it's not that,' she said, catching his hand.

'Well, what on earth is it?'

'I'm not ready *inside*.'

'I haven't come to that bit yet,' he said. 'When I've stroked you, *then* you'll be ready.'

Why couldn't she find the right words? 'Derry, do you love me?'

She could sense his body tautening. He paused. 'Of course. That's why I want to do this.'

'Say it then.'

'Say what?'

'Say you love me.'

'I love you.'

She shouldn't have asked him. It made it worse.

He held her tightly by the shoulders. 'Roe,' he urged. 'In a few months' time I'll probably be dead.'

'Dead?' she whispered. Her father's face came back with even more intensity. 'Oh, Daddy,' she blurted out, 'I'm sorry,' and she burst into tears.

'Roe,' stammered Derry. 'Don't cry.'

He gave her a pat on the back. 'There, there,' he said awkwardly.

His hands moved swiftly under the pillow. 'Damn!' he muttered.

'What's the matter?'

'Nothing,' he said, desperation in his voice. 'I can't find it.'

'Shall I draw the curtains?'

'No! Lift your head up.'

He pushed his hands well under the pillow again and around the top of the bed.

'Don't worry,' he said.

Rose sank back into the pillow. She listened to him padding around in the dark, the jangle of loose change in his shorts pockets, and the tearing of paper. Now she was more puzzled than ever.

'Oh no,' he cried. 'I've gone down.'

'What's the matter? Are you all right?'

'We'll just have to go back to the beginning,' he said shakily. 'Don't worry.'

The tremor in his voice warmed her to him. When he slipped back into bed, she reached out to comfort him.

'For goodness sake, give me a chance! *I'm* the one that's supposed to start it off!'

'Sorry.' She withdrew as though scalded. Bewildered she put her arms rigidly by her side, while he began to touch her again.

'It's all right,' he said, 'you can touch me now,' and he kissed her gingerly on the forehead.

It was then that Rose realised, that from the moment she had agreed to going to bed with him, they had not kissed once.

His hand dived under the pillow again and he began to writhe.

'I'm putting it on,' he explained.

'Oh,' she remarked, not knowing what else to say. 'I see.'

'Look, I'll explain later. All right?'

No, it's not all right, she thought, but he was pushing against her so hard, it was all she could do to concentrate on getting enough breath. Rose put her hand up to her face where her hair lay tangled across her mouth and pushed it aside. This wasn't wonderful at all, she thought. This was a nightmare. Everyone had lied.

'Roe?'

'Yes?'

'I still respect you. It was, you know, tremendous.'

She opened her mouth to speak but he interrupted her.

'It won't hurt so much next time.'

'Next time?' she exclaimed.

But Derry had already fallen asleep.

The door to Mrs Clarence's was open. Rose called out. A 'yoo-hoo' answered her. She stepped inside.

Dot was standing in the doorway of the kitchen which backed on to the garden. She grinned.

''Ello. Long time, no see.' She lowered her voice. 'Di's upstairs asleep. When Robert hadn't rung by midnight she and Mrs Clarence went to bed but Di crept down again. Mrs Clarence says she sat up all night by the telephone.'

'Oh. I was hoping to speak to her.'

Dot took a bowl of lard from the window sill and started slicing some bread.

'I should go up. She's probably still awake. Want some?'

'No thanks.' Rose dropped her bag on the floor and slumped into a chair.

'Bad news?' asked Dot gently.

'Yes.'

'It ain't your mum, is it?'

'No. My School Cert. results came yesterday. I failed one of the subjects again. So,' Rose said, shrugging, 'I haven't got it. I admit I didn't try very hard. I had no heart for it. But my mother will want me to have another go.'

Dot bit into her bread and lard.

'Do you want to?' she said.

'Yes and no. I'd like to, for my father's sake. He had such high hopes for me.'

'Such as.'

'Going to university to do a science degree.'

'Is that what you want?'

'No. I'd hate it.'

'Good job you didn't get it then,' said Dot licking her fingers. 'You can go on writing those stories.'

'Not if I have to go back to school for another year.'

'When are you eighteen?'

'November.'

'If you wanted, you could join up then.'

'I know. That's what Derry's done.'

'How d'you mean?'

'He registered for call-up yesterday.'

Sensing her face was growing warm, Rose glanced down at the floor, so that she didn't notice the puzzled expression on Dot's face.

'You sure?'

'Yes. He went off to Gynmouth. I won't be able to do that. When I'm eighteen I'll be locked away in school and the outside world will be out of bounds. There's always the Christmas hols though. I suppose I could sneak out and register then.'

'Are you sure Derry went into Gynmouth?'

'Yes. Why?'

'Oh nothin'. I probably got the times mixed up. I saw him

round the village yesterday. He must have got a lift in someone's car. He couldn't have borrowed Harold's horse and cart because it's being used for harvesting up at the Acres' farm.'

Rose felt sick.

'What's up, mate?'

'I'm just a bit tired. I haven't had much sleep.'

Dot leaned across the table and cut herself another piece of bread. As she spread the dripping on to it, she chatted aimlessly. Rose heard the words, but there was a fog between them and her brain. Could Derry have lied about going into Gynmouth? As soon as Dot began to talk about babies Rose started to feel panicky. If Derry had lied, he might not have told her the truth about not getting pregnant either. Did he really know what he was doing?

'Dot?'

'Yeah.'

'Do you mind if I ask you something personal?'

'Go ahead.'

'Do you really have no regrets about what happened between you and Jack?'

She smiled. 'No. I've got a bit of him inside me. It's a nice feeling.'

'But the other thing? When you . . .' She hesitated. 'Was it all right?'

'Yeah. It was lovely. Why?'

'I just wanted to know.'

'What's up? You look a bit done in.'

'Oh, I'm just fed up with failing at everything.'

'You're not in any sort of trouble, are you?'

'Trouble?'

'You know the sort of trouble I mean?'

Rose blushed. 'Hardly,' she retorted. 'No one would come within miles of me!'

Dot gave her an exasperated look. 'You don't need anyone to flatten you, love. You drive your own steamroller.'

Rose laughed. 'I suppose I do. Oh, Dot, you're a real chum.'

'A *chum*,' said Dot in a posh accent. 'Well, I been called many things in my time, but never a chum.'

The bedroom door was ajar. Diana was sleeping in the bed by the window. Standing motionless in the doorway Rose gazed round the room, breathing in the fragrance of the beeswaxed floorboards, and the flowers in the large jug on the washstand. The last time she had been in the room was the night of the dance. Part of her wished she could go back to that time and start all over again.

A breeze flapped the drawn curtains aside exposing the sea beyond. Such a peaceful room, she thought. I'd give anything to stay.

She made to leave but the floorboard under her feet gave a resounding creak. Diana stirred.

'Who's that?' she mumbled. 'Is it the telephone?'

'No,' said Roe. 'Just me.'

Diana pushed herself up to a sitting position, her mane of chestnut hair framing her pale face in a glorious tangle. She was wearing a patched nightdress of Mrs Clarence's. It looked wonderful on her, observed Rose enviously, but then, so would an old sack.

'What's wrong?' Diana asked anxiously.

'Nothing. I just popped in to see if you were all right. Dot told me you were up most of the night.'

Diana gave a dismal nod.

'I'm sure he's fine,' said Rose. 'I expect he's not allowed to phone. Perhaps he's on a secret mission.'

'That's what I'm hoping,' said Diana quietly. 'The awful thing is that if anything happened to him I wouldn't know, not being his wife.'

'Mrs Clarence would be told though.'

'Oh yes, of course she would,' she muttered. 'How stupid of me.'

Rose sat on the bed.

'Oh, Roe, I feel so sick all the time,' Diana confided. 'And every hour that goes by I feel worse. I've tried to sleep but I can't.'

Rose searched frantically for some reassuring words but every phrase which popped into her head was a cliché. She squeezed one of Diana's hands instead.

'I don't know what I'll do if he's killed. He's the only man in my life who's ever loved me.'

'How can you say that?' Rose protested. 'You've had men falling over their feet to get to you.'

'But they never loved me. They never got to know me as a person. Not even Father.'

'Diana!' interrupted Rose, shocked. 'Of course he did. He adored you.'

'Perhaps.'

A tear trickled down Diana's cheek. Rose hastily smoothed her sister's hair back. 'You're just exhausted. Everything always seems impossible when you're tired. Try and get some sleep. As soon as he calls, Mrs Clarence will wake you. You know she will. And you don't want to be in a stupor when he does ring, do you?'

Diana smiled sheepishly. 'I suppose not.'

'I'll stay here till you're asleep, all right?'

Diana nodded.

Rose tucked her up snugly like their father used to do when they were small and watched her sister close her eyes. She would tell Dot not to mention her exam results. Diana had enough to cope with already.

A book on the bedside table attracted her attention. To her surprise she noticed it was about childbirth. She picked it up and settled herself down in an old wicker chair.

Inside the cover she found a slip of paper. It read:

'For Dot,
    Rose told me you might find this useful.
    Good luck!
      Alec'

She began reading.

Rose paused for a moment outside the bookshop. She could see Alec seated at the table in the alcove. He was scribbling. She pushed the door open. The bell above it jangled. He looked up.

She placed her books on one of the piles on his table and immediately he handed her four more.

'Found these,' he said. 'Thought they might be handy. They're about life in England at the beginning of the century.'

There was an open book on the table.

'What are you reading?'

'That book of D. H. Lawrence poetry I lent you. As you can see by the chaos,' he added, waving his arm at the mounds of books all over the floor, 'I'm attempting to sort them all out.

'But it's hopeless. I get so far and then I pick one up and start browsing.'

She moved round behind the table and looked over his shoulder. It was open at a poem called 'Fidelity'.

'It's one of my favourites,' he said.

'I loved that one too, even though I didn't understand a lot of it.' She pointed. 'These lines here. I'm not sure what they mean but when I read them, they made me feel so sad.'

'"And a flower it takes a summer",' read Alec. '"And love, like a flower, will fade, will change into something else or it would not be flowery".'

'Love can't really be like that? It can't just fade, can it?'

'I think he means that falling in love is very intense, but that it can't remain at that intensity; that we have to let it change into something else, otherwise we're clinging on to something that isn't real.'

She drew away from him. 'I'm not sure I really know what love is,' she murmured.

'Yes,' he agreed. 'We usually look around for other people to tell us what it is.'

'You mean in films and magazines?'

'Yes. I'm sure we spend half our lives trying to make our feelings and actions fit someone else's ideas.'

'Including D.H. Lawrence's,' she muttered, and she looked away.

He caught her by the hand, and gave it a tug, so that she was forced to face him.

'What's up?' he asked. 'Story not going well? Losing confidence?'

'Not exactly.'

'Then what is it?'

'I failed School Certificate again.'

He gave her hand a sympathetic squeeze. 'Bad luck!'

'Do you think I should bother about writing stories? I mean, if I can't even get my School Cert . . .' Her voice trailed away. 'I'd be miserable if I didn't carry on.'

'Of course you would.' He released her hand.

She watched him search for his pipe amongst the books and then she noticed the scraps of paper on the table with lines of illegible scrawl on them. She looked away hurriedly, not wanting to invade his privacy. He was writing again! She felt pleased for him. She gazed around the bookshop. At the bottom of the steps were some of the pictures she had seen propped up under the window upstairs. A framed sketch of a young man was in the front.

'I'm sure I've met that man,' she said.

'You have.'

She crouched down to take a closer look. The eyes were familiar. 'Is it someone in Salmouth?'

Alec gave a grin and stuck the empty pipe in his mouth. 'Yes.'

'Someone I've met recently?'

'Very recently. More than recently, in fact.'

She stared at it. 'It's not . . .?' she began. 'Oh! It's you.'

He nodded.

'But you look so different.'

He ruffled his hair and beard with his hand. 'I didn't have all this camouflage then.'

'When was it drawn?'

'Two years ago.'

'Two years!'

'Afraid so.'

'But your hair. You've got grey bits in it.'

'Given to me by kind courtesy of the war.'

Rose stood up. 'I can't believe it!'

'I can see.'

'I'm sorry. That's not a very nice thing to say.'

'But truthful all the same,' and he began lifting up the books again. 'Where's my tobacco?'

'Why did you bring them down here?'

'The pictures?'

'Yes.'

'I rather liked the idea of having a few pictures in amongst all these words.'

Rose sat on a stack of books by the table. 'It's beginning to look marvellous here now.'

He raised his eyebrows.

'No, seriously. Oh, I know it's still a bit chaotic.'

'A bit!'

'But some of the shelves are really well organised. I noticed it as soon as I came in.'

'Good. It might attract more customers.' He gazed down at her thoughtfully. 'Now that's an idea.'

'What?'

'Stools,' he commented. 'Two or three stools or chairs placed about so that people can sit and browse.' He snapped his fingers. 'There's that old stepladder Hilda gave me. It turns itself into a chair. Yes. If customers knew they could sit down it might entice the ladies from *Hôtel Maternité*.'

She laughed.

'Talking of which,' he continued, 'how's Dot?'

'Bigger than ever. It should be any day now.'

'Is she still determined to keep it?'

'Oh yes.'

'She'll have a hard time.'

'I know. She's very brave.'

'Why on earth do people make it so difficult for unmarried mothers? You'd think they'd suffered enough.'

'They make them suffer even more at the hotel,' said Rose. 'You know it was an accident putting marrieds and unmarrieds in the same building?'

'I had heard,' he said grimly.

'The unmarrieds are treated like criminals or as though they have the plague. And there's no mixing with the marrieds. They're kept in separate sections. You wouldn't believe some of the stories Dot tells me.'

'Oh, I believe you. I had one of the sisters here one day, asking me to report to her, if any of the unmarried girls came in here.'

'You're not serious!'

'She was afraid an unmarried mother might walk in here while a married lady was choosing a book; that the girls had been specifically told not to come in here. That was another thing which infuriated me. The marrieds were called ladies, the unmarrieds were referred to as girls. The whole thing was ludicrous.'

'Alec, what did you say?'

'That I'd welcome anyone here; that what happened in my bookshop was none of her business.'

'Good for you.'

'I also told her there was no difference between a legitimate child and an illegitimate child; that a child was a child and life was complicated enough without adding extra complications, that I was a bastard and that my father had died in the last war fighting for this country like some of the men who had fathered the babies of the women in her charge.'

He began lifting up the books again. 'Where are those damned matches?'

'Here,' she said, picking a box off the floor. 'Is that true?' she began uncertainly, 'that you're a . . .?'

'Yes,' he said. He lit his pipe and peered down at her.

Rose stared aghast at him.

'Is this the end of a wonderful friendship?' he asked.

'No. I'm just a bit shocked, that's all.'

'I can see.'

'I don't understand. You mean your parents weren't married?'

'That's right.'

'But Derry said his uncle and aunt had you when they were much older.'

'They adopted me.'

She sank her chin in her hands. 'That's why he was so evasive when I asked him.' She swung round. 'He does know?'

'As soon as I knew, I told him, I was twenty-one before I found out.'

'But that's terrible!'

'Yes. It was pretty shattering.'

He fell silent for a moment. 'It felt as though there'd been a huge conspiracy going on behind my back, which I suppose there had been. I couldn't trust or feel at home with anyone. I felt rootless. The thought that they'd been deceiving me all those years . . . And I wondered who else had known. I decided to tell Derry straight away. I don't know if it was the right thing to do. He was only about thirteen, just starting public school. He soon picked up very quickly that "bastard" was a low form of insult. He made me into a kind of hero figure, bragging about me to the other boys. I think it was his way of compensating for the shame he felt.'

Rose had never heard him talk at such length and she realised then, it was because she was the one who was usually pouring out her soul to him. But her head was swirling.

Alec, illegitimate? To her surprise she found that she wasn't appalled. It was Miss Hilda's diary which had changed her attitude. It had already made her see Dot in a more sympathetic light. With a sense of shock, she realised that if it hadn't been for Miss Hilda, her friendship with Dot might never have blossomed, and she might now have withdrawn from Alec entirely.

'Were you up writing last night, too? You look as if you haven't slept for days.'

Suddenly Rose wanted to pour out the night's events to him and ask him if she could possibly be pregnant. But when she looked at him she found it impossible and that saddened her.

'No. I was just thinking a lot. It kept me awake.' It wasn't too much of a lie, she thought. She picked up her books hurriedly and shoved them into her bag.

'You'll end up lopsided carrying all that on your shoulder,' he said. 'I've an old army knapsack lying around somewhere. I'll look it out for you.'

'Thanks,' she said, and made a hurried exit.

Rose stumbled rapidly along the path, swopping her shoulder bag from one side to the other. Why had Alec suddenly decided to tell her about his illegitimacy now she wondered. She stopped. Had he suspected what had happened? Had Derry told him? Could this be Alec's way of warning her of the difficulties of being an unmarried mother so that she wouldn't risk it happening to her?

What would happen if she *did* become pregnant? Diana was bound to blame herself for staying at Mrs Clarence's. And her mother would be distraught. Rose would have to keep it a secret. But how? The teachers at her school would find out sooner or later and then her family's name would be disgraced.

She collapsed on the grass by the path. Overwhelmed with shame she sank her head into her hands.

It wasn't just the acute embarrassment at what she had done with Derry which swept through her. It was a shame far deeper than that. She didn't know what the shame was about but it seemed to be dragging down every ounce of her energy.

With difficulty she raised her eyes. A swim, she thought. After a good swim perhaps she would be able to see things more clearly.

She pulled herself to her feet.

Thirteen

It was late afternoon when Rose returned from swimming. To her relief Derry hadn't turned up at the cove so that she had been able to swim for as long as she wanted.

As she approached the gate she noticed that it was already open. Her heart sank. She stood still for a moment fighting a strong desire to run away until she caught sight of a pair of threadbare bloomers draped over the hedge. She gaped at them. She had never seen so many patches on one garment.

'Ello,' said a jaunty voice.

She found Dot sitting on a cushion on the steps. 'Scuse me knickers,' she said, 'I 'ad a bit of an accident. I was taken short on the way 'ere. All of a sudden. Woosh! Sorry. Thought I'd wash 'em here. Hope you don't mind.' And she blushed.

Rose plopped down beside her and flung her arm around her. 'Of course I don't. You can have a pair of mine.'

'S'all right. I got clean ones on. I keep pairs handy, see. In case. But I could do with some sanitary towels. In case I have another accident.'

She gave a sudden gasp and clutched her stomach.

'Did it kick you?'

She nodded and then relaxed. 'Phew! That's better.'

'Did you walk all the way along the coastal path? On your own?'

''Course I did, I'm a big girl now.'

'Isn't that a bit risky?'

'No. I won't have it for a while yet. You don't mind me comin', do you?'

'Of course not. Stay for ever.'

Dot reddened again.

'Are you feeling all right? You look a bit flushed.'

'Yeah. I expect it's the weather,' and she dabbed her cheeks with her hand.

'There *is* something worrying you,' Rose insisted. 'What is it?'

Dot glanced anxiously at her. 'I'm just a bit scared, that's all. Still, at least we've been told what's what at the first-aid class and I reckon I know that book about having babies by heart.'

'Me too,' said Rose.

'You?' said Dot surprised.

'I found it upstairs at Mrs Clarence's this morning. It was

quite an eye-opener. I thought babies came out of your navel.'

'That's nothing. I thought they came out yer bum. I still can't believe it happens the way they say it happens. I hope I can do it all right.'

Rose put her arm round her. 'You'll be fine. Remember you'll have me and Diana near by.'

'Stay *here*, whatever happens,' she blurted out. 'Promise?'

'Dot, whatever's the matter?'

'You *will* stay 'ere?'

'If you want,' said Rose puzzled.

'I'll be all right then.' She looked away for a moment. 'I wish Di was here, too.'

So do I, thought Rose. She stood up. 'I'm just going to rinse my sheets and hang them out so they'll be dry for tonight. I won't be a minute.'

Dot pushed herself to her feet. 'I'll help, I'm dying to do something. Cleaning? Got any cleaning I could do?'

'You're not supposed to do anything.'

'But I feel like it. I'd much rather do something, otherwise I'll sit here and worry.'

Rose smiled. 'All right.'

Once the sheets were on the line they took a pot of tea and some bread and jam out into the garden. In spite of having to stop intermittently when the baby kicked, Dot looked happy. She sat on the cushion, her face flushed, her mousey hair sticking up in spikes.

Rose leaned towards her and touched her arm. She was about to tell her about Miss Hilda, but Dot froze again as if to gain breath. Rose realised the kicks made it impossible for Dot to speak, so she waited till the baby had stopped. Before she could tell her, she heard the gate open.

It was Derry. He stopped uncertainly and wiped his hands on his shorts.

'Good afternoon.'

Rose stiffened. 'Hello,' she muttered awkwardly.

Derry noticed the sheets from Rose's bed hanging over the hedge. He blushed.

'He's seen me knicks,' Dot whispered. 'I never would have put them up there if I'd known he was comin'.'

'We're just having tea,' said Rose brightly. 'Would you like some?'

He stumbled on to the lawn and sat next to them.

'You've got jam on your nose,' he informed Dot.

They chatted politely about gardening and the stall Dot's parents ran, and then Dot said, 'I hear you've gone and signed up for the R.A.F.'

Derry looked evasive. 'Yes.'

'When do you think you'll be called up?'

'Any day now. When do you have to go back?' he blurted out.

'Not yet. I'm enjoying meself 'ere.' She brushed the crumbs from her lap. 'Roe, got any weeding I could do? I fancy doin' a bit of that.'

'Lie back and relax.'

'I can't. I want to move about. It's uncomfortable on me back.'

'Weed away then.'

Rose picked up the plates and teapot.

'I'll give you a hand,' said Derry eagerly, and he followed on behind with the cups and jam.

Rose felt sick. As soon as they reached the kitchen, he closed the door. He watched her put the crockery into the sink. 'Will Diana be staying at Mrs Clarence's again tonight?'

'Only if Robert hasn't called,' she answered staring fixedly at the washing up. 'If she does I'll stay there too after I've walked Dot back.'

He seized her elbows.

'Please stay here,' he begged. 'For my sake.'

'I'm worried about Dot. Her baby seems to be kicking harder than usual.'

And for longer, she thought. She glanced out the window. Dot was standing by the lettuce bed, her face contorted with pain.

'She'll be all right.'

'Shush a minute.'

They looked into the garden.

'What on earth's the matter?' he said irritated.

'She's in pain.'

Rose watched her blow out a few breaths and ease herself into a squat. Then Dot noticed her at the window.

'Kicking again?' yelled Rose.

'Yeah.'

'See,' he commented. 'She's used to it.'

'Derry, it's a two-mile walk on that coastal route. If anything happened to her . . .'

'What could *you* do?'

'I could run for help.'

'I'll walk back with her. Then I'll return here.'

'You mean you'd walk two miles there and two miles back . . .?'

He squeezed her hands tightly. 'Of course. If it means we can spend some time together alone. Remember,' he added hastily, 'this will probably be the last year of my life. I've got to make the most of it.'

'Yes, yes, of course,' she interrupted.

He patted her hand genially and gave a broad smile. 'So that's settled.'

Dot didn't ask to stay for supper but when she was still pottering about the cottage, making tea, and laying the fire in the living room, Rose didn't like to ask when she was leaving. Also, the longer Dot stayed, the longer she could put off being alone with Derry.

'I expect you'll be heading back soon,' he commented, as they sat over vegetable pie in the kitchen.

'It's nearly eight o'clock,' added Rose. 'They won't be worried, will they?'

'No. I told 'em I were going to a WI meeting with Mrs Clarence. They'll just think I'm there, and Mrs Clarence will think I'm just puttin' me feet up at the hotel. Anyway, I'd like to stop a bit longer, if you don't mind. This little blighter is giving me a bit of trouble.'

And then Rose had a brilliant idea. 'You wouldn't be allowed to stay here overnight, I don't suppose?'

Dot smiled. 'Yeah. 'Course I would.'

Derry was horrified.

'I could ring the staff nurse from the Acres',' said Rose excitedly.

'I shouldn't bother. I told 'em if the WI meeting went on too late, I'd stay the night at Mrs C's.'

'And they agreed? I thought they were terribly strict about that sort of thing.'

'They are, but I sort of persuaded them.' She stared down at her pie and hastily began to cut it up into small pieces.

Derry shook his head.

Rose pretended not to notice. 'I'll make up the spare bed in my room,' she said.

Dot looked up quickly. 'Thanks. I was wondering,' she added, 'if I could take a butcher's at the notes Diana took when the doctor gave us that talk.'

'Good idea, we'll look at it together.'

They beamed happily at one another.

Derry gazed at them in desperation. 'I'll sleep on the couch,' he blurted out.

They turned and stared at him.

'Can't have the two of you sleeping here on your own,' he said.

'There's no need. Dot and I can manage perfectly well on our own.'

'I won't hear of it,' he said gallantly. 'You'll be much safer with me around.'

After supper they went into the living room and turned on the wireless. Derry took one of the armchairs, and Dot sat cross-legged on the floor with her back against the sofa where Rose was seated. Rose brought some pillows down from the bedrooms to make her more comfortable and they sat and dipped into Diana's notes.

As the evening progressed, Dot grew restless, wandering dreamily to and from the garden and making frequent visits to the latrine. At first Rose suspected she might be deliberately leaving her and Derry alone together, but on her way to the kitchen Rose saw her through the back door on the lawn. She was gazing into the distance, her hand resting on her abdomen, quite motionless.

Rose observed her, half-silhouetted in the twilight. She wondered if Miss Hilda had ever stood there when she was pregnant.

She was startled by a hand on her shoulder. 'As soon as

she's asleep, come downstairs,' Derry whispered.

'Whatever for?'

'You know.'

'Derry, you can't be serious? Dot could come down at any time and catch us.'

As if she had heard her name, Dot turned and saw Rose in the doorway. 'It's lovely out here,' she said, 'so peaceful.'

Eventually they decided to go to bed. Derry was left with blankets on the couch.

Dot had brought her nightdress and wash bag with her.

'I thought I might be staying at Mrs C's,' she explained swiftly.

They were halfway up the stairs when Dot gripped Rose's arm and leaned into her. She gave a small moan.

Rose kept quite still. 'Are you all right?' she asked.

Dot relaxed her hold. 'Yeah. It just caught me on the hop.'

Rose draped Dot's arm across her shoulders. With her own arm round Dot's waist, they squeezed their way up the narrow staircase. They stopped on the landing for a moment while Dot rested against her.

'Thanks, mate,' she murmured.

Rose was woken violently by someone shaking her. She sat up sharply to find Derry standing by her bed.

'Go away, Derry! You'll wake Dot.'

'She is awake. She's downstairs. Come quick!'

Dot was in the kitchen clutching the sink with such ferocity that it looked as though she might wrench it away from the wall. She was staring at the blackout curtains, making strange panting noises.

Then it dawned on Rose. The strange 'kicks' coming at

intervals. She took a deep breath. 'Dot,' she began. 'when you had that accident it wasn't your waters breaking, was it?'

Dot nodded guiltily. 'I've been wetting myself ever since.'

Rose stared at her aghast.

Derry was standing by the range white-faced.

'Go to the Acres' and phone for help,' she told him.

Dot gave a frantic cry and shook her head.

Rose touched her shoulder. She must keep her calm. 'What do you want me to do?'

'Di,' she gasped. 'Just you and her. No one else.'

'Would you like Derry to fetch her and Mrs Clarence?'

She nodded vigorously. 'Not the hotel,' she begged.

Derry backed away from them. 'I don't know,' he said reluctantly.

Rose struggled to keep her voice from wavering. 'You'll have to. I can't go. Take my bike.'

'It's a girl's bike,' he protested.

'It still has wheels,' said Rose exasperated. 'Please, Derry. Just go!'

'But they'll want to know what I was doing here.'

'Chaperoning us.'

'But you don't understand.' He glanced at Dot. 'If anyone knew I was here with . . .' He stopped.

'Just go,' said Rose quietly. 'Now.'

As soon as Derry had left, the cottage seemed almost to sigh with relief.

Dot still clung to the sink, her cheeks flushed, the sweat streaming down her face. Rose noticed her feet had a blue tinge to them. At first, her feelings of helplessness were so acute, she began to panic, but one look at Dot and she realised she couldn't run away.

226

'Dot, let's go into the sitting room, it'll be more comfortable there.'

Dot nodded.

'And remember to breathe out,' Rose added. 'And relax.'

Once in the sitting room, Dot sat in one of the armchairs in a half-reclining position with her knees up. Rose dragged the blankets from the sofa, wrapped them round her, lit the lamp, and brought down pillows and socks from upstairs. Gradually Dot pushed the blankets away in an effort to make herself more comfortable. Rose clasped her feet. They were freezing. She rubbed them vigorously before putting the socks on.

'I'll go and fill the hot-water bottle,' she said. 'I won't be a minute.'

She stopped in the doorway. 'And don't forget to breathe.'

Out in the kitchen Rose put the kettle on the primus and quickly laid the range ready for lighting. She placed saucepans of water on top, returned to the living room with the hot-water bottle and tucked it under Dot's feet.

As soon as the fire was lit, Dot climbed out of the armchair and leaned against one of the alcoves, her head buried in her arms.

'Want to move.'

Rose gently draped Dot's arms round her neck. As Dot's grip tightened she sank into Rose her weight heavy against her. Rose dug her heels into the floor and held her.

Soon, Mrs Clarence and Diana would arrive to help them, thought Rose. All she had to do was to take each moment calmly and give Dot moral support until they did.

She stroked the base of Dot's spine. 'Any good?' she whispered.

Dot nodded into her shoulder.

'I often do it to myself when I have my period,' Rose explained.

'It's nice,' murmured Dot.

They began rocking together, moving around in a slow circle in front of the fire, blowing out air. Rose gazed down at Dot's damp untidy hair, and rested her cheek on her head, conscious only of Dot's warmth and the sound of the flames spitting and crackling through the logs.

'Want to kneel,' Dot blurted out, and she broke away.

She lowered herself on to her hands and knees and leaned back on her heels.

'Pillow,' she ordered.

Rose grabbed one from the armchair and handed it to her. Dot hugged one, rested her head into it and moaned.

Rose dashed upstairs to her bedroom, snatched the notebook with the childbirth notes in it and dragged the mattress off the spare bed. Gripping the canvas handles, she hauled it determinedly through the doorway, slid it down the stairs and leaned it over the sofa in the living room.

She had no time to open the notebook, for once she was back in the living room, Dot needed to hang on to her. They moved once again into their strange rocking dance and then Dot broke away and settled herself into a comfortable position, and Rose did what she had often longed for someone to do to her. She massaged the frown away from Dot's forehead, stroked the base of her spine and unclenched her toes with kneading movements.

Occasionally Dot's eyes glazed over and she became floppy, and Rose had to force her to look into her eyes again. Then Dot would suddenly regain her strength and cling vehemently to Rose or lean against the propped-up mattress for a rest. And all the while Rose kept adding logs to the fire, refilling the hot-water bottle and stoking up the range.

'I'll go and make some tea,' and she ran into the kitchen.

Scanning Diana's notes on the table she saw blood mentioned. That and the necessity of a 'slop pail' alarmed her a little. 'Roll up carpet. Put down newspaper,' she read. Taking the lamp she moved swiftly to the locked room, opened the door and clambered in. If the doctor said they needed newspaper, then newspaper Dot was going to have. She tore it off the ornaments and plates and hurled it out into the corridor.

Dot was leaning on her elbows on a pillow in front of the fire. She gazed at the pile of crumpled papers in Rose's arms.

'There's more to come,' Rose informed her.

'I could do with that cuppa now,' said Dot. 'Me mouth's as dry as a bone.'

'Oh, my goodness, the tea!'

She dropped the armful of paper, and dashed into the corridor. Steam was pouring from the kitchen.

It was later, when Dot lost courage. The carpet had been rolled back, and the newspapers smoothed out and laid on the floor. Surrounded by pillows and cushions and towels, Dot was resting her arms on a pillow again, on all fours, while Rose sat cross-legged in front of her. Dot was tired. Rose dunked her face-flannel into a cup of water, squeezed it out and placed it on Dot's forehead. Suddenly Dot flung it to one side.

'That's it,' she snapped. 'I've changed me mind.'

Rose leaned over to rub the base of her spine.

'Don't touch me!' she yelled. 'I'm not goin' to have it. And that's that. I just can't do it.'

'You can, Dot!'

'No, I bleedin' can't.'

Stay calm, Rose told herself. 'You're doing fine.'

'No I ain't,' and she sank her face into the pillow. 'Leave me alone.'

Rose didn't move. She felt too hurt.

'Go!'

Rose stood up uncertainly. She had just reached the door when she remembered a phrase in Diana's book. 'When she starts telling you to go and take a running jump,' the doctor had said, 'that's when she needs you the most.'

Rose hovered in the doorway.

'I'm no good. I'm no effin' good,' Dot was grunting into the pillow. 'I can't bleedin' well do it.'

Rose knelt down in front of her and forced Dot to look up at her.

'You *can*,' she said fervently. 'I think you're in transition. I'm sure that's what it is. Honestly, Dot, you *can* do it.'

Dot closed her eyes and gave a small moan.

'Look at me, Dot.'

Dot did so.

'I'm not leaving you, so you're wasting your time telling me to go.'

Dot gave a bashful smile. 'If I could just have a break,' she murmured.

Rose suddenly had a brainwave. 'Do you fancy a bath?'

'A bath?' she exclaimed. 'Would I just!'

Obviously, thought Rose, this was what they needed all that hot water for in those films she had seen. She carried the tub into the sitting room and put it in front of the fire, poured the saucepans and tureen of hot water into it and hung some towels on the fireguard.

'All yours,' she declared, and she turned to go.

'You ain't leaving me, are you?' cried Dot.

'I thought you'd want some privacy.'

'Please stay. I'm scared I might have the baby in the tub.'

'All right. I'll just refill the saucepans and put them back on the range.'

As Dot splashed leisurely in the water, they drifted in and out of conversation. Rose poured fresh water into the tub and added some logs to the fire, while Dot concentrated on breathing out and relaxing. She seemed to have less pain in the tub. She leaned back, her bony knees sticking up from the water. Rose brushed back her hair in long languorous strokes away from her forehead.

When Dot was ready to step out of the tub, Rose wrapped the warm towels round her. Dot had hardly finished drying herself when she gripped Rose's shoulders, and clung fiercely to her.

Rose used every ounce of energy to support her.

Please, Diana, get here soon, she thought.

'I can feel it pushing inside me,' Dot said. 'It's making me want to push. What shall I do? I don't know how open I am.' And she gave a loud moan.

It was then that Rose realised that Diana and Mrs Clarence and the cavalry were not going to come galloping over the hill to their rescue. Having accepted the fact, she felt calmer. 'I'll have a look, shall I?'

Dot nodded.

Rose had never even seen her own genitalia, let alone another woman's.

Dot leaned back against the cushions, her knees drawn up, her legs wide apart. Rose gazed at Dot's vulva. The lips had opened out like a petalled flower. She put her fingers up against them.

'It's only two fingers open,' she said. 'It says in Diana's notes you have to wait until it's four or five.'

'But I feel everythin' rushing down inside me,' said Dot.

'That's right. The doctor said you would, but that you'd probably need to hang on for a bit. And there was something about blowing candles out,' she added puzzled.

'Oh yeah, I remember!' and she began blowing out short breaths. But not for long. 'Want to move!' she snapped.

The slow dance began again with Rose supporting her. She grew so hot that she changed into her swimsuit. Dot remained naked. She was more comfortable that way.

And then it happened.

Dot was on all fours and Rose was behind her staring intently at Dot's vulva. A tiny dark-haired dome appeared between the lips.

'I can see the head!' cried Rose. 'I can see black hair.'

'I don't believe it,' gasped Dot.

'Touch it,' she urged. 'Go on, touch it!'

Dot tentatively put her hand down between her legs. 'Oh, my sainted aunt!' she whispered. And then she gave a moan. 'I've got to push! I've just got to!'

'Go ahead!' said Rose excitedly.

The baby's head was out. Rose held it there in her hands. It was blue. She swallowed. Should it be that colour? But it was a perfectly formed face, an exquisite tiny face, and she was the first person to see it.

'Is it all right?' asked Dot.

'Oh yes,' whispered Rose. 'Don't forget to breathe out,' she reminded her.

Dot blew out a few breaths and then gave a long loud scream. The baby twisted. Its shoulders slipped out and it slithered into Rose's outstretched arms.

'It's a boy,' she murmured. 'A darling little boy.'

She watched his skin change colour and grow pink, observed the umbilical cord which resembled a soft multi-coloured rope. It was still warm and pulsating. It seemed extraordinary to think he was breathing both from outside and inside Dot. Dot turned round and Rose handed the baby to her, and Dot put him on top of her. His eyes were closed and his small lips moved in tiny kissing gestures as liquid oozed from his mouth.

Dot rested her hand tenderly on his tiny buttocks, and then she started to cry. Within seconds they were both crying.

'Ain't he a darlin'?' she choked out. 'Ain't he beautiful?'

Rose blew her nose.

The baby moved his head slightly and opened his eyes.

''E's lookin' at me,' Dot whispered. ''E knows who I am. Yeah, my little 'un. I'm yer mum.'

Rose glanced down at the sheets. They were awash with blood. She couldn't see if Dot had torn. There was too much mess.

'Come closer,' said Dot.

Tentatively Rose touched the baby's skin. It was covered in a creamy substance. They talked in low voices, stroking the baby's limbs. In the soft light of the oil lamp and firelight, they were completely mesmerised by him. Rose slid her finger under his fingers, and he gripped it. For a moment, she wondered if he knew her, too. 'Hello,' she murmured. And she wanted to leave her finger there for ever.

He gave faint gurgling noises.

''Elp me get him to my breast,' said Dot. 'I don't think I got any milk but I want to have a go.'

They fumbled gently with him till eventually his lips touched one of Dot's nipples. They glanced at one another excitedly.

'I ain't got the hang of it at all. Funny, I don't even care. Mrs Clarence'll show me what's what, eh?'

It was soon after, that Dot released the placenta. Rose put it into the bucket, tied sewing thread round the umbilical cord and cut it.

She stared at the placenta. It resembled an enormous piece of liver. It lay shiny and dark at the bottom of the bucket, its task completed.

After Rose had banked up the fire, she bathed Dot with warm water, and placed a couple of sanitary towels between her legs. As far as they could see, she hadn't torn at all, and it was a great relief.

Rose brought down one of the drawers from upstairs, and made up a bed for the baby in it. They wrapped him in a towel which had been warmed by the fire and made a toga-like nightdress for Dot out of a clean sheet.

Outside, a bird began singing. Dot moved towards the window, the baby in her arms, and drew back the curtains.

'It's nearly light,' she exclaimed.

She shuffled dreamily out of the sitting room and opened the back door.

'Dot, don't you think you should be asleep in bed?'

She turned and smiled. 'I dunno. I s'pose so. The thing is, I feel too excited to sleep.'

Rose followed her out to the doorway. She was a strange sight, standing on the steps in an old sheet and woolly socks, the small bundle in her arms.

'Funny,' she murmured, gazing out at the garden. 'Last night I was standin' out there all on me own. Now there's two of us.'

Leaving Dot to stare out into the garden, Rose removed the newspapers from the sitting room, carried the mattress upstairs and rolled back the carpet. She left the blood-stained sheets and towels to soak in hot salty water in the kitchen and made up a bed on the sofa, placing the drawer beside it. She flung back all the curtains and opened the windows. It was a sunny morning, but she decided to keep the fire burning for the baby's sake.

She called Dot in, and tucked her up on the sofa, but Dot preferred to keep the baby with her, rather than put him in the drawer.

'If you give me the ration books,' Rose said, 'I'll go into Salmouth and get some more tea. And I'd better see if Diana's all right.'

'And call at the hotel to let them know I'm safe,' added Dot.

Rose lowered her cup. 'Whatever for?'

Dot looked away and sipped guiltily at her tea.

'I told you a few whoppers last night,' she confessed. 'The waters didn't break on the way 'ere. They broke at the hotel, so I knew me labour would be starting soon. I hid me knicks in me bag. If the nurses had found out I'd have been under supervision, so I told 'em I was off to a Red Cross meeting, and then started to walk 'ere. Bedtime's at nine o'clock, so I just 'oped they wouldn't get suspicious till then. I had no idea Diana would stay again at Mrs C's. I didn't think she'd leave you on your own again, see. And I *never* expected Derry to be here, either. You could 'ave slapped me face with a wet fish when he said he'd stay. I thought we'd never get rid of 'im.'

Rose turned away hastily and gave the fire a poke. 'I wonder what happened to him.'

'Lost his nerve, I expect.'

Rose came and sat on the sofa, by Dot's feet. 'Dot, why did you do it?'

'I was frightened.'

'But the nurses are used to women giving birth. They know what to do.'

'I wanted to be with me friends.'

'But if something had gone wrong you might have died.'

'I know, but I didn't see I had a choice.'

'But weren't you scared here?'

'Sometimes. But it was different. At the hotel I was scared I'd never get to hold him, that I'd never get to see 'im. I dreaded it. I really dreaded them taking the baby away, and watching them dangling him in the air like a piece of meat. I know it's what's normal and that everyone gets treated the same. And I know they take the baby away so's you can have a good sleep, but I couldn't let them do that, see.'

She peered down at him. He was asleep.

'He looks almost regal, doesn't he?' said Rose.

'Yeah. I thought that, but I thought that was 'cause I was his mum.' She pressed her lips softly against his head. 'Yeah. That's what I'll call him. George. After the King.'

She looked up and grinned. 'When me and Jack was little, we waited for hours to see King George, the last George, I mean, on his Silver Jubilee. Do you remember?'

'Yes,' said Rose. 'We had Silver Jubilee cups given to us.'

'Me and Jack went to see the procession. Jack only came to see the horses. Yeah, I think Jack would like that. I think George is a good name.'

'Dot, I must drop in at Mrs Clarence's and find out what's happened. Derry's taken my bike so I'll have to walk. Do you think you'll be all right on your own?'

"Course I will. Anyway I won't be on me own, will I?' and she grinned.

By the time Rose reached the coastal path she was aware of feeling different; lighter yet more earth-bound. She couldn't stop smiling. She was so happy she was convinced her chest would burst. The sky looked vast and wonderful. She almost felt as if she could soar up into it. Suddenly she saw things clearly. She understood what her shame had been about, and why she had felt it with Derry. Dot hadn't lied about what it was like to make love, neither had Miss Hilda. She had lied to herself. She had pushed her own feelings aside as though they were of no importance.

'Of course,' she muttered. 'That's why it felt so wrong.'

All the time, she had been worrying about Derry's happiness, believing these might be his last days alive. But what about her own happiness? With Derry she had felt small and insignificant, frightened. Now she felt proud.

'I like being female,' she said aloud.

And she laughed. A strange excitement welled up inside her and she began to run wildly, yelling it out over and over again.

'I like being female!'

Fourteen

Rose slowed down. From the beach she spotted a tall thin nurse slam Mrs Clarence's gate and stalk angrily up the road towards *Hôtel Maternité*. As soon as the nurse was out of sight Rose ran for the cottage. The first thing she noticed was her bicycle leaning up against Diana's, in front of the window.

Mrs Clarence threw the door open.

'Yes?' she shouted. 'Oh, it's you,' and she laughed.

'I saw her leaving,' said Rose. 'Did she come about Dot?'

'Yes.' She looked anxious. 'Dot didn't return to the hotel last night or this morning. I just had a telling-off as though it were my fault. They thought she was here. She's gone to phone the police.'

'We'd better stop her,' said Rose. 'Dot's at Lapwing Cottage.'

'Oh, thank goodness. Is she all right?'

Rose nodded. 'So's George.'

'George? Who's George?'

'Her son.'

For a moment Mrs Clarence stared at Rose transfixed. 'Oh my!' she gasped suddenly and she flung her hand across her mouth.

'Will you come and help her with the breast-feeding?'

'Course I will. You'd better come in. I don't want next door knowing. Leastways, not yet.'

Diana was in a nightdress in the kitchen, drinking tea.

'Roe, I am sorry,' she blurted out, 'I never meant to spend another night here but Robert didn't ring till after midnight. He's safe.'

'That's wonderful!' cried Rose. 'I told you, didn't I?' She threw herself into the chair beside her and gave her a hug. 'I'm so pleased for you.' She turned to Mrs Clarence and laughed. 'And you, too, of course.'

'Roe,' said Diana suspiciously. 'There's nothing wrong, is there? You seem very excited about something. And why are you here so early?'

Rose just beamed.

'What's going on?' said Diana, looking from her sister to Mrs Clarence.

'That's what I'd like to know,' said Mrs Clarence.

Immediately after Rose had told them what had happened, Mrs Clarence phoned the doctor and the hotel.

Within a short time Dr Clarke turned up. Vague and somewhat bemused he stood on Mrs Clarence's doorstep, his white hair dishevelled, a pipe and tortoiseshell spectacles sticking out of the top pocket of an old tweed jacket. Mrs Clarence, Diana and Rose squeezed into his tiny Morris, their two bicycles tied under the boot.

They arrived at the cottage to find Dot sitting with George on a rug in a shady patch in the garden.

She and the doctor went into the sitting room with the baby while the others emptied out groceries on to the kitchen table. It was there that they discovered the OHMS envelope addressed to Diana. It contained her call-up papers.

Diana sat bleakly at the table staring at the letter, then at Rose and back again to the letter. 'I have to be there tomorrow,' she exclaimed. 'What are we going to do?'

'Go to the post office and arrange for me to collect the money,' said Rose swiftly.

'We'll have to tell Aunt Em now.'

'We can manage. There's no point in worrying her. She can't do anything about it.'

'She's going to smell a large rat when Miss Hutchinson doesn't contact her.'

'No, she won't. You know the outside world makes no impression on her once she's rehearsing.'

'Wait a minute,' said Mrs Clarence. 'Does *anyone* know about Miss Hutchinson?'

Diana looked guilty.

'No,' said Rose.

'Not even your mother?'

'No. We didn't want to worry her.'

'Oh dear,' said Mrs Clarence, and she looked at Rose with concern.

'We've managed all right so far, haven't we?' said Rose brightly.

The door opened. It was the doctor. 'I'd like a word with you, young lady,' he said.

He and Rose stepped out into the garden.

'Is she all right?' asked Rose.

'Yes. But you realise your young friend might have haemorrhaged. What would you have done then?'

'I don't know.'

'You've both been very foolish. You're lucky she's so fit, otherwise your little conspiracy might have ended in tragedy.'

'It wasn't a conspiracy,' Rose protested. 'If I'd had any idea that I'd be around when Dot had her baby I would have run a mile.'

He sighed. 'And I suppose you couldn't have left her to make a phone call.'

So Dot hadn't mentioned Derry, thought Rose. That was a relief.

'You've coped remarkably well. I'll give you that,' he admitted. 'But now she's got to face a lot of unpleasant music.'

'That's what I'm afraid of. You don't have to take her back to the hotel, do you? We can take care of her here.'

'I have ears, you know. Your sister's been called up.'

'But I'll be here.'

'How old are you?'

'Eighteen.' She paused. 'Almost.'

He shook his head.

'It's not that I don't think you're capable of looking after her, it's just that I'd be nagged by the church committee, and the voluntary services and the nurses at the hotel . . .'

'But they'll put her into a home for unmarried mothers away from all her friends,' interrupted Rose. 'And they'll keep going on about how she should put the baby up for adoption. It'll be just like a prison. They'll tell her when she can eat and when she's allowed to see the baby. And they're bound to try and punish her.'

He put up his hand. 'I'll see what I can do.'

Rose slipped her arm into his and gave it a squeeze. 'Oh, thank you. I knew you would. You look the kind sort.'

He peered at her over his glasses and smiled. 'You're a minx, young woman.'

And so somehow, while Dot and George snoozed in the sitting room, Rose and the doctor, Diana and Mrs Clarence thrashed out their plans over the kitchen table. Dr Clarke agreed to recommend that Dot stay with Mrs Clarence.

There was talk of Rose moving in with Mrs Clarence after Diana had left but Rose declared she wanted to stay at the cottage and, to her surprise, she met with little resistance. It seemed that her ability to cope with George's birth had made her more level-headed in their estimation.

When Dot strolled sleepily into the kitchen and found them all still there she was delighted.

And so the day proper began, and they bathed the baby in the tub in front of the fire. Mrs Clarence showed them both how best to hold him, and they sat round him, splashing his small limbs with the warm water, unable to keep their eyes off him, talking quietly or not at all, so that Rose felt as though she was being drawn back into the timeless dance again, where there were no words, only sound.

'He's a happy little soul, ain't he?' whispered Dot.

Blissful, thought Rose. She remembered his frown when he had been born, and how they had found themselves stroking him; the creamy substance on his skin easing their fingers effortlessly down his spine and across his limbs, while he made faint snuffling sounds. Now his face was unlined, the corners of his mouth imperceptibly curved upwards.

'Ain't he beautiful?' sighed Dot.

And he was; it was no mother's bias. His thick downy hair stuck out wildly, still sticky from his birth, and his dark eyes gazed out in their direction, almost as if he was searching them out.

After Dot had breast-fed him in the garden with Mrs Clarence's coaching, he fell asleep in Dot's arms, completely oblivious of the laughter and talk around him. Rose wondered, as she pressed the tips of George's tiny fingers to her lips, if he would grow up to be a soldier. She hoped not. People talked about this war being the end of all wars but then they had said that about the last one. How many fatherless men had died in this war, never to be fathers themselves.

It was mid-afternoon when they heard a horse and cart in the lane. Rose ran to the gate. So this was the famous Harold, she thought, gazing up at a short, elderly man in a battered hat. He gave her a broad smile, crinkling up a mosaic of wrinkles, and called out something that sounded like, 'Ans gunoogin awl oola cumfin arlin, in e?'

As soon as he spotted the baby in Dot's arms, he clambered down from his seat and trotted over to her, making clucking sounds. Muttering incoherently in his soft lilt, he stroked the side of the baby's face with his fingers.

Mrs Clarence translated for them. 'He says he's got an open face and good strong arms, and that the name George suits the little chap.'

Harold grinned and nodded vigorously.

Rose held George while Dot climbed into the cart to join Mrs Clarence and Diana, and then handed him up to her.

'I shouldn't be too late,' said Diana. 'I'll leave a message asking Aunt Em to ring back as soon as possible.'

'Send my love, won't you?'

'Of course.'

'And ask her about Mother.'

Diana nodded. The cart jogged forward slowly. Rose waited till it reached the top of the hill before turning back to the cottage.

It suddenly seemed unnervingly silent. Rose hurried into the kitchen to where Diana's washing lay stacked by the sink, picked up the pitcher and headed for the pump.

There was already a tinge of pink in the sky when she heard the whirring of a bicycle in the lane.

All afternoon, every movement of a stone or crack of a twig made her expect Derry to walk in. She wasn't sure what she was going to say to him. One minute she was angry with him for not waking Diana and Mrs Clarence, the next grateful that he hadn't. Through the open doorway she saw that it was Diana. She hurried to meet her at the gate.

'How was it?' she asked.

'You can stay at the cottage as long as you visit Mrs Clarence daily.'

'Thank goodness! And the post office?'

'Mrs Clarence is to pick up the money for you.'

'Has Aunt Em heard from Mother?'

'No. She's been in touch with E.N.S.A. headquarters and they don't think there's anything to worry about. They've told her that they don't know the whereabouts of Mother's theatre troupe because that would give away where the troops being entertained were.'

'We knew that already.'

Diana sighed. 'I still don't understand why we haven't heard from her.'

'She warned us we might not receive her letters till after she got back.'

'Yes, I know.'

'Did you tell Aunt Em about Robert?'

'Yes.'

'Was she pleased?'

'Yes,' laughed Diana.

'Come on in, I've actually cooked you a meal.'

'Really?'

'It's a sort of stew. I'm afraid there are burnt bits at the bottom but if we eat the top bit I'm sure it'll taste all right.'

'I'll open a bottle of that blackcurrant wine I had for my twenty-first.'

'I hoped you were going to say that,' said Rose. 'We'll need it to drown the taste.'

As she and Diana chatted over the congealed stew, Rose was tempted to tell Diana about Derry but every time she was about to, she didn't know where to begin. In the end she decided that, since it was their last night together, she wouldn't give her sister anything extra to worry about. And she might not be allowed to stay at the cottage if Diana knew Derry would be visiting her unchaperoned.

Unfortunately, Diana had detected there was something on her mind. 'You seem a bit sombre,' she commented. 'What's up?'

Rose quickly forced herself to smile. 'I'm just a bit tired. I didn't get much sleep last night.' She paused. 'I'm going to miss you.'

'Are you really?' Diana gave a shy laugh. 'That's nice of you to say so.'

'Actually, there is something. My exam results arrived two days ago. I failed geography which means . . .'

'Oh, Roe, I'm sorry,' cried Diana. 'Why didn't you tell me?'

'Because you were so worried about Robert.'

'And you spent the night, all on your own, without having anyone to tell?'

'Yes,' said Rose, reddening.

'You silly thing. Why didn't you come to Mrs Clarence's?'

'Too lazy, I suppose.'

'Liar. You were too upset, weren't you?'

'A bit.'

'I should have been here.'

'You weren't to know.'

'I'm responsible for you.'

'You couldn't have done anything.'

'I could have given you a hug.'

'I'm afraid I pinched some of your wine to cheer me up.'

'That's all right. You probably needed it for the shock. Oh dear, what's Mother going to say?'

'"Take it again, dear!" At least Father's been spared being disappointed in me again.'

'He was never disappointed in you.'

'Don't you remember his face when he read my school reports?'

'But he never lost faith in you. He just didn't understand why you weren't doing well. It was a mistake sending you to the same school as me. If you'd gone somewhere else, you'd have got on far better.'

'Perhaps.'

'Oh, Roe, you look so miserable.'

Rose was just allowing herself to wallow in self-pity when she remembered Diana's phone call. 'How did Robert sound?'

'Tired. Happy. Now there's just Mother to think about.'

'If anything had happened to her, Aunt Em would be the first to know and we'd be the first ones she'd tell.'

'I know, it's silly to worry,' Diana said.

'You were born worrying. I think, when you first popped your head out of Mummy, you looked around, frowned and said, "Oh dear".'

Diana smiled and then picked at the skin at the side of her fingernails.

'There's something I have to tell you. About Robert. He's writing a letter to Mother asking . . .' She hesitated. 'And I've written one, too.'

'Diana,' breathed Rose. 'You mean you're engaged?'

She smiled. 'Yes. It's all unofficial. We'd like to wait till Mother gets home but if she's delayed we'll get married without her.'

'But you've only known him a fortnight.'

'I know. It doesn't make any sense. But I knew on my twenty-first I was in love with him.'

'You mean it was love at first sight?'

'Not exactly. It took about an hour,' and she laughed.

'"And a flower it takes a summer",' Rose murmured thoughtfully. '"And man and woman are like the earth, that bring forth flowers in summer, and love . . ."'

'What's that?' interrupted Diana.

'It's from a poem called "Fidelity".'

'It sounds beautiful. Who wrote it?'

'D. H. Lawrence.'

'Roe!' said Diana, shocked. 'You haven't been reading *him*, have you?'

She laughed. 'Oh, Diana, you are funny.'

'I keep forgetting how old you are. I always think of you as my baby sister.'

Rose lifted her plaits up. 'These don't help,' she commented. She gazed fondly at her sister. It was funny to think of her about to become Mrs Clarence.

'About Robert,' she began. 'What if Mother refuses permission?'

'Then we'll just have to get married without it. I'm twenty-one now. But Mrs Clarence's letter to her should make a difference. As soon as she says yes, we can start making arrangements.'

'Diana,' began Rose hesitantly. 'Do you mind if I ask you something personal?'

'What about?'

'You and Robert?'

'Go ahead.'

'I don't know how to put this without sounding snobbish.'

'You mean him being from a different class.'

Rose nodded.

'Yes. I don't think it's quite what Mother had in store for me.'

'Doesn't that worry you?'

'No. I feel relieved. If I'd married someone "more suitable" I would have ended up being a decoration at the dinner table. I couldn't have faced that loneliness.'

'You're not running away, are you?'

'On the contrary. I've stopped running.'

'But how can you be sure that Robert is the right person?'

'You think I'm making a mistake, don't you?'

'No.' She paused. 'I'm not sure.'

'Don't you like him?'

'I hardly know him. The short time he was home he spent mostly with you. He seems nice enough. And he obviously makes you happy. It's just . . .' She stopped.

'What?'

'What makes *him* so special?'

Diana looked thoughtful for a moment. 'I feel I'm an equal with him and I stop feeling self-conscious. I forget what I look like. Believe it or not, he also treats me as if I'm intelligent. He's demonstrative and he makes me laugh. That do?'

Rose laughed. 'Yes. That'll do.'

'About the letter to Mother, do you think I should have told her about Miss Hutchinson?'

'No.' She frowned. 'I suppose I ought to drop her a line now. I feel a bit mean, writing postscripts at the bottom of your letters. It's just when I'm working on a story I find it difficult to write letters. Daft really. I should be able to write anything.'

'Why?'

'Because I want to be a writer.'

'Seriously?'

'Yes.'

'Earn a living at it?'

'Eventually.'

'But couldn't you do it as a hobby?'

'No. I want to have a proper stab at it. Then if I'm a hopeless failure, at least I'll know that I've had a go. I'll have to do some other kind of job to earn money first.'

'Four years ago I'd never have dreamt that either of us would be working. Now, here I am, about to go into the WAAF and you're thinking of being a writer.'

'Diana, do you think you'll be able to cope with working in a hospital? They might ask you to help on the wards if they're busy and make you do . . .' She hesitated.

'Bedpans and cleaning up? Yes, I know.'

'Won't you mind?'

'Not if it means that the nurses can get on with looking after the patients.'

'But what if it's a burns unit,' said Rose quietly. 'They get terribly disfigured. Do you think you'll be able to stand it?'

'I hope so. It'll be far worse for them.'

'You're very brave.'

'So are you.'

'Me? Whatever for?'

'For standing by Dot.'

Rose laughed. 'Let's have a toast,' she said. 'To ourselves.'

They refilled the glasses with blackcurrant wine and raised them. They opened some elderflower wine and chatted about the past, laughing over the dreadful idiosyncrasies of the school mistresses. They talked of their father and discussed how they might best cope with their mother on her return to England.

Then, while Diana soaked in a tub, Rose packed her clothes into her bicycle bags. They had agreed to say their goodbyes privately that night. Station farewells reminded them too much of going back to school. Diana was to spend the night at Mrs Clarence's so that she would be nearer the station. The doctor had offered to give her a lift from there.

Swaying and laughing they stumbled out of the kitchen into the garden. It was dark.

'Are you sure you'll be able to ride your bike?' asked Rose, checking the tissue paper over the headlights. 'I don't want you crashing into a car.'

'There aren't any cars here,' giggled Diana. 'Only the doctor's. And he can patch me up if I do.'

'There are trees,' pointed out Rose.

They stood by the gate and gazed at each other.

'Oh, Roe,' said Diana, 'I don't want to go and I do want to go.'

'I don't want you to go either,' said Rose.

'It had to come some time,' said Diana quietly.

'I know. Thank goodness Miss Hutchinson was called up. If she'd been supervising us we wouldn't have got on so well.' She looked guilty. 'I haven't liked you very much in the past.'

'Why?'

'I was fed up having you rammed down my throat at school. And I thought you were a bit too good.'

'I wasn't,' said Diana. 'Since this is confession time I might as well tell you that I've been jealous of you for ages.'

'Jealous? Of me?' Rose was astounded. 'But why?'

'For being Father's favourite. Because of my looks he thought I was featherbrained. I longed for him to discuss things with me the way he did with you.'

'Oh, aren't we idiots?' Rose exclaimed.

Diana smiled and nodded. 'Are you sure you wouldn't rather stay with Dot and Mrs Clarence?'

'No. Dot needs some mothering now. I don't.'

They stared shyly at each other for a moment and then flung their arms round one another.

'Bye, old thing,' said Rose.

'Goodbye,' whispered her sister.

They held on to each other.

'Roe,' began Diana tentatively, 'you will eat properly, won't you?'

Rose burst into laughter.

'Oh, Diana,' she said, squeezing her tight, 'you never change!'

Fifteen

She had slept for eleven hours! It was the longest sleep she had had the whole summer. She stretched out her limbs like a cat and wallowed in her laziness. It was also the first time she had slept naked, having felt too awkward to try it before.

As she slipped out of bed she noticed a line of blood trickle down the inside of her thigh. It was four weeks to the day since her last period; one week earlier than usual. What was even more extraordinary, it had arrived with no pain.

And then she suddenly realised. 'I'm not pregnant,' she whispered. Overwhelmed with relief, she sat back on to the bed. It was as though she had been given a second chance.

She found herself thinking about Miss Hilda and her baby. She was disappointed that Dot hadn't been allowed to stay. She had wanted her and George to sleep in Miss Hilda's bedroom as a way of redressing the balance.

She grabbed her clothes and headed downstairs. She had

intended to put the china she had unwrapped back into the packing cases but once she had opened the door she changed her mind.

'Miss Hilda,' she announced, 'I'm going to unlock you!'

She had no plan; no idea of where she would put everything, but bit by bit, she dragged out the cane chair, the gramophone, the small tables and the wooden record cases. She eased out the many pictures which had been packed in at the sides. Blankets had been thrown carelessly around them. She stacked them under the sitting-room windows and examined them. The glass was still intact.

There were old photographs of children playing on a beach in Edwardian dress and a painting of Salmouth harbour, pale watercolours, prints of old boats, and sepia photographs of Tindlecombe and Gynmouth. Rose noticed that many of the pictures were of little boys, and she wondered if that was how Miss Hilda consoled herself for the loss of her son.

She hauled out rugs and curtains and armfuls of books and dumped them on the living-room floor. It was chaos; glorious chaos. She dragged out bookcases and tables. In the sitting room she put the books and ornaments on the shelves in the alcoves, covered a table with a crimson fringed shawl and placed the gramophone on top. She wound it up, selected the newest-looking needle in the small metal cradle and replaced it in the arm. To the strains of violin music she drifted from room to room sorting out what to take upstairs. Once her books and notes were stacked in a bookcase in her study, and the blue Persian rug was on the floor, all it needed was a few pictures on the walls and some prettier curtains to complete it. She placed the statuette of the dancing girl at the corner of her table. It was still her favourite.

By the time she had tidied up, waxed two wooden tables and polished the brass fire irons downstairs it was already late afternoon. Too late to visit Mrs Clarence. The sky grew leaden and a strong wind began to blow in from the coast. She brought in the curtains she had washed and attempted to read a book in one of the armchairs. Finding it impossible to concentrate she turned on the wireless and listened to the news. Italy was being invaded by British and American troops! She danced like a lunatic round the room, longing to be dancing with someone else and sharing the excitement.

The following morning she awoke to find her room flooded with light. She leaned out of the window and gazed seaward. She would visit the bookshop, she decided. She had to confront Derry sooner or later.

She set out for the coastal path, her shoulder bag and sandals swinging between her fingers, her jersey tied round her waist. She felt tall, surefooted.

Outside the bookshop she stood still to stare. The windows had been cleaned. Heavy red velvet curtains were hitched up at the sides and on the polished wide wooden shelf beneath, was an inviting display of books. What was even more surprising were the Lloyd Loom chairs dotted round the bookcases. Even the brass bell above the door had been polished.

Alec was sitting in the alcove shuffling papers about. As soon as he spotted her he stood up and beamed. 'What do you think?' he asked, and he flung his arms out wide like an actor on a stage.

Rose gaped at the organised shelves; the pieces of paper with typed headings on them: Gardening, Crime, Sea Stories, Magazines. 'It looks marvellous,' she exclaimed.

She looked round at the rugs on the floor, the cushions on the chairs, the pictures on the walls, and laughed. 'It's more like a sitting room than a bookshop!'

'Come on up and tell me about you and Dot.'

Upstairs she leaned in the kitchen doorway, as he was bent over the sink rinsing the teapot.

'Who told you?' she said nonchalantly. 'Derry?'

'The woman from *Hôtel Maternité*.'

'Oh. Where is he by the way? Still in bed?' She asked as casually as she could.

'Didn't he tell you? He left two days ago.'

Rose paled, 'So the R.A.F.'s finally called him up,' she stated flatly.

He looked puzzled. 'Not with his eyesight, I'm afraid. He failed their medical several months ago. No. When they still refused to take him in spite of his exam results he just decided it was time to go home.'

Rose burst into tears.

Alec led her to one of the armchairs. 'You look terrible,' he said.

She sank into the armchair sobbing and shivering uncontrollably. Alec tucked a blanket round her. Gradually the colour returned to her face. Alec sat in the armchair opposite and watched her with concern.

Rose could hardly bear to look at him.

He leaned forward. 'You'd better spill the beans,' he said gently.

'You'll hate me!' she choked out.

'I doubt it.'

'He said he loved me,' she began, 'that he was going to be a pilot and that he'd die soon and . . .'

'How long has this been going on?'

'Ever since he took me to the cinema.' She paused. 'It doesn't seem very long ago, does it?'

He shook his head.

'But now no one will ever want to have anything to do with me and . . .' She swallowed.

'Why?'

'It's just, well . . .' She struggled to find the right words. 'I'm not pure any more, if you know what I mean.'

'I could wring his neck. You realise he could have got you into serious trouble.'

'He made it safe,' she whispered, and glanced quickly down at her feet. 'Oh, Alec, aren't you disgusted with me?'

'No.' He took his pipe from the mantelpiece. 'I'm going to ask you a personal question. You don't have to answer it. All right?'

She nodded.

'Have you missed a period?'

She reddened. 'No. I've got it now.'

'Well, that's a relief.'

Rose pulled the blanket round herself. 'Alec, I'm so confused. I feel terrible at Derry leaving like this without a word, but I feel relieved, too.' She sniffed. 'He was going to take me out in his boat. I suppose that was just another of his lies. Now I'll never . . .'

'I'll take you.'

'You?'

'If you like.'

'I didn't know you could sail.'

'Whose boat did you think it was?'

'Derry's.'

'He doesn't live here. He just stays in the summer.'

'Yes, I know, but I thought it was his. I only ever saw him in it.'

'He didn't want my company this year. I knew he was heartbroken at being turned down by the services so I let him have it for as long as he liked. I didn't have much heart for sailing anyway.'

'I've only just learnt to swim, I'm afraid, but I can still cover quite a long distance.'

'That's not important. Anyway I have a spare Mae West you can wear but we shouldn't have any trouble today. It's hardly gale-force winds.'

'Today!'

'We'll go this afternoon. Think you can wait that long?'

'Oh yes,' said Rose laughing almost hysterically. 'I think I can wait that long.'

At the end of the beach several small boats were moored in a sheltered inlet. Alec's boat was lying on a stretch of sand.

He rolled back the piece of canvas which had been tied over the boom. 'This will fly like the dickens when we're out at sea.'

'Fly?'

'Swing across, to be exact. You have to do a lot of ducking and jumping about when you sail.'

'It all looks so complicated.'

'You'll soon get the hang of it. This large sail here,' he said, hauling up the one connected to the boom, 'is the mainsail. I'll be handling that and the tiller. You'll be handling the jib sheets. Those are what the two ropes connected to the jib sail are called. That's the smaller sail in front.'

At first Rose was too nervous to take her eyes off the sail.

After a while she began to relax. Occasionally they had to sit on the edge of the boat and lean out together to help what little wind there was fill the sails. As they glided past 'her' cove, she glanced quickly over her shoulder. To her utter astonishment Alec suggested they sail round the peninsula. She could have wept.

There were more cliffs and rocks on the other side but it was obvious that Alec knew the coastline well. Clusters of secluded coves stretched out before her and, in the distance, a small harbour rose up to a hill top. Tiny cottages were stacked tightly together up its slopes.

Alec headed the boat into the eye of the wind and they came to a halt.

Rose leaned over the side and dipped her hands into the water. Alec lounged back and gazed skywards.

'It'll start getting choppier from now on,' he said, 'and then it'll be the end of summer.'

'It doesn't feel like it,' she remarked. 'I hope it stays like this until . . .' She stopped.

'Until you go back to school?'

'I suppose so,' she said slowly.

She pressed her wet hands around her neck and across her forehead.

Alec stared at her. 'You're not going back, are you?'

She whirled round. 'How did you guess? I hadn't decided until this moment.'

'Intuition.'

'Don't tell anyone, will you? Not till I've sorted out what I want to do.'

'Of course not. Is it the thought of retaking School Cert?'

She shook her head.

'Derry?'

'No. It's because I stayed with Dot when she was in labour. I can't go back to being a schoolgirl now. When I saw George being born, it was the most wonderful experience, actually to be there at the start of someone's life. I'd forgotten what a gift it is, just being here!'

'Snap,' he said quietly.

'I don't want to waste it, do you?'

He gazed at her steadily. 'No.'

'My mother can give the money my father put aside for my university studies to Diana for a wedding present. She'll need it more than I will, especially if she has children.' She sighed. 'Isn't it sad? My father will never see them. I hope Robert survives. There are too many fatherless people already. Me. You. Though I suppose you have your adoptive father.'

'He died two years ago.'

'Oh. I'm sorry.'

'Yes. I was quite fond of him in a funny sort of way. He was a kind man, but I often felt as though I was letting him down or embarrassing him. Derry's very much like him. A conformist. That's why he wanted to be in the R.A.F. so desperately. It must have been devastating when his friends left him behind.'

'He lied so many times to me just to get what he wanted.'

'He lied to himself,' said Alec. 'He was convinced his poor eyesight and flat feet would be waved aside once he got his Highers. I tried to tell him they wouldn't be but he didn't want to hear. I suppose when he was given that very definite "No" a few days ago he couldn't pretend to himself any longer.'

'Or to me,' she interrupted.

'If only I'd known what he'd been telling you.'

'It wasn't your fault.'

'Or yours,' he added. 'Reading between the lines I would guess that losing his cherry was one way of proving his manhood.'

'Losing his what?'

'His virginity.'

'Oh, I see. On me,' she added bitterly. She stared angrily out at the sea. 'He lied about Dot, too,' she muttered. 'The hypocrite. He just pretended to like her to get nearer me.' There was a moment's silence. 'Has he really got flat feet?'

'Yes.'

'Good. He deserves them.' She turned to look at him. 'I've just remembered,' she said suddenly, 'Louise left you too, didn't she?'

'That's right.' He smiled. 'And we've both survived.'

'Yes,' she laughed. 'Yes, we have.'

They sunbathed until late afternoon. The sky had grown cooler and there was more of a breeze to fill the sails. Rose felt calmer than she had in weeks. Jumping about in the boat, and sitting beside Alec when they leaned out she was conscious only of the fine spray from the sea, the taste of salt on her lips and the warmth of his arm as it bumped accidentally against her.

They sailed into the inlet and quickly lowered the sails, leaping out a fraction too soon into a dip in the seabed, so that by the time the boat had been hauled up on to the sand and made fast, they were both drenched. They sprinted across the beach, their clothes flapping against their skin, their shoes squelching, on towards the jetty and into the lane. As soon as they were inside, they tore up the stairs. Rose peeled off her clothes in the bathroom, washed, and pulled on one of Alec's large white pullovers.

She was on the way out when she caught sight of herself in the old mirror on the wall. Staring back at her were two large eyes in a dark brown face surrounded by sopping black plaits. Her skin felt hot. She pressed her hands against her cheeks.

Downstairs Alec had lit the fire. She watched him fry mackerel in its own juices over the flames while she sat on the hearth rug and turned over her clothes to dry on the clothes horse.

Her wet plaits stuck to her neck. 'It really is your best feature,' she remembered Derry saying. 'You'd look like a boy if you had it cut.' She felt a tap on her shoulders. Alec was holding out a plate of bread and mackerel for her to take. Tomorrow, she thought, I'll go to the hairdresser's in Gynmouth. Tossing her braids aside, she took the plate, and began to eat.

She gripped her handkerchief and looked into the mirror, not at her face, but at her hair. The hairdresser leaned over her with a pair of scissors. 'Goodbye,' she whispered inside her head. She watched the scissors open and close around a clump of hair. And then it was gone. The girl picked it up from the floor and held it out.

'Do you want to keep it?' she asked.

'No.'

The girl smiled. 'The best choice, if you don't mind me saying.'

'You're not from these parts, are you?' remarked Rose.

'No. Evacuee. Only I done a bit of training and when I asked at this place for a job, they grabbed me. Everyone else here is middle-aged or elderly. I bring in the young, see.'

Rose nodded, her eyes still transfixed to her disappearing hair.

'Much better,' murmured the girl. 'Long hair pulls your face down. It's lovely and wavy. I think you've got a natural Even-Steven there.'

'What's that?'

'Short hair with a parting down the middle and permed. There's girls'd give their eye teeth for that.'

The hair was gone. There was nothing she could do about it.

'It'll take about six weeks for it to be its full bouncy self,' explained the young hairdresser as she combed it out. 'It's been pulled down at each side for years, see, so it takes a bit of time. The centre parting will stay for the same reason, but that'll go in time, too, if that's what you want.' She fluffed it up with her fingers and went to fetch the hand mirror.

This is it, thought Rose. She turned from side to side, examining the back of her hair in the mirrored reflection. 'It's lovely!' she exclaimed. 'You've done marvels.' And she laughed. 'What an idiot I am. I should have done this years ago.'

After leaving the hairdresser's, she bought some olive green slacks, and a pair of khaki dungarees. Then she treated herself to tea in the Tudor Tea Shop. She couldn't help glancing at her reflection in the glass. Her eyes seemed larger than ever; her face more oval, less drawn.

Harold was waiting for her outside the blacksmith's with the horse and cart. At first he just gaped at her, and then he gave a delighted chuckle. Rose stood in front of him, her arms full of packages, unable to stop smiling. On the journey back, she slipped her arm into his and gave it a squeeze. He gave such a broad grin that his eyes disappeared into a crease amongst his wrinkles.

'You knew Miss Hilda, didn't you?' she commented.

'Oh yars,' he drawled. And he muttered something which had a word in it like 'babby'.

'You knew her since she was a baby?'

He nodded vigorously.

'I wish I'd met her, though I suppose we'd never have come here if she hadn't died. And I would never have known anything about her. Not that I do know much,' she added hurriedly, 'but the cottage has such a lovely atmosphere that I'm sure I would have liked her.'

'Oh yars,' he agreed. 'You and 'er'd uv . . .'

And the rest, Rose didn't understand. 'You think we would have got on?'

His head bobbed up and down. And then he said something she did understand.

'Could've bin her dotter,' he remarked. 'Ooh yars. Two uv a kind.'

Rose stared at him flabbergasted, not knowing whether to be flattered or frightened.

He looked up at her hair, his blue eyes misting up with laughter.

She touched it awkwardly with her hand. 'I don't think I look that funny,' she protested.

'No,' he said, shaking his head. ''Tis biderful.' And he smiled to himself.

Rose had left her bicycle at Mrs Clarence's. Harold offered to put it in the cart and take her back to Lapwing Cottage, but Rose said she would prefer to cycle home later. She was afraid he might see Miss Hilda's furniture through the windows and although she didn't think he would tell anyone, he might be angry with her.

They had hardly pulled up outside the cottage when Dot's

face appeared at the window. Her mouth agape, she began to wave frantically. Within seconds Mrs Clarence had flung open her front door.

The secret was out, thought Rose.

Harold handed her shopping down to her.

'Thanks for everything,' she said earnestly.

He grinned and looked over her head towards the cottage, muttering incoherently again.

'Oh my goodness!' cried Mrs Clarence aghast. 'All your lovely hair! Gone!'

'You look crackin',' said Dot beaming. 'Don't she, Mrs C?'

Mrs Clarence gazed sadly at her, and nodded. 'You look so grown-up,' she remarked.

'Thank goodness for that.'

Mrs Clarence glanced at the parcels.

'Slacks and overalls,' Rose explained.

'You didn't use up all your coupons, did you?'

'Practically.'

'Whatever will your mother say?'

'I dread to think.'

Mrs Clarence shook her head and tutted but Rose could see she was fighting down a smile. 'You naughty girl,' she said. 'Diana hasn't been gone a day . . .'

'How's George?' Rose asked, quickly changing the subject.

'Asleep,' said Dot.

'Can I see him?'

He was upstairs, lying in an old cot. She and Dot gazed down at his flushed little face.

'Have you written to your parents about him yet?' she whispered.

Dot shook her head. 'Mrs Clarence says I should but I told

her I'm dead in me father's eyes. He'd just burn the letter.'

'What about your mother?'

'She's scared stiff of him, and anyway she's got enough to think about, with me brothers and sisters to look after.' She looked sad. 'I know it sounds daft, but I really miss Walthamstow. It's lovely 'ere. And Mrs Clarence is ever so nice to me, but, I dunno, I miss all the excitement, and seeing all me old mates from school, and the market and yelling out at the stall.'

She lowered her head. Rose saw some tears escape down her face.

'Anyway,' Dot said, 'chin up, eh? I got George, 'aven't I?'

Rose put her arm round her shoulders.

'I 'ope I'm doing the right thing by him. We've had people round from the church and the hospital and voluntary workers, and they say I'm being selfish keeping him and that I'll never be able to look after him because no one'll give me a job and I'll have no money and how will I feed him? And that he'd be much happier with a nice young married couple. And that I can't stay here for ever.'

'And what does Mrs Clarence think about that?'

'They say all these things when she's out of the way. One of them even suggested I go take a walk and that they'd remove him while I was out, so I wouldn't have to hand him over meself.'

'Oh, Dot, that's awful.'

'Mrs C. thought there was somethin' up when I got nervy about leaving him in the cottage with her so I told her.'

'Good.'

She smiled. 'Yeah. She's the best. But what if I can't cope? And what if something happens to Mrs C? Or me?'

'There's me and Diana, remember?'

Rose cycled back on the inland route, her parcels stuffed into the bags at the side of her front wheels. The evening had grown cool so that it wasn't till she had been cycling for some time, that she began to feel warm again.

It was such a delight to have no plaits flapping round her neck or stuffed into her blouse. She gave her head a shake.

When she arrived at the cottage, she could sense Miss Hilda welcoming her back. Suddenly she was relieved that Derry had gone. She gave a laugh. Derry, she realised, had been shed with her hair.

When she woke the following morning she was surprised to find herself thinking of Alec. And she realised she missed him. Miss Hilda would have to keep her company, she decided. She leaned across to her bedside table and picked up one of Miss Hilda's journals.

I asked Harold if he would take me into Gynmouth, she had written, *and to my utter delight he agreed!*

I had little to spend but it didn't matter. I peered into windows, stopped and watched people in the streets, went and had tea in a small tea shop and eavesdropped on conversations.

Eventually I slipped on my wedding ring and plucked up enough courage to go into the post office.

I made enquiries about my account, the one I had opened in my 'married' name, Mrs Matthew Tomlinson. I explained that I had been abroad and had forgotten to close it and asked if it was still valid.

The woman behind the counter was astonished when she saw my post office book. 'You can keep it if you like,' she laughed. 'It'd make a good museum piece!'

She handed me a new savings book. Not only did I still have an account but my savings had actually increased with interest. I fairly waltzed out of there, another tiny bit of independence in my hand.

In between sporadic accounts of gardening, the rest of the book described Miss Hilda's return visits to Gynmouth.

They were my source of sanity, she had written. Once again I had a focus to my life and one which always left me feeling recharged. My appetite grew, not just for food, but for life itself. Every small risk taken was an achievement, every pleasure I granted myself helped me grow in strength.

I decided to rid myself of my brother's dreary cast-off furniture. With Harold's help we would lift a piece of it into the back of the cart, cover it up with sacking, take a detour, as usual avoiding Salmouth, and head for Gynmouth. Once there I would put it into the auction. Ideally it would be sold first so that I knew the amount I could bid for something I liked.

While reading a magazine in town one day I hit on an idea of making money, she wrote. I wrote a romantic short story, drawing on my own experiences, and sent it away under an assumed name. I combined Matthew's name and my own, thus making 'Matilda Matthews' and arranged for any mail to be sent to the Gynmouth post office.

I didn't hold out much hope of it being accepted, but on my fourth try, it was taken up. I was paid for it and asked to send in another.

Rose was amazed. It was the most extraordinary coincidence, that they should both send a story to a magazine. She returned to the diary. It didn't take her long to realise she was reading a success story. Readers of the magazine wrote in saying how much they enjoyed Miss Hilda's stories.

And so I began writing on a regular basis, she wrote, setting most of the stories in different periods.

I remember at one of the Gynmouth auctions, bidding for two trunks filled with old clothes. No one wanted them, so I bought them for a song. As soon as I got them home, I had a dressing-up session, getting the feel of them. They helped me enormously by making several of my stories more realistic.

When I had saved up enough money I bought myself a pair of comfortable brogues, and so at last was able to walk with ease along the coastal path into Salmouth. I put on weight, which forced me finally into buying my beloved tweeds.

Rose closed the diary and fled into Miss Hilda's room. The trunks were unlocked. Folded at the top of the first one she opened was a powder blue dress which had been exquisitely embroidered along the hem and round the neckline. Wedged in beside it were ankle-length boots with buttons down the side. The leather was soft and scalloped.

She slipped out of her shorts and blouse and into the dress. It did up in the front into a small ruff. The buttons were soft and handmade, the sleeves leg-o'-mutton – huge from the shoulder to the elbow, close-fitting from the elbow to the wrist. She pulled out another dress and a laced corset.

As she tried on each costume she raced upstairs to her bedroom to gaze at herself in the mirror. She even put on a man's summer suit, complete with waistcoat. It was Edwardian in style and off-white. As she studied herself in the glass she remembered how nervous she had been when she had first put on her new slacks and overalls, the day she had had her hair cut. She was as relieved as she was then to see that she didn't look like a boy at all.

In the other trunk she found evening dresses and suits, going up to the twenties. It wasn't till she had tried on every-thing that she plucked up the courage to open the large leather suitcase in the corner. She knelt down in front of it and raised the lid, sitting quickly back on her heels, not daring to touch the contents. Then, very tenderly, she lifted up the old cream and crimson Chinese dressing-gown which was lying on top. Underneath were two pairs of brogues, sandals, dresses and cardigans, old tweed jackets, blouses and some strange Greek-tunic-style dresses, which hung loosely in folds from the shoulders. She put the garments back neatly and closed the lid.

Outside it was hot; Indian-summer weather. She took one of the Edwardian petticoats from the first trunk and put it on. She did up the tiny buttons on the bodice and untucked the lace at the top which had folded itself under the sleeveless straps. Glancing down, she couldn't help but notice her cumbersome bloomers bulging dark and conspicuous under the cotton.

'I'll put on my shell pink ones,' she murmured.

Feeling cool and comfortable, she took the cane chair out into the garden and continued reading again.

And I discovered that the people in Salmouth were not unfriendly at all. I had never given them a fair chance. I had hardly even looked them in the eye. I suddenly became aware of them nodding and smiling at me when I went into the shops and I found myself able to say, 'Good morning,' and even, 'How are you?'

And then the bombshell dropped.

It was last year, on 6 May, the day before my son's birthday. I always liked to do something special on that day and had prepared for it by making cakes and replenishing my sherry and port supply. I had just finished hanging new curtains when I heard a car draw up outside. Soon after, there was a loud knock on the door.

I opened it to find my sister-in-law standing outside, flanked by the vicar and Dr Clarke.

So it wasn't the doctor's first visit to the cottage when he came to see Dot, Rose thought. She remembered the telling-off he had given her and smiled.

It was the first time in five years we had set eyes on one another, continued Miss Hilda. *As for her companions, we had merely exchanged nods of heads, on the rare occasions I saw them in the village. I realised that someone must have seen me in Gynmouth and word of it had reached my brother. Bluff, I felt, was my only hope.*

'Good afternoon. What a lovely surprise!' I said. 'Do come in.'

I thought my sister-in-law's eyes would pop out of her head when she saw the kitchen dresser, the pictures and pretty plates on the walls, the lace curtains at the window, the sink, the matting on the terracotta floor. As we walked through the corridor into the living room I distinctly heard her shudder.

The fire was laid. Chatting heartily over my shoulder, while my heart thumped seemingly thunderously against my breastbone, I lit it.

'There's no need to trouble yourself,' exclaimed the vicar.

'Nonsense!' I exclaimed jovially. 'Do sit down.'

I watched my sister-in-law like a hawk; observed the horror in her face as she gaped at my odds and ends of furniture, my English country things mixed in with the rich Oriental. I had long ago decided not to furnish the cottage in any particular style but merely choose what pleased me. Books and periodicals were piled high in the alcoves and in the mahogany bookcase; scraps of leftover material from the curtains were draped over the back of a chair for cushion covers. As she huffed and puffed in her ridiculous town outfit, wide-brimmed hat and gloves, I fought down a strong desire to laugh.

After an awkward silence she informed me that I had been spotted as far away as Gynmouth and that I was seen actually having tea there and buying material in a department store.

'I know what a terrible experience it must have been for you during

the war with all that nursing, and we feel that you really shouldn't overtax yourself by making long journeys or you might have a relapse, and it is Mr Partridge's duty to keep an eye on your welfare and so,' she babbled on, 'when he happened to see the inside of the cottage through the window he felt it his duty to . . .' She paused and waved her hand about.

'Charming, if I may say so,' put in the vicar. 'Very cosy.'

I saw my chance. 'Yes. Thanks to my brother. He gives me a generous allowance. I consider myself fortunate.'

'Ah yes, Major Withers is a good man.'

Out of the corner of my eye, I could see that my sister-in-law was completely stumped. She wouldn't dare reveal how little he really gave me, since that would make him seem harsh.

'And your roses,' he went on. 'Such magnificent specimens. But how soon did yours start flowering?'

'Six days ago. I leaned out of my bedroom window and there was one single deep red rose. I thought, what a wonderful start to the month!'

'Indeed,' he agreed, nodding and smiling. 'They're really quite remarkable.'

He caught sight of Mrs Withers' stony eyes and reddened.

'Such a shame,' he stammered, 'we don't see you in church.'

So that was it! It was not only what I'd been up to which had caused disapproval, but also what I hadn't been up to!

'Yes, isn't it? But what am I thinking? I haven't offered you any sherry!'

The doctor rubbed his hands. 'I couldn't help noticing it in the corner there. Spanish, isn't it?'

'Yes.'

I grabbed some glasses from the top of the bookcase and began pouring.

'Most kind of you,' said the vicar. 'But are you sure?'

'Absolutely. I don't often have the pleasure of visitors.'

'Well, as I was saying,' he added, noting Mrs Withers' gesture of refusal, 'you don't visit the church much, do you?'

'I thought I might frighten away the congregation if I attended services. I'm quite mad, you know.'

I wasn't scared any more. I suddenly realised that 'madness' was my liberator. By declaring myself to be mad, I could be as eccentric as I wanted. I felt so happy that I threw back my head and laughed.

Dr Clarke raised his glass. 'Cheers!' he said.

My sister-in-law looked utterly confused.

'Ditto,' added the vicar.

'Are you sure you won't have some?' I asked her.

She pursed her lips and shook her head.

'Cheers, then!' I echoed.

I remember, as I raised my glass, thinking, good old sherry! Good old English roses! Good old country tweeds! I knew I had won.

Rose was startled to hear someone calling her name. She shut the diary quickly and slipped it under the cushion on the seat.

'I'm here,' she shouted.

She stood up and ran round the corner to the path. It was Alec.

Sixteen

He was standing in front of the door holding several empty boxes. On his back was a bulging knapsack.

'Your hair!' he cried. 'It's wonderful.'

He gazed at her long white garment.

Rose blushed. 'You're embarrassing me.'

'Sorry.'

She stared blankly at him. It was the first time he had visited the cottage, and it seemed strange.

'Have I interrupted you in the middle of writing?' he asked. 'You seem a bit dazed.'

She shook her head. 'Here, let me take all those boxes.'

'I thought they'd be useful for your apples.'

As they walked into the kitchen Rose noticed him glance at the blue and white vase of flowers on the table and the white teapot standing beside it.

'I thought you said all Hilda's things had been locked away.'

'Yes, that's right.' And she hastily dumped the boxes on to the floor.

Alec quickly undid the straps of the knapsack. Flabbergasted, Rose watched him pull out cold roast chicken, boiled eggs, tomatoes, bread, lettuce and other salad fare.

'How on earth did you get hold of that chicken?'

'Never you mind, me dear,' he replied in the local manner. 'You'm livin' in the countree nah.'

He plonked a corked stone jar on to the table.

'Cider!'

'Ooh, ah. That'll put the colour in they'se cheeks.'

She smiled. 'Then you'd better be the one to drink it.' She hesitated. 'Alec, I'm afraid I have the most awful confession to make.'

'Don't tell me. You're not hungry.'

'No,' she said, stifling a giggle. 'It's serious.'

He sat at the table and solemnly joined hands. 'What is it, my child?' he murmured. 'Confess it all.'

'It's about Miss Hilda and the locked room.'

He frowned. 'What about it?'

'You remember I told you I'd found a way in and that I liked to sit among her things.'

'Yes.'

'Well, I thought it was rather a shame for them to be hidden away so I thought I'd give them an airing, just until I leave here. I'll put them back at the end of the month.' She paused. 'What I'm saying is, that I've taken them out and spread them around a bit.'

After a moment's silence he started to laugh.

'You don't think she'd have minded, do you?' Rose asked.

He shook his head. 'She'd have loved it.'

'I didn't carry everything out, of course. Some of it was too heavy.'

He pushed up his sleeves. 'We can soon rectify that.'

'You really don't mind? I mean, I know she was a good friend of yours.'

'I'd like to see her things, too. I haven't been up here since last year. I couldn't bear the thought of seeing strangers living here.'

'Oh. I see.'

'It's different with you. I think you two would have hit it off famously.'

'That's what Harold said yesterday.'

They carried the mahogany bookcase into the living room.

'You realise,' she said, when they were taking a rest, 'I'll have to put this back again when I leave.'

'Don't worry, I'll still be here to give you a hand. I have one and a half months left before my check-up.'

They opened the small drawer in the base of the bookcase. Inside they found picture hooks and old nails.

'Oh good,' Rose said. 'We can hang the pictures up.'

Later, out in the garden, they spread out Miss Hilda's white damask tablecloth in the centre of a rug and set out bone-handled cutlery, the vase of flowers, cut-glass wine glasses and delicate china, surrounding it with cushions. Alec prepared the salad while Rose carved the chicken and threw chunks of bread on to plates. They settled down on the cushions, and Alec poured cider into their glasses.

He raised his one high. 'To Hilda,' he said. 'May her spirit live on.'

Rose lifted her glass, and took a mouthful. 'It's so cool,' she murmured.

They piled salad and potatoes on to their plates and ate the chicken with their fingers.

'Where did you find that extraordinary dress?' he asked.

'In one of the trunks. It's a petticoat. Edwardian, I think.'

'It suits you. Do you know, Hilda used to dress up, too. When it was hot she'd wear these Greek-tunic affairs. She said she found them more comfortable to work in, especially when gardening. The farmer who delivered her milk and eggs nearly crashed his van when he first saw her in one.'

'I suppose it was all over the village.'

'Of course. But everyone accepted she was mad anyway. They had a field day when she took in evacuees. When her "vaccees" went to the village school, the local children would gather round them and bombard them with questions. "You'm stayin' wi Mad Hilda, ent you?" they'd say. "What's it like?"'

'Didn't the billeting officers mind her having them? I mean, if people thought she was mad . . .'

'It's more acceptable to be a bit loopy if you're upper class. Also, she usually took in children no one else wanted. She'd turn up late at the village hall, after most people had chosen theirs from the latest batch of arrivals, and invariably she'd find a stubborn group of scruffy brothers and sisters who had refused to be separated, or a scowling unattractive little specimen of humanity. "I go for the ones that are rejected," she'd say. "They're usually more interesting to live with anyway."'

'Did they like living with her?'

'Most of them did. Some were scared of her. Others were just plain homesick. I used to pop in and play with them when I was on leave. Sometimes she would have as many as eight children in the cottage sleeping top and tail in the beds. Her brother hadn't dared to object since he had managed to wriggle out of taking in any evacuees.

'She used to be sad to see them leave,' he said, 'but she always used to say, "It doesn't matter if I've only managed to have them for a fortnight. They've had a holiday and a taste of a different kind of life. They've seen the sea and heard it from their bedrooms at night. They've been able to run wild, pick flowers, and make castles out of sand."'

'Did the village children come anywhere near her?'

'Oh yes. Only they used to snoop behind the wall. Hilda said they were rotten stalkers. They giggled and whispered too much for a start. She sometimes used to sneak up behind them and say, "Boo!" and they'd run off shrieking. She'd catch them scrumping, too.'

'Scrumping?'

'Stealing apples. One day, she caught two of the Clarence boys by the scruff of the neck and announced that they could either choose to flee empty-handed and she would tell their mother or they could help her pick them, stay for tea and take some apples with them.' He gave a broad smile. 'Of course they stayed. Tea with Mad Hilda was too good a chance to miss. It made a good story for weeks.'

'But I thought the Clarence boys are all in the services.'

'They are. This was well before I arrived.'

Rose leaned across the tablecloth and picked up a potato. 'How did you first get to know her?'

'Very dramatically. She came into the bookshop, took one look at me and just crumpled to the floor.'

'Why?'

'I don't know. She was terribly apologetic about it afterwards, but she was shaking so badly at the time, that I took her upstairs and gave her a brandy. We got talking, found we were both mad about books, and just hit it off.'

'Did she ever talk much about her past?'

'Not a lot. As you know she spent eight years in a mental institution thanks to her father, and her brother got her out.' He took a gulp of cider. 'She'd obviously caused the family acute embarrassment which is why I suppose they wouldn't have anything to do with her. People have strange reactions to nervous breakdowns. I discovered that with Louise. She gave me a very hasty farewell.'

Rose hesitated. 'But that's all Miss Hilda told you?'

'Yes. I had the feeling she was afraid to tell me more, so I didn't push it. I respected her privacy.'

Rose blushed deeply. If Alec had been reticent about asking Miss Hilda personal questions, he would be appalled if he knew Rose had been reading her private journals. She couldn't tell him about the diaries now. Not yet, anyway.

'I'm surprised this place hasn't been requisitioned since her death,' she said.

'It's her brother's property. As long as he officially keeps

some sort of evacuees here he can get away with it, I suppose.'
He smiled. 'I'm pleased he has done, aren't you?'

She laughed. 'Very pleased.'

After they had eaten, Alec climbed up one of the apple trees
and shook the branches. Rose stood underneath attempting
to catch them in the skirt of her dress and shrieking with
laughter every time they missed and hit her. They packed the
apples in the boxes in layers and cleared up the leaves. Over
a tea of picnic leftovers, they chatted aimlessly about what
to do with the fruit, whether to make cider or apple jam
from it, or exchange it for someone's peas, which were in
plentiful supply that year, and then went indoors to hang up
the pictures.

When they had finished, they gazed at the walls, pleased
with their hard work.

'It's good to see them up again,' Alec murmured, and he
touched Rose gently on the shoulder.

They sat on the floor amongst the books and attempted to
put them in some kind of order. It was slow work because they
kept browsing and reading bits out to one another.

Rose turned the wireless on, and it was while they were
listening to the nine o'clock news that they heard that Italy had
surrendered. Before they realised what they were doing, they
found they were hugging one another. They let go hurriedly,
both blushing furiously.

'It's wonderful news, isn't it?' said Rose eventually, but they
knew she was only speaking to break the silence.

They returned to putting the books into the bookcase.

'Have you thought any more about what you want to do
after the end of this month?' Alec asked.

'Not yet.'

'Only, in about six weeks' time I shall have to go for my medical. Chances are that I'll be passed as fit. Before I go, I'd like to complete the opening chapter of a novel. It's taking for ever at the moment. I haven't put pen to paper for two years, so it's rather like riding a very rusty bicycle uphill. Added to which, I keep having interruptions from customers. Thanks to Dot, word's been spreading about my collection of thrillers so there's a steady flow of visitors from *Hôtel Maternité*. He paused. 'So I was wondering, if you'd be interested in working in the bookshop. Part-time, if you like, so you'll have time to write, too.'

'Alec!' she cried. 'But are you sure you need me? I mean, couldn't you take your typewriter downstairs?'

'And have people peering over my shoulder? No thanks. I'd pay you, of course.'

'But you can't afford it.'

'I have my army salary. You don't have to give me an answer straight away. But you will think about it, won't you?'

'Yes, of course.'

She placed the books in her arms in the alcove nearest her. Alec gazed at her for a moment.

'How extraordinary,' he murmured, and then stood up quickly. 'It's late. I'd better be going.'

'Could you pop in to Mrs Clarence's and tell her I haven't been savaged by wolves, or kidnapped.'

'Of course.'

As he was leaving she noticed his knapsack on the chair in the kitchen.

She tucked it under her arm and ran outside. He had already reached the coastal path.

'Alec!' she yelled. 'Alec!'

He turned and waved.

She held up the knapsack.

'It's for you,' he called. 'I mentioned it earlier, remember?'

She stood in the doorway and watched him walk down the path.

'Thank you,' she said softly.

For the rest of the week Alec and Rose continued to spend every available afternoon or day in the boat. The bookshop was left unattended. They had to make the best of the good weather, he explained. At times they wouldn't talk at all, and Rose was surprised not to feel awkward. They would sit quietly in the boat, daydreaming as the boat rocked from side to side and then drift back into conversation.

Rose decided she would work at the bookshop, broke the news to Mrs Clarence and left a message for Diana to phone. After a long talk, Mrs Clarence agreed to back her decision and Rose sent another letter to Aunt Em, explaining and confessing all, even the non-existence of Miss Hutchinson. She waited anxiously for the reply.

One morning, she was in the garden carrying a pitcher of water from the pump when Mrs Potts flew by the hedge on her bicycle.

'Blustery mornin', ent it?' she said, referring to the sudden influx of wind from the sea.

'Yes,' agreed Rose. She pulled the sleeves of her jersey down and left the pitcher by the kitchen door.

'You got a letter,' Mrs Potts announced.

The address on the envelope was in Aunt Em's handwriting. Rose picked up the pitcher and went into the kitchen, closing the door hurriedly behind her.

There was a knock at the door. She flung it open. Mrs Potts was still standing there.

'Yes,' said Rose abruptly.

'You ent got any other names, 'ave you?' she asked. 'Only you're the only Rose I know round 'ere.'

'Other names?'

'The name Jolliffe,' went on Mrs Potts. 'Mean anything?'

'Why, yes. It's my mother's maiden name!'

'Only I got a letter for a Rose Jolliffe.'

'That'll be me. You'd better give it to me.'

'I 'ent got it 'ere.'

'Why not?'

'She didn't 'ave this address on her, did she?'

'Who didn't?'

'The letter.'

'Well, where is it?' cried Rose, growing more exasperated.

'At the bookshop. It had the bookshop's address on the envelope. Care of, it said.' She paused. 'I got a feeling it's from London. Just a feeling, mind.'

'London?'

Rose grabbed her gabardine cape from behind the door. My story, she thought, it must be news about my story.

'Know what it is?' asked Mrs Potts eagerly.

'No,' she lied.

Drat, she'd have to go into Salmouth on the coastal path by foot. If she cycled, Mrs Potts would be sure to accompany her and interrogate her about her family's life history. She'd have to read Aunt Em's letter on the way. She stuffed it into her pocket, and ran down the path, leaving Mrs Potts to stare after her, at the gate.

*

Alec was standing at the window. As soon as he spotted her in the lane, he flung the door open.

'There's a letter,' he began.

'I know,' she gasped. She rested her hands on her knees, her chest heaving. 'Mrs Potts told me.'

He held the envelope out to her.

She shook her head. 'No. You open it.'

He ripped the envelope apart and dragged the letter out. She noticed he was trembling. He smiled.

'You've done it,' he yelled. 'You've done it!'

He grabbed her round the waist and whirled her round, shouting and whooping. Rose flung her hands round his neck. At that moment, the old woman from the fishing-tackle shop happened to be passing. She peered at them through the window.

Rose started to giggle. She tugged at Alec's shirt sleeve and pulled him round. They broke apart, unable to stop laughing.

Alec waved the letter at her. 'Good news!' he shouted, but she was already walking away, her head shaking.

'Oh, Alec, I can't believe it. It's like a fairy tale.' She wiped her eyes hurriedly. 'You're sure they've sent it to the right person. They might have got hold of the wrong story.'

'Read it yourself.'

Rose stared at the letter and blew her nose.

'I know I'm being silly,' she blurted out, 'but you see I don't even know this person and he doesn't know me and yet he's been swept along by the story, and he likes the characters. Even if he didn't want to publish it but just believed the story, that would be enough, but this . . .' She glanced back down at it. 'And the money. It couldn't come at a better time. Alec, you won't need to pay me!'

He stopped smiling. 'I'm not a charity case,' he muttered.

'I'm sorry, I didn't mean . . .' Her voice trailed away.

He touched her shoulder. 'Sorry. I'm a bit touchy about that sort of thing.'

'Are you sure you still want me?' she asked quietly.

'Of course I do. But don't feel you have to work here now. Having this money will mean you can take more time off to write.'

'I want to work here.'

'Then you must let me pay you.'

'Alec, why don't you just feed me instead?'

He frowned.

'And let me have the odd book,' she added.

'No. If someone else worked here I'd pay them. Just because you're a friend I don't see why I shouldn't.'

'But it might spoil our friendship.'

'On the contrary. You can't buy groceries with sandwiches or books. I don't think it would go down very well with the grocer.'

'All right,' she laughed. 'You win.'

He turned the sign on the door round to 'Closed'.

'What are you doing?'

'I'm not opening until we've had a celebration breakfast.'

He insisted on opening a bottle of homemade wine. The bottle was covered in dust, as were the glasses from his junk room. While he fried bread and tomatoes and his week's ration of bacon, Rose sat at the table rereading the letter. Alec poured the wine into the rinsed glasses.

'I still can't believe it,' she said. 'I mean, for years I've told myself I'm no good and every time I handed in an essay, the teachers told me I was no good, too, though I did do reasonably well at English in my School Cert.'

'Cheers,' he said, 'and congratulations.'

She raised her glass and swallowed the dark liquid. 'Oh, it's lovely!' And she took another mouthful.

'Blackcurrant wine. I made it my first autumn here. It's 1938 vintage.'

She twiddled the stem of the glass in her fingers. 'I was just thinking of all the other things I've convinced myself I'm hopeless at,' she went on, 'that I've never even dared to try or I've kept a secret because I couldn't bear anyone to see how awful I was at them. If you hadn't persuaded me to submit this story, it'd be lying in a box somewhere with all my other bits and pieces. I mean, there might be lots of other things I can do that I don't know anything about. I might be quite a different person underneath.' She looked at him. 'It's a bit frightening, succeeding at something when you're used to failing.'

After breakfast Alec saw her to the doorway and turned back the sign on the door.

'Will you be working on your book today?' she asked.

'Yes.'

'How's it going?'

'It's like squeezing porridge through muslin.'

'I know the feeling,' said Rose.

Elated, she ran up the lane, giggly and giddy from the wine. She knew having her story accepted wouldn't turn her instantly into a professional writer. But it didn't matter. A stranger had liked it; had liked it so much that he wanted his magazine to print it, so that hundreds of other strangers could read it.

1 October, the day Rose was to start work at the bookshop, fell on a Friday. Aunt Em had agreed to let her stay after a further

pleading letter from Rose and a long phone-call conversation between them.

It was a crisp morning. The mist drifted across the sea and cliffs like an icy fog. As she cycled towards the village she had such butterflies in her stomach that she had to stop for a moment to steady herself. She took a deep breath and pushed herself off again.

It was odd watching Alec turn the 'Closed' sign round to 'Open'. She had seen him do it so many times, yet it seemed altogether different. They beamed at one another like a couple of children, and after a joint breakfast, went their separate ways, she downstairs, he upstairs.

Why Rose panicked at the thought of receiving money for a book and giving back the change was a mystery, for it was really quite simple. By the end of the day she was looking for something more complex to do. She found some old account books with paper stuck at random in them and underneath, several boxes filled with dated receipts.

The next day, while they shared a sandwich lunch, she asked Alec if she could sort them out.

'It's all yours,' he said. 'I'm afraid it's another of those jobs I've been putting off. All the information is there. It just needs to be put in order and entered into the books.'

Rose enjoyed working at the bookshop. She soon grew used to leaving a book as soon as the doorbell jangled and returning to where she had left off once the customer had gone. Although she loved reading and scribbling down ideas, at times she felt restless and would have reorganisational purges or make displays behind the well-washed window.

Alec typed out her new story. Until Rose had learnt to type more proficiently he had insisted on doing it.

A bundle of chatty letters arrived from her mother although any clues to her whereabouts had been heavily censored. They were two months old. The last letter broke the news that she would be unable to come home in September and that further letters to Rose would be forwarded to her school. Luckily, Aunt Em had already informed the headmistress that Rose would not be returning there.

Diana still hadn't written but had phoned from Harrogate promising to do so soon. General Training and Duties now occupied most of her waking hours.

One day in the shop, Rose asked Alec if she could finish early on the following Saturday. 'There's a dance in Tindlecombe,' she explained. 'And I'm bursting to go. I've got so much energy.'

'Do you mind if I come, too?' he asked.

'No. I didn't think you liked that sort of thing.'

'You do have some funny ideas about me.'

Mrs Clarence gave her some pale pink floral curtain material and Dot made it up into a dress. Her lace-ups were far from elegant, but so many women wore them that she hoped they wouldn't look conspicuous.

On Saturday evening, she bathed and changed at Mrs Clarence's and Alec picked her up in Harold's horse and cart.

Alec had trimmed his beard. He was wearing brown corduroy trousers, a tweed jacket and trilby hat, a white shirt with a tweedy tie and a grey waistcoat. The journey passed remarkably quickly for she and Alec hardly stopped talking. Soon Harold's cart was clattering down the cobbles towards the square.

Hordes of young people were heading for the town hall.

Village girls sat on the benches round the square, surrounded by G.I.s who were offering them cigarettes and gum.

After depositing the cart at the blacksmith's, Alec held out his arm for her to take.

She slipped her arm through his, and they smiled at one another.

'Shall we go?' he said.

She nodded happily.

As they entered the hall, she glanced round quickly for a familiar face. Spotting the Land Army girl who had yelled out at her about her knicker elastic she waved, but the girl only gave a puzzled look.

'Oh,' she said, squeezing Alec's arm, 'she doesn't recognise me.'

They made their way through the crowd in the hall and sat down on some chairs by the wall. The band tuned up, there was silence for a moment, the piano player gave them a nod and the music began. It was a foxtrot. At first Rose felt awkward but Alec's touch was so firm that she soon found herself relaxing into it. The lovely thing about dancing with him was that they fitted together. All she needed to do was to tilt her chin slightly and they were eye to eye.

She gave a laugh.

'What's the joke?' he said, manoeuvring her slowly round a farm labourer who was bravely attempting to persuade one of the village girls to dance.

'I was just thinking about the dance evenings in the school gym. Me leading Miss Cuthbertson, my geography mistress, past the horses and wall ladders.'

They whirled into a quickstep. He whisked her out of the way of a large couple.

'Heaven, I'm in heaven,' he sang as they drifted into the next number.

At the end of two more dances they took a break. Rose collapsed into a chair and attempted to fan herself with her hand while Alec went to fetch them a drink.

'Care to dance, lady?' drawled a boyish voice.

She looked up to find a tall freckled G.I. with spiky brown hair smiling rather bashfully at her.

'I'm sorry but I'm sitting this one out.'

'Oh.'

She could see he was disappointed. Suddenly she remembered how kind Tony had been to her at her first dance. She wondered what had happened to him. Under her dress she could feel the silk underwear he and the other G.I.s had given her. She smiled.

'What about one quick dance?' she asked. 'Will that do? It's just that my friend is getting me some scrumpy and I'd like to be back to drink it sometime.'

'Oh sure,' he said excitedly.

Once they reached the dance floor he began to grow awkward.

'Listen, I ain't so dandy at dancing,' he confessed. 'It was a nerve asking you, seeing as you're so good. And if you don't mind me saying so, ma'am,' he gulped, 'you're the prettiest girl I ever did see. Sure are the prettiest here. All the guys think so, too.'

'Stop it,' she laughed. 'You're embarrassing me.'

They rose and shuffled rhythmically into a foxtrot. Once or twice Rose noticed Alec gazing sadly at the young soldiers, for although there were only five or more years between them, he seemed much older.

Towards the end of the evening the floor was cleared for fifteen minutes while a half a dozen couples threw themselves wildly into the jitterbug.

'I'll just sit this one out,' said Alec.

Unknown to Rose, the Land Army girl had suddenly recognised her and was whispering to the group at her table. Within seconds a stocky G.I. was standing in front of her.

'Excuse me, ma'am,' he said politely, 'but I hear you're kinda good at this. Care to join me?'

'I'd love to,' Rose laughed, and she walked swiftly with him to the centre of the hall.

'Attagirl!' yelled the Land Army girl as he hurled her over his back and on to his hip. 'No orange peel this time? Shame.'

Alec watched astounded.

Soon the remaining couples backed away, leaving Rose and her partner. The drummer hammered away in an incessant rhythm as Rose's dress went flying.

'Yahoo!' hollered the pianist. 'Look at 'em cats go!'

As the number rose to a crescendo and ended, the hall erupted into applause.

'You're good!' exclaimed the soldier as he walked her back to her chair.

'You're not so bad yourself,' she panted back.

A crooner stood on the platform and the slower sentimental numbers began; 'Dearly Beloved', 'Moonlight Becomes You', 'A Nightingale Sang in Berkeley Square'.

> 'I'll be seeing you,' he sang,
> 'In all the old familiar places
> That my heart and mind embraces
> All day through.'

Rose rested her head on Alec's shoulder as they glided into the last waltz.

'You know,' she murmured, 'you're so comfortable.'

Hot and sticky, they poured out with the soldiers and women, through the blackout drapes and doors, and into the chill night. They walked briskly towards the blacksmith's stable where they picked up the horse and cart, and jogged slowly out of Tindlecombe. In spite of the tartan rug over her knees, Rose began to shiver.

'Put my greatcoat on,' he said. 'It's in the back.'

She wrapped it round herself, her arms lost in the heavy sleeves.

Alec let the reins hang loosely in his hands.

'Thank goodness we lied to my mother,' said Rose happily.

'About Miss Hutchinson?'

'Yes. Otherwise . . .' She stopped.

'Otherwise you would have been just a clumsy shy schoolgirl who one day happened to fall in and fall out of my bookshop and I would never have seen you again.'

'I was so embarrassed that day. I hated myself for it.' She smiled. 'I'm glad I came to Salmouth.'

'So am I.'

'Why did you decide to live there? Had you gone there for holidays?'

'No. I came across it when I was trying to find out who my parents were. My mother told me that the orphanage I'd been collected from was in this county. I went there to make enquiries but they refused to give any information. Legally I didn't have a hope in hell of forcing them to tell me anything either.

'I still had ten days' holiday left so, rather than turn back,

I thought I'd try to walk the fury out of my system. I took the coastal route. Days later I walked into Salmouth and fell instantly in love with it.'

'And you came across the bookshop?'

'Yes and no. It wasn't a bookshop then. It was empty and up for sale. It was pretty dilapidated at the time so was going cheap. I had some savings and when my father saw how enthusiastic I was, he offered to help set me up.

'I think he was relieved I'd found something I wanted to do; relieved I was going to be out of his sight,' he said, 'so he wouldn't have to be confronted with all his years of lying to me.'

'You don't believe that, do you?'

'I don't know. He did try to get on with me. And later he came and visited me in Salmouth. I tried to bring my adoption out into the open. I thought if we discussed it, it would relieve the tension, but he couldn't talk about it. After his death, my mother talked more openly about it. That's how I know my real father died in the last war.

'Anyway, I bought the shop in the autumn of 1938, and in between army postings, I've been there ever since. When you turned up, I'd only been there two months after it had been empty for nearly a year. And I'd already left it in a bit of a mess.'

'I think you've done wonders with it. I love it.'

'So do I,' he added quietly.

They passed dark fields and ducked under archways of branches.

'Your adoptive father?' began Rose.

'Yes?'

'Do you miss him?'

'I suppose I do. And my mother. Though I'm still angry with her.'

'I miss my father. I wish he'd known about my story being accepted. Perhaps then he would have been proud of me.'

'From the little you've told me, I suspect he already was.'

'Do you think so?' She paused. 'I was his favourite. I didn't try to be,' she added hastily. 'It just sort of happened that way. Poor old Diana. He rather left her out of things. With me he could have a good argument or laugh. But with Diana, he just admired her like a lovely ornament you weren't to touch. I never knew she was so cut up about it until she told me the night before she left. And I'd been jealous of her because I thought she was loved for herself, that she never had to earn his love. But I remember now, I was the one who got the hugs. And I was the one he stuck up for when I got into trouble for being unladylike. I'm afraid it caused a lot of friction. There's no one to stick up for me now. Except for Aunt Em. But she's often away.'

'And me,' he said.

She laughed. 'Thanks.'

They fell silent for a moment.

'Alec,' she said slowly, 'when you bought the shop what did Louise think about it?'

'I didn't know her then. We met the following summer. She used to stay in the hotel in Salmouth every year with friends and relatives.'

'In the one you call *Hôtel Maternité*?' Rose asked.

He nodded. 'One rainy day she visited the bookshop and we got talking. The next day was sunny but she popped in again and invited me to join her and her friends for drinks that evening. I was flattered. She was very attractive.'

'Oh,' said Rose dismally.

'Would you rather I stopped?'

'No. Go on.'

'Knowing she was only in Salmouth for a short period we saw each other every day. Her holiday came to an end and I thought that was that. Within weeks I was called up and sent to an army barracks not far from where she lived.

'I think I was in love with love. The odd thing was that I never really felt comfortable in her presence but I thought that was what being in love was all about. Of course her parents weren't too happy about it.'

'Why?'

'I was "in trade". Her father offered me work in his business after the war was over. Work in the city.'

'You mean bowler hats and pin-striped suits?'

'That's right.'

'I couldn't imagine you doing anything like that.'

'Neither could I. I explained that I already had a business of my own. Louise thought that, in time, I'd change my mind. After Dunkirk we were officially engaged, and she said she didn't mind living in Salmouth as long as there was a separate kitchen, and a place for the maid to sleep. I was stumped. Then the house next door came up for sale. You don't earn a lot of money selling second-hand books so I had no savings. But I had the most extraordinary stroke of luck: the kind of luck that only happens in detective novels. An old lady, who had holidayed in Salmouth and had enjoyed making use of my bookshop, died and left me a considerable amount of money.'

'What! But who was she?'

'I haven't the faintest idea.'

'Didn't you try and find out?'

'Oh yes. I traced the solicitor in London but he was under oath to keep her name anonymous. In the end, I was forced to give up.'

'And you bought the house next door?'

'Yes. I let the fishmonger stay in the shop part. He was delighted. Harold appeared out of the blue saying, "Got any odd jobs then?" Word had obviously got round.

'With his help we put an adjoining door in the wall of the first-floor room and turned one room into a sitting room and the other room above the fishmonger's into a kitchen. Then we took down a wall upstairs, hence the long corridor with the bedrooms leading off it.

'Louise and her mother came down. Her mother said it was fine for a summer residence but . . .' He shrugged. 'It wasn't long before they were suggesting it might be better to sell it all and buy a proper house, instead of one that was above a shop. I was posted abroad for a while so I procrastinated.'

'But I don't understand. If Louise and her family were so critical about the way you lived, why did she want to marry you?'

'I was doing well in the army. Moving swiftly up the ranks. Having nice things said about me. Louise had this image of me and unfortunately I didn't fit it. I'm not blaming her. We were both letting each other down. I expected her to be less conformist, she expected me to be more so.'

Rose looked away. 'Did you ever . . .' she began. 'With her?'

'Yes.'

She wrapped his greatcoat tighter round herself. 'Alec, how do you feel about me and Derry having had . . .'

She couldn't say the word.

'Sex?'

'Yes.'

'At first I was furious. Then I was jealous.'

'There's nothing to be jealous of.' She paused. 'Do you think you can have strong feelings for someone and not love them?'

'Yes. Don't you?'

'Yes. That's how it was with Derry.' She sighed. 'Oh dear, it's all so complicated.'

They took a circular route round Salmouth and turned out of the lane and on to the one which would take them to Lapwing Cottage. As the horse pulled them over the brow of the hill they looked down the lane and beyond to the sea. A full moon shimmered across the surface of the water. A light rain started to fall.

'I'm putting the boat into the shed tomorrow,' he murmured. 'I'll be there all day if you want to find me.'

'That means autumn's really here, doesn't it?'

'Yes.'

As he shook the reins and they moved forward she was conscious of not wanting to leave him, of not wanting him to leave her.

When they reached the cottage she turned to look at him. Tiny drops of rain were scattered on his beard, and one of his collars was sticking up over the lapel of his jacket. It was frayed at the edge. He was smiling, his dark eyes laughing, his damp crumpled hat tilted to one side. He looked so beautiful she was unable to speak. How was it she had never noticed him like this before? But of course she knew. It was because she felt so at home with him. He had always accepted *her* in spite of her ugliness. But then strangely enough, she had never felt ugly with him; never even given her looks a thought.

She realised then, that aside from being on her own, he was the one person with whom she could feel totally herself.

I'd go anywhere with you, she thought. If you were lost in a jungle the other side of the world, I would search it till I found you.

'I'll see you tomorrow then,' he said gently.

Dazed she nodded and clambered down.

She watched him turn the cart round; watched him as he climbed up the lane towards the hill.

'I love you,' she whispered.

It wasn't till he had disappeared from sight and she went to open the gate that she glanced down and realised she was still wearing his voluminous greatcoat.

Seventeen

In the morning she left the cottage as usual for work, her head lowered to counteract the strong wind which was blowing inland. She mounted the bike and pushed off, while the wind sent her wobbling in zig-zags up the hill. Above her the sky grew leaden. She pedalled faster.

By the time she had reached Alec's yard, the sky had opened and the rain tipped down. She ran with the bike into a small lean-to shed, unbuckled the bicycle bag with Alec's overcoat in it and peered outside. It was teeming. She sprinted through the yard and alleyway, and into the bookshop. The door above the steps opened, and Alec poked his head out.

'I'm not late, am I?' she asked.

'No. Come up and dry off.'

Upstairs a fire was burning in the grate. She dumped the damp bicycle bag on the floor.

'Your greatcoat's squashed in there,' she explained. 'I forgot to give it back last night. I must have had my head in the clouds.'

Realising what she had said, she hastily lifted her cape over her head to conceal her blushes.

'You look like a drowned rat,' he said snatching the dripping cape from her. 'I'll put this up in the bathroom. Go and stand in the warm.'

He returned with a towel.

'Here,' he said, pushing her into the armchair. 'Let's dry your hair.'

Before she could protest he clasped her head in a handful of towel and began rubbing vigorously. For a moment she felt as though she was six again, and it was her father drying her after a bath. The song he used to sing to her came flooding back.

Alec leant back and surveyed her tangled mass of blue-black curls. 'What's that you're humming?'

'I can't remember all the words–

'"You're as pretty as a picture",' she sang.
'"Has anyone ever told you before?
You're the image of an angel from above
And you are just meant for me to adore".'

'Why, thank you.'

She laughed. 'There was a bit about "your eyes, your hair" and "you must have walked out of a dream". My father used to sing it to me.'

Just then the window gave a loud rattle and the room grew dark. They stood up and walked over to it. The rain was falling heavily.

'It's a real old storm,' remarked Alec, and without thinking he slid his arms round her waist and rested his chin on her head.

'I love this kind of weather,' he murmured. 'When I was a boy I used to go camping and sometimes I'd sleep in the boat under a tarpaulin. I'd stretch it over the boom and tie it down, and I'd curl up in my sleeping bag underneath. It was like sleeping in a floating bivouac. When it rained I used to lie there listening to it pattering on the canvas and feel so snug and warm that I wanted to stay awake for ever.'

'I've never been camping. I'd love to.'

By now the rain had almost obliterated the bay and peninsula from view.

'We could pretend this room is a tent,' she said, leaning back happily.

'And the bookshop is the boat,' added Alec, 'and the village is the sea.'

'And we're in the middle of nowhere.'

They were interrupted by a loud hammering from downstairs. He released her.

'Must be a mermaid,' he said.

She laughed. 'And a large one by the sound of it. I'll answer it.'

The mermaid was Harold twisting his soaking cap in his hands. He looked distraught and gabbled out something which Rose could not understand.

'I'll go and fetch Alec,' she said.

He gave a brief nod.

She ran up the steps to the sitting room. 'Alec!' she yelled. 'Alec!'

He peered round the kitchen doorway. 'What's up?'

'It's Harold. He's in an awful state. Come quickly.'

She jumped swiftly down the steps, Alec following closely behind.

Red-faced and gasping for breath, Harold garbled out some frantic message.

'Wait there,' said Alec and he ran back up the steps and reappeared quickly with an oilskin, boots and sou'wester in tow.

'What is it?' asked Rose.

'There's been an accident up at Heathercombe Farm. Two men are trapped under a tractor. They need all the men they can get to lift it.'

Rose watched them make for the door. They were about to leave when Harold gripped Alec's shoulder.

"Tis messy,' Harold muttered and the rest was incomprehensible.

'Leave my feelings out of it,' said Alec quickly. 'I said I'm coming and that's that. Let's hurry. We're wasting time,' and they bolted into the lane leaving the door swinging noisily behind them.

Rose spent the afternoon attempting to read but found it impossible to concentrate. Every time anyone walked into or past the shop, she looked up sharply. At a quarter to six Alec still had not returned. At six o'clock Mrs Clarence opened the door.

'Jest came to see if you was all right,' she said, shaking her umbrella over the step. She glanced at Rose's head. 'Your hair's certainly got a bit of bounce to it now, hasn't it?'

Rose smiled. She imagined it must look a little extraordinary after Alec's rubbing.

'Alec's gone up to Heathercombe Farm. There's been an accident.'

'I heard,' said Mrs Clarence, quietly.

'I know about his breakdown,' Rose said, 'but it's all a bit confusing. I mean, Derry called him a coward, his fiancée thought he was unmanly, and yet people turn to him in a crisis. And there's this tremendous respect for him in the village.'

'People haven't forgotten Dunkirk, my love.' She paused. 'It's none of my business but since you came here he's been much happier. You've brought him back to life.'

Rose was about to point out it had been the other way round, but she couldn't get a word in.

'He's started to look his old self again,' Mrs Clarence continued. 'Why he kept that Derry living with him this summer, I'll never know. Nice enough boy but a bit too high and mighty.'

Mrs Clarence eyed the clock. 'Won't stay,' she said. 'I promised Dot I'd look after the baby. She wants to study her arithmetic.'

'Arithmetic?'

'Yes. She's got some idea of working in the market when she goes back to Walthamstow. It makes her feel nearer home if she works on her pounds, shillings and pence or whatever.'

After Mrs Clarence left, Rose felt even more alone. Outside, the sound of the rain grew louder. She moved restlessly, keeping the fire going in the kitchen range, filling the kettle with water, fetching towels from the bathroom and hanging them on the fireguard. She attempted to read, but was too jumpy. She was just giving the fire another prod when the door into the shop jangled. She grabbed the oil lamp and ran out of the room. He was standing at the foot of the steps drenched and covered in mud. His streaked face was ashen.

'Alec, are they all right?'

He nodded.

'Are you?'

It was a stupid question. He looked devastated. As she raised the lamp, he gazed up at her, struggling to speak.

'I c. .c. .can't s. .s. .seem . . .' he stammered.

'It's all right,' she reassured him, 'you don't have to say anything.'

'It's l. .l. .late,' he began. 'You, you should have g. .g. .gone home. You must, must . . .'

He started to shake uncontrollably.

'Come on,' she said, and she stepped down and took his arm.

She guided him into the sitting room, peeled off his oilskin and removed his caked boots. His clothes were soaking. He had no sooner sat down in an armchair than he sank his head into his hands.

Rose flung her arms round him.

'Sorry,' he gasped. 'All that blood!'

She held him tightly. 'You're wet through. Why don't you go and have a bath while I make us some toast? I've kept the range going, so the water should be hot.'

He gave a tired smile. 'That sounds good.'

While Alec retreated to the bathroom, Rose cut up some bread and stuck them on the end of a toasting fork over the fire. Her happiness seemed to swim deep into the pit of her stomach. She loved the feeling of her and Alec being cocooned together by the rain. She found herself singing, unable to stop. She turned the towels over on the fireguard. This simple action felt more intimate than all the wretched business she had experienced with Derry.

She held the piece of bread she was toasting near the bars of the grate. Just then he called out to her.

She jumped and dropped the fork on the hearth. 'Idiot,' she muttered to herself and she pressed her palms against her flushed face.

She grabbed the towels and ran out of the room.

'Is it unlocked?' she said, hovering outside.

The door opened and an arm appeared.

'I've shut my eyes,' she said quickly and held the towel out for him to take.

She was kneeling on the hearth rug pouring out tea when he came into the sitting room. She kept her eyes on the cups.

He sat cross-legged beside her. 'I'm a new man,' he announced.

She glanced aside at him.

He was smiling, his hair damp and tangled. He had put on a pair of old woollen trousers and a heavily knit roll-neck jersey.

She offered him the plate of toast.

He took her hand and kissed it.

'I shall have that hand stuffed and framed,' she said, attempting to cover her confusion.

After they had eaten they added some wood to the fire and leaned back against the foot of one of the armchairs. Alec put his arm round her and Rose sank happily against him.

He kissed the top of her head. 'I think it's too late for you to go home now. And you'd get soaked if you did. You're welcome to stay. You can sleep in the spare room.'

'Where Derry slept?'

'Yes.'

'No. I'd rather not if you don't mind.' She looked up at him. 'In there, I mean.'

'Because of Derry?'

'Yes. I suppose I'm still angry with him for leaving without saying a word.'

He brushed her face with his fingers. 'You can have my bed.'

'Alec.'

'M'm.'

'Did you and Louise ever . . .' She swallowed. 'I mean, up there?'

'No. Why do you ask?'

'I don't know. I just wondered.'

'Would it make any difference if we had?'

'Yes.'

'To us?'

'No. To me sleeping in it.' She gazed down at the floor which was now blurred.

'I'll go and change the sheets then,' he said.

'No, don't,' she said quickly. 'I don't mind that you've slept in them.'

She turned to meet his eyes.

'You don't have to sleep in the spare room,' she whispered. 'I mean, you could . . .' She stopped. 'We could . . .'

'What?'

'I'm afraid of saying it. It's just I'm a bit scared.'

'Me too.'

They smiled bashfully at one another.

'Let's go to bed then,' he said.

They were halfway up the stairs, their arms wrapped

round each other's waists, when Alec halted.

'What is it?' she asked.

'You and Derry. When you went to bed, was it . . .?'

'It was ghastly,' she interrupted.

He smiled.

'Alec,' she protested. 'You look *pleased*.'

He laughed. 'Do I?'

'Yes, you do.'

'I'll try not to,' he said still smiling broadly, 'but it'll be difficult.'

Rose woke to find Alec's knees tucked underneath hers. He was holding her round the waist. As she snuggled back into him, he kissed her shoulder. She tucked her head under his chin.

'And don't tell me you're going to have that shoulder stuffed as well,' he said.

She laughed sleepily.

'Do you know,' he remarked, kissing her between words. 'It looks as though you have pink straps where the lines of your tan end.' He peeped under the bedclothes. 'Yes. You're wearing a pink bathing suit.'

'I was too shy to lie naked in the cove.'

'Are you shy now?'

She turned to face him. 'A little.'

He was smiling.

'I can't believe this is happening to me,' she said.

'Me neither.'

They nestled into one another and for a while lay motionless, too exhilarated to move. She drew away from him gently. In the semi-darkness she saw his skin. It was pale. She touched his shoulders, letting her fingers trail through the hair on his chest. He was so smooth and warm, she thought.

Suddenly they found they were kissing, their mouths moving round each other's mouth, on and on and on till they collapsed apart into the pillows for breath, beaming at one another.

'I rather like your pink bathing suit,' he said rolling back towards her.

She clasped her hands loosely behind his neck. 'Do you?'

'M'm. In fact I like it so much I'm going to kiss it.'

'Not all of it though?'

'All of it. Every single inch of it.'

'You wouldn't dare,' she said laughing shyly.

'Oh, wouldn't I?'

The next night Rose stayed at the bookshop again. Alec didn't ask her to stay, or she him. They suddenly realised, when they were squashed up together in one of the armchairs by the fire that it was three in the morning, and were quite bewildered at how quickly the time had passed.

Early the next morning, Alec left Salmouth for his medical check-up. It was the first day of November; five days before Rose's eighteenth birthday.

Rose found the bookshop very quiet without him. She missed the sound of his typewriter from upstairs, the creak of the floorboards when he walked up and down the living room thinking, or his sudden appearances at the top of the stairs when he was taking a break.

When it came to locking up the shop and going home, she found she was trembling. She was certain Alec would be passed as fit, and she dreaded the possibility of him being posted abroad.

The ride back to Lapwing Cottage seemed long and lonely. At the top of the hill, overlooking the lane, she took her feet off the pedals and let the bicycle carry her speedily downwards. She hauled it through the gate and leaned it by the wall by the garden door. She paused to look at the garden, at the trees canopied in gold and russet leaves and the wild flowers lying bedraggled along the wall. A sharp gust of wind sent the leaves scattering like giant confetti across the tiny lawn.

She stepped into the cottage. The rooms were cold. After a scrappy meal, she lit the fire in the sitting room and turned on the wireless. She tried to listen but found herself staring at the fire. She waited until it had died out and then went to bed. She couldn't sleep. Wide awake, she lay in the dark thinking of Alec. She sat up, closed the curtains and relit the lamp. Outside, the wind was howling. She pulled the eiderdown up to her chin and looked round the room.

Beside her bed the cane table had a white lace tablecloth over it and on the nearest wall was a painting of a field filled with poppies. She felt a little better, as though Miss Hilda was trying to calm her. She picked up one of the diaries from the table and settled down to read.

It was obvious that Miss Hilda found it difficult to keep them going. After a few months of recording the day's events, there would be long gaps.

She kept up her trips to Gynmouth, made a few trips to London under great secrecy, and began to make friends, albeit not close ones, always having to be aware of her past. Rose carried on reading into the early hours, until she came across an entry written in the summer of 1938.

Hurrah! it read. *Rumour has it that a young man has bought up the old haberdashery next to the fishmonger's and is going to turn it into a second-hand bookshop. I've asked around and it seems pretty certain.*

Roll on the day!

Of course it's all the talk of Salmouth.

'What does Salmouth want with a bookshop?' they've been saying.

Fools!

'No one reads much round 'ere,' they keep pointing out.

Of course not. And why? Because they can't get hold of books.

With luck it'll be open by the autumn.

Oh, please let the rumours be true.

Bookshop, I shall be one of your first customers.

Rose closed the book.

No, she decided, it would be wrong to read about her friendship with Alec. She had read enough. She would definitely lock up the bureau. It would be different if she hadn't met Alec. But she realised that the next time she saw him, she would have to tell him.

Yawning, she opened the kitchen door to Mrs Potts.

'I got a letter for you,' she exclaimed. 'And two parcels. But I can't see where they'se from,' she added.

Her eyes fell on Alec's oiled jersey which Rose was wearing under the bib of her dungarees.

'Your buttons are still undone,' she pointed out.

'I know, Mrs Potts. I was just doing them up when you knocked.'

'How you gettin' on at the bookshop then?'

'Very well, thank you.'

'I 'eard you was stayin' on,' she went on. 'Don't you think you'se a bit young to be stayin' 'ere on yer own?'

'If I'm old enough to be called up, I'm old enough to stay here on my own, Mrs Potts.'

'How old are you then?'

'Eighteen. Well nearly.'

Mrs Potts beamed. 'I knew it! I knew it! Tis yer birthdeh, ent it! That's what all the parcels is fer. Well, well, well. Fancy that.'

'Yes, fancy that, Mrs Potts. Now can I have them?'

'What?'

'My parcels.'

'Oooh yes.' She handed them over gleefully. 'I wonder what's in there. I 'spect you can't wait to open them.'

'Well, I shall have to, won't I? Until my birthday. And now, if you'll excuse me, I'd like to finish dressing,' she added, closing the door.

She tore open the envelope. It contained a birthday card from Diana. Inside was a brief letter. Rose sat on the table to read it. Her sister sounded tired. She shared a room with lots of other women and from her account the women all grumbled together and rallied round if one of them went under.

'Next week,' murmured Rose, 'that might be me.'

Her birthday fell on the Saturday. She had decided to ask Harold to take her to Gynmouth on the Monday so that she could register for war work immediately.

Waiting for her at the bookshop was a letter addressed to Rose Jolliffe. She smiled. It was nice of Alec to have used her pseudonym.

'My darling Rose,' he had written.

'Apologies for hasty scrawl. All well on the medical

front. City diabolically noisy. Can't think for the racket. Takes me ten minutes to cross a road. And at night it's too quiet. Miss you and the sound of the wind and the sea. Don't know how many days I'll have to stay. Endless sorting-out jobs being done here. Bureaucracy is mad.

Longing to return to sanity and you,
Love Alec.'

It was the following morning, on her way into Salmouth, that she met Mr Partridge at the top of the hill.

'Hello, Mr Partridge,' she said casually. 'What brings you this way?'

He thrust his hand into his jacket pocket. 'I come to give you back half of this month's rent.'

'Oh, that's nice. Why?'

'You got to leave.'

Rose felt herself grow numb. He must have discovered she had got into the locked room. She swallowed. 'What do you mean?'

'Requisitioned. All this land, including the cottage. The major's got to be the same as everyone else now.'

'Oh, I see.'

He gave a smug grin. 'His influence in high places hasn't worked no more.'

'When do I have to leave?'

'Week Saturdee.'

'Oh well, there's nothing I can do, but it's a shame. I love living there.'

He peered at her. 'You do?'

'Yes. What's going to happen to it?'

'Hostel. Land Army.'

She took the money. 'What time Saturday week?'

He shrugged.

'I'd like to know when to clean up by,' she explained.

'Mrs Partridge'll see to that.'

'I'd rather do it myself. It's my way of saying a proper goodbye.'

He gave her a puzzled look. And then backed away slightly. Rose suppressed a smile. Did he think she was loopy? She remembered Miss Hilda saying once people thought you were mad, they didn't expect you to keep to the rules any more.

That evening she wandered round the rooms touching things as though seeing them for the first time. She had been full of good intentions about starting to return a few of them to the 'locked' room, but when she raised her hands to remove a picture from the wall, she found she couldn't do it. Instead, she sat by the fire and listened to Miss Hilda's records, endlessly rewinding the gramophone, and swopping the needles around.

Dot visited the bookshop the next afternoon. Rose held George so that she could sit on the floor and browse through the detective section in peace.

The bell above the door jangled. It was Mrs Clarence.

'Come for a book, Mrs C?' said Dot over her shoulder.

'No, love.' She gave Rose an anxious glance. 'Dot, there's a couple of people from London to see you.'

Dot rose slowly to her feet. 'Mum and Dad,' she whispered.

'No, my love. 'Tis Jack's parents.'

Rose saw the colour drain from Dot's face, saw her sway and clutch at the bookcase, and was unable to do anything with George in her arms.

Mrs Clarence caught hold of her. 'Now, my love,' she said. ''Tis all right. You hang on to me.'

She helped her to one of the chairs.

'He's dead, ain't he?' stated Dot dully.

'They don't know. They had a telegram sayin' how he was missin'.'

'Believed killed,' Dot finished for her.

'They haven't given up hope.'

Rose stood by the chair, and glanced quickly at Mrs Clarence.

'I don't understand,' said Dot lamely. 'What are they doing here?'

'They came to see you.' Mrs Clarence drew up a chair beside her and smoothed back her hair from her face. 'They didn't know you was expectin' Jack's baby.'

'But I thought everyone would've known.'

Mrs Clarence shook her head. 'Your father gave your mother, brothers and sisters strict instructions to tell everyone you were away on war work in a munitions factory up north. When Jack's parents got the telegram they came round to ask for your address, knowing how close you were. Your mother burst into tears, and it all came out.'

'But how did they find me?'

'Through the W.V.S. It's taken them months.'

'Months,' she whispered. 'So there's still no news.'

'No, my love.'

Dot grasped Mrs Clarence's hands. 'Are they angry with me?'

'They're angry that you didn't go to them for help.'

'Where are they now?'

'At my place.'

'Do I have to see them?'

'Yes.'

Dot stood up slowly. 'Me knees feel a bit wobbly.'

'You just hang on to my arm.'

'Can George stay 'ere with you, Roe?' she asked. 'I know it sounds daft, but they might have told the adoption people to be nearby to take him away from me.'

'They can't do that, Dot,' said Mrs Clarence.

'Mebbe not, but I'd feel braver if I knew he was being looked after, just till I know what's what.'

'He can stay with me for as long as you like,' said Rose.

'I'll leave his basket of nappies and things 'ere. It's by the table.'

Dot still hadn't returned by closing time. Rose shut up shop, lit the fire in the sitting room and put George in one of the armchairs. He had begun to cry. She had changed his nappy and sung him back to sleep, but she knew he would need feeding soon.

She was just shovelling some coke in the kitchen range when there was a loud knocking from downstairs. She stumbled down the stairs in the dark and unlocked the door.

Outside on the step stood Dot and a short squarely built couple in their forties. The man had a large bulbous nose and a crinkly sort of mouth. His stocky wife was round-faced with huge dark eyes.

'This is Jack's mum and dad,' said Dot. 'Mr and Mrs Wilson.'

She was smiling.

Relieved, Rose beckoned them in.

'Sorry about the dark,' said Rose, as they groped their way up the stairs behind her. 'I forgot to bring a lamp down.'

Once they reached the sitting room, they stood by the

doorway and stared at the baby in the armchair on the other side of the room. Mr Wilson hurriedly whipped out a handkerchief and pressed it hard into his eyes.

Dot was already crying.

'I'll make some tea,' Rose murmured, and she slipped out of the room to leave them on their own.

'So this is our grandson,' she heard Mr Wilson say hoarsely.

'Yeah,' answered Dot.

'George?'

'That's right. It reminded me of Jack, you know, when he was little, going off to see the last King's jubilee procession.'

'Yes, I remember,' said Mrs Wilson. 'You came round afterwards for tea.'

She broke off.

There was a long silence, and then Dot spoke. 'Mrs Wilson, would you like to hold him?'

'Are you sure that's all right, love?'

'Yeah. 'Course it is.'

Rose heard them move. She held her breath.

'Oh, Dot!' cried Mrs Wilson. 'He's just beautiful!' And then she heard her sniffing.

'I'm glad you fought to keep him,' said Mr Wilson gruffly.

'I couldn't do nothin' else, could I?'

'Your dad ought to 'ave some sense knocked into him. Anyone could see you and Jack was well-matched. If he'd have given his permission, this need never have happened.'

'All right, love,' interrupted Jack's mother, 'we've found her now.'

Rose heard Mr Wilson blow his nose.

'Are you sure you want me to live with you?' asked Dot hesitantly.

'Dot, you and George are all we got now.'

There was another long silence.

'Yeah,' said Dot at last.

Rose breathed easy again.

Dot peered into the kitchen.

'You're going back, aren't you?' said Rose.

'Yeah. We've talked it over. They're going to help me save up for a wedding ring, and make out me and Jack got married on the sly. As soon as I've got the ring I'm going to help out on Mr Wilson's stall. I'll have to get used to being called Mrs Wilson now.'

'What about your parents?'

She shrugged. 'I dunno. The Wilsons think they'll come round eventually.'

''Ere,' yelled Mr Wilson from the sitting room. 'We can hear every word you're saying about us. When are we goin' to be introduced?'

Dot grinned. 'I did introduce you,' she protested.

'No, you never. You introduced us to her, but we don't know her from a bar of soap, do we, Edie?'

Dot dragged her into the sitting room. 'This is Roe.'

'You're the writer, ain't you?'

Rose blushed. 'Well, not really. I've had a short story accepted, that's all.'

'Sounds good to me,' said Mr Wilson. 'Sounds very good. You can't start at the top, can you? It's rung by rung, ain't it? Now look at me. I started selling old apples off of a box when I was twelve. Now I got me own fruitstall. Well, I 'ad. Now it's what I can get, with rationing.'

Edie and Fred Wilson sat in the two armchairs and Dot and Rose sat on the floor with George between them, and they

313

talked; they talked about Walthamstow and how the market had kept going in spite of bombing, and reminisced over what Jack and Dot had done when they were children. They told Rose how they had been courting since Jack had left school at fourteen and how he used to save up his wages so he could take Dot out to the pictures.

'They was pictures mad,' said Edie. 'Sometimes they'd go three times in a week!'

And Dot told them how Rose had taken care of her at the cottage and how she had been the first to see George, until the sight of Mr Wilson's pale face caused her to stop.

'I think that's woman's talk, love,' said Edie. 'Men are such delicate creatures.'

Mr Wilson shot her a look. 'Me? Delicate?'

George began to cry.

'Mr Wilson,' said Dot, growing pink, 'I think George needs a feed.'

'What? Oh yes.'

'Come with me into the kitchen,' said Rose. 'You can tell me more about Walthamstow.'

'You'll be visiting us, of course. You're welcome any time, you know,' he said, following her eagerly. 'Any time.'

Rose lay back and wallowed in the bath. She hadn't told Dot about having to leave Lapwing Cottage for she knew she would tell Mrs Clarence, and she needed time to think. She gave a wry smile. Knowing how fast gossip spread, Mrs Clarence would hear soon enough anyway.

The water was already lukewarm. She was in the in-between stage, too cold to get out, too cold to stay in. She thought of her clothes warming on the fireguard downstairs. With one resolute movement she leapt out of the bath, wrapped a towel round her and fled out into the corridor and down the flight of stairs which led to the sitting room. She had just reached the doorway when she heard the door bell jangle. She froze. She could have sworn she had locked the door.

'Hello,' she said loudly.

Someone was in the bookshop. She heard the steps creak.

'Who's there?'

'Guess!'

The door swung open revealing a clean-shaven army lieutenant with close-cropped hair. Rose gripped the towel.

'Alec! Is that you?'

'Yes.'

'But where's your beard?'

'Lopped off. Beards don't go down well in the army.'

'But you look so different.'

'You don't like it.'

'It's not that. It's just you don't look like you.'

He took off his cap and threw it in the armchair. 'You're shivering,' he said.

He walked towards her and wrapped his arms round her.

'You'll get wet!' she protested.

He laughed. 'I know.' He picked her up and carried her to the fire. 'I'll dry you.'

Before she could argue he was rubbing her vigorously. 'Getting warmer?'

'A little.'

He removed the fireguard. 'That better?'

She nodded and then flung her arms round him. He gripped her tightly.

'Darling thing,' he whispered. 'Darling, darling thing.'

I never want to leave you, she thought. I never want you to leave me.

He held her face and covered her with kisses while she clasped his hands laughing, her eyes stinging.

'Don't cry,' he said, kissing her cheeks.

'It's because I'm happy.'

He kissed her mouth and she returned his kisses.

Scooping her up high above his head, he swung her round in his arms.

She buried her face into his cropped hair.

'How could they cut all this off,' she murmured.

He lowered her to the ground.

'And this uniform,' she added. 'It's so thick I can't feel you.'

'I'll take it off.'

They sank down on to the carpet, pulling the cushions off the armchairs, and lay in front of the fire with them scattered and tucked under their heads.

Rose felt herself dissolving into a delicious whirlpool, conscious of his fingers and arms stroking and caressing her and moving round her. She felt so fresh and alive, as though they were lying out in a field of high grass, kissing and kissing and kissing, drinking each other up in long heady draughts.

Rose flung back her head, rising on such peaks of delight that she almost tipped into unconsciousness. And then suddenly she was back on her childhood swing again but her legs and arms were round Alec and he was inside her, pushing her higher and higher till the pleasure was so exquisite that it caused her to cry out and she couldn't hold on to the ropes of the swing or Alec any longer. She threw her arms out high above her head, plummeting and soaring all in the same moment.

Eighteen

'Nine days,' she repeated quietly. 'Will they be sending you abroad?'

'No. It's a desk job. In London.'

They had dragged down the mattress, bedclothes and pillows from Alec's bedroom and put them on the floor in front of the fire. Stuck higgledy-piggledy on the mantelpiece and nearby table were several lighted candles. Relaxed, they lay with their limbs crooked round each other.

'I'll help you move before I leave,' he said.

'Where to?'

'Here. It'd be perfect. I'll need a rent collector and caretaker.'

'You know all the rent you get is fish. Anyway I couldn't. There'd be a scandal.'

'But I'll hardly be here.'

'I might not be either. I've made arrangements to go into Gynmouth on Monday and register for war work.'

'I see.'

'I could postpone it till you go away.'

He drew her closer. 'We'll go into Gynmouth together.'

She nestled happily into his warmth. 'That'd be nice.'

'Have you any idea what you might try for?'

'Not really.' She gave a yawn. 'They're not taking so many women into the services now so I suppose it'll be a factory of some sort.'

'They'll send you away, you know.'

'They'd do that anyway.'

'What about your writing?'

She tucked her head under his chin. 'I'll just try and

fit it in where I can. At least I've got started.'

She propped herself up on her elbow and gazed down at him. 'I wish you weren't going to London. Couldn't they send you somewhere safer?'

'Seems not.' He touched her face. 'If you work in a factory you'll be a prime target, too.'

He looked serious.

'I know, but I can't keep hiding in a hole forever. I think that's more frightening than being involved.' She sighed. 'I wish we could be together a bit longer, though. I never believed anything as good as this could ever happen to me. I was convinced nobody would even notice me.'

He nuzzled her ear. 'You silly goose.'

'Yes, that's me. A goose. And my sister is the swan.'

'Ah, but you're a wonderful wild goose.'

'Thanks.' She laughed. 'You know, I prefer being a goose. It's more fun.'

He drew her down beside him again. 'So do I.'

'What time is it?'

'Quarter to twelve.'

'What!' She sat up sharply amongst the tangled sheets and crumbs. 'I've got to get back to the cottage. It's my birthday tomorrow. Mrs Potts is bound to come knocking at the door. She might have a parcel for me. If there's no one there . . .'

She threw aside the bedclothes. Alec grabbed her arm. 'Wait until after midnight. Then you can have one birthday here and another one there tomorrow.'

She hesitated. 'Oh. All right.'

She pulled back the bedclothes and snuggled in beside him.

'Don't fall asleep,' he admonished.

She smiled at him. 'You are funny.'

He sat up and threw aside the sheets.'

'Where are you going?'

'All will be revealed soon. I'll be back in a minute.'

Rose leaned across the mattress to the pile of logs, and picked one up. She was just thrusting the poker into the fire, when something cold touched her shoulder. It was a glass goblet. Alec was holding two of them.

'Take these,' he said.

'But what on earth . . .?' she began.

He nipped out of the room on to the landing, only to reappear swiftly with a bottle.

'Champagne!' shrieked Rose. 'But, Alec, where . . .'

At that moment, the cork exploded, hit the ceiling and ricocheted off *The Mayor of Casterbridge*.

The bubbles swept down the side of the bottle.

'Quick!' he urged.

Rose leapt across the room with the glasses, and caught the liquid in them.

'Happy Birthday!' he said, taking one.

'Oh, Alec.'

'No slushy thank-yous, please. And now for something else.'

'What?'

He placed his finger on his lips, handed her his glass and fled from the room again.

This time he reappeared holding a flat square shape behind him. Rose laughed. She could see it was a record.

'I've seen it,' she cried.

She watched him wind up the gramophone in the corner.

'You're not supposed to look,' he protested. 'Turn away. Close your eyes.'

She did so. As the record crackled into life, he took away the glasses.

'What is it?'

'Shush!'

He gathered her in his arms and they swayed to the music.

'Here it comes,' he whispered. 'Listen.'

> 'A little sentimental tune,
> A melody I love to croon,
> I'm happy when I'm singing a little love song to you.
> As twilight falls the lights are low,
> 'Tis then my heart is all aglow,
> I hear the breezes singing, a little love song to you.
> It hasn't got a stirring strain
> Nor classic words by a poet of fame
> But every note just plays a part
> To show the passion that's in my heart.'

The singer paused, the music rose to a crescendo. Rose rested her head on Alec's shoulder, her arms draped around his neck as the last words of the song faded.

> 'Just like the stars up in the sky,
> That melody will never die,
> Now all the world is singing a little love song to you.'

The needle swished backwards and forwards and they rocked slowly round the room.

'Play it again,' she murmured.

'Is it slushy enough?

'Wonderfully slushy.'

They danced repeatedly to it taking turns to rewind the gramophone and then returned to the mattress with the blankets around their shoulders to sip champagne.

It was while they were sitting side by side that the subject of Miss Hilda came up.

'Rose, there's something I've been meaning to tell you for some time,' began Alec. 'It's about Hilda.'

'Yes?'

'You know the room outside your bedroom?'

'M'm.'

'She used to write there, too. Stories. Romantic stories.'

Rose couldn't look at him. 'Really?' she said lamely.

'Yes. She wrote under a pseudonym, mostly for women's magazines. She had to keep it quiet because of her brother. Not the done thing, you know.'

'Did you read any of them?'

'Yes.'

'What were they like?'

'Good. Some of them were very powerful.'

Rose said nothing.

'You don't seem surprised,' he commented.

'No.'

'What's up? Why won't you look at me? Are you cross because I've kept it a secret?'

'No. It's just . . .' She swallowed. 'Alec, I have the most awful confession to make. I've wanted to tell you for ages, but I couldn't seem to find the right moment. I didn't know you were friends when I started. And it didn't feel like prying then.'

She bowed her head.

'What didn't?' he asked. 'What is it?'

'You remember I told you I found a way into the locked

room? That's not quite true. I mean, I did find a way in, but I had a key. It was hidden in a piece of oilskin by the window in my bedroom. I discovered it by accident. It was wrapped in a letter with another key.'

'A letter? From her?'

'Yes.'

'I see,' he said slowly. 'And you read it?'

'Yes.'

'What did it say?'

'That it was her favourite view, that one of the keys opened the room next to the kitchen, that she'd overheard that all her belongings were to be locked away there when she died. I can't remember much else, except that she told whoever read it, that it would explain everything but to keep it a secret.'

'But it doesn't make sense. Why on earth would she tell a stranger to do that? Why not me? We were such close friends.'

'I don't know.'

He shook his head. 'I don't understand why she didn't mention it in her letters. We wrote to each other regularly,' he explained. 'She told me about her heart condition but she laughed it off. So did I. I thought she was indestructible. I was stunned when Mrs Clarence wrote and told me she'd died.' He fell silent for a moment. 'I wasn't able to attend her funeral. Somehow that made it even harder for me to accept it. Does that make sense?'

'Yes. It was like that with my father. I still sometimes think I'll receive a letter from him out of the blue saying, "I'm still here. They made a mistake".'

Alec pulled the blanket up round both their shoulders.

'When did she die?' she asked.

'October. Over a year now. I still find it difficult to believe

322

that she doesn't exist any more. I feel her spirit is still around.'

'Me too.'

'The letter. What else was in it?'

'Nothing as far as I can remember. I haven't looked at it for ages. She signed it "Mad Hilda."'

He smiled. 'She would.'

'I haven't told you the awful bit yet. It gets worse.'

'You haven't thrown any of her things away?' he said alarmed.

'No, nothing like that.'

'Well, what? Out with it.'

'There were two keys. The small one opened a writing bureau.'

'And you opened it?'

'Yes.'

'And?'

'It wasn't empty. Inside were several books tied together. Diaries.'

He swung round, incredulous. 'You didn't read them?'

She reddened. 'Not at first. As soon as I realised what they were I shut them straight away, but the letter seemed to indicate that she wanted whoever found them to read them; that it was important to her that someone should. So I did. I'm sorry.'

For a long time he said nothing.

Rose sat still, hardly daring to breathe.

'How far did you get?' he said at last.

'1938, when there were rumours of a young man who was coming to Salmouth to start a bookshop. I stopped reading them then.'

'Where are they now?'

'In the bureau. I put them back exactly how I found them. There's a box of photographs there, too.'

'I've probably seen those. She showed me several old ones of her and her family, and some she'd bought second-hand.'

'Alec, are you angry with me?'

'No. Just a bit stunned. Also, I'm shocked you've kept it a secret from me all this time.'

'I kept it a secret from everyone.'

'Even Derry?'

'Yes. I kept it for her, you see. I nearly told you when you first came to the cottage, but something stopped me.'

He gave her a squeeze. 'I suppose I can't exactly throw stones. I concealed the fact that she wrote stories for her sake, too. I was a little alarmed at first when you told me you were doing it, too, especially writing in the same room, sleeping in the same bedroom, by the same window. I wondered if her spirit was overtaking you.'

'How did you know that?'

'You told me.'

'No. How do you know exactly where she slept?'

'She was ill a couple of times, and I used to sit by her bed and chat or read amusing things out to her.'

'Alec, when we go back there, I think you ought to take those diaries. I'd hate to think of them getting into anyone's hands, like her brother or Mr Partridge. Would you? I'm sure that's what she would have wanted if she'd made a will.'

'She did make a will.'

Rose was astounded. 'But why didn't she leave anything to anybody?'

'She did. She told Mrs Clarence she'd made one and that she'd left details concerning it here in the bookshop. I gave her permission to look for it but she never found it.'

'Have you looked?'

'Oh yes. Not that I had much heart for it at first. By March I had started to crack up; bouts of fainting, the shakes, periods of inexplicable weeping. That's when Louise fled. So you can imagine the state I was in by the time the doctor sent me back here to convalesce. Not the best circumstances for hunting for her will. And you saw what a mess the shop was in. I had another look when I was sorting it out. But no luck.'

'But it must be here, somewhere.'

'I know, but where?'

'In one of these books?'

He gave a wry smile. 'That's the first place I thought of. I've looked in every one.'

'Perhaps it's still in the cottage somewhere.'

He turned sharply and grabbed her. 'You don't suppose she might have put it in one of the diaries, do you? No. You would have found it.'

'Unless it was in a later one. I told you. I stopped at 1938.'

They sprang to their feet. Rose dressed hurriedly by the fire, while Alec dashed upstairs. When she reached his untidy book-lined bedroom, she found him back in his corduroys and jersey.

'Oh good, it's nice to see you back in your old togs again,' she remarked.

It was in the last diary. Rose stood in the doorway of Miss Hilda's room while he opened it. Tucked inside was a large envelope with Miss Hilda's familiar handwriting on it. Alec tore it open. Inside were three other envelopes. He stared at them for a moment.

'I'll open the largest,' he said.

'What is it?' she asked quietly.

'It's a letter to her bank manager in Gynmouth, stating that she is Matilda Matthews and that the bearer of this letter, Alec Trelawn, is to be given the copy of her will. I have to take proof of her death and identification. It also gives the name and address of her solicitors.'

He opened the next envelope.

'It's a letter,' he murmured.

Rose could see he was shaken.

'I won't read it all out, if you don't mind.'

'No, of course not.'

'She talks about hiding the keys. She'd intended leaving this at the bookshop. It tells me where they are.'

He began reading.

Do you remember, when I was ill, and you used to read to me and how we used to laugh. Several times I woke from sleep to find you leaning out of the bedroom window, and I loved watching you, drinking in the view.

He stopped for a moment as if to take hold of himself.

I thought it would be a rather nice idea to hide the keys there.

'The letter I found under the window,' breathed Rose, 'it was meant for *you*.'

He nodded. 'I don't know what's in the will but I'll take the diaries back to the bookshop, just in case the bequests of the will don't come through till after my leave is over.'

She walked over to him and hugged him. 'That's a relief.'

They looked at the small envelope.

'Here goes,' he said.

It was a photograph of a young man in army uniform taken during the First World War. Scribbled across the bottom right-hand corner were the words:

'To my dearest Hilda,
    Fondest love and affection,
    Yours,
    Matthew.'

'May I look at it?' she asked, trying hard to conceal the tremor in her voice.

'Of course.'

As she took it from him she noticed that her hand was trembling violently. No wonder Miss Hilda had fainted, she thought. Alec was the spitting image of him. She stared transfixed at the face of the man she and Miss Hilda had fallen in love with.

'Are you all right?' asked Alec, concerned. 'Would you like to go outside? You're as white as a sheet.'

'I'm fine, honestly.'

'You're a terrible liar,' he said and he turned her round to face him. 'You know who he is, don't you?'

She nodded, shattered.

'But how?'

'From the diaries.'

'Tell me then.'

'I think you ought to read them yourself,' she whispered hoarsely. 'It'll be much better coming from her.'

'Please, Rose, I want to know now.'

She hesitated. 'He was her lover. Her father had her put into the asylum because she was bearing his child. The authorities took the child away from her. After the brigadier died, her brother got her out but he warned her that if she mentioned anything about it to anyone, he would say her "madness" had returned and have her put away again.'

Alec stared at her in disbelief. 'That's impossible. She would have told me.'

'You knew about the asylum, didn't you? She took an enormous risk even letting you know that much.'

'But she knew I was illegitimate. I would have been the ideal person to tell.'

'Alec, you were the last person....' She stopped.

'What do you mean?'

'If you'd known you'd probably have stormed up to the manor and wrung her brother's neck. He would immediately have had her put into the asylum, and have found a way of kicking you out of Salmouth. She couldn't risk that, not once she'd found you.'

'Found me?' he repeated, dazed.

She held the photograph out in front of him. 'Look at him,' she urged.

'So we're alike. It's an extraordinary coincidence.'

'When were you born?'

'1917.'

'What month?'

'May.'

'7 May?'

'Yes.' He took the photograph from her and shook his head. 'No,' he murmured. 'She would have said. She couldn't have kept *that* from me, not after she'd known what my parents had done.'

'She had to.'

'Why?' he cried. 'It doesn't make any sense.'

'What would you have done?'

'Raised hell.'

'Exactly.'

'I might not have done.'

She touched his arm. 'When you read what she went through in the asylum you'll understand why she couldn't risk being sent back there. If she had been, I think it would have killed her.'

He avoided looking at her.

'I'm sorry,' she began.

'Don't be. I'm glad you're here.'

They stepped out into the front garden, hugging one another for warmth and speaking in low tones. Leaning on the gate they watched the dawn rise up from behind the sea.

Alec remained subdued. Rose, observing his glazed expression, felt helpless to comfort him.

It was later while she was standing at the sink in the kitchen that she spotted Mrs Potts cycling down the hill, and she panicked.

'Quick,' she shrieked. 'Hide in the larder! It's Mrs Potts.'

'The larder? I can't fit in there,' said Alec. 'I'm not a gnome.'

'Next door. Go in there.'

Too surprised to protest he allowed himself to be shut up into the room where Miss Hilda's possessions had been stored.

Rose returned quickly to the kitchen and strolled nonchalantly up and down her heart pounding.

She waited till there was a knock at the door, counted to five, and then opened it.

'Hello!' she said brightly. 'What brings you here?'

Mrs Potts gazed quizzically at her.

'I've come with the post, same as usual. Ah!' she said suddenly. 'You don't fool me that easy,' and she wagged a finger at her. 'I knows what I knows, don't I?'

Rose, fearing the worst, was blushing violently and cursing herself for doing so at the same time.

Mrs Potts plunged her hand into the postbag and drew out a package and card.

'Happy Birthdee!' she cried. 'See, I remembered.' She lowered her voice "Course I guessed all along. Days ago. Even afore you let on.'

Rose grabbed the post. 'No one can keep a secret from you, Mrs Potts. You've got x-ray eyes. You know, you ought to be a detective. You'd be good at it.'

Rose watched her till she was safely out of sight. When she opened the door to the corridor, she found Alec crouched down outside.

'You can come in now,' she said.

'I feel like something out of a French farce.'

'Did you hear all that?'

'Every word. I had to stuff a handkerchief in my mouth.'

They sat at the table and Rose opened the parcels. There were exercise books and pencils from Diana. Inside Aunt Em's parcel were two packages; one of them was from her mother.

'I'll open Aunt Em's first.'

Aunt Em had sent her a red wool jersey together with a pair of bloomers made out of parachute silk. 'I don't know how she does it!' exclaimed Rose.

Pinned to the last package was a small card.

'Dear Rose,' it said,
    'I've left this with Aunt Em just in case I'm not back in time. Happy eighteenth!
    Love and best wishes,
    Mother.'

'Winceyette pyjamas,' she murmured.

She pulled them out. Tiny pink and red flowers were dotted about on a cream background.

'Roses.' She glanced at Alec. 'These must be the only pyjamas I haven't had handed down to me from my sister.'

She spread her hands along the material. 'It must have taken her ages to find this fabric. I feel a bit mean now, deceiving her.' She shrugged. 'Anyway I've burnt my boats now, though knowing my mother she'll insist on me going back to school even if it's the middle of next term.'

'And will you?'

'No. I'll just have to stand my ground. I'm not looking forward to that very much.'

'It might not be so bad. You said she sounded more easy-going in her last letter. She might be more understanding now.'

Rose gave a grim smile.

'I doubt it. What did your mother say when you joined up? I mean,' she added quietly, 'Miss Hilda.'

'Nothing. She just looked resigned. When Chamberlain finally announced we were at war she was relieved that all the waiting was over, in spite of her pacifist principles. She didn't think we had any choice. She'd been feeling that way since Czechoslovakia fell. I remember her asking me what I was going to do and looking very tired.'

'It must have been heart-breaking for her.'

'I suppose it must, but she rallied round once I'd registered for call-up. That's when she started taking in a stream of evacuees and doing voluntary work. Maybe she overdid it. Burnt herself out. If only I'd known,' he said bitterly. 'I would have spent more time with her. I'd have asked so many questions.'

'It's all written down for you.'

'That's hardly the same,' he muttered. 'Perhaps if I'd pushed her she might have told me.'

'I don't think so. She was probably relieved you didn't.'

'It must have been hard when I spent my leaves with Louise.'

'Did they ever meet?'

'A few times.'

'How did they get on?'

'Reasonably well on the surface but I knew she didn't like her.'

'Which way round?'

'Both. I actually confronted her with it one day. Hilda might have been wonderful at keeping secrets but she was hopeless at covering up her feelings.'

'What did she say?'

'That she didn't *dislike* her, that her opinion was irrelevant anyway, that I probably could see qualities in Louise she hadn't seen. That as long as we were both happy that was what mattered, that I wasn't to let anyone come in our way.'

'She and your father wanted to marry.' She paused. 'Do you mind me telling you?'

'No. Go on.'

'Her family were horrified.'

'Why?'

'All sorts of reasons. He was much younger than her and he worked for a publisher. But I think it was mainly because they had decided she was unmarriageable. Her mother sounded like one of those permanent invalid types. Miss Hilda was the only daughter so everyone assumed she would run the house and look after her parents till they died. I suppose they didn't like the idea of their plans for her being changed. Her father pulled a few strings and had the commanding officer of Matthew's regiment send him back to France.'

'But how did she get pregnant?'

'They managed to have a week together. They travelled as husband and wife.'

'Good Lord.'

'I think they realised they would never see each other again.'

'That must have taken extraordinary courage.'

'Yes. They had their own private wedding ceremony and made proper vows to one another. He even gave her a wedding ring.'

'Did you come across it?'

'No.'

'I suppose it's in her bank.'

'It can't be. She used to wear it into Gynmouth. She'd have to have kept it here. It's probably hidden under the floorboards.'

'Are you serious?'

'Well, she used to hide things there. I've never looked but . . .'

Under the floorboards of the storeroom they found a bundle of his letters together with the ring, some pocket classics, and small packets containing baby clothes.

Rose lifted the tiny cream garments from their nest of mothballs. They had been embroidered with fine white cotton. Handmade buttons trailed down the length of them.

Alec brushed off the dust from one of the classics and was about to open one when he noticed all the baby clothes strewn across Rose's knees.

She held up one of the little nightdresses. 'One day your children will wear these,' she said.

They stared across the exposed floorboards at one another. Our children, thought Rose.

'Yes,' he said quietly. 'I'd like that.'

The ring was lying in the palm of his hand. He glanced down at it.

'Rose, would you mind if we gave this to Dot?'

She sat back on her heels and laughed.

'No,' she cried. 'It's just what Miss Hilda would have wanted.'

They packed the diaries and letters into the knapsack and walked backed into Salmouth to open the bookshop. Alec called at Mrs Clarence's to let her know he had found the details concerning Miss Hilda's will, and to make phone calls to the bank manager and solicitor in Gynmouth.

In the afternoon he disappeared upstairs to read the diaries while Rose looked after the shop. No sooner had she dozed off in one of the wicker chairs than she was woken by the bell jangling and someone popping in to wish her 'many happy returns' and to press cards and home-made cakes into her hands.

A group of women from *Hôtel Maternité* burst in and stood in front of her in choir formation singing 'Happy Birthday' while one conducted. This was followed by 'For She's a Jolly Good Fellow'.

'What have I done to deserve this?' she laughed.

'You made it comfortable here for us,' they said.

'Alec did that.'

'But you let us sit by the fire,' they insisted, 'and you were nice to us.'

'Thanks,' said Rose quietly.

Between them the women had collected up balls of wool. They were all different colours. They dropped them into her lap.

Rose spread them out on the table with her cards. 'I'm going to knit myself the longest stripiest scarf in existence,' she exclaimed.

'You could knit yourself a hat and gloves,' one of the women suggested.

'Gloves! I'll have enough of a battle with a scarf.'

At closing time Alec reappeared. Together they went to Mrs Clarence's where Rose was to have her birthday tea. Mrs Clarence had laid out all her best silver and china for the occasion, and in the centre of a table of bread and jam stood a cake.

George was passed from arm to arm, from Jack's parents back to Dot and Mrs Clarence, to Alec and Rose and back to Mrs Wilson.

Towards the end of the tea Alec gave Rose a nod. 'Yes,' she mouthed.

'Rose and I have something to say,' he announced.

Hearing their names partnered, Rose found herself reddening.

'As you know, most people give the new-born baby a present but we thought George wouldn't mind if we gave his mother a present instead.'

'Me?' interrupted Dot.

Rose had wrapped it up in some of her birthday paper. She passed the small package over the table to her.

Dot stared intently at it. 'What on earth is it?'

'Open it and you'll find out,' said Mr Wilson.

She grinned. As she unwrapped the paper, Alec and Rose glanced quickly at one another.

'Oh my,' gasped Dot. She shook her head. 'I don't believe it.'

'It's beautiful,' said Mrs Wilson.

'It's a proper wedding ring, ain't it?'

She pulled off the old bent curtain ring from her finger and slid it on.

'I'm sure it can be altered if it's too big,' said Rose.

Dot held her hand out in front of her and gazed at it.

'I dunno what to say,' she began. 'It's like having a new start.' She swung round to the Wilsons. 'I can help you on your stall straight away. And I won't have to cover up me hand any more. Thanks ever so much,' and she laughed. 'Know what I feel like? I feel like I've been let out, like someone's unlocked this huge iron door and I've walked out of a prison.'

Rose glanced up at the clock on the church tower. She was sitting on one of the benches in the square attempting to read a book but was too excited to take anything in. She was wearing the new make-do-and-mend blanket overcoat that Mrs Clarence and Dot had finished for her birthday. She raised the collar and stuck her paperback into her bag.

Alec came out of the solicitor's and waved. He sprinted across the road, narrowly missing a cyclist. She sprang to her feet and walked briskly towards him. 'Is it good news?'

'She's left me everything! Her books, her furniture, her china, even the copyright on her short stories. Plus her savings. It's wonderful!' He gave a laugh. 'Sorry. I must seem very mercenary but it's just that they're hers and . . .'

She slipped her arm into his. 'You don't have to explain.'

'There's something else I found out, too.'

'What?'

'The identity of the mysterious old lady who left me that

money. She wasn't old and she wasn't dead.'

'Hilda?'

'Yes.'

'I didn't suspect her because I didn't think she had that amount of money. I suppose she did it because she was afraid of my selling the bookshop and leaving Salmouth. It also explains the swiftness of Harold's appearance as soon as I'd bought next door.'

'How soon will you be able to take her things out of the cottage?'

'As soon as I like. The solicitor rang Major Withers and explained it all. He said the major sounded delighted to be rid of the stuff. In fact he'd been meaning to dispose of it some time ago but hadn't got round to it.'

'Thank goodness.'

'So I don't have to wait for formalities. It appears that a Miss Rose Highly-Robinson will be leaving the said accommodation this coming Saturday, and it would be in my best interest if I could remove it as soon as possible after then, as it's to be taken over as a Land Army hostel the following Monday. They want me to take the beds, too, to make room for bunks. They're planning to put about ten or twelve in there.'

'What about the furniture in the sitting room?'

'They want me to clear that out, too. They're going to use that as a dining room. I told the solicitor I'd contact this Miss Rose Highly-Robinson and perhaps we could come to some arrangement. It was all quite absurd. The solicitor was acting almost as an interpreter, as if we were speaking in a foreign language. It would have been far easier if I'd spoken to him on the phone myself.'

'Did you feel angry with him?'

'No. He was just doing his job.'

'I mean with Major Withers.'

'Yes. But let's not talk about it now.' He kissed her. 'How did you get on?'

'Well, I'm registered.'

'What happened?'

'She asked about my parents. Had they given me permission? I explained that my father was dead and that my mother was abroad.'

'And?'

'She said, "I presume your mother knows," and I replied, "I'm eighteen." Then there was this long silence while she looked at me, and she said, "I see."'

'Did you mention that you wanted to work in a factory?'

'I didn't have to. She mentioned it first. I think she wanted to put me off. "Of course you wouldn't have a nice uniform to wear," she said, "if you worked in a factory." I said I'd had enough of uniforms to last me a lifetime and that I'd be pleased to work in a factory if that's where I was needed most. "You realise it'd be hard work and you'd have to get those nice hands of yours dirty and mix in with a very different class of gel."'

He laughed.

'"A girl of your type might do better in an office of some sort, like the Ministry of Information, in a clerical capacity. I presume you have School Certificate." When I told her I hadn't she nearly fell off her chair. "Oh," she said. "And you seemed so bright."'

'So you don't know if you're going into a factory, or not?'

'Yes, I am. My lack of School Cert. convinced her that I was stupid enough to work in one, which doesn't make sense to me. You'd think it'd be the other way round, that you'd need more wits about you to build an aeroplane than push a pencil.'

'Do you know when you'll have to start?'

'Next Monday, somewhere in the Midlands. There was a phone call from an aircraft factory while I was there, pleading for extra workers.'

'So we've a week together?'

'Yes.'

'We'll have to make the most of it then.'

She couldn't stop smiling. 'We will.'

Rose stood in the doorway and glanced round the empty room. Her bed, the cane table, the chest of drawers, mirror, wardrobe, rugs and pictures had all been removed. Leaning against the door were her bulging bags. She walked over to the seaward window and leaned out.

The sea was grey and choppy. Dark clouds lowered across the sky. She gave a shiver and slipped her hands into the sleeves of her jersey. By now Alec and Harold would have reached Salmouth with all the furniture in the cart.

She rested her back against the window and looked across to the garden window. They had decided to leave the blackout curtains. It seemed silly to take them since they fitted the windows.

She pushed herself away and picked up her bags.

'Goodbye, room,' she whispered.

Downstairs she stacked all the remaining books along the walls in the kitchen, packed Miss Hilda's china and ornaments into the packing case and dragged the trunks and suitcase along the corridor and through the doorway. Now all the rooms were empty except for the kitchen.

Outside, the wind whistled round the walls. Rose brewed up

some tea on the primus and sat on one of the trunks, warming her hands round the cup and putting her nose over the tip so that the warm vapours from the tea wafted into her face.

She was in the garden rinsing her cup out at the pump when she heard the horse and cart. She ran to the gate. It was Alec. She was relieved to see he was alone. She had hardly spoken a word to him while they were carrying the furniture out of the cottage. She didn't feel she could betray her sadness at leaving in Harold's presence, but he must have guessed for as he left, he said, 'You be comin' back, Miss Rose.'

And she had nodded.

She stood in the lane and waved. Suddenly the sky grew leaden and there was a loud rumble.

'Don't rain yet,' she muttered.

She looked at her watch. Eleven o'clock. At midday Mrs Partridge would be coming to clean out the cottage. Not that she needed to now. Tomorrow Harold would return loaded with bunks and blankets and trestle tables ready for the onslaught of Land Army girls and later he would take Alec and her to the railway station. Alec would begin his journey to London; Rose to the West Midlands.

When she had registered for war work she had pointed out that if they needed more people in the Land Army in the Salmouth area she wouldn't mind farm work. But the woman had said that they already had their quota of girls there. Anyway it would have been upsetting to have lived in the cottage when it was being run as a hostel. In that sense she was relieved.

Alec drew up at the gate. 'How are you doing?'

'Everything's in the kitchen ready for loading.'

'Good. I'll just turn her round.'

She was carrying an armful of books down the path when

she met him. He kissed her and took them from her.

'It's all right,' she protested. 'I can put them in the cart.'

'I want your hands free.'

'Why?'

'Because I have some post for you. It came care of the bookshop.'

'For me?' she asked, following him.

'For Rose Jolliffe. Know her?'

He pulled out a magazine from his pocket. A piece of paper with the name and address on it was sealed round it.

'My story!' she shrieked.

She tore the paper surrounding it and swiftly opened it to the index. Alec stood behind her and rested his chin on her shoulder.

At last she found the page. Written at the top were the words: 'Freewheeling by Rose Jolliffe. Set in Edwardian times. A humorous and moving story of a young girl's fight for independence.'

She stared down at it. It was strange seeing it there, something she had lived with in private, now out in public for anyone to read. She scanned the page. Yes it was all there. All her words laid out in print, dark against the rough yellowy paper allowed by the War Economy Standard.

'Congratulations!' said Alec warmly.

A strong gust of wind sent the pages of the magazine flapping.

'I think we'd better move fast,' he said glancing upwards, and he released her and dashed up the path.

Rose couldn't bear to let go of the magazine. She wanted to keep looking at her story, to convince herself that she wasn't dreaming. The sound of thunder spurred her into action. She lifted her jersey, slipped the magazine up inside and tucked the jersey firmly into the waistband of her slacks.

She and Alec ran up and down the path to the cart, carrying the boxes and books, the packing case and trunks, looking hurriedly upwards at the mists which were rolling in from the sea.

They wedged everything compactly at the end of the cart by the seat and covered it with tarpaulin and sacking, roping it in at the sides.

'Well, that's a relief,' she said leaning against the cart. 'We've beaten the rain.'

Alec touched her face. 'I've hardly said a word to you all morning,' he said.

'Me neither.'

'I just wanted to get the furniture away so we could be alone sooner.'

'I'm glad we have. I was scared Major Withers would suddenly appear to say he'd changed his mind and forbid you to take it away.'

'We won't have any problems there. I've already seen him.'

'What? Where?'

'He was waiting for me and Harold at the bookshop.'

Rose gripped his arm. 'What did he say?'

'He just introduced himself and we made polite conversation. I was all set to tell him how I felt and then slowly strangle him but the poor man looked half-strangled already. One look at him and all my fury went down the plughole.'

'What does he look like?'

'Tubby, nervy, red-faced. And rather sad. Not like Miss Hilda at all.'

'Do you think he's guessed?'

'No. I doubt he has that much imagination. But he's obviously a little curious as to why his sister should leave everything to a young man. He asked me if I knew that his sister had been selling romantic stories.'

'What did you say?'

'Yes. Then he said he could understand why she might leave me her books but not all her other things. And could I think of a reason?'

'Did you tell him?'

'No.'

'Why?'

'Because I'm going away. I don't want to return to find the bookshop burnt to the ground.'

'You don't really think . . .?'

'No. But if and when I decide to tell him I want to be on home territory.'

'So what did you tell him?'

'I was lucky. He supplied the answer himself. While I was thinking madly he suddenly asked me if I wrote, too. I said, "Yes, a little." "Ah," he said. "So you're a *literary* chappie. That explains it. Her writing and all that!" So I said, "Yes, I expect that was the reason."'

'Do you think he'll leave it at that?'

'No. I suspect he'll be taking an interest in second-hand books for a while to try and find out more. Poor Mrs Clarence will have the pleasure of dealing with him till I get back.'

He kissed her gently. 'Come on, let's go up to Hilda's room. In case it's the last time we're here.'

Upstairs they squeezed into the window frame and leaned out, their heads resting against one another.

'You know,' said Alec, 'when Hilda and I met, I think

she was right not to tell me, aside from the risk, I mean. She couldn't have made up for twenty-one years. If I'd known, we might have tried to act like mother and son, and that would have been disastrous. A good friend was the best she could ever be. And she was. It was my adoptive mother who brought me up. She's my real mother. In a funny sort of way, I feel much closer to her now.'

'Will you tell her about Hilda?'

'I don't know. I want to get to know her better first. There must be a lot that she probably hasn't felt able to tell me.'

'How did she react to your breakdown?'

'She was very concerned. She wanted to come and look after me but I wouldn't let her. I virtually cut her off. I felt so bitter about her deceiving me, I wanted to sort it all out myself. Be alone.'

'And then Derry came down?'

'Yes. A week before you arrived. Perhaps that was a mistake. I don't know.'

Rose looked away. 'Do you think he'll tell anyone about me?'

'You mean, brag about it to his friends?'

'Brag? There's nothing to brag about.' She blushed. 'I meant people in your family.'

'I doubt it.'

'I suppose one of these days I'll have to meet him again,' she went on. 'That's if we're still together.'

'We will be if you accept this.' He was holding an ornately carved silver ring inlaid with dark blue stones. 'They're lapis lazuli,' he said.

'They're beautiful,' she gasped. 'Was it the ring . . .?' she began tentatively.

'No. Louise wanted something less Victorian. My adoptive

mother gave this to me on my twenty-first. She had been saving it for the daughter she never had. Please say if you don't like it.'

'I love it,' she whispered. 'It's perfect.'

'I'm asking you to marry me,' he added.

'I know,' and she smiled.

'Does that mean you will?'

She nodded. It felt natural to accept.

He slid the ring on to her finger. 'And you don't mind that it's silver?'

'I prefer it. Gold is too conventional.'

'We can't have that,' he laughed, and drew her close.

Rose held on to him tightly.

'Oh, Alec,' she murmured. 'I'm so happy that I'm frightened. I'm afraid someone might come along and punish us for being so happy.'

'We won't let them.'

The sky gave a loud crash and then opened. The rain swept down like a great curtain of mist. They withdrew their heads quickly, their hair dripping.

'I'll get soaked,' she cried.

'It's all right, I've brought oilskins for us.'

At his insistence Rose waited in the kitchen while he made a quick sprint to the cart. Rose hovered in the doorway as the rain thundered loudly round the cottage. They dragged on the oilskins and plonked sou'westers on their heads.

'I can hardly see you under that hat,' Alec remarked.

They tore down the path, their heads bowed as if attempting to duck the storm. Immediately they had climbed up on to the seat of the cart Alec took up the reins and they jogged forwards.

Inside her oilskin Rose felt snug. She pressed her wet hand

against the buttons. Underneath her jersey she could feel the outline of the magazine.

Suddenly she was filled with such joy that she pushed herself up to her feet and balanced herself precariously on the foot rest.

Alec glanced aside at her, amused.

'I feel so light,' she exclaimed. 'I feel I could just, I could just . . .' And she waved her arms as if searching for the right word.

'Fly?' he suggested.

She sat down with a bump.

'Yes, I do. I do really.' She smiled. 'Oh, Alec, I do love you.'

'I love you too,' he shouted back through the rain.

The cart came to a halt and they slid into each other's arms. They clung to one another while the rain drummed on to their oilskins and streamed down their faces.

'Let's not go away,' she said. 'Let's stay in this lane for ever.'

'Goose,' he laughed, and he gathered her tightly to himself. 'Darling, darling goose.'

JUST HENRY

'A totally gripping novel about learning to question your prejudices ... It is beautifully written and highly satisfying'
Daily Telegraph

'A plot that is breathtakingly exciting and ultimately uplifting'
London Review of Books

'Only the greatest authors of children's fiction share this ability to touch the heart'
Amanda Craig, The Times

A LITTLE LOVE SONG

'Packs everything in opera style. Once I started reading it, I couldn't put it down'
Times Educational Supplement

'We feel real anger ... suspense, hope and pain'
Independent

'An engrossing and memorable novel'
Kirkus